Eutychus
Terminally Committed To Christ

J.Pauls

Terminally Committed To Christ

And a young man named Eutychus, sitting at the window, sank into a deep sleep as Paul talked still longer. And being overcome by sleep, he fell down from the third story and was taken up dead.

- Acts 20:9

Eutychus

Copyright © 2022 by J. Pauls

Cover design by Robyn Hodgdon

Interior design and formatting by Robyn Hodgdon

License Notes

Contents

Acknowledgments

Novel writing for me is always a team effort. First the Holy Spirit inspires. Then comes the conversation with Him and work together on plot, character, story details, and lots of research. The support from family, my wife Kathy, and son Caleb, and daughter Beth encourages and lifts me up. Then there are those inner circle friends who read the rough drafts and review. Then the website support and novel editing, formatting, and design team of Nathan and Robyn Hodgdon. Without all of this support you would not be reading this novel.

I hope this reading adventure guides you to read the Word more and makes you want to research those who walked the path before us. This is a work of fiction but I tried to be as close to the Biblical account and possible timeline and historical facts.

Many of the characters in this novel were real people in history, but as in all works of fiction their portrayal within the novel were imagined.

This novel is NOT scripture, but a researched fiction. Read the Bible for the real historical account.

Enjoy the journey!

Chapter 1
58AD

Life in the warehouse

T he wet spot of sweat grew larger on the stone floor as he sat on the crate watching the drops fall from his head. And it was only mid-morning.

"Let's go, son, the next ship just docked. Only two more ships to go today."

It's only Monday, thought Eutychus. His breathing had just returned to normal.

Eutychus sighed, got up, and slowly walked to the large open door to look at the men and his father helping with the ropes from the ship that he would soon be helping to unload into the family's warehouse. The port at Troas wasn't as big as others, but it certainly was big enough to keep his family's business extremely busy.

"You better get moving, Eutychus. Your father will need your strong young back on this one."

Eutychus nodded at Gaius and began trotting to the ship. Gaius was a Roman soldier from a squad assigned to guard the Roman treasury currently being held at his family's Shield of Iraklidis Warehouse. Eutychus then knew the ship most likely carried newly minted Roman coins and other valuables that he would be loading into the heavily fortified room at the back of their warehouse, which meant a lot of heavy lifting.

Today was like most other days in the warehouse with lots of heavy lifting, walking, carrying, inventory reports, bills of lading, and record keeping. Eutychus had become the natural foreman in the warehouse, staying long after the last ship was unloaded to update the warehouse inventory manifest and close down the warehouse for the night. His father, Nikias, was a well-respected merchant business owner in the city of Troas and had bought his Roman Citizenship just ten years earlier. The family now had three ships moving cargo with the largest vessel being captained by Eutychus' older brother Nicolaos. The Roman treasury account was a big win for Nikias, as the Proctor of the city had thought of just building a new building, when Nikias offered him a much more inexpensive option in using a portion of the family's warehouse by just fortifying one room in the back, and only for half the charge for the construction project. It was much closer to the dock, with a much less security need to load and unload because of the proximity. The last five years Eutychus had gotten use to the Roman guard presence in the warehouse. In fact, he actually liked a couple of them.

Just as the last crate from the ship was being moved into place Eutychus heard his mom call for his father and him to come get lunch.

"Corrina, you are a beautiful sight and an angel of blessing!" Eutychus could hear his father saying as he walked to the small warehouse office.

Fresh bread, thinly sliced meat, and fresh cheese were laid out on the back counter, with a bunch of freshly picked grapes.

"Thank you, Mom, I'm soooo hungry. What did you bring dad?" Eutychus grinned at his father.

"Hah. Hah. Funny, son." Nikias was digging into the fresh bread.

"He certainly is earning his keep lately and getting stronger by the day. But he'll need another bath tonight! I can smell him from here!" Nikias was smiling at Corrina, knowing Eutychus needed to hear his praise.

"When will Nicolaos be getting back?" Corrina asked Nikias.

"He just got there. Probably in about 30 days," Nikia responded. "It depends how well he does in Roma and obviously the weather."

"Well, I'm off to the market for some more wine. Xenia told me of a new winery, I want to try what they are offering. See you two tonight." And Corrina, smiling, glided out through the front door with a hand wave.

"Just one more today, Eutychus, then hopefully we'll get out of here earlier than yesterday." Nikias grabbed a handful of grapes and headed out the door in the direction of the dock.

Next one coming from Neapolis should be easier than the last one, Eutychus thought as he went back into the warehouse and began to move crates to make space for the next shipment coming that afternoon.

About midafternoon Eutychus could see the next ship docking. Down the plank walked some men Eutychus thought he recognized. Seven men came off the ship together, four headed down the main street and three headed towards the warehouse. A man waved in friendly greeting to Eutychus.

"Timothy!" Eutychus shouted and waved in response.

"Eutychus, you remember Tychicus, and this is Aristarchus," Timothy said, shaking Eutychus' hand and introducing his companions.

"Good to meet you." Shaking their hands firmly, Eutychus asked Timothy, "Are you here for Paul's box?"

"Yes, we are. I hope to have some time this week to come back and visit you, but now we've got to get to a meeting."

Eutychus ran to the back of the warehouse and brought back a mid-size wooden box and handed it to Aristarchus whose arms were outstretched to receive it.

"I'll come back sometime this week to visit you, hoping to have some time to talk. Is there a day less busy than others for you this week?" Timothy looked at Eutychus as Tychicus and Aristarchus turned and began to walk out of the warehouse.

"Wednesdays tends to be the slowest, but I'd have to check the preliminary docking schedule," Eutychus replied.

"Great. I'll hope to be back Wednesday late afternoon to visit you." Timothy turned and jogged towards his companions.

Eutychus headed to the ship to begin helping with the unloading of the cargo. The sun was just going down as the last of the cargo was being put away in the warehouse.

"I'll be home as soon as I can get the new shipment into the day's inventory manifest," Eutychus was telling his father as his father was gathering parchments for his walk home. The day warehouse workers had just left after Nikias had paid them their daily earnings.

"Sounds good, son, thank you. Don't be too long, you know what your mother will say." Nikias smiled at his growing son and was pleased at how Eutychus had taken over the warehouse inventory manifest duties.

I'm really proud of that boy, Nikias thought as he headed towards the family home. *He'll make a great businessman someday. He'll make our family name proud. He keeps the warehouse better organized than Nicolaos or I ever did. He sure has changed in the last year.*

Eutychus lit some lamps as he began to document the day's cargo in size, place, and merchant on the warehouse storage manifest.

"Gaius, that was a total of twenty-three crates and forty-seven bags of coins today correct?"

"That's what my bill of lading confirms, Eutychus. Nothing gets by your watchful eye kid." Gaius smiled as he turned to meet up with his night relief guard.

"Don't try anything, Crispus. Eutychus will find you out," Gaius said this with a grin and loud enough for Eutychus to hear.

"That kid knows every piece in here," Crispus replied and saluted Gaius and made a 'show' for Eutychus to see. Eutychus walked towards them.

"Crispus, I now am done and you now have the warehouse. Keep it safe and thank you."

"Don't worry, Eutychus, we've got your warehouse safe."

Eutychus still went methodically through the warehouse checking all the doors and windows again before leaving for the walk home.

Eutychus arrived home and it was already dark.

"I know, mom," Eutychus said as he passed her going through the courtyard.

"Dinner was... warm an hour ago. Your dad is really proud of you. He even told me that tonight. I am too. Now go get something to eat AFTER you get washed." Corrina smiled at her son.

"Thanks, mom." Eutychus headed to the bath area where he could wash off the day's sweat.

After eating a cold dinner, he collapsed into his bed and fell immediately asleep.

Chapter 2

Introduction to The Way

Family history.

"Wake up! Dad's already left!" Eirene shouted at the sleeping body on the bed as she passed by his room.

Nothing like the annoying voice of my little sister as a wakeup call.

Eutychus slowly rose and stumbled to the wash basin and splashed water in his face.

I've got to get going. Eutychus had to think hard what day it was, since everyday was so much the same routine of work. *Wednesday, right?* After he threw on a fresh tunic laid there by his mom, he walked to the main room and quickly grabbed some fruit from the basket before he had to talk to anyone, then slipped through their home's courtyard into the street on his way to the warehouse.

The main street was surprisingly full this morning. Street merchants were rushing to set up their stalls, produce suppliers were moving fast, one had to watch where the stepped or they would be hit. Eutychus loved the hustle and busyness of the main street. Many waved at him as he walked to the family's warehouse. Most merchants knew him, as many had used the family's warehouse at one point or another. Eutychus looked at the sun and realized he was a bit later than usual and picked up his pace.

"The boy wonder finally graces us with his presence!" One of the day workers named Steven called out as he saw Eutychus approaching. Eutychus liked Steven, as he was actually part of his group called The Way that met together on Sundays. Eutychus had convinced his father to hire Steven, even though his father had been somewhat reluctant in hiring Jews.

Two years prior, the family, minus Nicolaos who had stayed back to run the warehouse, had taken a trip to Ephesus for business. While Nikias was busy meeting with important merchants and Eirene stayed to play with their friend's daughter who was the same age, Corrina and Eutychus came upon a street preacher named Paul who HAD talked about an unknown God. Day after day they continued to go back to listen to this well-educated Jewish Pharisee speak of his Messiah named Jesus. This led to many conversations with others who were part of a group called The Way in Ephesus. Corrina and Eutychus eventually had accepted Paul's stories as Truth and had acknowledged that Jesus must have been the Son of God. They both had seen things beyond natural laws in some of those meetings. Miracles they called them. Then there was this ... Presence ... that everyone could feel but not see. When they had returned to Troas, a man who said he was sent by the Holy Spirit to deliver a message and news that the group The Way had begun in Troas and they needed to be a part of it. How it all happened was ... very different.

In Ephesus, Eutychus had met Timothy who was also part of The Way, and they instantly liked one another. Since that first meeting, Timothy had always stopped by to visit with Eutychus when he came through the port city. Timothy had deposited a box for Eutychus to store in the warehouse for safekeeping the year previous that contained copies of Paul's writings in it. Eutychus had always been curious as to the contents and often wondered if he'd be allowed to read them. In the past, year Eutychus found himself having more and more a desire to speak to God. The group called it praying. But Eutychus found it easier to just *talk* to God in private places and under his breath. Then he began to realize that God might be talking back to him, though he really couldn't describe it other than it was a *knowing* and an inner Voice guiding him sometimes. Some in his group talked about a baptism of the Spirit, but he didn't really understand what that meant exactly. Eutychus' problem was most Sundays were busy at the warehouse, and he often showed up late to the evening meetings if at all. He wanted to be there but the daily warehouse business was just so demanding and physically tiring, plus he wanted to move up and learn more of the workings of the family business.

Actually, this Wednesday at the warehouse business was fairly slow for arrivals, only one ship, although there had been plenty of outgoing pickups, but everyone enjoyed a slower pace than normal. The day workers were let go earlier than normal and were just leaving when Eutychus waved to Steven and he saw Timothy and Tychicus walking towards the warehouse.

Timothy greeted Eutychus with a hug and slapped him on the back. "How is my younger brother?!"

"Doing good, we had a slower day today and I actually have time to talk now." Eutychus led the two to a back area of the warehouse and they sat on some crates facing one another.

"It's so good to see you, Eutychus! I talked with your mom some, and she says you're doing really well here in the family business."

Eutychus shrugged his shoulders. "There's always lots of work to be done. I'm trying my best to learn the business."

"Speaking of business, I've got a lead for you. We just came from the city of Philippi before arriving here in Troas where we were meeting with a small group of The Way. In that group is a woman who has discovered a new way of producing a purple cloth and her business is exploding. Her name is Lydia and she may need your family's services, as she is looking to expand with trusted connections, especially with someone like your business which has so many wide and various merchant connections." Timothy was quite focused looking at Eutychus as he spoke these words, like there was a greater purpose in all of it.

"I could arrange a meeting with my father to discuss this opportunity with you, Timothy?" Eutychus offered.

"No." Timothy was quick and short.

"This opportunity is specifically for ... you. I've been discussing this with the Holy Spirit for a few days now, and His instructions to me is to keep this

specifically with you." Timothy had lowered his voice as he said this. "In fact --
Tychicus said that the Holy Spirit confirmed it with him as well."

Tychicus nodded at Eutychus. "The Lord has big plans for you Eutychus.
What they are He didn't tell me. But there is something big in your near future
with His plans for you," Tychicus spoke slowly and clearly.

Eutychus was quiet. He didn't know how to take all of this new information.
Timothy and Tychicus were so serious and earnest and he knew they were being
straight and honest with him.

"What should I do then exactly?" Eutychus asked, looking back and forth
between the two.

"We're not exactly sure either, Eutychus," Tychicus replied.

"You should pray and ask the Holy Spirit about it," Timothy replied firmly.

"How is your connection with Him lately? What has He been saying to you?"
Timothy gently asked.

Eutychus sat quietly trying to gather his thoughts and figure out how to
actually answer the question. "Honestly I don't know how to answer this question. I can say that I think God has been speaking to me sometimes ... I think.
There is this feeling of inner knowing and guiding sometimes, I just don't know
if it is really Him or not. I wish I had you two to talk about it more." Eutychus
was slow and halting in his words.

"I know I should be studying the scriptures more, but I just don't have the
time. I do.... talk to Him when I'm alone, I try to be as real as I can in my ... prayer
to Him. I wish I could somehow know Him better." Eutychus was looking
down at his feet as he said this.

Tychicus put his hand gently on Eutychus' shoulder and began to pray.
"Father, be with Eutychus, surround him with your Presence. I've experienced
your love for him, and it is powerful. Thank you for him. Now guide him in
the way You want him to go. Give him the words to speak, set up those divine
appointments You have for him."

Timothy then came over and put both of his hands on Eutychus and prayed
as well. "Father I love this man so much, but not as much as You do. I know that
You have big plans for him. Guide him Father. Be with him Holy Spirit. Jesus

baptize Eutychus with the Holy Spirit." Timothy then grabbed Eutychus in a bear hug.

Eutychus felt something strange as Timothy prayed for him. It was a warm buzzing type of feeling flowing from the top of his head down through his fingers and toes.

"Woah, that was ... weird," Eutychus said quietly.

"Yep, I felt it too," Timothy remarked.

"It was the Holy Spirit," Tychicus confirmed.

"I've got so much to learn." Eutychus sighed.

They all stood, and Timothy and Tychicus hugged Eutychus again.

"Paul and Luke who are already here will talk to your group on Sunday. I hope I will see you there, Eutychus." Timothy looked earnestly into Eutychus' eyes while keeping his hands on Eutychus' shoulders.

"I will try my best to be there," was all Eutychus could get out. He was strangely feeling too emotional.

"I'd really like to talk with you more, Eutychus. I look forward to getting to know you better," Tychicus said warmly.

Timothy nodded at Eutychus and turned with Tychicus to walk out of the warehouse.

"See you Sunday!" Timothy called over his shoulder.

Eutychus waved goodbye to them.

When Eutychus arrived home early, his mom made a big deal of asking who this strange man was; it couldn't be her son Eutychus because he never gets home before dark.

"Mom, did you know Paul and Luke will be here in Troas on Sunday?"

"Yes, son. I want you there. Our group is meeting at Xenia's home on the third floor, as her house has the most secure location and a room big enough for all of us."

"You know, mom, how busy we are right now at the warehouse. But Timothy and his friend Tychicus came to see me today, and I kind of told them I'd try to be there."

"Good. Now go wash up, you'll get actual warm food tonight!"

Eutychus was quiet during dinner and didn't say anything as he was pondering the whole afternoon meeting with Timothy and Tychicus.

"You okay, son?" Nikias asked.

"Yes, father. My thoughts and mind were about the warehouse."

"You need to relax, son, and enjoy this early evening."

"I'll try, dad." Eutychus got up and excused himself to go sit in the courtyard.

Eutychus found himself talking to God quietly.

"Jesus, I don't know what you want of me or what your plan is for me. Could you explain it to me?"

The only thing Eutychus could hear was the small wind in the trees.

He went to sleep that night wondering what God had in store for him.

Chapter 3

An Eternal Encounter

The Fall Out Of The Window

*L*ight was rushing all around him. Or was it that he was rushing through the light? He could sense the motion and intensity. Was that voices he was hearing in all the screeching that sounded just faintly in the background?

Eutychus jolted awake. He sat up in a sweat. *What a dream!*

"What was that?!" Eutychus heard himself say out loud.

He was internally shaking. It had been quite a few years since he had had a nightmare.

Was this a nightmare though? Or something else?

He got up like normal and tried to go through his regular morning routine, but the dream seemed so real and permeated his mind and thoughts. The walk to the warehouse was a blur, his body was on autopilot, he didn't even notice the morning greetings from merchants. Then he saw the day's schedule. He groaned. *Receiving eight ships? Two of the ships being official Roman cargo? Plus over ten scheduled outgoing pick-ups, four of which would be outgoing ship loads. On a Sunday? I hope father has hired some extra day workers for today, it's going to be brutal.*

And the day was exactly as he expected it. Nikias had actually brought on two extra men for the day, but Eutychus thought he should have brought on four more. Things were extremely busy. Eutychus had little time to do anything outside of telling men where to place and move cargo. He had four men rearranging inventory to make room for the incoming as well as staging the outgoing loads. Bodies of men sweating and moving quickly were everywhere. Nikias and Eutychus were heard shouting directions all morning.

When lunch time rolled around Corrina, could barely get her men's attention when she walked through the office and into the warehouse.

"Mom! It's dangerous in here! Please go back into the office." Eutychus was a little gruffer than usual, but he didn't want his mom to get hurt.

When Eutychus made it to the office, he apologized to his mom. "I'm sorry, Mom. Today is twice as busy than normal. Just leave the food. Dad and I will get to it when we can. Thank you."

"Remember, son, tonight's meeting, please be there." Corrina's voice was gentle. She could tell the warehouse was in full swing. As she said this, Eutychus was already walking back into the warehouse.

Corrina heard Eutychus' response as he walked away. "I'll try my best, mom."

The afternoon was the same as the morning, except another Roman cargo ship had arrived unexpectedly. Even the Roman guards were helping unload. Usually, they just barked orders at the men unloading the ship. The warehouse was a blur of men and cargo incoming and outgoing. Just getting a drink of water become a rare thing in the midst of the action. Nikias had to remind Eutychus to drink water.

Come late afternoon, Nikias pulled Eutychus aside and told him they had only one more ship scheduled to arrive, but they had two more outgoing ship loads.

"We've got to push, Eutychus. You're doing great. You work on staging the outgoing loads; I'll handle the final incoming ship."

"You got it, Dad."

"Breathe, son. We'll make it," Nikias and Eutychus both then began shouting orders to their men.

The sun was already down when the final outgoing load was finished. Nikias told Eutychus that he would help him with the evening's warehouse inventory manifest. Nikias had already lit the lamps an hour ago.

"I heard that Mom wants you at a meeting tonight. Maybe we can get it done before it's over and you can at least catch the end of it. You did great today."

It was much later when Eutychus found himself walking to the house where the meeting was taking place. Steven let him in the front gate and told him he was surprised to see him there after the day they had just had at the warehouse.

"I've promised a few people that I'd try to make it tonight. So here I am."

"The meeting has been going on for several hours already, Eutychus."

"I'll try to find a place where I don't offend people with my smell."

"Try a window, Eutychus," Steven suggested.

Eutychus slowly climbed the stairs to the third story. His legs felt like lead. He was so physically exhausted. And he had to admit to himself ... he smelled bad.

I'm going to NEED to find a window.

When Eutychus came to the doorway of the room, people were even sitting in the hallway. He whispered to the man closest to him, "Are there any windows in the back?" The man pointed. And Eutychus slipped around as many people as he could and made his way to the far back corner. A man near the window opened the window further and Eutychus climbed up on the windowsill and leaned back, with one leg outside and one inside.

Paul's voice was going on with somewhat of a monotone. People were quiet trying hard to listen to every word he said, so there was little noise coming from the crowd in the room. Eutychus saw his mom in the front row sitting next to Timothy and Tychicus on the floor. Luke was standing against the far wall taking notes.

I've got to stay awake. Oh, does that breeze feel good. Eutychus closed his eyes for just a second, or so he thought.

He was jolted awake.

He was standing in a green pasture in full light. About two hundred paces ahead of him was a rolling green, grassy hill. There he saw children in white clothing running and shouting in what looked like a game of tag. To his right about thirty paces away was a large, beautiful river. He turned around and saw the biggest mountain range he had ever seen. To his left about fifty paces away was a man sitting under a massive oak tree who was staring at him.

Then the man got up and began walking towards him. Eutychus was frozen in wonder; he had never breathed, smelled, seen, or felt anything like what was now all around him. The air even seemed alive. The man waved at him and kept coming towards him. Eutychus was just ... staring, seemingly paralyzed in shock. But he could move, he kind of flapped his arms to check. He heard the man laugh.

When as the man got about ten paces away from him he heard Him speak. "It's so good to have you here, Eutychus. I'm Jesus." Immediately Eutuychus fell to his knees and hands. Then Jesus grabbed Eutychus, lifted him to his feet, and gave him a huge hug.

Eutychus' mind was reeling, as his head was right next to Jesus' head in a hug.

Jesus?!! What is happening to me?? Where am I? What is going on??

"Woah, woah, woah, Eutychus, we've got time. In fact, I've all the time you need," Jesus said with a chuckle in His Voice. Jesus stepped back but kept His hands on Eutychus' shoulders. He spoke directly to Eutychus with a smile. "Yes, it is me. You are with me in my Kingdom. You might know it as Heaven. You fell out of the window, and now you are with Me."

Eutychus couldn't take his eyes off of Jesus' face and eyes. *What window?* He was trying to remember.

"You know. At the meeting and Paul was being long-winded?" Jesus laughed again. "I'm proud of you, Eutychus, the way you've been helping your dad."

Jesus stepped back and motioned for Eutychus to follow Him. They began to walk together. When they got to the large oak tree Jesus motioned to a rock for Eutychus to sit down, Jesus then sat with His back to the tree. "So what do you think?" Jesus tilted His head and just smiled.

"I ... I... this ... um ... is amazing." Questions began to form in Eutychus' mind.

"Relax, Eutychus, I'll answer most of what you want to know but not all of it because some of it you're not quite ready to understand. Just breathe," Jesus said slowly. The way Jesus said, "Just breathe," reminded Eutychus of the way his dad had said it.

"Eutychus, you've still got options and some choices to make." Jesus was more direct now. "But they're your choices. I'm not going to make you do anything you don't want to do. And, yes, you can stay here if you want." Jesus answered Eutychus's question before he could even say it.

Eutychus was just now figuring it out that Jesus knew what he was thinking without saying anything.

"See that big crowd of people over there?" Jesus pointed.

For the first time Eutychus saw the people. They were a lot farther away than he should be able to see them. *There must be something different with my eyes here.*

"Yes, Eutychus, your eyes are perfect here." Jesus laughed again.

"There are many in that crowd wanting to meet you. But I've told them I want some time with you first. You're mine."

Eutychus felt his heart melt. He had never felt such a feeling of love like he was now experiencing.

"I want to ask you some questions." Jesus looked at him directly.

"Don't You already know my answers?" Eutychus suddenly felt confused. Jesus just laughed again. Eutychus thought, *Jesus sure laughs a lot.*

"Here where there is no limit of joy? Of course. People laugh here all the time. I may know your answers before you give them, but I still want to discuss them with you all the same. I love you. This is about our relationship. You and Me.

I don't like shortcuts. In fact, when you have all of time at your disposal, why take them?"

Eutychus was beginning to feel the life of the place and he just laughed. It felt so good.

"Okay, Eutychus, let's walk to the river." Jesus got up and began walking towards the river. As Eutychus got up to follow Him, a girl ran up to Jesus, handed Him a flower and then just ran back to her friends. All the kids seemed to have boundless energy.

As they got to the river Jesus just began to walk into it. With water up to His knees, He motioned for Eutychus to join Him in the river. As Eutychus began to walk into the river, Jesus splashed him, and Eutychus without thinking splashed Jesus back. For a good amount of time a major splash fight ensued till they were both drenched and laughing. Jesus went to the bank and fell back on the grass. Eutychus followed Him and lay down next to Him.

What was that all about? Eutychus thought.

"I like to baptize people with the Holy Spirit in different ways. I never do anything the same way. I'm the most unpredictable Person you will ever meet!" Jesus laughed.

"Wait, what just happened?" Eutychus just said without thinking.

Can you hear me now? Jesus' Voice was now in Eutychus' head. And Jesus laughed again.

"You know that line would be funnier to you at another time. But it also works for now." Jesus smiled at Eutychus.

I can hear you so clearly. Is this the way it will be now all the time? Eutychus thought.

"Here, yes. On earth it will depend on a lot of other things. People are greatly and easily distracted there. But if you listen and be patient, you'll hear Me." Jesus was speaking out loud rather than in Eutychus' mind.

What do you mean on earth, am I going back?

"Don't get ahead of me here. That's what I want to talk to you about. I have a choice I want to give you." Jesus was looking at Eutychus intently and sat up. Eutychus sat up too. "I want to have people on earth who are willing to give everything to me knowing what awaits them here. There are many who will be coming here soon, but they will have to face terrible trials and suffer for my Name. I need someone there who will speak my Words to them when they will most need them, and because of the intensity of the situation, they may not be able to hear me very well, so I want to be able to send them someone who will encourage them to stay courageous through the very tough but short time they are facing."

Eutychus thought of Paul.

"Yes… Paul is one in my Army. But there are many others as well." Jesus was more serious now. "Eutychus, will you be one of my Messengers to those facing their … death on earth?"

Eutychus immediately had the thought … *Yes, of course.*

"Even if you yourself will have to face death sooner than most and suffer for my Name?" Jesus' eyes were piercing now.

Eutychus slowed down as if time stopped. Things seemed hyper-focused. He began to see pictures in his mind of earth. Places, people being tortured, killed, and torn apart. People in jail cells awaiting trial. People hiding in caves. Children being ripped away from their parents and killed in front of them. Men and women being led to the Forum Romanum and then being put in the arena where great cats tore them apart. So many things were quickly flashing through the mind of Eutychus.

"You okay?" Jesus brought Eutychus back to the present.

"Wow. That was intense."

"I wanted to give you enough to know what some of the things you'll be facing if you decide to be my Messenger. It won't be easy. But I will NEVER leave you, and you'll have to listen closely to the Holy Spirit and obey the instructions WE give you."

Eutychus then thought of his Dad, older brother, and his sister. *They need to know Jesus too.*

"You could have a big impact on their lives, Eutychus, if you go back, but it won't be right away."

"I want to go back, if You'll help me." Eutychus was beginning to realize how important this decision was.

"What do you think the splash fight was about?" Jesus laughed.

"What about all those people?" Eutychus pointed to the crowd in the distance.

"They'll have to wait a few more minutes till you get back here."

Minutes? Eutychus' mind skipped.

"It's a time thing. I'll explain more when you get back here." Jesus smiled.

Before Eutychus knew what was happening, he was flying down a tunnel of light at a speed beyond he could have imagined. He immediately thought of the dream he had had in the morning. *Was it this morning?*

"He fell!"

A woman screamed. Everyone turned and looked in her direction. A man was shouting loudly. Great confusion washed over the room.

Paul immediately rushed towards the door and headed for the stairs while lots of men followed him. On the way down the stairs Paul, began asking the Holy Spirit what to do. When he got down to ground level, he rushed out of the house and found the body of Eutychus lying on the stone courtyard. He right away scooped up the body and cradled it in his arms.

What do You want me to do, Jesus? What is your heart for this young man? Paul was focused in prayer for Eutychus.

The Holy Spirit spoke to Paul in his mind. *He's coming back. His life is in him now.*

A crowd had gathered around Paul. Paul then spoke. "Don't be alarmed, for his life is in him."

Eutychus began to move. He opened his eyes and looked at Paul and then saw all of the other faces looking at him in shock and wonder.

Chapter 4
The Flow Increases
A different life.

Luke began checking Eutychus over. Eutychus felt pretty sore in several places but he hadn't broken any bones—at least Luke didn't think so. People were amazed at what had just happened. But rather than Paul making a big deal about it, he headed back up the stairs and asked if the Master's Supper was ready to be served. It was after midnight and the meeting continued after Paul had served communion. Paul then launched into stories of faith and the meeting continued until dawn.

After the crowd dispersed in the courtyard around Paul and Luke had come to check on Eutychus, though, Corrina was in shock and shaking. She scolded Eutychus at the same time crying and hugging him. Eutychus now had a calm about him that seemed very different to Corrina. Eutychus helped his mom back up the stairs to the meeting after everyone had already went back upstairs. When they came into the room, everyone made space for them to be in the front. They sat down next to Timothy and Tychicus.

Eutychus leaned over and whispered to Timothy, "I'd like to talk to you when the meeting is over."

Eutychus had a different countenance than Timothy had seen before and just nodded at him. Timothy kept glancing over at Eutychus for the rest of the meeting. There was something definitely different about him.

As the meeting ended Eutychus told his mom to go home and to tell his father that he would be at work on Tuesday. Corrina who would have normally gave Eutychus directions and instructions about what was going to happen, just nodded at him and set off for home.

Timothy hung back until Corrina had left and then approached Eutychus. "You wanted to talk?"

"Let's get Tychicus," Eutychus said, "and find a secluded private place in the courtyard to talk."

Timothy was surprised Eutychus asked for Tychicus too.

When the three were sitting around a tree in the courtyard Eutychus began to tell his experience to Timothy and Tychicus. They listened with great interest.

After Eutychus had finished Timothy said quietly, "You've got a call now."

"Well, at least we know now what 'big plans' the Lord Jesus has for you Eutychus," Tychicus responded.

"I have a sense that my Master will use both of you in my life in the future," Eutychus added. "I'll need strong spiritual brothers to help me understand certain things in the coming days. Both of you are much more versed in the scriptures than I. As I said, Jesus is more to me now in every way. His Voice is very clear to me now since our splash fight. My life is now terminally committed to Christ."

Tychicus just shook his head in amazement. Timothy laughed and then said, "Just when I've thought I've heard almost everything about Jesus, He continues to amaze me. I think the Pharisees would find your meeting with Jesus very irreverent." All three of them laughed at once.

"Jesus told me He was the most unpredictable Person I would ever meet." Eutychus shrugged, chuckling.

"Well, I will be leaving Paul's box again to be stored in your family's warehouse. The Holy Spirit is telling me you are to read the contents and copy them by your own hand." Timothy was very direct.

"You'll need them for some of your assignments in the future," Tychicus added.

"Plus they will help you understand more spiritually now that you have the Holy Spirit to teach you as you go through them," Timothy said immediately after Tychicus.

"You having to copy them in your own hand will help the Holy Spirit bring them to remembrance as you face the assignments He will be giving you." Timothy and Tychicus were speaking fast back and forth and Eutychus was just taking it all in.

"You'll find another copy of every document in the box," Timothy instructed. "While we've been here in Troas we had scribes here who are part of The Way make three extra copies. One copy is going with us, one copy left with your group, another to be put back into the box alongside the originals. Be sure to be exact when copying them for your set."

Eutychus nodded.

"We've got to be going," Tychicus said as he began to stand up. "Luke is signaling me."

As they all stood up their hugs with Eutychus had much more meaning for each of them.

"I'll be in touch as much as I can," Timothy said as he and Tychicus walked towards Luke.

"We've got passage to Assos." Luke quickly laid out what was happening next for their group. "The ship will leave midmorning today. Paul has told me the Holy Spirit has instructed him to walk to Assos. We will meet him there when he makes it. Let's get going."

Eutychus slowly walked home. It was if he was seeing his city differently for the first time. He had a unique sense now about people and places as he walked by them.

Teach me, Holy Spirit, what all these new feelings are and what you want me to do. I'm listening.

When Eutychus came through the gate of his home, Eirene ran up and hugged him hard.

"What's this all about? This isn't like you," Eutychus said playfully.

"Mom said you died and that man Paul raised you from the dead!!" Eirene's voice was muffled as she said it into the tunic of Eutychus.

"I'm here now. And you're not going to lose me just yet little sister." Eutychus squeezed Eirene. "Could you lighten up your hug a bit? I'm still pretty sore in some places."

Eirene let go quickly and stepped back. "I'm sorry," she said quietly while looking at Eutychus.

"Hey, is there any breakfast? Did mom make any food? Let's go get some." Eutychus smiled at his sister.

"That's the brother I know. The bottomless pit." Eirene chuckled as they both walked towards the home through the courtyard.

Corrina had prepared a huge breakfast feast. She ran and grabbed Eutychus as soon he entered the room.

"Are you okay?" Corrina wouldn't let go of him.

"I'm a little sore, mom, that's all. But I am really hungry." Eutychus squeezed his mom. Corrina then let Eutychus go and went to a very full table of food.

"Okay. Well.... I've had some food prepared for you. You eat. Then I think both of us will have to get to bed much earlier than normal. Is there anything else you want?"

"I could use a hot bath?" Eutychus asked.

"Yes, of course. I'll get Martha to get the fire going to heat up the water right away. By the time you're done with your breakfast, the bath should be ready for you."

The family had quite a big retinue of servants to keep the home complex clean and supplied. Martha was Corrina's main kitchen servant and had been set over the other female house servants.

Eutychus was stuffed from eating a huge amount of food and was now completely relaxed soaking in hot water. It felt so good. He marveled at how many things had transpired in just the last day.

Timothy has already dropped off Paul's box at the warehouse. I want you to be about reading and copying the contents at the end of every day.

The Voice of the Holy Spirit was so very clear in the mind of Eutychus. He was gentle and firm at the same time in His tone.

I have much to teach you in the next few months. You are to be diligent and faithful. You will be learning of My Fruit I want to bear in your life, so that you'll be ready for the assignments Jesus wants to send you on. You will need a strong foundation for your tasks ahead.

Eutychus was still amazed how clear he heard the Voice of the Holy Spirit now. Then he thought how much he wanted his family to have this same relationship with Jesus and the Holy Spirit.

"Thank you, Holy Spirit, for your instructions. Please keep speaking to me though all of this," Eutychus replied out loud. He didn't know why exactly, but it just 'felt right' and better somehow.

"Did you say something, Master Eutychus?" Martha replied from the other room.

"Just praying, Martha. I'm okay," Eutychus said loudly enough so she could hear.

That night Eutychus' dreams were filled with wild mountains and beautiful rivers and waterfalls. It all was very peaceful and calm, but his dream changed and then he saw a girl being held in a jail cell crying out to Jesus, and then he saw others praying in hidden places, rooms, and caves asking for Jesus to help them. When he awoke early on Tuesday morning, he felt a purpose grabbing hold of his heart and a determination filling his body.

I'm here. Guide me. Speak to me, Holy Spirit.

"Thank you, Jesus, for this day to serve you. It's Your day now, not mine. Lead the way, " Eutychus prayed again out loud before getting ready to walk to the warehouse.

Before he left his home, he felt like he was supposed to have a handful of flowers as he walked. He asked his mom if he could have the flowers from the table. She looked at him strangely and said, "Of course Eutychus, what for?"

"Honestly, Mom, I don't know." Eutychus grabbed the flowers and headed out of the house.

As he began to walk down the main street, the hustle and bustle of the merchants were in full swing like always. But this time, Eutychus was so much more aware in a way he hadn't experienced before. It was like when he had walked home the previous morning, he could sense things more acutely.

Stop.

The Holy Spirit spoke the command loudly in Eutychus's head. It was so loud to Eutychus that he thought it was audible. Eutychus stopped in the middle of the street.

Turn to your right and look at the woman in the stall with the red head covering.

Eutychus turned and looked. There were several merchants' stalls. His eyes scanned until he saw a woman with a red head covering working in the back of one of the stalls.

Give her the flowers and say these words: Jesus loves you and hears you. He knows your name.

Eutychus walked towards the stall that was selling leather goods. The man in the stall nodded at Eutychus and asked, "Do you need a belt today, young master?" Eutychus walked right past him and stood in front of the woman whose head was down and was sorting items. When she looked up she was surprised to see Eutychus looking directly at her.

Eutychus handed her the flowers and said, "Jesus loves you and hears you. He knows your name."

The woman began to cry. Tears flowed greatly from her eyes. She grabbed Eutychus, hugged him, and said, "Thank you, thank you, thank you," and then turned and ran up the street.

The man in the stall who had just watched the whole thing asked Eutychus, "What was that all about?"

Eutychus just shrugged his shoulders and said, "Just following my instructions," and walked out of the stall and continued down the street.

What was that all about, Holy Spirit? Eutychus asked in his mind as he walked.

That's between Me and her. You did your part well. Many times, I will give you an assignment and you are to just do it without question. Your obedience is what I want. Your obedience will reap great things for Jesus and the people He sends you to. You may not always see the end of those assignments though, like in this case. You've just got to trust Me.

This is getting interesting, Eutychus thought to himself. And he smiled. And walked with a greater confidence in his step all the way to the warehouse.

Chapter 5
New Strategies
A new calling.

"Eutychus is dead?!!"

"That's not what I said. I said he died when he fell out of a third story window."

A confused and frustrated look crossed the face of Atticus. "You're not making any sense, Steven. I just asked you why Eutychus wasn't here yesterday and you say he died?!"

"Will you be quiet long enough to allow me to tell you what happened?" Steven said. "Sunday evening Eutychus and I were at the same meeting when Eutychus fell out of a third story window and hit the ground. I was standing at the courtyard gate and ran over to him. I checked his breathing and heartbeat. He had neither. Then a man who was speaking at the meeting ran down and grabbed Eutychus, and moments later Eutychus was up and walking."

"So ...what did this guy do to Eutychus?"

"He held him in his arms was all I could see, and then told everyone not to be alarmed that his life was still in him."

"That's it?!"

"Yep. A doctor who was there checked Eutychus out and found no broken bones."

"So is Eutychus going to be back here at the warehouse soon?" Atticus was not quite believing Steven.

"I don't know. Obviously he wasn't here yesterday. I had to muster all of my energy to be here yesterday, because I didn't sleep Sunday night at all. Yesterday when I got home I went right to sleep." Steven set down the box he had in his arms and pointed down the street. "Is that Eutychus I see?" Steven was smiling.

Atticus stared at the young man walking down the street. It looked like Eutychus.

When Eutychus got to the warehouse he went straight to the office and he greeted his father.

"Good morning, Father."

"Well, look who decided to show up today."

"I'm sorry, Father, I needed yesterday to recover and sort some things out. But I'm here now. And I have some suggestions for our business I'd like to propose to you after contemplating the events over the past two days."

"Go ahead." Nikias still had a serious look on his face.

"I think we need another foreman to begin to be trained to do the evening's inventory manifest duties and the other responsibilities I have here. At any point either you or I could be taken out of the situation, and that would greatly hinder our family business. We both know the business needs Nicolaos to continue to manage our ships. And, if the business lost either one of us at any point, we would have to most likely call Nicolaos off his current vital duties. Plus, Nicolaos could be pretty far away and wouldn't be able to get back soon. And if either one of us needs to travel to secure new business and accounts, we'll need another foreman." Eutychus paused.

Nikias' face had softened a bit. "Keep going."

"As I've went through the list of men here in my head as to who would be the best candidate for the position, my choice is Steven. As you know we need extreme trust in whoever we train for that position. We need a man whose ethics, principles, hard work, and honesty have been displayed here. Someone who the other men already look up to. I believe I need to begin to train him starting today."

Nikias was watching and listening to his son. He was seeing something different in him. There was a greater confidence and maturity that hadn't been there before. "Your mother told me as she was getting home from your all-nighter, that you wouldn't be making it in yesterday. Also, yesterday your friend Timothy came by the warehouse in the morning and dropped off this box for you." Nikias pointed at the box in the corner of the office. "Are you going to tell me your story?"

"I'm still processing all that happened to me. I will tell you the story, Dad, but not today. Let's get this warehouse running at full capacity now. Let's get this day going." Eutychus had walked over and picked up Paul's box.

"I think you are correct about the business's need to train another man in the foreman duties. Your logic makes sense. But put Steven on a month's probationary period for the training with extra pay, then I will determine if he can rise to the need and the job. It will be your job to train him."

Eutychus nodded. "I know this will mean longer days for me, and I also will be doing extra study each night. So... help me with mom. I'll probably be getting home later than usual for the next few months."

Nikias was liking this new Eutychus who sounded like a more mature focused business owner. *He's growing up fast.*

Eutychus walked out of the office with the box to put it back into the hidden place that he had always previously kept it.

Days were long for Eutychus in the passing months, but he found energy from reading and copying the documents in Paul's box. There was a spiritual wisdom growing in Eutychus as the Holy Spirit taught him throughout each day and helped him understand what Paul had written with the inspiration of the Holy Spirit. More and more the Holy Spirit had been giving Eutychus small 'divine appointments' with explicit instructions to carry out. Some were just words of encouragement, and some were just gifts he was to give to individuals the Holy Spirit specifically pointed out. Eutychus was always amazed at how each instruction and act of obedience to the Holy Spirit had a different effect on the individuals.

Nikias noticed Eutychus seemed to have increasing strategies of making the work and organization of the warehouse more efficient and profitable. What Eutychus didn't tell his dad was that the Holy Spirit was helping him by giving him the ideas. He also had uncovered several workers who had stolen from them in the past, as the Holy Spirit revealed the men's actions and led Eutychus to the proof. The business profits had risen greatly with the changes Eutychus had been making. Nikias had also given Eutychus the extra duties of hiring and firing of the workers at the warehouse. Some men didn't like having to work for such a young man, so there was some turnover in the first few weeks, but the new workers Eutychus and Steven had trained together seemed better than the ones who had left.

Steven had turned out to be the right man for the job and in three months had already been acting as new foreman without any help from Eutychus or Nikias. He had a good understanding of the logistics of the warehouse and was very detailed in his record keeping. Nikias had made him permanent after the one-month probationary period. Steven had been a great help to Eutychus each night with Paul's box and a strong encouragement to continue in what Jesus had called him to do. Steven usually left the warehouse each night praying for Eutychus as he watched him open up the box and begin his studies and copying. Although Steven was at least ten years older than Eutychus, their relationship had developed into a deep friendship and trust of each other.

"Thanks, Steven, I sure appreciate you," Eutychus said with his head down deep in the documents as Steven had finished closing up the warehouse for the day.

"Eutychus, I have to tell you what the Holy Spirit has been talking to me about."

Eutychus stopped and looked up at Steven.

"He's been telling me to be ready to run this warehouse without you as He is going to soon set you on a different path that will take you away from this day-to-day business. I don't get the sense that you're exactly leaving the business completely but will be filling a different role which will take you to many cites and hidden dangerous places. You'll be doing a dual role as His Messenger and as an agent for this business at the same time, at least for a while."

"Keep going, I'm listening." Eutychus knew Steven had more.

"He's been telling me to pray for your father. That he might become part of The Way. And I also include your other family members in my requests before Him. He's also been pushing me to be ready to serve Him in complete and quick obedience, as your life and mine, will depend on it."

"That definitely sounds like Him... everything you just said is confirmation to me. I know I'm going to need someone here that will be my advocate going forward, someone who will take over for me, as I get led far away from here with the assignments my Master gives me. My heart is for my father, that he would know the Truth. But as we both know the Lord's timing is not ours, and we've got to learn to wait and be patient, till He says 'Go'." Eutychus had gotten up from the desk and came around and gave Steven a hug. Steven returned the embrace. Both men could feel the Presence of the Lord in the office.

Both men began to speak words of worship and adoration to their Father their Creator and thanking Jesus and the Holy Spirit for the work in their lives.

As he walked home Steven could sense that Eutychus's time at the warehouse would soon be changing, maybe even in the next few days.

"Father, guide him and me as we try to be obedient to every instruction You give us." Both men had begun to pray this separately but also simultaneously as they both set about focusing on the days ahead.

Chapter 6

Departure and New Adventures

Dreams and travel.

He was flying over water, then over green hills. While in mid-flight he saw a blazingly bright individual flying up to him, as the individual got closer Eutychus could see he was like a man, but not quite, for he was bronze in skin color and he was much bigger than the average man. The glowing being waved him to follow him, and Eutychus followed him as they flew over a walled city.

Eutychus woke up. He had not had a flying dream in a long time, at least not for many years. He always had loved them, but this last one was very different as it was so much more detailed, and he had a sense the dream had a meaning beyond and it had spiritual significance.

Can you explain that dream to me, Holy Spirit?

Be ready to move. More will be revealed to you later, was the quick response in his mind to his question.

As he walked to the warehouse that morning, he was getting instructions from the Holy Spirit.

As this opportunity is presented to you, allow Me to give you the right words to say to your father, so that you will obtain favor with him in this new endeavor.

Eutychus had learned to be patient with the Holy Spirit and not jump to conclusions as to what He meant. The Holy Spirit would reveal what he needed to know when he needed to know it.

When he arrived at the warehouse office, he found he had a document that had been delivered by messenger for him. As he unrolled it, he discovered it was from Timothy, laying out the business opportunity he had told him about months before, right before his encounter with Jesus. It was about Lydia in Philippi, saying the opportunity was now at hand and he needed to pray about visiting Lydia in Philippi in person to secure the account and to learn of other future opportunities from her. Timothy had included actual numbers of possible inventory and business Lydia was ready to commit to his family's merchant and warehouse business. It was a substantial account if it could be secured.

This is what I was advising you about. The Holy Spirit was clear in Eutychus' mind. *Present to your father the facts and numbers first of the potential account. Then remind him of the work Steven has been doing. Then explain to him that Timothy has set up this prior connection specifically for you and no one else, and that time to secure the deal was now. And that you are ready to secure passage with Nicolaos to Neapolis as his ship is being loaded this week for his next delivery route. And that you will explain this whole thing to your mother and get her approval before you leave.*

Eutychus then did everything that he had been instructed to do and say to his father. But he was still surprised how fast his father had given his approval.

"Eutychus, you've done so well these last few months. Steven is ready. Even though you're really young in someone else's eyes, you've become a man in mine. It's time for you to fly the nest and test your wings," Nikias said with pride in his voice.

Eutychus wondered about the flying metaphor. He wondered if the Holy Spirit was even speaking to his father without him even knowing it. Eutychus was even more surprised when his mother agreed so quickly to the opportunity and plan. Because it certainly wasn't like her. With so many things falling into place so quickly and easily Eutychus knew the Holy Spirit was at work in his favor.

"I've been having these dreams of you on Nicolaos's ship. I think the Lord has been preparing me for this. Because I would have said 'no' without those dreams," Corrina confessed to Eutychus.

Eutychus spent the next two days packing and going through all the things he would need for the journey. The Holy Spirit was advising him about items he would need to bring with him, specifically his own copies of Paul's documents plus the extra copy set from box. Those instructions about the extra set of copies had been included in Timothy's letter to Eutychus. The originals were to remain intact in the warehouse for the time being. Eutychus hadn't quite finished his own complete set yet and was glad for the instructions to bring the extra copies, which allow him to continue to finish his own copies hopefully on the way or when he arrived in Philippi.

Departure day arrived and good-byes were said. Even Corrina and Eirene had come to see Nicolaos and Eutychus off. Steven had pulled Eutychus aside in the warehouse and quickly prayed over Eutychus. After Steven was finished, Eutychus grabbed him and hugged him. "Thanks, brother."

Nikias, Corrina, and Eirene waved from the dock, Corrina dabbing at her eyes with her shawl.

Steven said he had something in his eye as he watched the ship pull away from the dock, and then began barking orders to men to get moving.

"You're now in my world, little brother. Observe and learn," Nicolaos said quietly to Eutychus, and then turned and began shouting orders to his sailors.

The trip took several days of sailing to reach the Port of Neapolis, also known as Thrace. Nicoloas and Eutychus hadn't spoken much during the trip as Eutychus had been below the deck continuing to work on his copy of Paul's writings in Nicoloas' cabin. In the evenings Eutychus went above to spend the time watching the sun go down and his brother handle the ship and sailors. He was impressed at how the sailor's respected Nicoloas and how efficient the tasks were done.

"Do you know what to do when you will get to the port?" Nicolaos asked Eutychus.

"I've got to find a way to Philippi. I'm sure I'll figure it out," Eutychus responded.

"Look for a man with a golden turban, his name is Aabbas. He has the most secure transport wagons. Sure, he's more expensive but he knows me, so he'll take care of you properly and won't abuse you. Plus, his transports are the fastest. Use my name and tell him you're my brother, but don't let him charge you more than twenty-six denarii."

When Eutychus got off the ship, he waved to Nicolaos and Nicolaos waved back. And then he realized he was alone for the first time on this adventure.

You're not alone. Just listen.

Eutychus smiled. *Nothing like having the Creator of the universe as your Guide.*

The port was busy. Eutychus looked at the other ships being unloaded and realized it wasn't too unlike Troas. He figured the transporters would be near the port. He quickly found the area where many people were securing transport to other cities and areas. Scanning the transporter merchants for a man with a golden turban, he caught a glimpse of a man who might have fit the description as the man entered a fairly large tent. Eutychus just waited to see if the man would reappear.

As the man reappeared, Eutychus approached him. "Are you Aabbas?"

"What can I do for you, young master?" Aabbas bowed with flair, speaking with great enthusiasm.

"When is the next transport to Philippi?"

"That depends, young master." Aabbas was definitely putting on for show.

Ask him how his daughter is doing. She is very sick with a fever. The Word of Knowledge came quick to his mind with a picture of a girl about twelve years of age.

"How is your daughter doing? Does she still have a fever?"

Aabbas stopped his salesman face and flair and squinted his eyes at Eutychus. "How do you know that?" Aabbas became stern with Eutychus.

Ask him if he would allow you to see her. That you've come to help her.

Aabbas wondered how this young man knew this. He didn't look like someone with the wrong motives. His worry about his daughter had him off balance.

"Would you allow me to see her? I've actually come to help her," Eutychus said sincerely.

Aabbas for some reason, for which he didn't really know himself why, motioned for Eutychus to follow him into the tent. There in the back of the tent lay about a twelve-year-old girl being attended to by a woman. The woman was putting a cold cloth on the girl's head. Eutychus was now very attentive to the voice of the Holy Spirit, waiting for His next instructions.

Kneel down next to the girl. Place your hand on her head and tell the fever to go and tell the girl to rise in the Name of Jesus.

These instructions were the first time the Holy Spirit had asked Eutychus to do anything like this. All the other previous assignments had been words or gifts, but not asking for healing for anyone. Eutychus felt somewhat nervous about what the Holy Spirit had asked him to do. Questions began to fly into his head. *What if the girl doesn't respond? How will the man react if the girl doesn't get up?*

Trust Me. The Holy Spirit was firm in Eutychus's mind.

Eutychus went over to the girl and did exactly as instructed by the Holy Spirit.

The girl's eyes opened and she moved. "Mom, what am I doing here? Why are you here?" the woman gasped and then hugged the girl and began to cry. "Please let me up, Mom." The woman let go and the girl stood up and walked to her father. Aabbas then grabbed his daughter and hugged her tight.

"Andalee, are you feeling better?" Aabbas asked as he let go, his eyes wet with tears.

"I feel fine, Papa."

"Andia, why don't you get her some food and water." Aabbas looked at his wife who was standing looking at her daughter in shock. She rushed to the back of the tent. "Andalee, my precious, please go eat some food." Aabbas looked overwhelmed and relieved at his healed daughter, then turned and looked at Eutychus. "Who are you?"

"My name is Eutychus. My brother is Nicolaos, captain of the *Hercules* from the merchant Shield of Iraklidis Warehouse in Troas. I'm here to find transport to Philippi."

"Yes, I know Nicolaos. He's an honorable man. Good Captain. But how did you know about my daughter?"

What do I say to him? Eutychus was asking the Holy Spirit as to what to say. *Tell him the truth*, came the quick response.

"Aabbas, I was told about your daughter by the Holy Spirit in my mind. He instructed me to ask about her and He told me exactly what to do and say to her."

Aabbas was silent. His face softened. Tears began to roll down his cheeks.

"I know Jesus loves you and your family, and I'm sure now He set up our meeting today," Eutychus added.

"You will need to tell me more of this Jesus and this Holy Spirit as I personally transport you to Philippi tomorrow, but tonight you will be our guest and have dinner with us and stay the night. I know my wife, Andia, will want to thank you."

Say yes to his offer. The Holy Spirit was very gentle in response to Eutychus's question before he could even ask it.

That night Eutychus spent with the family with the Holy Spirit guiding Eutychus what to say and what not to say. For the most part, Eutychus showed genuine interest in their family, their business, and Andalee, and asked them lots of questions. The family found that they all liked Eutychus and his genuine and honest manner. Eutychus then went to sleep on the softest bed he had ever slept on.

What an adventure, Jesus. Lead on, Eutychus said in his mind before going to sleep.

It won't always be this easy or comfortable. But enjoy this for now. This time the Voice in Eutychus's mind sounded like Jesus.

Chapter 7
Philippi
On the road.

"**M**aster Eutychus, are you ready to go?" Aabbas was calling for him from the cart. There was a delivery of goods for Philippi from a recent ship arrival. Aabbas had taken over the delivery from his employee who usually made this roundtrip route.

"Andalee, you obey your mom and dad now, okay?" Eutychus told her as he tried to extricate himself from her tight hug. "Maybe I'll stop by on my way back."

"You are always welcome, Eutychus," Andia told him.

"Let's go, people! places to go, people to see, goods to get to market!" Aabbas was getting insistent.

Eutychus ran and hopped into the cart next to Aabbas.

The cart bounced along the road through the market. Aabbas played the tour guide as they went, pointing out many sites and details as they traveled the road.

"Philippi is a rich city with beautiful walls and a thriving economy. They say they've got gold mines in the hills, but only very few know exactly where they are located. We currently are on a major Roman road called the Via Egnatia. Philippi is still about half a day from the port in a cart like this. We will pass by some very rich farms. Some people even refer to Philippi as the little Roma."

Aabbas went on about many other things about the surrounding area but finally stopped. They both were silent for a time before Aabbas said, "And now we have time to discuss." Aabbas asked Eutychus all sorts of questions pertaining to the story of Jesus. He had heard of The Way but never really discussed the beliefs of the group with any members. Eutychus did his best to try and tell Aabbas about the story of Jesus, at least of what he knew, and how he and his mom had become members of The Way on their trip to Ephesus. Aabbas would often interrupt Eutychus with all sorts of questions about certain points of the story. Eutychus tried to answer all the questions but often said, "I don't know." But Aabbas became very silent when Eutychus told him about the events of that Sunday night, his fall, and his meeting with Jesus in Heaven, and then agreeing to be sent back.

"You've given me much to think about, young master. I have no doubt you are telling a real story as you have experienced it. The proof lies back home with my precious daughter Andalee." Aabbas paused. "So... you said Jesus caused you to become a host to a powerful spirit?"

"The Holy Spirit ... Aabbas. One of the Three in the ONE, as He told Moses 'I AM.' It is a great mystery beyond my understanding. But I'm learning more each day from Him. The Holy Spirit is the Spirit of Jesus. And I hear Him inside of me giving me directions, instructions, and wisdom. He also lets me know when I've done something wrong and I need to ask forgiveness. He really is my Teacher and many other things. He is the One who told me to ask you about your daughter and then told me what to say and do," Eutychus explained. "And now I have a question for you, Aabbas. Have you heard of a businesswoman in Philippi called Lydia? She has a large purple cloth textile business." Euthychus was curious to see whether Aabbas had any previous dealings with Lydia.

"I have heard of her," Aabbas said plainly. "In fact, one of my employees tried to procure her local business' transportation needs, but so far we've been turned down. I have yet to meet her. I hear that her business is getting quite large and profitable. I've been told she lives in a large house in the city of Philippi and has many workers."

"Lydia is who I am going to meet," Eutychus said boldly. "I have a contact that has set up the introduction and meeting. We hope to sign a shipping, storage, and merchant contract with her for my family's business in Troas."

Aabbas looked at Eutychus with serious expression. "You are very young to be having such weighty contractual negotiations. Your father... he sent you ... alone?" Aabbas was skeptical.

"My father has seen the difference in me since that Sunday night. And he as well cannot deny the profitable changes that I've made in the business in the last six months. As I have been relying on my Teacher to tell me what to do, I've learned to obey quickly and trust Him. Then there's the problem that most people think I'm younger than I actually am. Steven our warehouse foreman says it's because of my 'baby face'. We lost a few workers when I took over the warehouse crew duties from my father. But I trained Steven and we hired a better crew." Eutychus laughed. "It might help if I could grow a beard."

Aabbas chuckled and nodded in agreement. "I still think that the young master should have a traveling companion. Two is better than one, as the ancients say. And traveling brings much danger. I am well skilled with the Saif, as are all of my employees whom I have trained with it." Aabbas patted the long sword that was carried on his back in a type of sling.

"I've been wanting training with a sword. And your words and advice, Aabbas, are heard, appreciated, and will be thought about very carefully," Eutychus said with sincerity.

They were within sight of Philippi now and Eutychus marveled at the beauty of the wall and city. The farms surrounding the city were very well kept and had many workers in them. By his estimates it was almost midday when they reached the outskirts of the city. They were coming alongside a river where they saw many people.

"This river is called the Gangites," Aabbas informed Eutychus.

Eutychus saw a group of women washing purple cloth and hanging it on poles to dry. He motioned for Aabbas to stop. Eutychus climbed off the cart and walked towards the women. As he approached, he greeted them with a wave and asked, "Do you know Lydia? My friend Timothy told me I was to meet her. My name is Eutychus." A woman looked at the young man and didn't sense any danger or guile and walked towards him.

"Timothy!!! Yes. Well... Eutychus, you are welcome," said the woman.

"My name is Euodia. Let me get my friends taken care of and then I'll take you to Lydia." Euodia turned and went back to the area where they were working, then pointed at Eutychus and then walked back to him. It was then Eutychus saw a very large, dark-complected man sitting watching the women, like a guard, who nodded at Euodia.

"Is that man your guard?" Eutychus asked Euodia.

Euodia laughed. "Ermias? Our Ethiopian warrior protector looks quite intimidating, and he is quite dangerous to anyone who has evil in their actions, but he keeps everyone safe and is a friend."

Eutychus and Euodia walked backed to the cart where Aabbas was waiting.

"Aabbas, thank you so much for your advice and friendship. Please thank Andia and Andalee for their hospitality and wonderful food and comfort. Now let me give you the fare. Twenty-six denarii." Eutychus had gotten out his bag of coins.

"Stay your purse, young master!" Aabbas held up his hand. "Your money is not good with me. But your friendship is worth more and I value our relationship. Come and see us when you get back to Neapolis. I am still in your debt for Andalee." Aabbas then called to his horses and waved at Eutychus and began his assent into the city.

Euodia watched and listened to the exchange with interest.

"What does he mean that he is still in your debt?" Euodia asked Eutychus.

"The Holy Spirit healed his daughter when I just had met them for the first time yesterday," Eutychus said plainly.

Euodia's eyes got wide. "Oh... we have much to talk about, Eutychus!" Euodia said with excitement. She then led Eutychus into the city.

The entire city seemed like the rich neighborhood of Troas. Nice houses, some very large, with lots of well-dressed people; even the workers seemed to have nicer clothing. He noticed most all of the people smiling and genuinely happy. Euodia walked quickly and Eutychus had to jog sometimes to keep up as he was constantly being distracted from looking around at the city. They seemed to be walking into a neighborhood with even larger, nicer homes. Eutychus marveled at the affluent homes and streets.

"We're here." Euodia pointed at a very large home surrounded by a very large stone wall. "I guess I'll take you in through the front, since you're our honored guest." Euodia smiled at Eutychus. They both walked up the steps to a very tall, arched front iron gate which led to a huge courtyard filled with different fruit trees and manicured sitting areas with stone benches. They walked up to the home which had very tall front doors. Euodia pushed open the front door and motioned for Eutychus to enter.

Eutychus walked into the home and looked and stared at the grand ceilings, carpets, and large rooms.

"Euodia, who have you brought me?"

Eutychus turned to see a woman striding up to him. She was tall and thin, wearing a beautiful purple dress. He right away noticed she was barefoot as she walked towards them. Her hair was beautifully fashioned up on her head. Her face seemed friendly but also like she could see right inside of you. She had piercing green eyes.

"Lydia, this is Eutychus, the one Timothy told us about in his letter," Euodia told Lydia.

"He looks younger than I expected," Lydia winked at Euodia. "That's okay, Eutychus. Timothy often is thought of being too young as well to be a leader in The Way. If Timothy is your friend, you're our friend. Now let's get you settled." Lydia promptly spun around and began to walk towards the hall.

"See you later, Eutychus." Euodia waved goodbye at Eutychus. He had to jog to keep up with Lydia.

Lydia turned and headed up some stairs. "I'll give you a third-floor bedroom. It has great views you'll love." Lydia practically flew up the stairs. Eutychus tried his best to keep up.

The bedroom windows overlooked the city on one side and the mountains on the other and had a large balcony. Eutychus was overwhelmed at how beautiful everything was but also practical. The bed was also large and had many covers and pillows. There was also a nice table and chair next to a window.

"This is beautiful, Lydia, I .. I.. don't need such a nice room." Eutychus was still overwhelmed.

"Nonsense. Besides, this room is made for the young. After all those stairs, you might change your mind after many trips going up and down. After you're settled, come find me in the common room. And, oh, you might want to know I think Paul wrote his second letter to the group in Corinth on that desk. He liked his privacy when he wrote." Lydia then turned and practically floated down the stairs.

Eutychus put his bag in the corner and the holder of his documents and took off his coat. He explored the room some more and walked out onto the balcony and breathed deep.

"Okay, Jesus, I'm here. Now what?" said Eutychus under his breath.

Listen. Watch. Learn. Be slow to speak. Listen well before responding. Ask Me if you have questions. Remember the Fruit of the Spirit you've been reading about in Paul's letter to the Galatians. Let them be manifest in you by the Holy Spirit. Be yourself. Be honest. I'm with you.

Eutychus could feel the tension in his body leave, and he relaxed.

"Thank you, Jesus. Lead on," whispered Eutychus.

Eutychus slowly walked down the stairs. He got to the bottom and didn't know which way to turn. After he stopped and listened, he could hear voices towards to the right and rear of the home, so headed in that direction. He came to a large room with a big fireplace with lots of couches and padded chairs. He saw people in groups of two and three throughout the room talking with one another. Lydia then saw him.

"Over here, Eutychus." Lydia waved him over to her group which was by the fire.

"In about an hour dinner will be ready, but now I want to introduce Dawit, Phaedra, and Nikita. Eutychus, everyone you'll meet here is a part of The Way. Everyone, this is Eutychus, the one Timothy has told us about. Please excuse me. I want to see how Lia and crew are doing with dinner preparations." Lydia got up while Eutychus sat on one of the chairs that faced the couch.

"Dawit, you look like a man I saw today down at the river," said Eutychus.

"That was my brother Ermias." Dawit smiled at Eutychus.

"I'd like to hear your stories and how you came to be here and part of The Way. I'm sure I'll be asked when everyone is together to tell my story and how I came to be here," Eutychus gently suggested.

Euodia then entered the room, looked around, saw Eutychus, and headed over to the group. "So Eutychus I want to hear the story of Aabbas' daughter." Euodia plopped down in the couch as she said this. "Oh... I'm sorry did I interrupt?"

The others just laughed.

"Did he already tell you guys the story of how the Holy Spirit healed a girl yesterday?" Euodia looked at all of them and then at Eutychus. Then they all looked at Eutychus.

"Well... there's not much of story, pretty simple." Eutychus then went on the tell them of how the Holy Spirit helped him find Aabbas and his family and what had transpired. The group asked a few questions and Eutychus tried to answer them the best he could.

"Dinner is ready, folks, let's gather into the dining hall," Lydia called from the edge of the common room.

Chapter 8
New Friends
New Business.

Eutychus sat at the large dining table just after breakfast and the workers had left to begin their day. Lydia, Euodia, Syntyche, Junia, Phoebe, Dawit, and Ermias were also gathered for the meeting with Eutychus. It had been several days since Eutychus had arrived, and most of the team had gotten to know Eutychus and his story.

"Eutychus, this morning I wanted to discuss future plans with my leadership team and the opportunities you're bringing to us," Lydia said, setting the agenda for the meeting. "First, thank you for bringing the copies of Paul's letters. We already had the Thessalonians' and Corinthians' letters from Paul, but you brought us the letters to the Romans and Galatians. In exchange, you've shown great interest in the writing of James that we have. So... I'm making preparations for you to have a copy of that parchment as well."

"I'm so grateful Lydia to you and everyone here for your awesome hospitality, and friendship. But if you would just allow me, I'd like to make a copy of the parchment of James myself, in my own hand. It's a discipline the Holy Spirit has been teaching me. I learn so much from Him that way," Eutychus explained.

"That's fine and good. Yes, I'll make sure you have the supplies to do just that. Now second on the agenda, the contract with Eutychus' family business. Team, do you have any suggestions?" Lydia asked, looking at the other members around the table.

"Obviously trust is an issue with anyone we do business with," Syntyche said.

"How involved is the business with The Way?" Junia asked.

"We are not officially involved, but my mother, Corrina, and my warehouse foreman, Steven, are both members," Eutychus replied. "Obviously my heart and prayer yearn that all of my family know Jesus personally."

"I think one of us needs to visit the business and discern through the Holy Spirit what we should do," Dawit suggested. "There's nothing like being there in person. Then if the plan is agreeable with everyone here and the Holy Spirit we will then move forward. I've been revisiting the lessons we all learned from Paul."

"I agree with Dawit. And since he made the suggestion, I think he should be the one to go," Euodia suggested. Everyone nodded to this suggestion.

"I'm fine with a little trip across the water," Dawit said. "I can leave tomorrow if you agree Lydia. I should be back in a week or less."

"That's good," Lydia stated. "Tomorrow you will leave with the contract with the details and provisions I want included. If they agree, then you will have my seal to make the contract valid."

"If you would allow me to look over those details and provisions I might be able to help both parties come to an agreement faster," Eutychus suggested, "as I do know what we are able and not currently able to accomplish for you."

Lydia smiled with a surprised look on her face. "You're more like Timothy than you know, Eutychus," she said. "Eutychus, take the contract and look it over. When you're done, you and I will work it all out so Dawit will have the contract ready to go tomorrow. Okay... agenda item number three. Prayer. Let's take some time to pray together now for this opportunity and Eutychus and see what the Holy Spirit has to say."

Eutychus was surprised how fast everyone immediately launched into prayer. Dawit and Ermias were praying in a different language. Everyone seemed to be praying out loud at the same time. Some were praying in a tongue that Eutychus had never heard. It was different than the style of the people in the group of The Way at Troas. Eutychus was used to a much more singular style, where only one person prayed at a time out loud in the language everyone knew. Then everyone around the table stopped abruptly.

Eutychus waited and listened.

"Eutychus, I've been seeing scenes of you... in Roma, in some very dangerous places," Junia said.

"I saw him at a jail in Corinth," Euodia said.

"And with the group in Ephesus," said Lydia.

"Jesus will be taking you back to be with Him before any of us. It seems like it is not far off," Ermias said. Everyone seemed surprised at this information but Eutychus nodded in agreement. "And I am to accompany you for part of your journey. Plus, I am to train you in our way of fighting sticks, and then combine that with Saif sword techniques." Ermias looked directly at Eutychus.

"The Holy Spirit has lessons for you in the training that you'll receive no other way," Dawit said.

"These lessons will help you to learn how to navigate physical pain in the correct way," Ermias said.

"I've had a good foundation of that working in the warehouse with long days of lifting heavy boxes and bags. But I want to learn from everyone here," Eutychus added.

Ermias and Dawit smiled and nodded at Eutychus.

"Anyone else?" Lydia asked. Everyone was quiet and waited.

"Did anyone get anything about how long Eutychus will be with us here in Philippi?" Lydia looked around the table.

After a long pause of silence, Phoebe said quietly, "I think at least several months. I saw Eutychus interacting with almost everyone here in this business and house. I even saw him working with the cloth alongside us at the river. I can confirm what Ermias said, as I saw Eutychus doing fighting techniques and exercises down by the river with Ermias. I feel we all should help him any way we can."

Lydia smiled and shook her head. "It's always the quiet ones who bring the words of wisdom."

Eutychus could feel the Presence of the Holy Spirit and the love of Jesus begin to fill the room, and his eyes began to water. He realized he wasn't alone because everyone began to worship and praise the Father, Jesus, and the Holy Spirit. Some stood with their hands raised. Eutychus saw Ermias on his knees with his forehead on the ground, everyone was taking a different posture before the Presence. After a period of time of worship, everyone became quiet.

"I have so much to learn from all of you," Eutychus said quietly.

At his statement Lydia came over to him and put her hands on Eutychus' shoulders and began to pray. "Thank you, Father, for bringing Eutychus to us. I can see Your heart in him. Help us in the way You want us to help him. Make clear for each of us of how You want each of us to invest in him."

When Eutychus opened his eyes, he saw that everyone had gathered around Lydia and him as she was praying. "I need to write a letter to my father and family to go with Dawit tomorrow. Now that I know I will be here a while with all of you," Eutychus said quietly.

As Eutychus stood, Lydia gave him a hug as did Euodia. Dawit and Ermias placed their hands on his shoulder and nodded to him.

"This fellowship is to be continued later," Lydia announced. "Now let's follow the Spirit's instructions and walk with Him today." Immediately everyone went their separate ways while Eutychus headed to his room to write a letter.

He was in his room for just a few minutes when he heard a knock and Lydia came into the room with a parchment. "Here's the contract with my details and provisions. Look it over and come back with your suggestions. We'll put it into final form this evening after dinner." Lydia smiled at Euthychus and turned quickly and left the room.

Lydia is so quick. It seems like she floats everywhere. *Holy Spirit, guide me here. What should I say to my family in the letter?*

The months flew by. Dawit's trip was successful. Steven and Dawit became immediate friends after their first meeting. Even Nikias liked Dawit and his confident, honest manner. Several purple cloth shipments had already been delivered and sold by Shield of Iraklidis Warehouse in Troas, with plans of doubling the size of shipments. Both businesses were growing in profits from the joint venture. Nikias had begun setting aside money to be held for Eutychus for his portion of the purple cloth account.

Meanwhile, Eutychus had begun training with Ermias the next day and had continued every day since. Ermias remarked to almost everyone how fast Eutychus had picked up the techniques. Some days both Dawit and Ermias trained Eutychus in fighting styles ranging from lots of hard disciplines using weapons and close combat techniques with and without weapons. At any point of any day, Ermias and Dawit began to attack Eutychus with surprise trainings. It became a playful interaction that looked like brothers of the same family to anyone observing from the outside.

Eutychus also seemed to volunteer for every hard labor assignment he could within the Philippi operation. He took every humble job that he saw. In the evenings was when he really enjoyed the conversations. The group of The Way in Philippi were not shy of debate of the scriptures. Eutychus listened with great earnest. He even joined into the conversation and debate about what was the evidence of the Holy Spirit being in a person's life. The debate went back and forth with many people using the letter to the Galatians where Paul talks about the nine fruit of the Spirit and the first letter to the Corinthians and the nine gifts of the Spirit.

"Isn't the evidence of a tree the fruit it produces?" Eutychus asked.

"But if no one ever eats the fruit, what good is it?" another quickly shot back.

"But the gifts should be an outflow of His instructions to what He is asking any of us to do," Eutychus stated. "It's not like we can turn them on whenever we like, but we sure can shut them off if we're too fearful or stubborn. The fruit tells us about the real character of the tree, whether anyone ever eats the fruit or not."

There's wisdom in this young man, Lydia thought and smiled as she watched Eutychus get involved in the scriptural debates.

One morning Eutychus received a letter from his father asking about plans for the future and his possible arrival back home. In the letter Eutychus found a fairly detailed schedule of the shipping routes and days that Nicoloas had now established with the five ships now in the family's fleet.

You're not going home yet. The Holy Spirit was quick in response. *Your next stop will be in Corinth. Understand that Corinth will not be as easy or comfortable for you as Philippi. You must be ready for hardship—that's what your training was for, both spiritual and physical, to make you ready for the months to come. Lydia has some names for you to contact. I am sending Ermias with you on this leg of your assignment for Me.*

Eutychus walked down the stairs to find Lydia.

Chapter 9

Connections

On the sea.

"In three days, the next shipment to your warehouse is scheduled to be loaded from Neapolis. Here is the name of my contact in Corinth. He usually can be found in the financial district at the official Roman money exchange office." Lydia was going over details with Dawit, Ermias, and Eutychus. "If he is not there, they will know where he is. I've also included my contacts in Roma and the places they can most likely be found, as the Holy Spirit revealed to us that you will be sent there as well at some point, Eutychus. Please understand these names are only contacts, a place to start. You'll have to rely on the Holy Spirit as to what, how, and when to utilize them. Not all of them have I met in person, but they know me or of my reputation."

"We'll leave in two days, stay at our regular lodging for the night, and then I will send them on their way," Dawit replied.

"I can confirm that we will have two company ships in port." Eutychus was looking at the shipping schedule he had received in the letter from his father. "One for your shipment and the *Hercules*, which is bound for Roma but will stop in Corinth first."

"There is much to be done. Let's be ready to go," Ermias said and walked quickly towards his room. Dawit headed to the storehouse and stables.

"Eutychus, before you leave, can you think of anything you might need from me?" Lydia looked at Eutychus.

"Not at this moment, but I will ask the Holy Spirit for instructions. Thank you, Lydia, for all that you've done for me."

Lydia could tell Eutychus was truly sincere in his words. "I will ask Him as well. You may be young but remember Who called you. Stay true to His requests and calling. Now get going, there's lots to do before you and Ermias leave."

Eutychus wondered if he saw Lydia's eyes filling with tears just before she turned and walked away

The day arrived quickly and the whole household met in the front courtyard for the goodbyes to Ermias and Eutychus. They gathered around the three men, laid hands on them and prayed over them. Many stepped up to hug Eutychus one last time.

"May the grace of the Lord Jesus Christ, the love of God, and the fellowship of the Holy Spirit be with you," Lydia declared as the men climbed aboard the cart filled with the shipment of cloth.

"When we get to the port I would like to visit the transporter row. I think I'm to visit someone there," Eutychus said to Dawit when they were on the road beyond Philippi.

The trip seemed much shorter to Eutychus than the trip into Philippi. Maybe because his thoughts were so much on the current assignment on which Ermias and he were embarking.

Dawit turned into the avenue of tents known as transporter row.

"Go to the large tent second nearest the dock," Eutychus instructed. Eutychus spotted a man with a gold turban. *Yep, that's Aabbas.* "Aabbas!" Eutychus shouted and waved from the cart as they were coming towards his tent.

Aabbas turned and looked to see who called his name. He then spotted Eutychus. "Master Eutychus!" Aabbas waved and called out.

Eutychus jumped down and jogged to Aabbas and they grabbed forearms in greeting.

"It's very good to see you again Master Eutychus!" Aabbas paused was looking at Dawit and Ermias. "I see you come with formidable help." The brothers climbed off the cart and bowed to Aabbas.

"Aabbas, let me introduce you to Dawit and Ermias. They are my brothers in Spirit and my trainers."

Both Dawit and Ermias bowed again in greeting.

"Come. Welcome to my tent. Andalee will be so excited to see you, Eutychus." Aabbas turned and held the tent flap open.

"I will stay with the load," Dawit told Eutychus.

Then Ermias and Eutychus went inside, and Aabbas followed.

When Andia looked to see who it was she exclaimed, "It's so good to see you! Andalee, look who it is!"

Andalee then jumped up and screamed in joy and ran and hugged Eutychus.

"This is quite a welcome," Ermias leaned over and quietly said to Eutychus.

"You must stay long enough to break bread with us. Andia, prepare some food for our guests." Aabbas was motioning for them to sit down on some cushions.

Andia disappeared behind a flap in the back of the tent. Andalee wouldn't let go of Eutychus and sat down right next to him. Andia returned with some bread, aboard of fresh cheese, and a bowl of grapes.

"Tell us are you headed home? Have you been in Philippi this entire time?" Aabbas was speaking fast.

"Ermias and I are headed to Corinth tomorrow on the Hercules. Dawit has the next shipment headed to our warehouse in Troas," Eutychus explained.

Aabbas clapped his hands together loudly once. "Good! Then we have time to talk tonight! You must stay with us! All three of you. I will take care of your horses and cart and keep them secure for the night." Aabbas picked up bell and rang it. A man appeared. "Take care of the cart and horses out front. Be sure to feed and water them. Keep everything secure till tomorrow in our stables." The man bowed and exited through the front of the tent.

"I better go explain things to Dawit," Ermias said to Eutychus, and he got up and went out.

That night Dawit and Ermias heard from Aabbas the story of his daughter's healing from a different perspective than the one Eutychus had told. They didn't know the past history of Andalee and the previous year of sickness and serious health challenges. And that the healing had had a major impact on Aabbas and Andia. When all the servants had left after dinner, Aabbas said quietly to the three men, "Tell us more about this Jesus and Holy Spirit. And I can see that you two also have quite a story to tell." Aabbas was looking directly at Dawit and Ermias.

"Yes. I can tell you know of our marks and what they mean. We serve another Master now. The King of Kings, Jesus. Our lives are now completely In His Service. We've been serving Him at His operation in Philippi for the past year. Lydia paid for our release and we are free men now," Dawit explained. These were things Eutychus didn't even know and he listened with great interest.

"We have had the joy of training young Eutychus here in the ways of our homeland and some of your people's ways with the Saif. He's learned well in this last six months," Ermias commented, "but of course a lifetime of learning is never enough."

Aabbas' eyes widened at this statement.

"I have taken your advice, Aabbas, and Ermias my friend and trainer will now go with me on this next travel leg to Corinth," Eutychus said as he looked at Aabbas.

"I'm glad, Master Eutychus. And honored you have taken my advice to heart. All of you are welcome in our tent at any time." Aabbas bowed his head in their direction.

"I would have never expected Eutychus to show up with such men of renown and deadly abilities, and then to be trained by such masters. But with Eutychus I am always surprised at his connections and favor." Aabbas was looking at Ermias and Dawit.

Eutychus was filing all of this information away in his mind. *I'm going to have lots of questions for Ermias on the ship.*

The conversation continued into the night. Each of the three men telling their personal story to Aabbas, and Andia of their commitment to Jesus and their lives being filled with the Holy Spirit. They relayed as much of the story of Jesus as they had learned.

"Aabbas, tomorrow after they've left and I've secured my load onto the ship, I will come by to talk with you further," Dawit said. "The Holy Spirit is telling me to meet with you about sharing a teaching we have in our possession in Philippi."

"I would be very honored and pleased to welcome anything you have to offer to this humble family." Aabbas bowed extra low this time.

Nicolaos marveled at Eutychus as he watched Ermias put him through a fighting training exercise with swords on the deck of the ship.

"My little brother is gaining some pretty impressive skills. And you've grown stronger and faster," Nicolaos said as Eutychus took a break and was still breathing heavily from the last round.

"Ermias is a good teacher. I still have so much to learn," Eutychus said, still breathing hard. He got up and took a ready stance as Ermias motioned him forward.

"Enemies do not wait for one to catch their breath," Ermias stated with intention.

For the next hour the two went through rigorous rounds of different training exercises. Every day in the afternoon on the deck, Ermias trained Eutychus. In the evenings Ermias was found reading by lamp, parchments copied from the

Pentateuch. And Eutychus would engage Nicolaos about what he knew about the family's business.

"The purple cloth textile account is keeping us busy and has opened many new great opportunities and connections as well as increased profits. Father is even talking about buying the adjacent building to expand the warehouse. Steven is always ready and on top of things. He now runs the warehouse completely and has hired even another foreman. Father now has the time to explore even more connections and new business ventures. Father is traveling more, much to mother's concern. She always asks me if I know anything about you, which of course I say 'No.' I guess now I'll have something to report to her. Although I think she'd rather hear of any serious female prospects you or I may have for the future. Telling her that you are becoming a good fighter being trained by a skilled African weapons master won't be 'good news' to her ears." Both Eutychus and Nicolaos laughed. "I keep hearing bits and pieces about you and a fateful Sunday night where you fell from a third story window. What's that all about? And how did you become such a businessman securing our biggest account? What were you doing in Philippi for six months? How did you get an Ethiopian warrior to train you? I thought they didn't train anyone not from their tribe."

"That's a very long story. And someday I may tell you about what all has happened with me," Eutychus replied. As the Holy Spirit had already advised Eutychus not to say anything about his meeting with Jesus to Nicolaos just yet or how the Holy Spirit now completely guided his life. Eutychus changed the subject. "So... when are we going to make the stop for Corinth?"

"We should be there in another day," Nicolaos replied. "We've had good wind, and the seven-day trip was easy this time."

"Father gave me this shipping schedule in a letter." Eutychus handed the document to Nicolaos. "Could you make any changes that are needed to keep me up to date? You've got five ships now to coordinate?"

"As of next month, six ships. The next ship will be the biggest yet, and I'll soon be taking that one as mine. Sure, I'll look over the schedule and add anything that's missing."

"Thanks, Nico."

"Tomorrow don't let me forget, Father gave me a package for you. He gave it to me the last time I was home to give to you the next time I saw you."

Chapter 10
Corinth
Pride goes before the fall.

In the morning Ermias and Eutychus began discussing self-defense.

"One of the best pieces of advice I could give in defensive training would be to be aware of your surroundings at all times. Be observant of all the people around you. Learn how to size them up as to their potential." Ermias was being very serious. "The best place to be in a fight is ...not in it. I've been to Corinth. It's a very unpredictable place. There are lots of factions there. Most are not moral but are looking for ways to profit off of the innocence, ignorance, addictions, and weakness of people." Ermias was trying to get Eutychus to prepare himself for Corinth.

"Here's the package father wanted me to give to you and the updated shipping schedule. And I'd listen to Ermias; he is correct about Corinth." Nicolaos had walked up and heard Ermias' advice.

"Thanks." Eutychus took the package and document and opened the package to find a letter and money. The letter explained that Nikias was setting aside some profits from the Philippi account for Eutychus and this was a small amount for travel expenses Eutychus might encounter.

"You need to split up this money. One bag needs to be concealed in a belt next to your skin, and the other smaller amount needs to be in your external money bag. Any personally revealing documents also need to kept secret next to your skin and not in the external document holder." Ermias was trying to get

Eutychus to be prepared for when they disembark the ship. "Be very aware when we walk from the ship through the docks." Ermias was again warning Eutychus.

"I've been around the docks all my life. I'll be fine," Eutychus responded.

Ermias closed his eyes and prayed, *Lord Jesus help me with Eutychus.*

It was almost midday when Nicolaos guided the ship into the dock and the ropes were secured. Ermias followed Eutychus off the ship. Nicolaos was already barking orders to his crew to get the shipment for Corinth unloaded.

As the two walked through the docks, Ermias was scanning every person on the docks and street ahead. They were approaching the bars in the wharf district. The street was narrow and not made for carts but only people, and the street was crowded with men. The noise of the music and men in the various bars was loud.

Suddenly a fight had burst through one of the doors. Ermias stepped back just in time. But Eutychus was knocked down by the two fighting men into the bar across the way. Eutychus fell face down in the bar with his feet still in the street. Men were shouting, Eutychus felt a kick in his side, and he quickly turned over to his back. When he looked up, standing over him was a nude girl about his own age. She was one of the dancers in the bar and was quickly trying to get out of the way. Eutychus then felt someone grab his ankles and then pull him out of the doorway back into the street. Ermias had grabbed Eutychus and was now standing him up.

"Let's get out of here now!" Ermias guided Eutychus quickly forward up the street at almost a jog. When they had cleared the wharf district and found a larger open area, Ermias finally stopped pulling and shoving Eutychus forward.

"Are you okay?" Ermias allowed Eutychus to breathe and check himself.

"I'm missing my money bag, but everything else seems to be here," Eutychus said as he checked himself.

"This is why you greatly conceal certain items," Ermias said. "You still have your other money belt?"

"Yes. Everything else is still here." Eutychus was rechecking all of his bags and clothing.

"Then let's get to the financial district as fast as we can and find Regulus." Ermias motioned for Eutychus to go ahead of him. When they got to the front of Roman office of money exchange Eutychus asked some official looking men if they could tell him where to find a man named Regulus. They pointed to a building across the square.

"Are you Regulus?" Eutychus asked the man sitting at a desk in the small office.

"I am, and who are you?" Regulus was not friendly in his greeting.

"My name is Eutychus. I was given your name by Lydia of Philippi, manufacturer of the best purple cloth in the region. My family is a major distributor of her fine cloth out of Troas."

"And what exactly can I do for you?" Regulus still was very skeptical in his tone.

"My friend and I—" Eutychus pointed at Ermias who was standing just outside of the doorway. "—are looking for a meeting place, that Lydia said you'd know about. She said you'd know .... the way."

"I see." Regulus still had a stoic face. "Let me put some things away here. Wait for me outside."

Eutychus went outside and stood next to Ermias.

"Is he going to help us?" Ermias asked quietly.

"I think so," Eutychus responded in a whisper.

"Remember my advice about being aware of your surroundings? It should apply with everyone and everyplace we go in Corinth as long as we're here." Ermias was speaking very quietly to Eutychus.

"Follow me," was all Regulus said as he walked in front of the two. They wound through the streets and finally came to a plain building with no writing or windows. It looked like a warehouse. Regulus knocked five times in a certain cadence at an unmarked single door. A small opening in the door at eye level opened. Regulus then knocked two more times and said the word 'Wednesday' and they could hear the movement behind the door before it opened halfway. The three went into the building.

They climbed the stairs to the second story and went down a hall to another door at the end which Regulus opened to a large room. When they entered, they saw a circle of people in prayer in the room. Once Eutychus and Ermias were in the room, Regulus turned around and went through the door before closing it behind him. Eutychus and Ermias were left standing looking at the group in prayer. Finally, a woman looked up and saw them standing there, the woman motioned for them to join the group. Eutychus and Ermias came over and quietly sat down on the floor in the circle.

As Eutychus began to pray, he kept hearing a name in his mind. The group prayed silently for quite a while. Eutychus thought that this group was more like the group in Troas than the group in Philippi in their prayer manner. Then a man began to pray aloud, "Father, tell us how we are to be a help to these travelers." Everyone remained quiet. Then everyone began standing up. Ermias and Eutychus stood up as well.

"My name is Eutychus, and this is Ermias. We just came from Philippi as we were instructed to come to Corinth by the Holy Spirit." Eutychus and Ermias bowed. Slowly the group members came and greeted the two.

"Does the name Chloe mean anything to any of you?" Eutychus asked. "When I was in prayer here, that name kept coming to my mind."

A woman gasped. "That's who I was praying for. She is a slave who has been wrongly accused by her master's wife and is now in jail awaiting execution. I was trying to see if she would be willing to be a part of our group, but it is very dangerous for slaves to meet anywhere out of their master's sight or knowledge. She accepted Jesus as she listened to Paul when he preached in the streets here. I've been trying to encourage her for the past few years when I see her. Now it looks like she will be executed this week. I don't know what to do."

Eutychus looked at Ermias. "I guess I have my first assignment." Eutychus looked at the woman. "Where is this jail?"

"I can take you there and point it out. But I'm not sure I can get you in." The woman was looking hopeful but also was cautious in her voice.

"I'd better be the person to guide them, Dimitra. I don't want you exposed in any way." A man interjected into their conversation. "My name is Prophyrius. I know Lydia. Did she give you Regulus' name?"

Eutychus nodded. "Can you take us now?" He was feeling a strong urgency to speak to Chloe and that there wasn't much time left.

"Okay, I'll take you now." Prophyrius motioned to Ermias and Eutychus to follow him.

The three walked through the streets as Prophyrius led them. He stopped across the street from a large stone fortress, which was obviously a Roman jail.

"I can't get you in, but that is where she is being held." Prophyrius pointed.

Ermias looked at Eutychus then said, "I'll wait here with Porphyrius. Remember what I told you."

Eutychus was asking the Holy Spirit in his mind what he needed to do.

Get out fifty denarii and give them to the guard at gate. Tell him you have to speak to Flavius Aeneas about a prisoner being held there.

Eutychus wondered about the substantial amount of money needed. He had to go around a corner and extricate the money from his inside belt. He wondered if he would have enough money left over to make it through the time they were to be in Corinth.

Eutychus took some deep breaths and walked to the gate of the prison.

The guard at the gate looked at Eutychus and didn't move or speak. Eutychus held out his hand, took the guard's hand, and dropped the money into his hand, saying, "I need to talk to Flavius Aeneas about a prisoner being held here."

The guard turned and motioned Eutychus through the arched opening. The guard pointed to an opening where Eutychus saw more soldiers. As he walked he heard his next instructions.

Ask for Flavius Aeneas, then tell him you are here as a family representative of one being held for execution tomorrow, and that you have final words for the prisoner.

Eutychus did his best to remain calm and alert as he followed the Holy Spirit's instructions. Soon he was being guided into a long corridor of single stone cells holding single prisoners. He began to walk down the row of cells. The Roman guard watched him carefully.

Stop. Tell the girl on the left you are here with a message for her.

"Chloe, I have a message for you," Eutychus said to the figure in the back of the dark cell. "Guard, can you let me in so that I may speak to her in private?

The guard came and unlocked the iron gate and relocked it after Eutychus had entered the cell.

"Do I know you?" A small voice asked from the dark corner.

"No. But Jesus knows you. He sent me to give you a message", Eutychus said very quietly.

"Are you an angel?" asked the voice.

Eutychus moved to the back of the cell and found a young woman sitting in the corner. "I'm not an angel, but I'm His messenger." He could feel the Presence of the Holy Spirit come over him and begin to give him words. "Chloe, you need to know He loves you greatly and cares for you right now. You need to know you will be with Him tomorrow and not to fear what will happen to you. He will diminish the pain and will send His angels to escort you to Him." Eutychus could feel the love of Jesus for Chloe. Eutychus could hear that Chloe had begun to cry. He reached out and put his hand on her shoulder.

"I felt so alone and was crying out to God for Him to help me. I can feel Him here in this place with us right now. I've never felt anything like this before. What is your name?" Chloe was looking up at Eutychus.

"My name is Eutychus. The Holy Spirit has guided me to you for this very moment in time. I can tell He really loves you."

"I have a peace now that I've never felt before. This is so strange and won-derful." Chloe stood up and lifted her hands into the air. Eutychus watched her smile. "Thank you, Eutychus, for coming to see me." Chloe then grabbed Eutychus and hugged him tight. Eutychus gently put his arms around Chloe.

"Tell Dimitra I'm okay now. Tell her thank you," Chloe said as she stepped back from Eutychus.

"Tell her thank you for…?" Eutychus asked.

"I just know she was praying for me. I'm ready now. Thank you again Euty-chus." Chloe had a smile on her face.

Eutychus was in a sort of daze as he was escorted from the prison. *Did all of that just really happen?*

He found himself in the street at dusk. Ermias and Prophyrius found Eu-tychus somewhat disorientated. They grabbed him and escorted him down the street. Prophyrius brought them to an empty house and ushered them in quickly, as it was now dark.

"This is one of our safehouses. I'll bring food in the morning. Use only one lamp and then keep its light hidden as much as possible." With those instructions, Prophyrius left and locked to the door.

"Ermias, was it like this when you were here?" Eutychus asked quietly as they found the wooden cots in the room and sat down.

"No. When I was here, it was very different. But that is a long story for another time. Did you get to see Chloe?" Ermias was curious about what had happened inside the prison. Eutychus told Ermias as much as he could remember about the events and meeting at the prison. "Prophyrius told me Chloe's story that he learned from Dimitra," Ermias quietly began telling the whole story to Eutychus. "She was a slave owned by a wealthy merchant, the wife of the man was having an affair with another man. She was very suspicious of her husband also of having multiple affairs and never liked Chloe and always thought her husband had purchased Chloe because she had a pretty face and had other plans for her. So, when the husband questioned his wife about a different man's cloak being in their bedroom, she accused Chloe of having an affair in their bedroom. And then accused her husband of also having an affair with

Chloe. The husband felt trapped that Chloe might say that she had seen him with other women and agreed that Chloe was a problem and that she needed to be charged. The next day she was immediately arrested in the marketplace after she had just finished telling the whole story to Dimitra and then she was charged with multiple crimes, all of which she was innocent."

"She'll be with Jesus very soon. Her assignment is over here. Her life will continue in heaven," Eutychus said quietly.

Chapter 11

Missteps

Church meeting awkwardness.

*E*utychus *was seated at a table and was watching the nude dancers in the bar. The enticement of the dancers was palpable to Eutychus as they waved at him. He looked across his table and saw the face of Chloe. Chloe's face looked sad. He looked at another table and saw his mother and sister; their faces looked angry.*

"Aaarrgg!" Eutychus groaned with a type of yell in his sleep.

Ermias reached over and shook Eutychus. "Eutychus, wake up."

Eutychus sat up. "Bad dream." He rubbed his eyes and head.

"You want to talk about it?" Ermias asked.

"No," replied Eutychus. Eutychus wasn't ready to confess the images that kept coming to his mind ever since his fall into the bar when they first arrived in Corinth. He was embarrassed at his own weakness in this area. Now the images had begun to show up in his dreams.

Lord Jesus, can you take away these images from me? The secret, silent prayer became a regular one from Eutychus. He got up and could tell that the sunrise was close, as the light of dawn was rising. The response to Eutychus' prayer was still silence.

"I need to go for a walk." Eutychus began to put on his cloak and sandals.

"Whoa, whoa, my friend, slow down, I'll go with you. We don't have to talk." Ermias got up and quickly got ready. *Jesus, help Eutychus. Help me know how to help Eutychus.* Ermias was praying in his mind. The Holy Spirit responded quickly in his mind. *You're already doing it.*

The two slowly walked down the street together in silence.

"We shouldn't go too far, as we need to be ready to meet Prophyrius when he arrives," Ermias said quietly. He had been keeping the front door of the house in his sight.

Eutychus stopped and slowly sat down with his back to a stone wall, staring off into the distance.

Ermias went across the street and stood where he had a better vantage point of the entire street, house, Eutychus, and any potential approaching danger. It was only a short time till Ermias had spotted Prophyrius walking down the street towards the house. Ermias waved at Prophyrius and Prophyrius waved back. "Let's go, Eutychus. Prophyrius is coming."

Eutychus got up and began to slowly walk back to the house. *Forgive me, Jesus, I don't know how to handle this. I'm obviously weak in this area.*

"Here is some food, it's not much. This morning our group will be meeting all together in a large home of one of the elders," Prophyrius explained to Eutychus and Ermias. "I'll take you to it. They've already been informed that you're here in Corinth and are expecting you."

Of course I forgive you, Eutychus. I love you. Listen to Me. Trust Me. Keep talking to Me. Keep asking me questions. Eutychus had barely heard anything Prophyrius had said. But the response from the Holy Spirit had brought tears to his eyes.

"Thank you, Prophyrius, for everything. Our Lord supplies our need." Ermias smiled at Prophyrius.

"Are you okay, Eutychus?" Prophyrius looked at him.

Eutychus still was staring off into the distance but now he had tears running down his cheeks.

"He had a bad dream," Ermias explained quietly to Prophyrius.

Eutychus wiped his face with his sleeve.

"We need to leave in a bit to get to the meeting. You have some time to eat though." Prophyrius kept watching Eutychus.

After they had eaten, Prophyrius led them through the streets. When they arrived at the house's courtyard they were let in and they were led into a large home which had a large meeting room. Chairs had been set up, but the group was even larger than Philippi and Troas, so people were also standing and sitting with their backs against walls. The room was packed.

Eutychus was surprised to see Regulus step forward and address the crowd. Everyone came to a hush as they saw Regulus step forward.

"Let's begin with prayer. Everyone. . . please take some time to pray to the Lord."

The room was silent except for the sounds of people shifting in their seats. Eutychus began as he always had, in opening his heart and mind before the Holy Spirit and thanking Jesus for the opportunity to serve Him this day. Then as he was praying he began to see images of certain men sitting in bars, and then taking women back to rooms. The words "sexual immorality" kept coming. Eutychus asked the Holy Spirit if this was correct.

Yes. There are some here with this problem. It grieves My heart.

Eutychus heard Regulus then began to pray out loud for everyone to hear. "Father, You are our Creator. Jesus, You are our Savior. Holy Spirit, You are our Teacher and Comforter. We welcome You to our midst. Guide us in The Way. In the name of Jesus Christ, we acknowledge all these things."

Everyone could be heard shifting in their seats as the prayer came to an end.

"We have guests this morning. Eutychus from Troas and Ermias currently from Philippi. Do you have anything you'd like to share with us here?"

Everyone turned and looked at them.

Ermias stood up. "We greet everyone here with the love of our Lord Jesus Christ. We only strive to do His will each and every day."

Eutychus also had stood up beside Ermias. After hearing Ermias there was a long pause and Eutychus said, "As I was in prayer here this morning, all I was getting was that there is sexual immorality in this group and that it grieves the heart of Jesus."

The entire group was very silent, an awkward silence. . . for everyone. Ermias and Eutychus sat back down.

"Yes, well, thank you, Ermias and Eutychus. Let's listen and remember Paul's letter to us. Prophyrius, are you ready?" Regulus asked.

Prophyrius stood and began to read. "If I speak with the tongues of men and angels, but have not love, I am a clanging cymbal..."

The meeting went on but Eutychus couldn't hear it – because his mind was confused with all sorts of questions. His heart felt heavy. His stomach twisted inside of him. It seemed like it was an awkward long meeting to Eutychus.

After the formal meeting concluded, Dimitra came over to Eutychus. "Did you get to see Chloe?" Dimitra asked.

Eutychus nodded.

"Did she say anything? What did you tell her?" Dimitra looked at Eutychus with concern.

"Chloe wanted me to tell you, 'Thank you'."

"What for?" Dimitra looked confused.

"She said she knew you were praying for her." Dimitra's eyes began to tear up while he spoke quietly to her. "The Lord Jesus had me tell her that He was with her, and that He would send angels to escort her to Him. He had me tell her how much He loved her, and that He would diminish her pain. After that I don't remember much."

"Thank you, Eutychus." Dimitra then hugged him and turned and walked away.

While Eutychus was talking to Dimitra, Ermias overheard some of the men at the meeting talking about Eutychus.

"... probably projecting his own sins..." Another said, "... The boy needs guidance... he's too young to understand..."

Ermias felt disgust and turned to find Eutychus. He saw him talking to Dimitra and began to walk over to them. Just as he got to Eutychus, he watched Dimitra walk away.

"You ready to go?" Ermias asked Eutychus.

"Absolutely. Let's go." Eutychus and Ermias wound their way through the people. A few people nodded to them, but no one said anything to them.

As they passed Prophyrius, he said, "I will meet you at the house later."

Ermias nodded to him. Eutychus still seemed oblivious to his surroundings. Ermias gently guided Eutychus back towards the safe house through the streets.

The entire walk back to the house the conversation with the Holy Spirit in Eutychus' mind was going...

What did I do wrong?

Why didn't you ask Me what to tell the group?

But You were showing me images of things that grieved Your heart!

Yes.

But what did You want me to do then if not share them?

I wanted You to pray for them with... empathy. With My heart. You know how tempting those situations can be.

Eutychus' heart grieved. He knew that he had missed it.

What did You want me to tell them?

That time has passed. Focus on what I have called you to do. I did not call you to try and straighten out leaders or elders. Or to expose their sins... unless specifically and directed by Me. I would then only send you privately to the individual, with love with very specific words I will give to you. You should always ask what you should do with the spiritual knowledge and insight I give to you for each step of the way. I gave you that 'word' so that you could pray for them... with My heart and compassion, not with condemnation.

Please forgive me Jesus! Eutychus' heart grieved and ached.

Ermias and Eutychus had finally reached the safe house.

As they went inside Eutychus turned to Ermias. "I need to confess something to you."

Ermias sat down and just looked at Eutychus.

"I was prideful. I should have listened to you. Because of my pride, I didn't see the fight that knocked me into that bar. And because of being in that bar I now have images in my head that I can't seem to get rid of," Eutychus was saying with a humble voice. "Images of... girls. Those images also invaded my dreams last night."

Ermias listened intently and waited for anything else Eutychus might say, and when it seemed Eutychus was done, Ermias gathered his thoughts as to what he should say.

"Eutychus the Lord has sent me along with you on this trip. I'm unaware of all of His reasons. But I do know I am to train you in some things, even beyond the physical fight. You are showing your wisdom by realizing these things in you. I too am well aware of the temptations of the flesh. We as men will always be harassed by the enemy in this way of our humanly urges and passions. You have done the best thing a man can do to combat that harassment, and that is to bring it into the light, with confession to the Lord and another brother who you trust. Confessing and repenting quickly is our way to be free from the guilt and shame the enemy wants us to live in. But the battle will always be with us on this side of death. Let's learn how to fight it together. Together with His help and the Holy Spirit and each other we can win." Ermias placed his hand on the shoulder of Eutychus. "You've got more wisdom than most of the men I know, even though you are still young. Yes you made mistakes, but we all do. Let's confess, repent, and move on to the calling He has for us each day. Let's be good ground for the Holy Spirit to produce His fruit in us. His fruit of self-control will get better in us as we listen to Him." Ermias was trying to be as comforting as possible in his tone.

"Ermias. . . Thank you. You are truly sent by the Lord to teach me many things. I so appreciate your words of truth. You are such a good man of God. I am privileged and blessed to have you as my older brother. I promise to try and listen to you better."

This is another reason why I love you, Eutychus. This time the Voice in Eutychus' mind sounded like Jesus. *Every time now, when the enemy places those images in your head, pray immediately for the men at Corinth. Pray with My guidance and compassion.*

Yes, Lord Jesus. Eutychus unknowingly physically nodded to the Voice in his mind.

"What is going on in your mind, Eutychus?" Ermias asked.

"I'm supposed to pray for the men at Corinth every time an 'image', you know, comes into my mind," Eutychus shared with Ermias.

"Sounds like the enemy won't like that. Isn't that like our Master, to use the enemy's efforts against us against him?" Ermias laughed. "Sounds like battle training to me," he added.

Eutychus hadn't thought of that before. "You're good trainer, Ermias. Do we have time for some more fight training today?"

There was a knock at the door.

Ermias opened the door and Prophyrius came in with some more food. After he had set down the food he said, "Well, that was an interesting meeting this morning."

"I blew it, Prophyrius, please forgive me." Eutychus quickly said.

"Regulus and I spoke after the meeting. What you revealed was something both of us have known about some men in the group. We are seeking the Lord as to how to handle the situation, as we know it needs to be dealt with. That you brought it up in front of the entire group has pricked our hearts to be more sensitive to His leading to handle it very soon."

"Yeah, because I handled it so badly," Eutychus remarked.

"The Lord uses our brokenness and our weaknesses, Eutychus," Prophyrius stated plainly.

"I've been instructed to pray for the men of Corinth whenever my weakness is revealed by the enemy over and over," Eutychus confessed.

"We will always take and need honest and fervent prayer from our brothers in the Lord!" Prophyrius was smiling as he said this. "Let me know if there is anything else you might need. I've got another meeting to be at, plus I've got to get to work. I'll come by later this afternoon." With that, Prophyrius left the house.

"I think we need to spend some time together now in prayer to see what the Lord has for us next Eutychus."

"Lead on, Ermias. Lead on, Holy Spirit," Eutychus said.

The two men went to their knees in humility.

Chapter 12

A new work in Corinth

Expansion.

Eutychus and Ermias were deep in prayer together. After spending a time worshipping the Father and praising His works in their lives and thanking Him for Jesus, they then spent time bearing their most intimate hearts before Him, which led them to confession and repentance. Then they asked the Holy Spirit to guide them and show them what He wanted them to do next. They were quiet and waited for Him to speak to them.

Eutychus begin to see images in his mind. He was seeing images of people gathering in hidden rooms in small groups in Corinth. Ermias was also seeing people and he recognized that they were all slaves.

Teach them.

Just two words is all the words that came to Eutychus.

Eutychus said quietly to Ermias, "The Holy Spirit says to 'teach them.'" Eutychus hadn't told Ermias the images he had been seeing in his mind.

"Slaves," Ermias said.

"Yes. That is the sense I get too," Eutychus said.

They then shared with one another what images had been coming to their minds.

"I think we need to talk to Prophyrius," Ermias suggested.

"And Dimitra." Eutychus added. "I saw her in some of the images I received. It looked like she was teaching them. I also saw us on a ship sailing to another destination," Eutychus added.

"Ephesus," Ermias said. "You heard 'teach them', I heard 'Ephesus'."

"So do you think the slaves you saw were in Ephesus?" Eutychus asked.

"I'm not sure," Ermias replied. "I do think you need to check the schedule and see when your next family ship will visit Corinth on its way to Ephesus. But I also think we are to reach out to the slaves in Corinth. I don't think it's one or the other, I feel and think it's both. Considering the call Jesus gave to you, it would seem that most of His followers that would be facing death would be slaves in many places, like Chloe. It at least seems logical to me. But obviously we need the Holy Spirit to guide us to the individuals and places He has planned and prepared for us."

Eutychus got up to get the shipping schedule document. "Only ten days from today. The next ship docks in ten days."

"With Nicolaos?"

"No. A smaller ship," Eutychus replied.

"Then we better get started right away. Let's see if we can meet with Prophyrius tomorrow if he is available," Ermias suggested.

"And Dimitra," Eutychus added.

Their prayer time went fairly long into the night. The prayed for direction and further instructions. It was very late when they laid down to sleep.

The next morning they both were awakened by a knock on their door. The sun was already up. When Ermias opened the door, Dimitra walked in with a bag.

"I brought you two breakfast. Prophyrius told me which house you were in."

"Thank you, Dimitra," Eutychus said while he stretched his arms.

"I'm sorry, did I wake you two?" Dimitra looked at Ermias and Eutychus.

"We had a long time of prayer last night," Ermias responded.

"And we need to talk to you, Dimitra," Eutychus said looking at Dimitra. Eutychus got up and guided Dimitra to sit down. Dimitra didn't know what to think, and she had a worried look on her face. "During prayer last night, Ermias and I think we are called to teach and begin some small groups of The Way made up of slaves in Corinth, and that you too should be involved. I saw you teaching in some small groups in some images I received from the Holy Spirit."

At first Dimitra was quiet and just looked back and forth at Ermias and Eutychus. "That is confirmation to me. The Holy Spirit has been putting that specifically on my heart, but I didn't know what exactly to do about it, and honestly I was scared. I've never done anything like that. Women don't teach in our group. Although I've already gotten some ideas of how to reach out to a few women slaves. They knew Chloe." Dimitra looked hesitant.

"One group I saw you with were all women, Dimitra." Eutychus added. "I suggest you begin with women and follow His lead."

"That makes sense with the women I feel led to approach about it." Dimitra nodded as she said this.

"Do you think you could arrange a meeting with Prophyrius for us today?" Ermias asked.

"I think we need to discuss this with Prophyrius and maybe Regulus," Ermias suggested. "I don't want there to be any friction within your group because of us."

"Yes. I certainly have done enough of that already," Eutychus confessed.

Both Regulus and Prophyrius felt that the Holy Spirit was guiding in this future assignment in Corinth. They had also suggested to another woman about joining Dimitra in her efforts of beginning and teaching a small group of women slaves. The entire thing was kept secret within just the people involved. In the next ten days, Ermias and Eutychus had several meetings with both men and women groups of slaves in hidden places, teaching about Jesus and a life led and lived with the indwelling Presence of the Holy Spirit.

"But how does one exactly become filled with the Holy Spirit?" asked a man in a small group.

"You ask Jesus to baptize you with Him." Eutychus gave the simple answer. "While being baptized with water is an outward symbol of the death of your life and coming out of the water is a symbol of the new life you have been given in Christ, you then ask Jesus to baptize you with the Holy Spirit," Eutychus said to the small group.

"So that the Holy Spirit can teach you about spiritual things and give you guidance as to how He wants you to live and what He wants you to do," Ermias added.

"So that you can hear His Voice," Eutychus said.

"I had difficulty really hearing and discerning His Voice until Jesus baptized me with the Holy Spirit. Then it became much easier. He also teaches me and helps me understand as I read the scriptures and the letters from Paul and others. The Holy Spirit also guides me when I mess up and how to get back on the right path with Him. That usually involves me confessing and repenting before Him. It's not an unusual thing for me, I'm still learning so much, and I'm still making mistakes. . . almost every day, as I'm sure Ermias can confirm to you." Eutychus winked at Ermias. He was trying to be as real and honest as he could with the men and women in the small groups. "My life now is terminally committed to Him. Everyone here understands what that means to a depth that most others do not. Jesus has called us to serve Him here on earth. He has called us to serve you here and now. I am His bond-slave." Eutychus was gentle in his words.

At the end of the meetings, Eutychus and Ermias then did something that shocked every group. They both got up and got bowls of water and towels and began to wash each group member's feet. As Eutychus went to each member to wash their feet, he would pray for them, often giving the words he heard the Holy Spirit speak about each person. Many had never experienced the love of God like they did in those meetings. When Eutychus washed Prophyrius' feet, both had tears in their eyes.

Prophyrius told Eutychus and Ermias that the Presence of the Lord was so strong in those small group meetings. He too experienced the Presence and workings of the Holy Spirit in ways he not had before. Prophyrius became terminally committed to Christ at a level he hadn't experienced before. Prophyrius felt a deepening of love, joy, peace, and courage growing in his heart.

The ten days before their departure from Corinth went fast. Lots of long days and secret meetings. The Holy Spirit continually amazed Eutychus and Ermias how He had prepared their steps and meetings each day. Both Regulus and Prophyrius had come to the docks to see them off. Dimitra had shown up as well. Lots of hugs and quick prayers of thanks were offered by everyone. Eutychus had quickly made an extra copy of the words from James in those last ten days, copying late into the night. Along with that copy of James, Eutychus left a copy of Paul's letters with Dimitra to share with the secret slave groups of The Way in Corinth.

"Just a little over a three-day journey," the captain said in answer to Ermias' question as to how long the journey would take. "Master Eutychus and yourself are welcome to my cabin for the duration of the trip. It is my honor."

Some of the crew were eyeing this deadly-looking Ethiopian warrior that had come aboard accompanying Eutychus and were wondering if Eutychus had acquired a slave. In the following days they watched as Ermias trained Eutychus on the deck in fighting exercises. They noticed a relationship that was very close, certainly not a slave-master relationship, but more like an elder-younger brother relationship. Their view of Eutychus was changing greatly. He was no longer this boy who worked in the family business in the warehouse. When they learned that the purple cloth account had been secured by Eutychus, it raised their respect to even another level.

"Do you have any direction as to whom we are to meet with in Ephesus?" Eutychus was asking Ermias.

"Have you heard the names Priscilla and Aquila?" Ermias asked Eutychus.

"I think I somewhat remember those names. I think I've heard Paul mention them," Etuychus replied.

"I've heard Lydia talk of them of being in Ephesus. You've heard Paul mention them. I think they would be a good starting place," Ermias suggested.

"Well, let's ask the Holy Spirit and see what direction and instructions He will give us," Eutychus replied.

Ermias smiled and nodded.

That night in the captain's cabin, Eutychus kept getting statements in his mind that reminded him of how he had made mistakes in Corinth and that had ruined the plans that Jesus had wanted him to do. Those thoughts made him twist inside.

Please forgive me, Jesus, for all those mistakes I made in Corinth! I'm sorry that trip wasn't very successful, Eutychus was praying in his mind.

Those thoughts are not from Me! came the loud response in Eutychus' head. *Rebuke those thoughts in My Name. When you've done that, I have some questions for you.*

Eutychus rebuked those negative thoughts out loud in the Name of Jesus.

Ermias looked at Eutychus when he heard Eutychus say those words and just watched and listened. He could tell Eutychus was having a conversation with the Lord.

What is your definition of success, Eutychus?

Eutychus knew Jesus well enough to know that Jesus already knew the answer to every question He asked but wanted to have a conversation with him about what he knew and thought. Eutychus was hesitant to answer the question. *Obviously my definition of success needs to change. So, it's probably not what I think it is or I'm used to.*

Chloe was greatly encouraged by your obedience and the words I told you to give to her. She is with Me now and loving life! That is success! Those new groups of followers in Corinth are learning to walk with Me. That is success. Your perspective of success and Mine are vastly different. Success to Me when I was on earth was to obey and complete the Work the Father had for me there. In earthly terms and by a human perspective, My life was not a success. But to my Heavenly Father, I was a complete and total success. Your eternal success will be to do those things I have asked you to do. Isn't that enough? Who has the real perspective of eternal success? How much of the successes recognized and received on earth do you think will be rewarded in heaven? Whose life are you living?

Eutychus immediately was reminded of the time he had spent with Jesus in heaven. He knew this life he had was actually the life Jesus had given back to him. He knew with every fiber of his being that the life he lived now was Jesus' life. That last question he was asked was quite the reminder.

"Ermias, do you ever get schooled by the Holy Spirit?" Eutychus asked sincerely.

"Sometimes, Eutychus. Sometimes. I know He sometimes sounds like my former weapons trainer, taking me to task, but somehow with love in His Voice when He wants to correct me in my ways or thinking. And other times His Voice is comforting and gentle." Ermias was speaking slow with a thoughtful tone in his voice.

"Yeah, the Holy Spirit sure has His ways. And they definitely are not like ours," Eutychus said with sureness.

Chapter 13
Aquila and Priscilla
Ephesus.

Ermias was scanning the masses around the docks in Ephesus. As the center for Roma in Asia, Ephesus was an extremely busy and large city. "Some say Ephesus is the fourth largest city in the world presently," Ermias remarked.

"Paul was a tent artisan, correct?" Ermias asked Eutychus.

"Yes, I believe so," Eutychus replied.

"Let's get directions to the craftsman's district and ask around to see if anyone knows of him. Maybe Paul is here," Ermias suggested. "That is if you don't have any instructions from the Holy Spirit to do otherwise?"

"Lead on, Ermias." Eutychus motioned with his hand. "I've been here before but my knowledge of the city is fairly limited as we didn't go many places but stayed in the city center most of the time. It's been a few years ago," Eutychus explained.

They traveled through the busy streets to the craftsman's district where the leather, canvas, and textile artisans set up their shops. They looked for the leather tentmaker shops. They asked at the first shop and the man pointed them to a larger tent, saying that artisan might know of him.

They went to the shop, a young man told them to wait there as he went into the tent. Another man came back with the first. "You were inquiring of Paul? How do you know him?" the man asked.

"I listened to him the last time my family visited Ephesus. My mother and I became students of his teachings. Is he here in Ephesus now?" Eutychus asked.

"Come into my shop." The man motioned for them to enter.

Ermias and Eutychus looked at one another. Both trying to figure out what to do next.

Go, came the response to their simultaneous prayer request. Ermias nodded to Eutychus and Eutychus nodded back, and they walked into the tent.

"I didn't want to discuss Paul until I had direction," the man said.

"And we didn't want to enter until we also did," Eutychus replied.

"Well, good then. My name is Aquila. And who are you?"

"I'm Eutychus and this is Ermias," said Eutychus by way of introduction. "I'm from Troas, and Ermias has been in Lydia's operation in Philippi of late. We've just come from our assignment in Corinth. We left Regulus and Prophyrius just four days ago. You are who we were led to find when we first arrived in Ephesus."

"Brothers in The Way, welcome. How can I serve you?" Aquila had a big smile on his face. "And to answer your question, Paul is not here. He currently is in prison in Caesarea near Jerusalem. That story is one we can talk about when you meet with our home group." Aquila looked at a nearby young man. "James, you've got the shop. I'm going to take these brothers home and settle them in." Looking back at Eutychus and Ermias, he said, "Follow me." Aquila motioned for them to follow as he walked out of the tent and down the street.

"The fellowship of The Way is growing very fast in Ephesus. There are multiple home groups." Aquila was talking low as they walked through the streets. "There really isn't a place that we can gather all at once now that isn't out in the open, so we just have multiple meeting places. So, we're somewhat discrete with our meeting places. We do have several Romans in our fellowships who have city positions and some are part of the active Roman military that help us know what we can do, but we keep their identities secret. I'll introduce you to some of our elders when they come to visit the house. I'm sure they'll want to hear what the Holy Spirit has been doing in Corinth with the fellowship there."

The three men walked into a nicer housing district within the city. Eutychus raised his eyebrows at Ermias as the homes kept getting bigger and bigger the farther they walked.

"Here we are." Aquila pointed at large home with lush green trees and plants with a large forward courtyard. The gate was big enough for large carts to move through. Aquila walked them around the back of the home to a large stone patio area which had a lot of padded couches that looked over a large lush garden area.

"Have a seat." Aquila pointed at some couches. "I'm going to see what Priscilla is doing. I'll be right back."

"Wow. This place is huge and beautiful," Eutychus remarked.

A woman came walking out the house wearing a beautiful purple dress and shawl followed by Aquila. The couple sat down across from Ermias and Eutychus. They looked like the extremes of each another, with Aquila the rough skilled manly artisan and Priscilla looking so feminine like royalty but with a piercing look that reminded Eutychus of Lydia.

"Aquila says you are Eutychus from Troas. Let me guess... from the Shield of Iraklidis warehouse." The woman smiled at Eutychus. "And you must be. . . either Dawit or Ermias?"

Eutychus and Ermias glanced at one another.

"Lydia is a dear friend. And as you can tell, Eutychus, Lydia's cloth has made it to our city via your warehouse." Priscilla winked.

"Ermias, my lady. I am here to serve." Emias stood straight and bowed low.

"It is our honor to have both of you here. I've already ordered to have rooms made ready for both of you," Priscilla said with authority. "Tonight, after dinner, we'll want to hear all of your stories."

"I'm going to ask some of the elders to come over for dinner tonight," Aquila said. "I'm sure they'll want to hear the stories as well."

Priscilla and Aquila then stood and motioned to the house. Eutychus and Ermias followed them into the large white stone home. A servant girl walked them to the second floor led them to their rooms.

As Eutychus and Ermias had come down from their rooms after a much-needed afternoon rest, they looked at the patio that had been transformed and looked like it was ready for a large dinner party.

Tables and chairs were set up on the patio. Garden lamps were lit. There were enough places for at least thirty people. Several people were already sitting on the couches in small groups.

As Eutychus and Ermias walked out of the home, they heard their names being called. They turned and saw Timothy and Tychicus walking towards them.

"Timothy! Tychicus! Wow! It's so good to see both of you." Eutychus grabbed each one and hugged them in turn.

"What have you been feeding this guy, Ermias? He's bigger and looks stronger than ever!" Timothy remarked.

"He's a good student." Ermias bowed.

"You've been training him?" Tychicus looked shocked.

Eutychus nodded. "I've received lessons from both Dawit and Ermias, more Ermias as he's been traveling with me and being my teacher and trainer. Ermias is a very wise man with wisdom guided by the Holy Spirit, I'm honored to be taught by him."

"Well, it seems your adventures have begun," Timothy said with a big smile. "I know I'm excited to hear what the Holy Spirit has been doing in both of your lives."

Tychicus motioned them to a set of couches. Just as they sat down, Priscilla made an announcement.

"Dinner is now served. . . please find a place at the table."

The four of them got up and moved to chairs at the table. Timothy and Tychicus took chairs straight across from Eutychus and Ermias.

The evening was filled with food, laughter, and love. After dinner and the tables were cleared the party arranged the chairs into a large circle. Eutychus and Ermias were able to tell their story of Chloe. And of the Holy Spirit leading them to begin secret groups among the slave population in Corinth. They mentioned that some of the groups even had "Corinthian girls" in them.

Many were looking for a way out of the life as a "dancer" in the bars. Eutychus went on to say that they felt that the Lord and the Holy Spirit wanted them to begin the same type of work in Ephesus among the slave population. And to minister to those with a death sentence placed upon their lives. Everyone knew how dangerous of a work Eutychus was describing.

After Eutychus and Ermias had given their story, some of the elders left and a smaller group remained behind. They then learned about the current status of The Way as the elders currently knew it. Timothy and Tychicus had returned with the elders from Ephesus after meeting with Paul in Miletus. Luke was supposed to arrive in a week from Jerusalem and Caesarea after being with James and Paul who had been arrested and put in jail. No one knew how long Luke planned to stay in Ephesus but knew that Luke had been compiling as much of the history of Jesus as he could. He was also recording as much of the teachings and miracles of Jesus from personal witness first-hand accounts. Luke had developed a relationship with the main historian and librarian for the Roman Library in Ephesus which was the biggest in all of Asia, and some believed that the individual was close to becoming a follower of The Way. He was named Theophilus.

Timothy then directed questions back to Eutychus.

"How can we help you in your calling?"

"I think I need to rent a small apartment here in the city, out of which Ermias and I can have as a place that is not known by any attachments. I would expect our meetings will never be held in the same place, and never at the apartment. I'll be sending correspondence to my father for the funds he's set aside for me, so that we won't be in need from the work here. Any help in directing us to the right place to rent would be helpful. And until I receive those funds we're extremely grateful for everyone's hospitality here."

"You can stay as long as you like," Priscilla offered.

"Thank you for your gracious offer, Priscilla, and for the rooms we already have been so blessed with," Eutychus said politely. "But as of tomorrow, I think I'll accept Timothy's offer to stay with Tychicus and him at their apartment."

"We'll make sure your space is ready," Timothy said, smiling.

"You're both welcome here anytime. I'm sure we'll be seeing each other much more as the Holy Spirit directs both of your steps," Priscilla said with graciousness. "At least we have you both for tonight."

"I've got some ideas for that apartment you will need," Aquila offered. "I'll be over to Timothy's later this week and we can go look at a few options."

The next day after arriving at Timothy's place, the four sat down to find out what each was doing.

"Tell me the story of Priscilla and Aquila, Timothy," Eutychus asked.

"Priscilla is basically Roman elite status. Her family had great wealth. She inherited her family fortune. She made a lot of waves when she married outside of her class and a Jew. She's a very smart and shrewd businesswoman. She is one best teachers of Paul's material that I've ever known. Add to her ability to size up a person or a situation with the Holy Spirit's gifts and abilities and she's an extremely formidable person in so many ways. Aquila and Paul immediately became friends when they first met. In so many ways they think alike, work alike, and even laugh alike. The three of them together, oh my, it's really hard to keep up." Timothy laughed.

"So the house here in Ephesus is their lifestyle?" Eutychus asked.

"I've seen Priscilla out work in labor quite a few men. She's a tough woman," said Tychicus. "She's worked side by side with Aquila many times. But she can also mingle in the elite society if she has to. Actually, this home in Ephesus is small in comparison to her family's compound in Roma from what I hear."

"If you would see her in work clothes alongside Aquila – you might not recognize her," Timothy added.

"It really doesn't surprise me Lydia and Priscilla are sending correspondence back and forth. Those two seem like they have a lot in common," Tychicus said.

"She actually reminds me of Lydia," Eutychus remarked while Ermias nodded in agreement. "I've been thinking a lot of the situation we encountered with so many women in Corinth who need a way out of the life they've been trapped in, either by slavery, or by family debt, and they're made to sell their bodies as currency for their owners or employers. I think I'd like to talk to Priscilla about it and what suggestions she might have. If we were able to free women trapped in that lifestyle somehow in Ephesus …what exactly would happen next for them." Eutychus was pondering out loud.

"I think she's the perfect person to ask that question, Eutychus," Timothy said.

"Well, when and if the situation arises here, she'll be the first person I'll seek out. Thanks, Timothy." Eutychus nodded at Timothy. "What does the Holy Spirit been having you do here in Ephesus, Timothy?"

"Mainly it's been teaching people about Jesus, and the Holy Spirit in the different home groups. I've been able to utilize some of Luke's notes that he's been compiling for the book he wants to write. He has gathered as many parables of Jesus as he could, from as many sources as he could meet with. I've been using those parables to teach people here in Ephesus. And, of course, the letters Paul has already written when teaching people about the Holy Spirit and how He is involved in our lives. I've been asking Paul to think and ask the Lord about about a list of qualifications for elders. I too have been praying and seeking the Lord about it. The tentacles of religion seem to grab ahold of that issue so tightly and want to maneuver it to a status thing rather than a character and maturity issue." Timothy was in a thoughtful mode as he discussed these things with the three.

"Tychicus, what about you? What has the Lord set in your heart?" Ermias asked.

"I wish I had such a narrow-focused call like yours, Eutychus, but mine is just to serve the Body of Christ," Tychicus replied. "I've set my heart to serve Paul in any fashion I can. To be there for him. I was really surprised when he told Timothy and myself to return to Ephesus with the elders when we were in Miletus. But then I guess the Holy Spirit had already talked to Paul about what was coming for him in Jerusalem. I'm praying and asking if I can visit Paul and maybe travel with Luke the next time he leaves. But for now, my job is to support and help Timothy here in Ephesus."

"That call is vitally important, Tychicus. Ermias may have been told by the Lord to go with me, but I think he's been more of a mentor to me than me taking the lead. . . in what the Lord has for us. Without Ermias, I would have made so many more mistakes in this last trip. When Paul talks about the Body and how vital each part is. . . I've actually experienced it now to a big degree," Eutychus confessed. "We need one another."

"He's a tremendous blessing to me." Timothy smiled as he talked about Tychicus. "He has insight about people and situations I often don't have. He also knows how to ask good questions. To me it's obvious in so many ways that he has a strong intimate relationship with the Holy Spirit because he is able to get the heart of a matter so quickly."

"Enough of the love fest. Let's go to prayer and ask Him what we all need to do next." Tychicus went to his knees. The other three followed him.

Chapter 14
The Gospel and New Business

More expansion.

The days flew by for Eutychus and Ermias. It took about three weeks for Eutychus to receive his funds from Troas. Aquila had set them up with the owner of an apartment building almost immediately and had paid their rent till Eutychus' funds arrived. The building's rooms were rented to workers and located just outside of the city proper. The rooms were small but adequate for what Eutychus and Ermias wanted. Just a simple room with wooden platforms to sleep on, one chair and a single lamp on a small table. The building was on the same street as the bars and where the more dangerous elements of society were gathered for "business" and other purposes. It was not uncommon to see unconscious bodies lying in the streets. Beggars were found at every busy place of foot traffic. In the city proper the Roman soldiers wouldn't allow beggars in the streets.

Eutychus had set up an agreement with Priscilla for his funds to be kept at their home and given to the owner of the building as needed for rent. And he often dropped by to pick up just enough funds for food for the week for the two of them. He also stored his important documents at their home rather than the apartment. Eutychus and Ermias only kept the bare essentials with them. Ermias even stored his swords and knives at the home. He told Eutychus at the apartment they would only use their staffs for protection. The staff was a long wooden pole that could be used as a walking stick or a weapon when needed. The Ethiopian warriors were masters of the wooden staff, and Ermias had trained Eutychus on the basics of using a staff for self-defense.

Ermias and Eutychus had to listen moment by moment to the Holy Spirit of everyday. The two could often be seen talking to the most-filthy beggar, or prostitute in the street. Miracles happened as they were led to pray for an individual. Those miracles opened doors to other relationships and secret meetings. Slowly by slowly groups began to form. They would meet in an individual's apartment, tent, and even near the city dump. No place was off limits for them. Tychicus sometimes joined them for a day as they had their secret group meetings to bring certain parchments. Eutychus had to tell Tychicus to wear work clothes when he joined them and not the finer clothes he usually wore.

Discussions with Priscilla became a regular weekly meeting. As Eutychus and Priscilla had begun a secret route and path for women who were escaping their lives of degradation and slavery. Secret payments were made as the Holy Spirit provided to secure the freedom for certain women. These women then were moved to other cities to begin new lives with new identities and become part of The Way in that city. Priscilla and Eutychus worked on opening an orphanage with the help of the Church in Ephesus to provide for children who had no other place to go.

The membership of The Way in Ephesus exploded with the efforts that the Church was taking in reaching out to the poor, orphans, and needy, mainly led by Eutychus and Ermias, and organized by Priscilla. The number of women joining their ranks grew and grew, as the followers of The Way held all life as precious, forbade the practice of abortion, and did not treat women as second-class human beings. Priscilla held meetings at her home strictly for women for teaching them in spiritual matters. It was one of the largest group meetings in the Church at Ephesus.

Eutychus and Ermias had secured a pass to the main city jail through a Roman contact that was a secret member of The Way. They began weekly trips to the jail to speak to the prisoners about Jesus. At first most of the prisoners mocked them, especially Eutychus for his age, but after seeing what had happened with certain prisoners most became open to talking with them. Both Ermias and Eutychus had gotten used to being spit on, and struck, and having insults hurled at them as they were at the jail.

It was the condemned prisoners on death row that Eutychus seemed to be drawn to most. So many of these individuals became terminally committed to Christ in their final days on earth. But there was the occasional prisoner who was already a follower that Eutychus and Ermias felt sent to and to pray for with greater earnest. Their heart was that these individuals would be freed somehow by God's divine help. The story about Peter being escorted out of jail by an angel sat in the minds of Eutychus and Ermias on so many occasions while ministering to a believer on death row. But they had yet to see God move in that way, but their hearts yearned for it all the same.

The spring and summer in Ephesus had gone by very quickly for Eutychus and Ermias. It was one particular fall evening while Ermias and Eutychus were in prayer in their apartment after a long day, when they heard the Holy Spirit tell both of them at the same time that their work in Ephesus had come to an end. That others would now continue the work that the Holy Spirit had begun through them.

The next morning, they set out for the home of Priscilla and Aquila. Priscilla was very surprised to see them that early in the morning.

"The Holy Spirit has confirmed to both of us that our assignment here in Ephesus has come to an end," Eutychus told Priscilla.

"We'd like to make arrangements to give up our apartment and move back into the city as we seek Him as to what next He has for us," Ermias explained.

"Of course," Priscilla replied. "I will make the arrangements with the owner. And we would be so blessed if you would stay with us until you get your next marching orders."

"So many of the women that meet here weekly would be so happy to see both of you again. You both have had such a huge impact in so many of their lives. Please say you'll stay." Priscilla almost pleaded with them. "Plus, the children at the orphanage would also love to see you again, Ermias. They all seem so drawn to you."

"Okay. We'll stay," Eutychus replied to Priscilla. "But we don't need separate rooms, and we don't need lots of space or comforts."

"Thank you. I'll have your rooms made ready this very moment." Priscilla rang a bell and a girl ran to her side. "Please have the two suites on the second floor made ready." The girl dashed off.

"But we don't need...." Eutychus began but stopped as Priscilla put up her hand. Eutychus had learned not to try and fight with Priscilla. He would always lose.

Being back in the city proper was quite a change for both Ermias and Eutychus. They had to work hard at being very aware of the Holy Spirit's instructions and directions as things were so much more comfortable and seemingly less dangerous. They settled on trying to help Aquila in his shop while waiting for further instructions on where the Holy Spirit would send them. One morning as they were walking to Aquila's shop, Eutychus saw a textile shop with a type of purple cloth that was different than Lydia's. He then headed over to talk to the individual at the street booth.

"How much for this bolt of purple cloth?" Eutychus asked the man.

"You have a very good eye and such good taste. But this cloth is very, very expensive." The man had bowed low and looked at the 'youth' of Eutychus. Plus, Eutychus didn't really seem like a man of wealth, his clothes really weren't that nice.

"Where did you get it from?" Eutychus kept asking the man questions.

"This comes from Roma. It is highly sought by my patrons in Roma."

"So do you sell much of it here in Ephesus?" Eutychus kept the questions coming. Ermias just watched from across the street with a silly grin on his face. *That man doesn't have a clue who he is dealing with.*

"I have a few patrons here in Ephesus who enjoy this cloth." The man was becoming more confused by this persistent young man. What does this young man really want?

"What if you could get the same type of purple cloth, in different textiles, at one third the cost?" Eutychus asked.

The man stopped and squinted his eyes at Eutychus. "What exactly do you mean?"

"Do you know Aquila over there?" Eutychus pointed at the large tent of Aquila's.

"I don't know him personally, but I know he is a fine tent maker," the man said. "I've seen his clients."

"Tomorrow morning meet me at his tent," Eutychus said. "I want to show you some cloth you might be interested in becoming a seller of."

The next morning Eutychus had taken Priscilla's entire personal stock of Lydia's cloth down to Aquila's shop.

Ermias approached the man in the cloth textile booth.

"Master Eutychus would like to invite you to Aquila's shop this morning." Ermias bowed to the man. The man eyes had gone big at the large imposing Ethiopian warrior standing before him.

"Master who?" The man asked with an unsure tone.

"The man who inquired about your purple cloth yesterday," Ermias explained.

"That young man?" The man asked.

"Master Eutychus is the account holder for the Shield of Iraklidis in Troas of the finest purple cloth in all of Asia. The cloth comes from Philippi. You will not find it's match anywhere," Ermias said these things with an air of importance. "Come with me." Ermias motioned for the man to follow him. And turned around and walked to Aquila's tent. The man just followed along.

Eutychus the previous night had asked Aquila for a finer set of clothing for the meeting in the morning. Of course, Priscilla overheard and they both set about dressing Eutychus like a wealthy Roman elite businessman.

When Ermias led the man into Aquila's tent he saw racks of the finest purple cloth in every type of weave and make. And the same young man was now dressed as one who looked like his very wealthy patrons in Roma.

"Please come... look this cloth over." Eutychus motioned with his hand.

The man slowly looked over the cloth. Feeling the different textures and the seeing the rich hues of different purples. "You have so many different rich samples here. How did you..." The man was stunned and just kept feeling the different cloth samples.

"Tell me exactly. How large is your operation? How far does your business extend?" Eutychus asked with an air of authority.

The man looked at him differently. *He obviously is not who I thought he was.*

"I'm the son of a very powerful sheikh in Egypt. I run my father's textile business. He has textile operations in Roma and here in Ephesus, but he would like to expand into other cities as well. My name is Nephi, my father is Sheikh Masud." Nephi bowed to Eutychus.

Ask him if he would join you on a trip to Troas via the ancient coastal road. The Holy Spirit broke Eutychus' train of thought. Eutychus was silent and began to ask the Holy Spirit more questions in his mind.

When? Eutychus prayed. *What is Your plan? What do I need to do?*

You'll leave next week, the Voice replied, *by wagon. He'll become a major seller for you in Africa. Listen well.* The Holy Spirit was clear in His instruction.

"Nephi, would you like to be a seller of this cloth? Would you consider coming with me to my family's business in Troas? You could become our first merchant seller in all of Africa as well as any other place your father wants to expand to. We could secure all the details and the needs you might have in Troas. I would like to give a bolt of this cloth to you to send to your father."

"Give...?" Nephi hesitated.

"Yes. As a sign of my goodwill and hopes of a prosperous future for both our families," Eutychus said as he bowed towards Nephi. "I'll be leaving next week for Troas via the ancient coastal road, with my friend Ermias." Eutychus pointed at Ermias.

"I will secure a wagon for our trip, so that I can bring back inventory right away." Nephi bowed low to Eutychus.

"I will be here tomorrow and we can talk about any details or questions you might have," Eutychus replied.

Nephi bowed low and practically ran from the tent.

"Well, he seemed excited." Aquila said laughing.

"Aquila have you ever thought about exporting any of your fine leather work?" Eutychus asked. "I know you have James and a few other apprentices, but what about expanding your operations to having someone sell your work in many other places? You could employ more men and families..." Eutychus was now thinking about a leather works account.

"Obviously I'll have to talk to Priscilla. You've even got my mind now thinking." Aquila scratched his head.

Ermias just smiled and then laughed. *Watch out, Aquila, you've just entered the Eutychus zone.*

Chapter 15

On the Road to Smyrna

Finding The Way.

Three sat in the wagon going north and the air had a chill in the wind. The wagon was filled with leather goods and other supplies for the trip. Eutychus had used a substantial amount of his money to buy the leather goods from Aquila hoping to spur further sales in export. Eutychus had given the remainder of his money, except for the travel expenses they had calculated they would need for the trip north, to Priscilla for the orphanage expenses.

It was rather late in the year to be making such a trip, but they were determined to push through. The cold at night would require a fire and shelter for themselves. They also were carrying a canvas tent and poles Nephi had brought.

"My father always wants us to have our history with us. We were nomads for many centuries. We are still a people of the tent," Nephi said proudly.

They also had planned to stay in Smyrna, Pergamum, and Assos in lodging along the way. Aquila also had given Eutychus and Ermias the names of contacts of elders in The Way in the cities along the road and where to find them.

As they were going so late in the year, the amount of people and traffic on the road was very minimal. They both knew that this could mean greater danger from bandits along the way. Ermias was always on a state of high alert and scanning the horizon in all directions for potential danger. They had figured on three days travel time to Smyrna. Two nights on the road. By the third night they should be able to find lodging and stables in Smyrna.

Conversation was mainly between Nephi and Eutychus. Eutychus was asking Nephi about his family and his past history, and what had brought him to Ephesus, and other information. Nephi seemed very willing to talk about anything and was very open about many subjects of conversation. Then the opportunity came when Nephi began to ask Eutychus questions. At the beginning it was about the family business. Nephi was extremely excited to learn of the family's shipping capabilities with the fleet of ships they had under the direction of Nicolaos. Eventually the topic turned to more personal questions about Eutychus. Eutychus answered all of them as honestly as possible.

But when Eutychus told his story of that Sunday night, and his meeting with Jesus in heaven, Nephi became very quiet. He listened with great focus and interest. After Nephi figured Eutychus was completely done with his story, he began to ask questions.

"You and your mother had become part of The Way before that night correct?"

"Yes. About two years before."

"And none of your other family is part of this group?"

"No, not yet."

"Isn't that hard for you and your mother? Doesn't that bring tension in the family?"

"Yes it does, but the Holy Spirit helps us navigate those relationships with love. It has become much easier since Jesus baptized me with the Holy Spirit."

"What do you mean by that ...exactly?"

"It means being able to hear His Voice with much greater clarity. To be completely filled with Him. He lives inside of me."

"His voice?"

"In your head. In your thoughts," Ermias said.

Nephi was so surprised at the response from Ermias because he had been silent the entire time.

"Ermias is correct," Eutychus said.

"You can hear this... Holy Spirit in your head? In your thoughts? How do you know it's Him and not your own thoughts or some other... thing?"

"That usually takes time," Eutychus said, "like in any relationship. How do you know when anyone is speaking the truth to you? It takes time, to know the individual, and how they are, and speak, and their personality. We have the scriptures to tell us of many thousands of years of history about our God's interaction with people, and what He is like. He does not violate His Word. He does not change."

"Eutychus had a very unusual experience in that he got to meet with the risen Jesus personally in heaven," Ermias said plainly. "Paul met Jesus on the road near Damascus in a vision."

"Just because I did, doesn't mean I get everything correct now. I still make lots of mistakes, which you can personally confirm. Jesus, the Holy Spirit, and you are still teaching me so many things, Ermias."

"This Jesus is alive now... and in a place not on this world?" Nephi asked.

"Yes," Eutychus confirmed. "He called it His Kingdom and some describe it as the third heaven. But as you learn more, you come to understand that this entire world and sky is His Kingdom, there is no place one can go that isn't His."

The conversation continued in these same lines. Ermias began to speak more and began to talk about the history of the faith. Adam, Noah, Abraham, and Moses. He then told the story of King Solomon, and a wise Queen that had visited him and how that history and faith became mixed with the Ethiopian people. Eutychus listened enraptured. These were things he didn't even know about Ermias. *I need to do more road trips with Ermias.*

"I knew of the 'faith'. It was my ethnic history. I knew all the stories. But I didn't really know God... personally. It wasn't till a woman named Lydia intervened into my brother's and my life that we really got to know Him, meaning Jesus, personally and become filled with the Holy Spirit. Then my history and people's stories took on new meaning for me. The Holy Spirit has been teaching me His Will and Way in me. I no longer do things out of tradition for tradition's sake, but out of instruction and direction by the Holy Spirit. My history now has a much greater meaning and spiritual depth for me." After saying all of this, Ermias became quiet again.

After a while Nephi said, "I think I need to know more of this Jesus and His Story."

"I think we need to find a place to set up camp," Ermias said.

"So early?" Eutychus asked.

"We've been making good time. And Smyrna should be reached easily on the third day. This first night will take us a little longer as it's the first time we'll do it," Ermias was explaining. "Each successive night should go much faster as we learn a good routine. I also want to find a place that is somewhat defensible and off the road a way so that we won't be easily seen."

"I'll get the tent set up and a fire going," Nephi volunteered.

"I'll get out the food and get dinner going," Eutychus said.

"That looks promising." Ermias pointed ahead to a ridge and trees.

They came upon a campsite that already had travelers set up there. There was a clean water source, and good flat spots to set up tents. They set up camp a bit away from the other travelers. The other travelers looked at Ermias and his swords and decided to stay out of their way.

Ermias after dinner decided Eutychus needed some training. They went through three rounds of staff and sword exercises. Nephi watched in awe. Nephi wasn't the only one watching.

While they were getting ready to go to sleep Eutychus asked Ermias a question. "Why the weapons training tonight? I'm not complaining, just wondering."

"We had an audience," Ermias simply replied.

Eutychus knew then that Ermias was being wise to let everyone who saw know that they were not going to be easily messed with.

The next day the conversation continued. It was a nice sunny day and Eutychus was enjoying the countryside and views on the ride but soon the conversation turned again to the story of Jesus. Luke had taught in various meetings of the 'apostles' as they called them. The original twelve who traveled and were taught by Jesus. Luke was compiling their stories and eyewitness accounts.

There was a younger man Mark who was also working on writing an account of Jesus, who Luke had also conferred with. Eutychus tried hard to remember all the stories Timothy and Luke had shared about Jesus and His disciples. Both Ermias and Eutychus did their best to tell the story of Jesus to Nephi. Often they would fill in certain stories or parables the other did not know about. When they told of Matthew, Nephi wondered.

"My father wrote to me about hearing a man speak about a Jesus in my home city. I think he said his name was Matthew. He said that Matthew was on his way to Ethiopia to tell the story of Jesus. My father said he was quite moved by his stories of this man Jesus. Would this be the same Jesus you are talking about?" Nephi asked.

"Matthew is going to Ethiopia?" Ermias was now curious.

"That's all I know Ermias," Nephi explained.

Oh Heavenly Father – reach out to my family! Ermias was praying in his heart and mind.

"Matthew was in your country on the way to Ethiopia?" Eutychus asked Nephi.

"If it's the same man," Nephi replied. "I don't know for sure."

"I strongly believe this is same Jesus we are talking about Nephi. He was prophesied to be the Messiah by many Jewish prophets," Eutychus said.

"I don't think we are together by chance," Ermias said quietly.

They rode together in silence for a good while thinking about what Ermias has said, when they were passed by several riders on horses going fast in the opposite direction. Ermias kept an eye on them until he could no longer see them.

"Must be messengers," Eutychus said.

"They didn't look like bandits to me," Nephi replied.

"Never presume on outward appearance," Ermias said.

"Many times in the scriptures that kind of warning is given. Man looks on the outside. God looks at the heart of the individual," Ermias stated. "It's also part of warrior training. Never underestimate an opponent. Never be over-confident by what you see." Ermias was slowly speaking his thoughts out loud. "Your pride will kill you. Both physically and spiritually, especially in a fight."

"I'm reminded of what I thought of you Eutychus, when I first saw you. I was very wrong," Nephi confessed.

"You're not the only one to make that mistake, Nephi. I've made that mistake too many times myself," Eutychus said. "It's helped to have the Holy Spirit to guide me with situations like that. My problem has been not to ask Him when those situations arise. I could have avoided many painful lessons if I had just asked Him for help. Hopefully I'm learning."

That night when they set up camp they were alone. And the process did go faster than the first night. But the wind made it very cold and they just wanted to get some sleep. But during the night the three were awakened several times by wolves howling in the distance. It was a rough night for all of them. They got up early and packed up and set out with the goal of reaching Smyrna as soon as possible.

The wagon came over a rise just after mid-day and they could see the city of Smyrna.

"Do you have the parchment with the names of our contacts?" Ermias asked Eutychus.

"I'm getting it." Eutychus was going through the leather pouch to find the document.

As they rode into the city they could tell how well designed the city streets were. This city definitely was planned out with very straight streets. Almost all the buildings were of the same architecture, with white walls and orange clay-colored roofs. It seemed almost like a Roman military garrison but on a much larger scale, it in fact did have a large Roman military presence. It was quite easy finding the street that Aquila had given them to find their contact.

Ermias stopped the wagon in front of a building in the warehouse district not too far from the second harbor. Eutychus noticed that it looked like Smyrna had two large harbors, one for the military and the other for regular commerce. There were a lot of people on the street. Business was in full swing. Many men were loading and unloading in the building's warehouse. Eutychus stopped one of the men who he figured looked like the foreman.

"Excuse me do you know a Dashan?" Eutychus asked. The man pointed to the office. Eutychus went to the office while Ermias and Nephi stayed with the wagon. Eutychus entered the office and asked the man at the desk. "Can you tell me where I can find Dashan?"

"Who's asking?" The man looked at Eutychus.

"My name is Eutychus. I'm an agent for the Shield of Iraklidis in Troas. I've been told to meet with Dashan concerning business. My contact in Ephesus, Aquila, gave me this address and name."

"Dashan will be back shortly. He's checking an incoming load at the dock."

Eutychus walked back out to the wagon. He then saw a man walking towards the building from the dock carrying a tablet. Eutychus walked towards the man and asked, "Are you Dashan?"

"And who are you?" asked the man.

"My name is Eutychus. I'm an agent for the Shield of Iraklidis in Troas. We too have a large import and export business and warehouse. My contact in Ephesus is Aquila; he gave me your name."

"Aquila?" asked the man.

"Priscilla and Aquila, who made tents with Paul," Eutychus said with a half knowing smile on his face.

"Come with me." And the man walked into the office of the warehouse.

"Joseph, will you please excuse us and see to this next shipment for me?" Then the man handed the other man the tablet. The man at the desk got up and went through the front door.

"I am Dashan. I do know Aquila. What can I do for you?" Dashan asked Eutychus.

"My partners and I have just come from Ephesus by wagon on our way to Troas. We are looking for lodging and stables for the night and a secure place for our wagon." Eutychus was direct.

"I can definitely arrange that for you. Ask Alexius out in the warehouse. He'll store your wagon and get your horses stabled for the night. When your done with him come back here and I will set you up for the night."

After the horses and wagon were secured Dashan led the three to an inn just down the street. They booked two rooms and came down to get some supper. Dashan was waiting for them after they secured their rooms, on the main floor where the meals were served. He was sitting at a table in the corner with his back to the wall.

"Does this establishment know …the way?" Eutychus asked Dashan.

Dashan waited till he could tell no one could overhear them. "Yes. But only to those who know it as well," Dashan said with a straight face.

Nephi was definitely lost and had no clue as to what was being said.

"I was hoping to talk to someone who knew the way. Maybe tomorrow you could guide us?" Ermias asked.

Nephi looked confused. Eutychus watched Dashan's face closely.

"I think I can arrange something," Dashan said. "Do you remember the man in the office? In the morning ask for Joseph, he'll help you find … the way."

Chapter 16
The Risk

Ruth.

Nephi had set out first thing in the morning to check out the artisan district in Smyrna. Eutychus and Ermias had found Joseph and were now sitting around his table in his home discussing The Way and the problems they were facing.

"We've got significant opposition here in Smyrna. First, the Roman military garrison rules the city, so mandated weekly sacrifices to the gods and monthly taxes are strictly enforced. The Jewish sect in the city has been able to gain a religious exemption, making them our opposition as well by always informing the Roman authorities on any Jew that joins our group. This makes the individual subject to the weekly Roman enforcement. They usually end up leaving the city to escape the persecution. That's why the majority of our members are not of Jewish descent. Our meetings have to be totally secret and always moving." Joseph was trying to be as clear as possible.

"So that's why we had the greeting we did?" Eutychus asked.

"Yes." Joseph nodded. "We have to be very wary of anyone seeking information about .... The Way." Joseph paused. "But my current problem is something that we'll have to deal with by tomorrow at the latest."

Eutychus and Ermias looked at one another. Ermias asked, "How can we help?"

"I hope you can," Joseph said with some skepticism, "but I'm not sure if you're ready for the size of the problem."

"Currently one of our members is hiding a young woman. Her name is Zosime. Here's the story I was told. Her father died when she was eight and left behind significant debts. They went to her mother to collect. But in their words they had 'mercy' on the mother and only required her to turn over her daughter for the debt. Her mother then left the city as soon as she could. Zosime was a house slave for four years and then was put into the owner's bar to be a 'dancing girl'. She's been entrapped there for three years and being sold nightly to the patrons of the bar. Two nights ago, the owner was murdered. The young women fled immediately. She broke into one of our member's home and was found hiding there by the homeowner. The Roman authority has been investigating the murder and also looking for the young woman. She says she did not kill her master. And when I questioned her, the Holy Spirit confirmed that she was innocent. So now we not sure how to proceed. The only instructions we get from the Holy Spirit is to 'wait'. If we turn her in, not only will she be put back into the same pit she was in, we also will come under severe scrutiny for hiding her. The Roman authorities are now searching house to house. It's just a matter of time." Joseph looked at Eutychus and Ermias with hope.

Eutychus and Ermias again looked at one another and nodded.

"We'll take her," Eutychus said quietly.

"We'll leave as soon as we can load up," Ermias replied.

"Really?!" Joseph sounded surprised and thankful.

"We've been dealing with these kinds of problems both in Corinth and Ephesus," Eutychus replied. "I get the sense that sending her to Ephesus is too close for her safety. We'll rely on the Holy Spirit to guide us on how to proceed."

"I'll have her brought to the warehouse within the hour," Joseph promised.

"Okay, let's get moving," Ermias said and stood up from the table. Eutychus and Joseph also stood up.

"I'll go find Nephi and bring him to the warehouse to get him ready to go," Eutychus said to Ermias.

"I'll get the team hitched and the wagon ready to go," Ermias replied.

"Can you pick up some food for the next several days?" Eutychus asked Ermias.

"I'll handle that for you," Joseph interjected, "after I get Zosime to the warehouse."

The three men left the house in a fast walk going in different directions.

Less than an hour had past and the three were sitting in the wagon headed out of Smyrna. Zosime was completely hidden under the rolled-up canvas tent and leather bundles. She was told she would be gotten out after they were out of sight from the city. The Roman guards at the city gate just waved them through.

The three didn't say much for the next hour. Nephi asked a few questions but realized both Eutychus and Ermias were not in a talking mood. After going over a rise and out of sight of Smyrna, Ermias pulled the wagon off the road.

"Why are we stopping?" Nephi asked.

Both Eutychus and Ermias had gotten down and began to unload the wagon.

"It's way too early to camp..." Nephi began to say, when he noticed the young woman being taken out of the wagon. "Who is this?"

Eutychus and Ermias said nothing and just began to reload the wagon. Eutychus had gotten out one of his longer cloaks with a hood and handed it to Zosime to put on. She put it on and was shown to sit just behind the bench of the wagon.

"Well....?" Nephi was getting somewhat angry as Eutychus and Ermias were not explaining anything.

"Nephi, for your own good, we kept Zosime a secret from you," Eutychus explained. "That way you could be completely innocent if we got caught. We will be taking her to Troas with us unless the Holy Spirit directs us otherwise."

Zosime up until that point had been completely quiet. "Thank you," was all she said while looking at Ermias. She really didn't know what to think, not knowing if she was in even a worse situation than before. But she so wanted to leave Smyrna that she would have taken any opportunity that was presented to her.

"What if we encounter Roman patrols? What are we going to say then?" Nephi was nervous.

"Well, I guess were going to have to have our story straight then." Eutychus smiled.

Nephi didn't like how both Eutychus and Ermias weren't showing any signs of concern.

Eutychus had been in prayer the entire time as they were in the wagon. Praying through the gate. Praying as they rode out of the city. Ermias had been doing the same.

"She needs a new name," Ermias said.

"I agree. And the story that keeps coming to me is Ruth," Eutychus replied.

"Ruth. I like it," Ermias said.

Zosime quietly spoke up just then. "What's the story of Ruth?"

"You want to tell the story, Ermias? I'm sure you know more details, since I'm sure you've read it more than I have."

"Ah... the kinsman redeemer. Such a wonderful story. Saving the woman, an outsider, and making her his. Reminds me of Jesus, doesn't it?" Ermias just smiled.

"And the leap of faith Ruth made. My favorite part," Eutychus said, smiling.

Ermias then launched into the story of Ruth. Eutychus loved the way Ermias told it. Nephi and Zosime listened with great interest. Many times, as Eutychus looked back at Zosime, he saw tears in her eyes as she listened to Ermias and his passionate way of telling of the story.

After Ermias had finished his story Zosime said, "Ruth. I like it. I'd be honored to have that name."

"You are now Ruth to us. From this point forward, we'll call you Ruth," Ermias said smiling.

"We will protect you just like Boaz protected Ruth," Ermias said.

"But like our little sister instead of our wife." Eutychus laughed, but then got serious while looking at Ruth. "We won't let anyone touch you or hurt you. You're safe with us."

Tears began to fall down the cheeks of Ruth. She wiped them with her sleeve.

"Thank you. All of you," Ruth said.

As it turned out, Ruth was a really good cook. She immediately took over the food duties for the group. The four easily fell into a good routine of unloading, setting up, cooking, and then cleaning. Because of the lateness of the season, they had not encountered any other travelers on the road. This actually made Ermias even more wary and alert, and more determined to make good time towards Pergamum. Ruth was very quiet the entire time and didn't speak unless spoken to, and then her answers were short. Eutychus was very aware of how much Ruth was watching and listening to each of them.

On day four around mid-day, they could see Pergamum.

"Okay, everyone, remember Ruth is my little sister," Eutychus reminded. Eutychus was searching for the parchment that had the contact names from Aquila. The document actually was disguised like a manifest and the names were part of the buyers list.

Ruth began rehearsing the details she had learned from Eutychus about his family in Troas, just in case she ever was questioned. But her strategy was simple and that was to stay silent as much as possible, and just let the men speak and defer to them about any questions she might be asked.

Pergamum was easily seen now by the group, sitting on the hill with a good wall and fortifications. It actually was quite a large and busy city. As the wagon entered the city they were very aware of how religious the city was. Everywhere there were sellers of religious talismans, and potions. Large ornate temples to various gods were in high places.

"Eutychus, do you have the location of our contact?" Ermias asked.

"Head to the artisan district," was Eutychus' reply.

Ermias asked a merchant in a street booth from his seat on the wagon where the artisan district was. The merchant just pointed. Ermias kept going in the direction he was pointed.

Nephi then said, "Turn right, I think I see artisan booths."

Ermias turned and headed down the street. He stopped the wagon next to the tent making merchants. Eutychus got down and began to ask the different merchants if they knew a Heron. Most did not, but finally a merchant pointed them to a small booth at the end of the street that sold leather items.

"Is there a Heron here?" Eutychus asked the man manning the booth.

"How can I help you? Do you need some leather items? If you don't see what you need, we can make it." The man just smiled. Eutychus figured he needed to use the businessman's approach.

"My name is Eutychus, I'm an agent for the Shield of Iraklidis in Troas. I need to find a man by the name of Heron. I have a prosperous and urgent proposal for him and only for him. I've been sent by Aquila in Ephesus who is my contact in that city." The man stopped smiling and turned and when into the tent behind the booth.

Soon a woman came out and bowed low to Eutychus. "My husband is not here, but I can take you to him."

"Is your husband Heron?" Eutychus replied with a serious look on his face.

"Come with me," the woman said, and began walking away, she motioned Eutychus to follow her.

Eutychus held up his hand to Ermias and the others, letting them know they should stay where they were.

The woman walked another block and turned into a courtyard behind a large stone wall. The courtyard held a medium size home and what looked like a large warehouse. She motioned for Eutychus to sit down on a bench and then went into the warehouse building. Soon a short stout man came walking out followed by the woman. Eutychus stood up and greeted the man with a bow.

"Are you Heron?" Eutychus asked.

"I am. I'm told Aquila gave you my name."

"Yes. He told us … The Way … to find you." Eutychus was watching, praying, and listening all at the same time.

Heron just looked at Eutychus. Eutychus recognized that look, as if Heron was having an internal conversation.

"I have my wagon, partners, and my sister with me, back at your booth. Can I go get them?" Eutychus asked.

"Yes. Bring them to this courtyard. Then we'll speak further," Heron replied.

Eutychus quickly turned and jogged back to the wagon.

As the group turned into the courtyard they were met by five men who were waiting for them. As Ermias got down from the wagon the usual looks were observed. Some were quite surprised and wary by this imposing Ethiopian warrior.

"This is my partner, Ermias. This is my friend, Nephi. And this is my sister, Ruth." Eutychus introduced each of his group. "We're on our way to my family's business in Troas. The Shield of Iraklidis. We're import-export merchants. Nephi here is considering becoming our northern Africa contact and broker," Eutychus explained to the men. "We've just come from Ephesus where we spent time with Aquila and Priscilla. We worked with their entire operation and group. They showed us ... the Way... all around Ephesus."

"We've been expecting you," one of the men said. At this both Nephi and Ruth looked very surprised but both quickly tried to hide their reactions.

"We've already been informed and have a place for each of you," another man said.

"You and Ermias will stay with me. Gaius will give Nephi a room. And Ruth with stay with Heron and his wife," the third man said. "My name is Antipas. Won't you please come with me. Gaius and Heron will take care of your wagon and horses." Antipas led them to the warehouse building.

"How did you know?" Ermias asked very quietly to Antipas so that no one else would hear as they walked to the building.

"You're not the only one who hears His Voice.... brother," Antipas whispered and winked at Ermias. "We were told to expect three men and a young woman today and to keep them safe. The Holy Spirit told us yesterday in our prayer meeting," Antipas said quietly. "We've learned to obey Him quickly here in Pergamum, our lives depend on Him."

Chapter 17

Pergamum

Antipas.

Eutychus and Ermias sat at the table while Antipas' wife Miriam served them breakfast.

"The Way here in Pergamum has big challenges." Antipas sat down next to them.

"I suggest that you leave today, and you should know that the evil spiritual forces here know that you have arrived. You have two in your group that will be subject to their lies before you leave the city walls. They also will mock you two, but both of you know that mocking us means nothing as our lives are His and His alone." Antipas was serious in his speech.

"Here in the city, we have many factions. There is a small but deadly group of Jewish Zealots who work on disrupting the Roman forces here. We also have what I call Balaam's crowd, those that turn in followers of The Way for money, they claim to be followers of The Way but they betray us. Then we have the Nicolaitan way – those who are always trying to introduce other religious ways, traditions, and practices into the group, either blatantly or covertly. On top of it all are the demonic forces who possess human flesh and constantly attack us in every way that they can. This summary sounds bad, but it is a daily reality for us. The followers here must be able to hear His Voice clearly or they become deceived very quickly. Because of the darkness that pervades our city, the light of Christ in us shines extremely brightly here. My work here has been to make sure every member of The Way here has a very intimate relationship with the Lord and is indwelt completely by the Holy Spirit." Antipas paused and looked at them.

"Do you have any words of advice specifically for us?" Eutychus asked.

Antipas closed his eyes and was silent for a time. Everything in the room came to a hush. "The enemy is setting up an ambush for you on the road outside of the city. He wishes your destruction," Antipas said with his eyes closed. "That's all I get at the moment. I saw you and Ermias fighting men off with long staffs."

Ermias looked at Eutychus. Eutychus had his head down and eyes closed too.

"My work here also is to free people from the demonic possession that is so rampant here in Pergamum. We have several in our group who have been freed from demonic possession. The many various temples here who rely on that demonic power and information are constantly trying to get to me. I've made them very angry because they have lost valuable conduits to their power." Antipas was sober as he said all of these things.

"I hear that you, Eutychus, have met Him personally. And that He has you on a mission for Him. Don't stray from that path. Stay true to your calling from Him." Antipas looked directly at Eutychus and Ermias.

"I had the blessing of meeting with and learning personally from the apostle John. His words ring brightly in my heart and mind. Before you go, I give to you his words he gave to me: 'The anointing that you received from Him abides in you, and you have no need that anyone should teach you. But as His anointing teaches you about everything, and is true, and is no lie—just as it has taught you, abide in Him.' Shalom, brothers." Antipas stood along with Eutychus and Ermias, grabbing first Ermias in a hug and then Eutychus.

"Thank you, Antipas, for being obedient to the Holy Spirit. Thank you, Miriam, for your gracious hospitality. We are extremely blessed to have been with you, and to receive your wise words Antipas with joy. I will always remember them." Eutychus bowed.

"You are in my heart. Your words and actions will also ring in my mind." Ermias bowed.

The group of four met back at the courtyard where they loaded up and were headed out by mid-morning.

Antipas had given them the most direct route out of the city to the north, but that also meant going by a large temple. They traveled the streets in the wagon without really talking. It seemed everyone in the group was high alert and watching. The people along the way were also looking at them, and unlike most other cities, none of them smiled or seemed friendly towards them.

As they were passing a crowd and man jumped out in front of them with wild eyes and began shouting and pointing at Nephi, "Son of Abram, your fate is fire, just like mine!" The man then laughed almost with an unearthly laughter. His finger then pointed at Eutychus, "What are you looking at boy?!" He sneered at Eutychus. "You are just a child ... you are just so childish in everything you do!" Again, he laughed maniacally.

Ermias then urged the horses forward. The man then sneered at Ermias as they passed. "Son of a dog, you are not worth anything." Then the man spat on the ground.

"Well, that was interesting," Eutychus remarked. He looked back at Ruth and her eyes were big and filled with fear. Eutychus put his hand on her hand and looked at her. "You're okay, remember what we told you."

As they turned the street and were approaching the temple the crowds in the street got thicker and the wagon had to go very slow. Ruth looked at the steps going up to the temple. She saw a young girl wearing only a very sheer garment surrounded by what looked like priests. The girl was staring at Ruth directly.

The girl then began to point and shout at Ruth, "You are one of ours. You cannot escape us. You belong to us. You are not his sister. Don't believe that lie. You are not one of them. You belong to us. You serve us. Your body belongs to us. No matter what you do or where you go, you cannot escape us."

The people in the street began to turn and point at the group and Ruth. Ermias urged the horses to go faster, people began to curse and yell at them. Eutychus and Ermias were praying now and listening for any instructions the Holy Spirit might have for them.

Keep going, don't slow down, Ermias heard in his mind.

Eutychus then said to Ermias, "Keep going, don't slow down. That's what I'm hearing."

Ermias nodded and spurred the horses to go faster. Then several rocks began to hit around them. The people were throwing rocks at them. Ermias put the horses into a trot.

After they got away from that crowd and had turned the street Ermias slowed the wagon down.

"Everyone okay?" Ermias asked.

"I only got hit once, but it was a small rock, every other rock missed me," Nephi said.

"Ruth?" Eutychus looked at her. Ruth looked dazed. "Ruth, are you okay? Did you get hit by any rocks?"

"No rocks," was all Ruth said with a blank look on her face as she stared off into the distance.

They made it out the northern city gate without any interference as the Roman guards were only checking incoming travelers. After the city the road seemed very sparse of travelers. The mountains on their east began to rise in height. They traveled in silence for quite a distance. Then Nephi began to speak.

"What do you think that mad man meant?" Nephi asked quietly not directed at anyone specifically. It was almost as if Nephi was thinking out loud.

"You are a descendent of Abraham, Nephi, that is so. Abraham is called a 'father of nations'," Ermias said plainly.

"What about the fire?" Nephi sounded confused.

"All I know is we will all have to stand before God at the end of our lives and give account. We will be justly judged by Him," Ermias said again plainly.

"Yes, Ermias, you are correct. And that's why Jesus died for us. To pay the price for us that was justly ours to pay. Our sin was paid by Him. He is my redeemer now. He has redeemed me from the fire and my from my sin." Eutychus said quietly.

"How does Jesus become my redeemer? How do I know?" Ruth spoke directly. It was the first words she had spoken since the temple.

"You accept and believe who He is. The Son of God, who gave His life for you. You ask Him to forgive you of your sin, and ask Him to come live inside you, and to fill you with His Holy Spirit," Ermias was quick to respond.

"Is anyone allowed to do this?" Nephi asked.

"Yes, anyone, Nephi," Eutychus responded.

"I want to belong to Him. Not to anyone or anything else," Ruth said firmly.

Eutychus and Ermias began to praise God out loud. Nephi and Ruth just listened.

"Father, You are our Creator, giver of Life! Jesus, we praise You, our Redeemer who gave Your life for us! Holy Spirit, we worship You, as You are wisdom and power beyond measure!" Ermias was speaking loudly.

"Jesus, I thank you for giving me this chance to serve You further in this life," Eutychus chimed in.

Back and forth Ermias and Eutychus continued to pray and thank God. Then Nephi and Ruth were surprised to hear their names being lifted in prayer.

"Father, help us explain what Jesus did specifically for Nephi and Ruth so that they will understand," Eutchus prayed.

"Holy Spirit, I ask You to explain it to their hearts and minds as only You can," Ermias prayed.

"Ermias, stop the wagon," Nephi said loudly.

"What is it Nephi?" Ermias and Eutychus almost said at the same time.

"I want to accept Jesus now," Nephi said.

"I do too," Ruth also said.

As the wagon came to a stop, the four got down and stood in a circle. Ruth was between Ermias and Eutychus.

Ermias and Eutychus led Nephi and Ruth in prayer to accept Jesus.

"Do I need to confess all my sins?" Ruth asked.

Eutychus shook his head. "The Holy Spirit will prompt you as to what you need to confess, Ruth. He will lead you and comfort you and tell you when and what you need to ask forgiveness for."

Ruth began to ask Jesus to forgive her for all the hatred in her heart towards her former owners and men that abused her. Tears began to roll down her face.

Nephi was tearing up as well and confessing his own shortcomings and feelings he had for his own father.

After a good time of prayer, Nephi and Ruth looked different.

"I feel so light," Ruth said.

"I feel love," Nephi said.

Soon everyone was hugging and laughing.

"We need to get back on the road," Ermias said.

"I've got so many questions for you two," Ruth said looking at Ermias and Eutychus.

"I'm going to have my own questions too," Nephi chimed in.

"We've got at least six more days on the road, with lots of time to talk and discuss. I'm sure Eutychus and I are willing to answer all your questions to the best of our abilities. You've just joined the family of God. You really are our brother and sister now in the Lord, as it's by His blood that we are now a spiritual family," Ermias said smiling.

"Can you tell us more about the Holy Spirit?" Ruth asked.

"What exactly do you want to know, Ruth?" Eutychus asked.

"How does He speak to me? How do I know what He is saying to me? What does it mean that He lives inside of me? Is it like those people in Pergamum who had spirits in them?" Ruth was going fast with her questions.

"Yes. I'd like to hear those answers too," Nephi said.

"Well, then I guess we'll have a good discussion then as we set up camp for the night," Ermias replied.

Ruth and Nephi then realized how late in the afternoon it had become.

Ermias looked for a good spot off the road to make camp for the night.

Chapter 18
Baptisms
New life.

Remember to stay on the path. Remember the calling Jesus gave you. Don't settle into being comfortable and sedentary. Many need to hear His Words. Keep going, He will lead you. Be ready at all times. A figure glowed so bright that Eutychus could only make out the outline of the being in front of him in his dream.

Eutychus awoke from the dream and it was early morning, just as dawn was breaking. He got up and went for a walk. "Lord Jesus, help me," was the simple prayer Eutychus uttered under his breath. He walked to the edge of the camp area and looked out at the horizon and the light coming from the rising sun.

"Lord Jesus, I confess I don't have what it will take to complete this path. I so need the Holy Spirit's guidance, and strength. I need His wisdom." Eutychus was quietly praying out loud.

"What are you doing?"

Eutychus was startled by voice behind him, he turned around and saw Ruth. "I was praying and asking for His help. I had a dream that ... made me think ... about the path ahead of me."

"I certainly need His help," Ruth said quietly. "So, what is the right way to pray?" Ruth asked Eutychus.

"The only right way is from your heart," Eutychus said simply. "It doesn't have to be with big or religious words. Just simple, real heart feelings and thoughts expressed to Him. That's how you begin in your relationship with

Him. Being honest with yourself and Him. Start that way. As your relationship grows He teaches you what prayer is and can become." He paused then added in summary, "Just speak to Him the way you would speak to your best friend."

"I've never had a best friend," Ruth confessed.

"You do now. And you have brothers and sisters now. A real family." Eutychus smiled. "And family fights, and disagree with each other, and get mad at one another, and all sorts of messy things." Eutychus laughed. "But... with the Holy Spirit guiding us we learn to love one another the way He loves us. So, we learn to ask for forgiveness and also forgive one another. Family can be hard and wonderful all at the same time." Eutychus chuckled as he said these things.

"I've got a lot to learn." Ruth looked down.

"I do too, Ruth. The more I learn the more I realize the less I know," Eutychus said. "But with the Holy Spirit as Your Teacher, learning becomes fun again. Full of adventure, and new opportunities, and passion. He will give you glimpses of what He wants with you. Life is exciting as He leads. I was a follower of Him for almost two years before He really got my attention. Falling out of third story window and meeting Him in His Kingdom did it for me." Eutychus laughed. "I was too busy with my own agenda. I was so sure that my way was right. I was going to make my mark on the world," Eutychus said with a much more serious tone. "Now I just follow His lead. Listen for His instructions and obey. And I'm learning to ask Him a lot more questions before launching out in the way I think I should go. I have messed that up many times. Thinking I knew what He wanted without asking Him. I've made so many mistakes. But I'm learning."

"I'm all ears. I want to learn," Ruth said quietly.

"Well... let's get breakfast going for the others," Eutychus suggested. "Often when I'm waiting on His instructions, I just work on serving those around me. I think of how I can help them, serve them." Eutychus shrugged his shoulders.

Eutychus went to get the fire going and Ruth went get the food and cooking pan.

The morning's conversation was around the story of John the cousin of Jesus, and how he baptized people in the river, and how he also baptized Jesus. And what the Voice from the heavens said to everyone who saw that event happen.

"You said something about being baptized with the Holy Spirit. Eutychus, is that what John was doing?" Nephi asked.

"John's baptism was for repentance," Ermias explained. "To believe in the One who came after him, which was Jesus."

"The baptism of the Holy Spirit is what we ask Jesus to do to us," Eutychus also said. "It's a spiritual baptism. The Holy Spirit fills a person with His Presence. He takes residence within our own minds and hearts. Paul says our bodies become the temple of God when we do this."

The conversation was shortened by Ermias telling everyone they needed to pack up and get going, the conversation could continue once they got on the road. Everyone pitched in and they got it done quicker than they ever had before.

The entire time on the road Ruth and Nephi were asking questions. Ermias and Eutychus did their best to answer them. The conversation never seemed to stop. Ermias was acutely aware of the absence of any other travelers on the road. It was colder now, and everyone was bundled up in extra layers of clothing. The road in the late afternoon was now along the coast and they could see the sea.

"So, could we get baptized now?" Nephi suddenly blurted out.

"Isn't it too cold now to get dunked in the sea?" Eutychus asked eyes wide.

"We could find a place to camp, build a big fire, and also get baptized," Nephi said hopefully and nodding his head vigorously.

Ermias and Eutychus looked at one another. Eutychus shrugged, and Ermias turned off the road and on the next path towards the sea.

Lord Jesus, guide us here on what to say and do. Protect us as we seek You with all our hearts. Eutychus was praying in his mind.

The path led to the bluffs and then down to a hidden beach area. When they looked south they saw an area with some trees that looked like a perfect camping site for the night tucked up right next to the rock cliff of the bluff.

Nephi quickly got the tent set up and a big fire going.

"Not exactly a cooking fire, Nephi," Eutychus laughed.

"Hey, we're going to need to get warm after we all are done being wet from the sea," Nephi said.

"Okay, everyone wears something you can get wet," Ermias said as he set up a line near the fire that would be used as a drying line.

The four huddled together near the lapping water of the sea on the beach.

"Let's go up to our waists. Ermias, you take Ruth, and I'll take Nephi," Eutychus suggested.

The four waded into the sea. There were a few gasps of breath and involuntary sounds as they walked in up to their waists. But everyone was determined to make it through no matter what.

"Ruth, do you believe that Jesus is the Son of God and died for you?" Ermias asked Ruth.

"Yes. I believe that," Ruth responded.

"Nephi, do you believe Jesus is the Son of God and died for you?" Eutychus asked Nephi.

"I believe," Nephi responded.

"Then I baptize you in the name of the Father and His Son, Jesus," Ermias said and dunked Ruth under the water. When Ermias lifted her up he said, "Ruth, the life you now live is His life. Ask Jesus to baptize you with the Holy Spirit."

"Jesus, baptize me with Your Holy Spirit."

Ermias and Ruth then watched Eutychus and Nephi go through the same questions and actions.

"Jesus, I too want you to baptize me with the Holy Spirit," Nephi said after standing back up.

Suddenly Ruth began to speak in another language. Her arms and hands lifted to the sky.

When she was done speaking, Ermias asked her "Do you know what you were saying?"

"No, I don't… but it was wonderful!" It's like the Holy Spirit was guiding my tongue what to say.

"I'm not sure what all of it was but your first words were in my native tongue and you were saying 'Worship the Creator'" Ermias said.

Eutychus and Nephi were just staring at Ruth.

Nephi then said, "I can translate the rest. The next line she said was Arabic and she said, 'Worship the Son' and the next line was in Aramaic which was 'Worship the Spirit .. for We are One.'"

The four began to walk out of the water. They headed to the fire. They allowed Ruth to change first in the tent. She came out and put her wet clothes on the line. Then the three men went in to change. Soon they were all talking around the fire.

"What just happened?" Nephi asked. "How did Ruth know how to speak in different languages?"

"Paul explains those things in his letters to the followers in Corinth. He calls them the 'gifts of the Spirit'. One of those gifts is the 'gift of tongues'," Eutychus explained.

"I have to confess something," Ruth said. All eyes turned towards her.

"I've been praying. And since coming out of the water my prayer has also been in a different language. I don't know what it is – but my spirit sings when I pray like that," Ruth said quietly. "I'm just so happy!"

"Paul talks about that too, Ruth. It just means you're are filled with His Spirit now. Paul prays in tongues too. And you can still pray with words you know too. I've heard from those that the Spirit uses that way that when they run out of words they know they just continue praying in tongues," Eutychus explained.

"There are eight other 'gifts of the Spirit' that Paul talks about in those letters to Corinth," Ermias said. "It would be good to have Ruth and Nephi read Paul's letters."

"I agree, Ermias, but we should also remember the nine fruit of the Spirit in Paul's letter to the Galatians," Eutychus said. "Those fruit need to be grown in us by Him so we don't misuse His gifts."

"I can't read," Ruth said quietly.

"Well, then one of us will read them to you," Eutychus said.

"I willing to teach her how to read if she wants me to," Nephi said.

"Can you do both? Read me the letters while I learn to read?" Ruth asked.

"Sounds like the right thing to me." Nephi nodded and smiled.

The fire had died down some and the coals were hot. Everyone had regained their warmth again.

"Let's get supper going," Ermias said.

Everyone then realized how hungry they were and they all scrambled to get the meal going.

After supper was finished and they packed up the utensils and food, Ermias brought out the bag which had the copies of Paul's letters.

"I think I'll just read a few pages tonight. Everyone can just listen," Ermias said.

Ermias got out Paul's first letter to Corinth.

"Paul, called by the will of God to be an apostle of Christ Jesus, and our brother Sosthenes, To the Church of God that is in Corinth, to those sanctified in Christ Jesus, called to be saints together with all those who in every place call upon the name of our Lord Jesus Christ, both their Lord and ours: Grace to you and peace from God our Father and the Lord Jesus Christ..."

"I have got so many questions. You're going to have to help me." Ruth had leaned over to Eutychus and whispered to him.

Ermias kept reading until he had finished the letter.

"There was so much there. I'm going to need help understanding it all," Nephi said.

Ruth just nodded. "Plus, doesn't Paul know how to take a breath?" she asked. "He talks so long."

Eutychus just laughed. "You should hear him in person."

"First, I've learned this. My number one Teacher is the Holy Spirit. He helps me understand these things Paul talks about. I can try to explain what He has taught me about these things. But you need Him to teach you about what He means about these things for you. How He wants you to carry out His wishes for you." Eutychus explained. "My faith can't be your faith. He wants to you to walk with Him personally too," Eutychus explained.

"Why don't we all go spend some time alone talking and praying with Him tonight." Ermias got up and had put away the documents. Ermias began to walk down the beach.

All of them had difficulty going to sleep that night. Their minds were all racing from the big events of the day.

Chapter 19

Attack

Trials.

Nephi was tending the breakfast fire when the others heard him yelling for them to come. Ermias and Eutychus were in the tent and came out immediately. They looked down the beach and saw four men on horses riding towards them. Ermias and Eutychus immediately went back into the tent and retrieved their long staffs.

"Ruth, stay in the tent," Eutychus said. "Don't come out 'til one of us comes back in to get you."

Ermias and Eutychus had taken up a stance before their wagon with Nephi behind them. The men stopped their horses at the beginning of the grove of the trees. Ermias and Eutychus lost sight of them for a moment behind the trees.

"Calm. Remember your training. Breathe. Focus." Emias was giving Eutychus direction.

Soon there were yelling men with drawn swords running at them. Ermias engaged two men at once. Eutychus engaged with another. Soon the two men Ermias had engaged were lying flat unconscious. Eutychus was still fiercely battling his opponent.

But Eutychus all of sudden remembered a certain training exercise Ermias had put him through over and over. Eutychus moved quick and disarmed his opponent and struck him squarely in the forehead, rendering him unconscious.

"Weren't there four? Where is the other one?" Nephi asked. Ermias and Euthychus looked around. Ermias nodded his head towards the tent. Eutychus understood and slowly approached the front of the tent. As he looked in he saw a man with a knife to Ruth's neck.

"Lay down your stick, boy. Or the girl dies." The man was menacing in his speech.

Talk to him. Ermias needs time, was the statement in his mind.

"No need to do anything rash. We don't have much but what we have is yours." Eutychus was calm in his voice. He very slowly crouched down, holding his staff out like he was going to lay it down all the while moving so that the man would turn as well leaving the rear tent flap out of sight.

Eutychus watched Ermias slip into the tent through the back flap in total silence behind the man. Then, quicker than Eutychus had ever seen Ermias move, his staff snuck under the man's arm, pushed away his forearm and hand with the knife, spun the man around, and hit him in the forehead. The man toppled, completely unconscious. Ruth just stood there shaking.

The entire incident was over in the span of a moment, though each second-had felt more like an hour. Eutychus stood still, catching his breath and prayed in his mind as his hands surrendered to the jitters. *Holy Spirit, what do we do now?* he thought in his mind. Eutychus had seen head injuries before during accidents on the docks. The staff strike could smash a gourd with ease.

They are in My hands, came the answer of the still, small voice. *See to those I have placed in yours.*

Eutychus saw Ermias checking the vitals of the men on the ground. "How are they?" he asked.

"We do not enter conflict with the intent to kill or not kill," Ermias said, pulling his fingers away from the neck of each man. "We merely aim to stop the threat, just as a good shepherd should. In this way we do not repay evil for evil but overcome evil with good." He lingered as he counted heartbeats from the last man before nodding with approval. "Their life is still in them."

The irony of the words gave Eutychus pause. That was what Paul had said when he'd fallen out of the window. Perhaps good may yet come out of these men's evil actions. *I hear You, Holy Spirit.* "What should we do with them?" he asked Ermias.

"Let's move quickly and get them all tied up," Ermias said to Eutychus as he began to tie up the nearest man. Eutychus quickly walked out of the tent and found that Nephi had already tied up two of the men and was working on the third. Eutychus went back into the tent.

"Nephi has got the other three tied up. Let's get packed up and out of here." Eutychus was looking at Ruth but Ruth still stood in the same spot in shock. "Ruth, it's okay. We need your help. Get all the things into the wagon and packed." Eutychus was calm but firm.

Ermias dragged the unconscious man from the tent and laid him down with the other three. One of the men began to groan. The signs of them stirring was bittersweet to Eutychus. They had intended violence, yet they had not been slain either.

Holy Spirit, please grant them repentance and the knowledge of You, even if it's not from us. Eutychus had stopped to bow his head in thanks and supplication.

You need to hurry, the Holy Spirit prompted.

"We must hurry," Ermias said aloud at nearly the same time.

Nephi and Eutychus began moving as fast as they could, taking down the tent and packing the wagon while Ermias got the horses hitched up. Ruth was now helping but completely silent. Once packed and ready, the four climbed into the wagon. Ermias stopped at the edge of the trees.

"Get their horses," Ermias said. "We'll tether them to the back of the wagon and turn them into the Roman authorities in Assos. We can't have those thieves catching up to us right away again."

Eutychus and Nephi got down, gathered the four horses, and tied their reins to the back of the wagon. Soon the group was back on the road with the wagon. Ermias purposely sped up. Not too fast but definitely faster than normal pace.

"Ruth, are you okay?" Eutychus looked back at Ruth as the wagon was going down the road.

Ruth had a faraway stare on her face. She just looked at Eutychus and nodded. It was obvious to Eutychus that there was much she wasn't saying.

Lord, speak to her. Holy Spirit comfort her. Teach her. Eutychus had begun to pray in his mind for Ruth.

With the extra speed they spotted Assos on a hill just after midday. It was early afternoon when they stopped a Roman officer in the street of Assos.

"Sir, we were attacked by thieves this morning. We rendered them unconscious. Here are their horses. Please take them. We took nothing from those four men. We did not kill them. We tied them up – but I think by now they are free and probably walking this way." Ermias bowed low before the Roman officer.

The Roman officer looked at the four, slowly noticing the wide differences in each of the individuals.

"Where are you headed? And what's your business here?" the officer asked.

"We're headed to Troas. My family owns the Shield of Iraklidis warehouse. My name is Eutychus, my father is Nikias. Ermias here is my friend and mentor." Eutychus held his hand out towards Ermias. He then pointed at Nephi. "This is Nephi also my friend, who will become our contact and broker for Africa. He is coming from Ephesus to sign a contract with my family business." Eutcyhus then pointed at Ruth. "This is Ruth my sister. We are on our way to my home to Troas."

The Roman officer listened intently, looking at all of their faces closely and into their eyes. "Okay, I've heard of your warehouse. Can you describe the men that attacked you?" the officer asked.

While Ermias was untying the horses from the back of the wagon, Eutychus described the men the best he could. Ermias filled in some more and Nephi gave a very detailed description of their clothing. Ruth said nothing.

"Okay. I will alert my superiors of the situation," the officer said while taking the reins from Ermias.

"Are we free to go?" Ermias asked.

"Yes. But I don't suggest you stay in Assos tonight. Be on your way," the officer responded.

"Thank you, sir. We'll be on our way," Ermias replied. He climbed back onto the wagon and urged the horses forward.

They went north straight as possible through the streets to the other side of the city. They passed through the city gate and wondered why there was no Roman presence there.

"So, we camp outside the city then?" Nephi asked.

"Looks like it," Ermias said.

"Please everyone, begin praying and asking the Lord Jesus for help and instructions," Eutychus requested. "Let's keep going until we have some instructions from Him."

Ermias was actually glad to see more travelers on the road going in the direction of Assos.

"It looks like we won't be so alone on this last leg of the trip," Ermias commented.

The road out of Assos was downhill and they made good time and got a good distance away from the city and it was now out of sight, but the sun had just set and they still had not stopped to make camp.

"Anyone get any instructions on where or when or what we should do?" Eutychus asked the group.

"I've had a weird picture in my head of a group of people camping with a larger fire, and us coming up to it," Nephi said hesitantly.

"Okay. Now ask the Holy Spirit what we're supposed to do with that picture and information?" Eutychus said gently. "Are we supposed to camp there with them or avoid it? I've learned the hard way that even though I have some spiritual information, I need to bring it to Him and keep asking questions until I know specifically what I'm supposed to do. I've made the mistake too many times jumping to my own conclusions and moving ahead with my plan instead of His," he confessed. "Ermias can certainly confirm this."

"Yes, I can confirm you've made some bonehead mistakes," Ermias said, poking Eutychus in the ribs.

Ruth actually laughed out loud. Nephi chuckled.

"I keep getting the feeling we're to camp alone," Ermias said. "Maybe the group Nephi is seeing is a marker for us somehow?"

"I keep hearing in my head the word 'pass'," Nephi said.

"Was that before or after you saw the 'weird picture'?" Eutychus asked Nephi. "Did the word 'pass' come to you after you asked the Holy Spirit questions?"

"It was during the time I saw the picture," Nephi said. "And still now."

"Well, that's kind of a big clue, Nephi," Ermias said.

"Okay, let's be on the lookout for a group of people with a big fire," Eutychus said.

"How are we going to set up in the dark?" Ruth asked.

"I think we'll be fine. Nephi, you work on first getting a fire going," Ermias said. "Ruth, you work on getting out some food. Eutychus and I will work on unloading and begin to get the tent set up. The fire should give us enough light to work."

"Is that a fire I see in the distance?" Nephi remarked. Everyone looked.

"Towards the mountainside?" Ruth asked.

"We need to go past the fire and find the small stream that we will cross," Ermias said. "We just need to go slightly off the road and up the stream. I think that's what the Spirit is prompting me to look for. I kept hearing 'stream' in my head."

"The fresh water will be good. We're almost out," Ruth agreed. Everyone began to hear Ruth quietly praying in another language under her breath. When she looked up and saw everyone staring at her she said, "It helps keep me calm. And I really don't know what to pray for ... so I pray in my prayer ... language, if that's what it is called."

"You keep praying in the Spirit, Ruth. I'm glad you are," Eutychus encouraged her.

When they were looking at the group to the right on the mountainside with a large fire, Ermias said, "Begin looking for a stream."

They had gone about a thousand paces past the group when Ruth spotted the stream. There was a grove of trees just a hundred paces off the road near the stream.

"Let's see about that grove of trees and if we can make camp near there," Ermias suggested.

Camp was actually set up quite easily and quickly. All four were working really well with one another. They were learning and appreciating the skills and talents of each member. After supper Ruth and Nephi began asking Ermias and Eutychus spiritual questions again.

"How do we know what is us and what is the Spirit of God in our heads? How do I interpret any pictures that I see in my head? Does the Spirit also use dreams?" Ruth and Nephi kept going fast with the questions without allowing Eutychus or Ermias to answer before asking the next question.

"Well, it helps to read and know of some of Paul's writings," Eutychus remarked.

"It's also good to read the ancient scriptures as well," Ermias suggested. "Lots of good stories about dreams in them."

"I guess spiritual learning takes time, effort, prayer, and lots and lots of questions. Just like most things in life." Nephi sighed.

"Yes, it does, Nephi," Eutychus agreed. "But I'm finding it's not so much a hard task as much as it is a relationship and a willingness to go beyond what I'm comfortable with. Like self-defense training with Ermias. There is always so much more for me to learn."

"The more I know, the less I know," Ermias said thoughtfully.

"And what the Holy Spirit seems to be constantly reminding me about are three areas I need to be continually learning, humility, gratefulness, and repentance," Eutychus confessed. "Humility to examine my ego and pride to keep me in check. Gratefulness to lead me to peace and contentment wherever He has me and whatever state I find myself and to ward off envy. And repentance to keep short accounts with Him so bitterness and unforgiveness doesn't grow in me and turn my heart against Him and others. This means I have to confess my faults to my brothers, like in the book James wrote."

"Sometimes you amaze me, Eutychus," Ermias remarked. "Obviously you've been listening to Wisdom. Because you are certainly too young to know these things on your own."

"You said 'Wisdom' like it was an entity, Ermias. Is it a separate being?" Nephi asked.

"The Holy Spirit is sometimes referred to as Wisdom," Ermias explained. "It definitely is one of His traits. There is a 'gift of wisdom' listed by Paul that comes from the Holy Spirit."

"You'll learn the Father has been spoken about with many different names and attributes," Eutychus said. "Jesus as well has been given different names and titles. The same goes for the Holy Spirit. The root of the word 'spirit' is breath. I'm still learning so much."

"I am that I am," Ermias said quietly. "That's what He said to Moses at the burning bush, when people would ask him what His name was."

Ruth just sat listening and soaking up all she could. She wondered how she would ever learn it all. "Nephi," she said, looking at him, "you said you could teach me to read. Can we start tonight?"

"Why don't you start with the book James wrote. His sentences are shorter than Paul's." Ermias got up and went to get the document pouch.

"I think we need to start with the basics first, Ermias." Nephi first began teaching Ruth the Greek alphabet letters by drawing in the dirt with a stick.

Chapter 20
Back Home
With new friends.

When Eutychus got up that morning, dawn was just breaking. After the non-thinking, normal morning habits were taken care of, he found a log to sit on and look out towards the western horizon to pray.

Father, You are my Creator. I know You are Love. I know You are merciful. Thank you for Jesus. Jesus, my friend, thank you for this chance today to serve you. Holy Spirit teach me in Your ways. Guide my steps. Show me Your plan for today. Speak to me.

Eutychus was staring at the horizon and praying. He eventually looked to the right and saw Ruth standing on rock about fifty paces from him. He got up and walked towards her. As he got closer he could tell she was praying. He stayed back and waited till she went silent.

"You're up early," Eutychus said.

Ruth turned quickly and relaxed. "Couldn't sleep," she responded.

"I think we're close to Troas. We should make it today if nothing slows us down," Eutychus said.

Ruth didn't say anything but just turned and looked back out towards the horizon.

She's scared. The thought was very clear in his head.

Eutychus prayed in his mind, *Holy Spirit comfort her. Let her know You and Jesus are with her ... always.*

"My mother and sister are going to love you," Eutychus said quietly.

Without turning Ruth asked, "How do you know?"

"Because I know them," Eutychus said gently.

Ruth didn't respond back.

Eutychus then began to walk back to the campsite and stoked the coals before adding some smaller wood pieces to get more coals for cooking breakfast. He got out some food and began to cook when Ermias and Nephi came out of the tent. Ermias began his usual morning stretching exercises, while Nephi just watched.

Everyone was fairly quiet throughout breakfast and they packed up rather quickly. They all seemed to be contemplating what was going to happen next. The fall morning air was crisp, but there was no wind. They could smell the sea air. They all rode in silence for quite some time. Any conversation that was had was short and not about anything important, and in the late afternoon they could see the outskirts of Troas.

"Ermias, let's head to my family home first. I'll get the horses taken care of," Eutychus said, "and we can let the wagon set. We'll unload it in the morning." He began guiding Ermias along the most direct way to his family's home.

When the Eutychus opened the gates, and Ermias urged the wagon through them into the courtyard, they were greeted by Corrina, followed by Nikias and Eirene who came to see who was there.

Eutychus ran up and hugged his mom.

"You're back!!!" Corrina said with great joy.

Eutychus then stepped back and began introductions.

"Everyone, this is Ermias, my friend and trainer who has been on this adventure with me since Philippi. And this is Nephi, a friend who I met in Ephesus and could become our contact for all of Africa." Eutychus looked at his dad when he said this. "And this is Ruth, my sister in The Way." Eutychus looked at his mom as he said this. Corrina immediately went to Ruth and hugged her.

"Welcome, Ruth, to our home. Welcome, everyone! We're so glad you are all here." Corrina then looked at Eirene who immediately knew what her mom wanted and went into the house to prepare extra rooms, accommodations, and food for their guests.

Nikias had walked over to Nephi and had immediately struck up a conversation with him. As Eutychus looked at both of them, he saw genuine smiles on both their faces.

"Come on, Ermias, let's get the horses unhitched and the wagon put away." Eutychus then guided Ermias around to the back of the house. Soon they were all settled around the table as a large amount of food and wine was spread on it. A fire was blazing in the fireplace.

Nikias was talking with Nephi. Eirene was talking with Ruth. Ermias and Eutychus were talking with Corrina.

"Ruth had nowhere to go and was facing either death or lifetime slavery in Smyrna, and Ermias and I decided to help her," Eutychus explained to his mom. "We had helped women in Corinth and Ephesus previously get out of their terrible situations the best we could. Both Nephi and Ruth have become followers of Jesus on this trip from Ephesus. Ermias and I baptized them in the sea, and it was cold! But Nephi and Ruth were determined to do it as soon as possible. Both of them have asked Jesus to baptize them with the Holy Spirit."

Eutychus continued. "Mom, you would really love Priscilla and Lydia. They are such wonderful smart strong women, ... like you. I think you should write them. You're close enough to Philippi that maybe you should even consider visiting Lydia or have her come here for a visit. You should pray and ask the Holy Spirit about it." Eutychus was excited in his voice.

Nephi was telling Nikias about his family history, his father the Sheikh, and their textile businesses around Asia. Nikias probed Nephi about resources he might have through his family that they might import. Ruth and Eirene had slipped into a conversation about art, and beauty, and creativity. Ruth had avoided or sidestepped any questions dealing with her past and was careful not to ask any uncomfortable questions of Eirene about why she wasn't part of The Way. They had settled into the current conversation on fashion trends and where they thought they were going. Eutychus heard them both genuinely laughing and felt good Ruth was able to feel somewhat comfortable.

In the morning, Nikias and Corrina were awakened by knocking noises coming from their back patio. Nikias got up and looked out the bedroom window to see Eutychus and Ermias fight training with long staffs. Nikias was surprised at the skills Eutychus was showing. He smiled and said, "Corrina, you need to see this." He waved for her to come look out the window.

She looked and was surprised. "Why so early? I hope he doesn't get hurt."

"From what I see, they've been doing this for quite a while. Our son is no longer a 'boy', but a man to be respected," Nikias said while smiling. He was surprised as Ermias and Eutychus had put down the staffs and now had switched to long swords. "I'm going down to observe closer."

By the time Nikias had gotten dressed and down to the patio, Ermias and Eutychus had moved on to hand-to-hand training on the grass just off the patio. He was amazed at the speed they both moved from one position to the next. After the training, Ermias and Eutychus pulled up chairs near Nikias and were breathing heavy.

"That was amazing," Nikias remarked.

"Your son is a good student," Ermias said.

"I'm very thankful and humbled to be taught by such a master like Ermias. I have so much more to learn from him, and not just self-defense." Eutychus said, looking at his dad.

"Thank you, Ermias, for all you have done and are doing for my son," Nikias said with serious smile and piercing eyes. "Let me know if you need anything."

"It's been an honor to be a friend to Eutychus. The Holy Spirit is obviously guiding him, that is when he'll listen to Him." Ermias winked at Eutychus.

"Both of you must be ready for breakfast. I'm sure Corrina has the cook making a big table full of food for everyone." Nikias had stood up and bowed to Ermias and motioned towards the home.

"We'll be in shortly, Dad. Ermias and I will wash up and then join everyone."

Nikias had gone into the house when Eutychus asked Ermias a question. "I keep thinking about Ruth and what she'll do here. What her place will be. The idea that keeps coming to me is all of Aquila's leather goods we hauled all the way from Ephesus, and that asking her if she would like to open her own business of leather goods. She could have her own business and income. I think she would be good at it. What do you think?"

Ermias sat quietly listening and didn't respond right away. "Two things. I think you need to ask the Holy Spirit on all things about this, and obviously ask Ruth about it. I think it would be good for her, I just don't know if she's ready. I think she'll need help, and a mentor, and someone looking out for her."

"I keep seeing Eirene with her in my mind, in the leather booth with her," Eutychus said. "I'm not sure how that's going to work though. I not sure if Eirene would like to do that."

"You've given me something to pray about," Ermias said to Eutychus. "If I receive anything from Him I'll let you know."

"Thanks, Ermias. Let's get some food."

Nikias welcomed them to an extremely full table of food. The morning breakfast was hearty and filling. "I think Steven will want to see you today, son. Are you going to come to the warehouse this morning?" Nikias asked.

"Yes, my plan was to show Ermias and Nephi around the warehouse if you don't mind," Eutychus responded.

"I'll see you there!" Nikias then kissed Corrina and headed out the door.

Eutychus leaned over to Ruth and said quietly, "I have something I want to talk to you about. It's a business idea. Maybe when I get back from the warehouse we can talk about it."

"Okay?" Ruth didn't have any idea what Eutychus was thinking about.

"You just relax today. I'm sure my mom and sister will have all sorts of plans for the day doing things with you and showing you around." Eutychus smiled at Ruth.

"Let's leave unloading of the wagon for later while we go visit the warehouse. I want to introduce both of you to Steven. He is our business's foreman, a good friend, and a strong member of The Way. I'm sure both of you will deal with him if you do any business with the Shield of Iraklidis." Eutychus was looking at both Ermias and Nephi.

The three walked down the street to the warehouse. Nephi was surprised how many street merchants went out of their way to greet Eutychus when they saw him.

"Do you know everyone?" Nephi asked.

"I grew up here. Many of these merchants get almost all their exported goods through our warehouse. I've dealt with all of them." Eutychus shrugged his shoulders.

"Well, well, well, look at the long-lost boy, who has come home," Steven said when he saw Eutychus with friendly sarcasm in his voice. He then walked over to Eutychus and hugged him hard, lifting him off the ground. "It's so good to see you."

"You too brother," Eutychus said laughing. "So, how's business?"

"Better than ever, somewhat ... because of your efforts," Steven said with more sarcastic smiling. "Let me show you around." Steven then proceeded to lead the group into the warehouse.

Eutychus saw immediately the much larger expansion of the secure Roman room. "Well ...doesn't that cut into the space," Eutychus remarked.

"Sure does, ...in this warehouse. This warehouse is mainly now only official Roman business. We have almost tripled in Roman business and shipments." Steven then led them out of the warehouse and down the street to even a larger building where the space was three times the size of the previous building.

"You father began the process of buying this building after you secured the purple cloth account. I'm sure glad he did, because we needed it almost immediately. I've now got two foremen under me who run each building. Your father promoted me to manager. I also now have a fulltime clerk who does the night inventory manifest for me, as well as all the other record work. He too is part of The Way." Steven said the last part quietly.

Eutychus was really impressed at all the work Steven had done.

"So, what do you think, son?" Nikias said as he walked up behind the group and joined them.

"This is incredible, Dad," Eutychus said.

"If we have another year like the last, I may have to buy another building." Nikias laughed. "And seriously ...I'm already looking. If Nephi and I can dream a little bit together, we might need it sooner than later," Nikias said looking at Nephi.

"I think we'll need to discuss about the port at Alexandria and how many shipments you can accommodate in a year, Nephi suggested as he motioned for Nikias to walk with him.

Nikias walked over to Nephi and they went into the office of the warehouse. When Nephi was sure they were alone he looked at Nikias and said, "I need your advice and knowledge of who I can trust to exchange this for local currency." Nephi then brought out a small leather pouch from which he pulled the largest ruby Nikias had ever seen.

"I know the person who I would trust," Nikias replied, "but he deals mainly with the Roman elite though. He comes to Troas about once a month for a few days to do business. He has several homes and properties in various cities, but his main home is in Roma."

"Could you help me get this done? I've learned to trust Eutychus. I can see that he has been raised with good values and principles... by his father." Nephi nodded his head to Nikias.

"I'm very willing to help," Nikias replied. "In fact, he should show up at any time. This is usually the time of the month he arrives to do business in Troas."

"Good! Good! Thank you so much! I'm very much looking forward to the business we can do together," Nephi said bowing low to Nikias.

"Let's go now and see if he has arrived in Troas, and if not when he is expected to arrive," Nikias said.

Nephi and Nikias left the warehouse office and began walking down the street together as Nikias led the way.

Chapter 21
Dreams
A new challenge.

The wind was blowing hard, the sail was flapping wildly, and the sea spray was stinging her face as the sky filled with dark angry clouds. She was scared, not knowing what to do. A man was shouting orders to a crew, but his voice could barely be heard over the wind. She was holding on tightly to a rope as the ship pitched under her feet.

Ruth jolted awake. She sat up. It was still dark out. It took her a minute to remember where she was. After that dream it was hard for her to go back to sleep. She lay back down and began to pray.

Lord Jesus, what was that all about? Can you help me to understand this dream? Ruth was still trying to calm herself down. She began to breathe deep breaths and slowly let them out. Ruth was then surprised at the clarity of the Voice in her head.

Oh, how I love you. There are many lessons in this dream, and I will reveal them and teach you as you need them. Life can be like a storm, but I will always be with you. Don't be afraid, for I will strengthen you when you need it. I am your Captain in the storm. I am your Peace in the storm. Rely on Me. Call out to Me. I will never leave you or forsake you.

Ruth felt her heartbeat begin to slow down.

Was this really you, Lord? Ruth felt a strong peace come over her that was like she had on the trip when she gave her life to Jesus. Ruth began to pray quietly in her prayer language. She slowly was getting over the intensity of the dream that had jolted her awake.

Ruth prayed for a good amount of time in her prayer language when dawn began to break through her window. After she decided to get up and get dressed, she put on a big wool shawl she found in the closet, then went downstairs onto the back patio. The light was growing to her left while she sat in a chair on the patio. She bundled up with the shawl pulled up around her nose and with her knees drawn up to her chest.

"Lord, I don't know what You have in store for me, but please help me know what to do. I want to serve You, but I don't really know what I'm good at or what my skills are. All my life I've just been told what to do, what to give, what to suffer through no matter the disgust or pain or humiliation. Lord, I feel used up. Please give me a new life. Show me who I am to You?" Ruth was praying quietly aloud. She sometimes felt her prayers in her mind could be too distracted by other things. Ruth was surprised as the door to the patio opened and Eutychus walked out.

"Here you are ...up early again," Eutychus said quietly. "Please excuse me for interrupting your morning time with the Lord, I'll go somewhere else." Eutychus began to walk away.

"No, please stay. I had an intense dream last night. It brought up so many feelings and issues, I'm just trying to make sense of it all." Ruth confessed quietly.

"I actually know that feeling," Eutychus said quietly.

"You? You struggle with dreams?" Ruth looked surprised at Eutychus.

"I struggle with many things," Eutychus said quietly. "I've had dreams that have been hard to understand and that have been scary too. But I've also learned to just ask the Lord about them. He's taught me many lessons from those dreams. I am learning more and more to rely on Him ... in all things."

Ruth sat quietly not saying anything, but Eutychus could tell she was thinking.

"You've confirmed some things to me. Thank you," Ruth said simply.

"Can I ask you a question?" Eutychus looked at Ruth.

Ruth nodded her head.

"What do you like to do? What kind of life excites you? What do you see yourself doing in the future?" Eutychus was gentle in his tone. Tears began to form in Ruth's eyes. Eutychus could tell he had touched a sensitive area. "I don't mean to offend you, Ruth," Eutychus said gently.

"You aren't offending me, Eutychus. I was just praying to the Lord on that very thing. I don't know what I'm good at. All my life I've only done what I've been told, and what I had to do to survive. I really don't know what I'm good at." Ruth now had tears falling down her face.

"I know this... the Lord Jesus loves you," Eutychus said plainly. "And whether you know it or not, He has a plan for you. He wants to use the talents His Father designed in you even if you don't know what those abilities are just yet. The Holy Spirit that you asked for is in you to guide you and teach you all the things He needs you to know. He will send His messengers and words to you. He will give you dreams that will teach you lessons He wants you to learn. These few things I do know."

"What do you know about me?" Ruth asked, desiring to hear more as she wiped her face with her sleeve.

"Lately I've been seeing things in my mind concerning you," Eutychus said looking at Ruth. "I've been asking the Lord for the proper time and place to tell you and ask you."

Ruth was trying to discern the look on Eutychus' face. He looked like someone who was concerned for her, rather than someone who wanted something from her.

"Remember yesterday when I said I wanted to talk to you?" he asked. "That I had a business idea?"

Ruth nodded her head.

"I keep seeing you in a booth here on the street with all the merchants, and you're in the tent we bought from Aquila and the booth was filled with leather goods," Eutychus said with a thoughtful look on his face. "But there were other things too. You were the one running the business." He paused before asking, "What do you think Ruth?"

Ruth was somewhat in a daze. She had never considered the option. She didn't know how to process the information. "I don't know what to think," Ruth said.

"When we left Ephesus, I bought a tent and leather goods from Aquila, hoping somehow of opening another import business utilizing Aquila's leather goods. I'm beginning to think now that those leather goods we brought back with us ...were meant for you." Eutychus explained. "Obviously I'd help you with setting up a regular import of leather goods from Ephesus from Aquila via our shipping schedule. I'd give you a 'family' discount." Eutychus laughed and winked.

The more Ruth thought about it, the more the idea grew in her heart and mind. All of a sudden it's as if ideas began to pop off in her head about future possibilities. *A business of her own.* The thought intrigued her and excited her. *Woah ... that's a weird feeling. Am I actually excited about this possibility?*

"The other weird idea that keeps coming to me is that you are to go with us to Philippi to visit Lydia and her people and business. Why exactly I'm not sure," Eutychus said with his head cocked to one side.

"Wait. Doesn't that mean going on a ship?!" Ruth looked stunned and somewhat scared.

"Yes?" Eutychus didn't know why Ruth reacted the way she did. "Our family has several ships that sail the sea to many ports. I made that trip to Philippi last year around this time," Eutychus said, wondering what had set Ruth off.

Just then Ermias and Nephi came through the door onto the patio. Ruth and Eutychus turned to see who was coming out of the house. Ermias began his morning stretching routine.

"There is this hot drink called 'tea' in the kitchen. My father had some once, but this is good," Nephi said as he sat down in one of the chairs holding a mug.

"That sounds really good to me." Eutychus got up and then asked Ruth, "Can I get you some?"

"Really? I was never allowed anything like that ... before, my master didn't ... and we didn't have any on the trip. Can I try it?" Ruth asked.

"Tea is on its way." Eutychus turned and went into the house.

Eutychus came out with two ceramic painted mugs with steaming hot tea. He handed a mug to Ruth. "One of the benefits of being in the import and export business. Tea from the far east."

Nephi and Eutychus just watched as Ruth took her first sip. They were trying to read her face, but Ruth didn't show any emotion or facial changes.

"I think I like it," was all Ruth said.

"Usually someone has a stronger reaction to it the first time," Nephi said.

"Sorry. But I've taught myself not to show any reactions if I can help it," Ruth explained. "I've probably showed more emotions in the last week than I have in years." She looked downward. "I guess old habits...."

"You're here now ... Ruth." Eutychus then whispered to her, "You're not Zosime anymore. You now are Ruth and belong to Jesus." He smiled at her.

Nephi leaned in close to Eutychus and said, "Tough girl."

"You should pray for her. She's got a lot to think about and adjust to, so do you for that matter. I've learned to pray for others when I know I need prayer in the same areas," Eutychus said quietly to Nephi. Nephi nodded.

"Hey, is there anyone out here who wants breakfast?" Corrina had opened the door and called out to everyone on the patio.

"Sounds great, Mom!" Eutychus said and began to get up. Ruth and Nephi got up too.

"Just a few more and I'll be in," Ermias said to the group.

"Where's Dad?" Eutychus asked his mom as he was sitting down at the table.

"He's already left for the warehouse. Some early shipment or business or something." Corrina just shrugged. "You know Dad."

The others were finding chairs around the table. Again, the table was filled with wonderful food.

"I could get use to this. This is so wonderful, thank you," Ruth said to Corrina directly.

Eutychus suddenly stood up and said, "Before we begin ... let's give thanks to Jesus for all of this." Eutychus motioned to the food and to each person around the table.

After the prayer the conversations were lively and full of laughter. Eirene had come down to find everyone welcoming her to the table and making a place for her.

This certainly is different having all these people here. But I think I like it, Eirene thought.

"Excuse me everyone?!" Eutychus said loudly. Several turned and looked at him surprised. Slowly everyone got quiet. All eyes turned to Eutychus. "I think everyone around this table needs to go together to Philippi. I think we should leave within the week. And we should spend at least a week there," Eutychus said in all seriousness.

"Are you serious?" Corrina asked.

"Yes. I am, Mom. That includes you. And Eirene." Eutychus was looking at his sister when he said it.

"I think that's a great idea!" Eirene said immediately. Eirene had often secretly wanted to go on the adventures both her brothers were experiencing. But being a girl and the youngest she didn't see any opportunities coming. But this one immediately excited her.

"I think it would be fun, Mom," Eirene said.

"Ermias can visit his brother. Nephi can meet with Lydia and talk business. Ruth can see how Lydia runs her business. And you and Eirene get to see what our family business is really about ... first hand," Eutychus explained to his mom.

Everyone began to talk to each other. At first everyone didn't know what to think of the idea, but the more they considered it and thought about it, each person found a desire to go, except for Corrina. After breakfast was over Corrina pulled Eutychus aside to talk.

"I'm not sure this is a good idea," Corrina said to Eutychus.

"Just pray about it, Mom," Eutychus said gently. "I'm not going to try and convince you of anything, and I'm certainly not going to force you. But I think you would benefit talking and sharing with Lydia. You have more in common than you think."

"Okay, I'll pray about it," Corrina said to Eutychus. "But I'm more opposed than I agree at this point. But I think you know that."

"Yes, I know, Mom." Eutychus then kissed his mom on the cheek before turning away to find Ermias.

Eutychus found Ermias in his room.

"Would you like to train?" Ermias asked.

"Yes, I would, but maybe tonight? I think I need to begin to plan and rough out all the details of the trip. I need to talk to Steven and look at the current shipping schedules and well as ship availability."

"I agree that this trip needs to take place. I had to ask the Lord about it, as my heart badly wants to see my brother, and I wanted to know if it was His will for me. I was very happy to find out that I was to go. When you mentioned it at the table I felt my spirit leap in joy," Ermias confessed.

"I feel pretty strongly that my mother and sister are to go too. There are certain connections and lessons that can only be secured on a trip like this one. But my mother is hesitant about it, which I expected. Please agree with me that she'll hear exactly what the Holy Spirit wants her to do ...whatever that is." Eutychus said with earnestness in his voice. "The Lord wants to do something in Eirene too... but He hasn't filled me in on exactly what that is..." Eutychus paused.

"I get the feeling this is going to be more of an adventure ... than expected," Ermias said thoughtfully. "There's something about this that feels right... but also ... like we'll be facing ... tests. I haven't felt like this since Ephesus when we lived on the outskirts and had to be focused entirely on His agenda and wishes. I'll get ready to go with you now."

Eutychus and Ermias found Nephi and set out for the warehouse.

Chapter 22

Business and Life in Troas

Steps of faith.

"Nephi, just the man I need to talk to." Nikias greeted Nephi as the three entered the office of the first warehouse.

"Is Steven here?" Eutychus asked.

"Other warehouse." Nikias replied.

Ermias and Eutychus left through the front and began walking to the next warehouse.

"The man who I referred to earlier as the one you need to meet about your special stone is now here in Troas," Nikias said to Nephi.

"When do you have time to visit him? Will today work?" Nephi asked Nikias.

"Now works. Let's go." Nikias opened the front door and motioned for Nephi. Nephi stepped through the door and followed Nikias down the street.

"I want to stop by two other dealers I know first, just to see what kind of offers they would make," Nikias said quietly to Nephi. "Then we'll know for sure if the dealer I'm suggesting will offer a better value for your stone."

"That sounds very wise," Nephi agreed.

At the first two dealers, Nikias made sure the stone was kept in plain sight at all times. The offer from the second was better than the first. They then headed to the man from Roma.

As they entered the building of the man from Roma, Nephi noticed many fine items from many different places in the shop. Nephi couldn't quite place the man's ethnicity. He looked like a mix of races and wore extremely fine clothing. The man greeted them with a bow.

"Nikias good to see you again. Who is your friend with you?" the man asked.

"This is Nephi from Egypt," Nikias answered. "I think he has something you might be interested in."

"Good to meet you Nephi. I'm Alrazi." Alrazi bowed low to Nephi.

"Are you from Persia?" Nephi asked.

"My father was, yes" Alrazi said. "My mother was Greek. I was born in Roma and am a citizen of Roma."

Nephi observed his piercing green eyes and tightly cut black beard. Alrazi was a big man and tall. He definitely could be intimidating. His manner was confident yet welcoming.

"What can I help you with today?" Alrazi asked Nephi.

"I have something I'd like to convert to local currency." Nephi got out the small leather pouch and brought out the large ruby stone.

Alrazi had no reaction but took the stone and began to look through it carefully. He checked the stone in sunlight, and lamp light. Nephi was surprised as Alrazi went through many different processes as he inspected the ruby. Finally, Alrazi spoke.

"This is a very fine stone. One does not usually see a ruby of this size and quality." Alrazi then put the stone down on the table and went into the back room, leaving Nikias and Nephi alone.

Nikias and Nephi just looked at one another. Nephi's hand went instinctively to the hidden knife in his waistband.

Alrazi returned right away. "I'm sorry I had to make sure I had the currency to fulfill my offer." Alrazi then said plainly, "I will offer you a hundred gold coins and four hundred fifty silver coins."

"I accept your offer," Nephi answered. Nikias just smiled, for Alrazi's offer was more than three times higher than the others.

"Good. I will bring out the coins, and we can count them together." Alrazi then left again and returned with leather pouches filled with coins.

"Nephi, you complete the transaction with Alrazi and I will be back. Don't leave this building until I return." Nikias said after he heard the offer Alrazi gave to Nephi.

Nephi and Alrazi were still counting coins when Nikias returned and outside the building stood two Roman guards.

"I figured we needed an escort," Nikias said to Nephi and nodded at Alrazi.

"I was just going to send my boy to get a Roman officer, but you are ahead of me, and I see you have good security. I should have remembered the Shield of Iraklidis is well maintained with Roman security," Alrazi said.

Nikias and Nephi left the building handing a sack to each Roman soldier. When they got back to the warehouse Nikias told the soldiers to ask Gaius to come to the office. The soldiers put the sacks on the desk and went out to get Gaius.

"Gaius, this is Nephi. He is a good friend to the Shield of Iraklidis and will be doing a lot of business with us. Please take these coins and put them in the secure room. Log them into the secure room's inventory manifest." Gaius nodded and looked surprised as he lifted both sacks off the desk.

"Steven, when is the next ship leaving for Neapolis?" Eutychus asked after he snuck up on Steven and grabbed him from behind.

"Who else would do that?" Steven just shook his head. "Let's go to the office and look at the shipping schedule."

"He never would have tried that with me." Ermias laughed.

"I have learned, Ermias." Eutychus just smiled at Ermias.

"Maybe we need to train tonight on situations like this." Ermias scratched his head.

"Oh boy, I think I'm going to pay for that." Eutychus laughed.

"Looks like in six days the next shipment from Lydia should arrive," Steven said while referencing the schedule. "After that the ship doesn't have another previously scheduled appointment. At least for another several weeks as it goes back to Neapolis for another cloth shipment. Although I haven't got Nicolaos' updated schedule yet. He's actually scheduled to be here in the next few days. As you know, the late fall and winter months are our slow time for sea shipments, because the weather makes it too dangerous." Steven was informing Ermias more than Eutychus as he knew Eutychus already knew the seasonal changes and how they affected their business.

"So, who is the captain of the ship now who makes the cloth run?" Eutychus asked.

"Milos. Nicoloas found him in Corinth," Steven answered. "He became a deck hand, then a first mate, and then he was quickly promoted to captain. He has made this run to Neapolis more than any other in our business. He knows those waters well and is a very good sailor."

"I look forward to meeting him. Can you please let me know when the ship arrives? I think we will ask him to make the trip to Neapolis after the shipment is unloaded and he's had a day to rest. There will be six of us going to Philippi," Eutychus told Steven.

"Six?!" Steven was surprised.

"My mother and sister will be joining us," Eutychus replied.

"Isn't a bit late in the season to be going especially for the sailing novices?" Steven asked. "Weather at this time can be very unpredictable."

"You said Milos knew the waters and was an experienced captain," Eutychus said.

"He is. I just was thinking of your mother and sister, and if something went wrong," Steven replied with concern in his voice.

"Ruth, I must have you see what the next merchant has in the latest fashions. Here ...it's this way." Corrina and Eirene were showing Ruth the different merchants which had the latest textiles and women's fashions. Corrina had decided Ruth needed some nicer clothes and Eirene was more than happy to go along and help. The three women went from stall to stall, tent to tent looking through all that Troas had to offer.

"Are there any merchants that deal with leather goods for women? Like sandals or bags?" Ruth asked the two.

Ruth and Corrina looked at one another. Ruth could tell they were thinking. "Isn't there that stall that had sandals down the street?" Eirene asked her mom.

"Not anymore. They closed up and left," Corrina answered Eirene. "There is Seneca's tent. But he caters to both men and women with his sandal selections." Eirene wrinkled her nose at that suggestion. "He's not good with women, I never feel comfortable in his tent."

"We usually get our sandals from Ephesus," Corrina said to Ruth, "which we ask Nikias to get for us, when he has a shipment coming from that city."

Ruth was actually liking the responses Corrina and Eirene were giving her. There actually might be a space for another leather goods merchant here in Troas. Especially one who catered to women. Her mind was now racing with all the possibilities.

"Here it is!!" Corrina was lifting up a brightly colored cloth and holding it up to Ruth.

"I like that one!" Eirene said. "It will make your eyes stand out. Now if I can just find the right accessories to go with it!" Eirene began to look at the handmade jewelry on table.

"That looks too expensive, I don't have any money," Ruth was hesitant.

"My dear, this is our gift to you. You're one of us now." Corrina smiled at Ruth.

"This necklace will go good with this cloth." Eirene was holding up a necklace with beads that complemented the dress colors.

"I like that!" Corrina said when she saw the necklace Eirene had picked out. Corrina then went to the table and picked out a hair comb that matched the necklace.

Ruth didn't really know how to feel about all that Corrina and Eirene were doing in purchasing all the items for her throughout the day. She had heard Corrina's words, but still wondered what strings might be attached to these gifts or what would be expected of her.

That night at dinner Ruth wore her new outfit and accessories Corrina and Eirene had bought for her. Eirene helped Ruth in pinning the outfit in a very flattering way.

Ermias remarked how beautiful she looked. Ruth just blushed. Eutychus told her she looked now like Eirene, who obviously is a fashion expert.

Eirene smiled, nodded and said, "I think she looks really good."

"She's one of us now," Corrina announced to everyone.

"After dinner there's a meeting, Eutychus." Corrina had pulled Eutychus aside and said this quietly to him. "If you four would like to join me in going, I know the group here in Troas would love to hear of your travels."

"I'll ask them," Eutychus replied and nodded.

Later that evening the four followed Corrina to the home in which The Way was meeting that night. It actually was the same home that Eutychus had fallen out of the window. Eutychus looked for Steven at the gate, but it was a younger man who he didn't know that ushered people into the property. Corrina let the four know that a prayer meeting had been going on for a while before the official meeting so that there would be quite a few there already.

Steven greeted the group as they entered the third story room.

"This one does not get to sit in the window," Steven told Ermias as he winked and pointed at Eutychus. Corrina rolled her eyes at Steven.

Just then Corrina was greeted by Annella who pulled her quickly aside.

"While we were in prayer just this evening, I got this picture in my mind of you on a sailing ship. Then Anat said that she heard from the Holy Spirit that you were going on a trip and that we were to pray for you. Where are you going?" Annella looked at Corrina.

"I haven't decided yet if I'm going," Corrina said with a furrowed brow.

"So then there is a possible trip in your near future?" Annella asked.

"Yes. My son and his group are going to Philippi, and he has asked if Eirene and myself would join them." Corrina said plainly.

"So you will be going on a trip," Annella said. "When will you be leaving?"

"I still haven't decided if I'll go or not," Corrina said with a little irritation in her voice.

Steven then was heard announcing to the group that they were going to get started and shared with everyone that Eutychus had returned and with friends. The people took their seats on the floor. He then asked Eutychus to tell his story.

The group of The Way in Troas listened as both Eutychus and Ermias told of their experiences in Philippi, Corinth, Ephesus, and their trip on the road to Troas through Symrna, Pergamum, and the confrontation on the beach near Assos. The marveled at the work the Holy Spirit was doing through them especially in Corinth and Ephesus. They rejoiced at the story of the baptism event in the ocean after Pergamum. They greeted Nephi and Ruth with encouragement and love and welcomed them into The Way.

After the meeting, several made their way to greet Nephi and Ruth and to welcome them.

"Everyone was so friendly. I've never been to a meeting like that," Ruth said quietly as the five walked home.

"Neither have I Ruth. That really was different. Good but different," Nephi said.

Corrina was quiet as she walked home. She was thinking about what Annella had told her before the meeting. And then she was thinking about all the stories she heard from Eutychus and Ermias. She was really surprised at who Eutychus was becoming. He was certainly different now than just a few years ago. Who was Eutychus now? She heard the others talking about the evenings event and wondered about this trip to Philippi.

Lord, do you really want me to go? You know how much I don't like going on any boat, Corrina had begun to ask the Lord in her mind.

Eutychus had slipped around and was now walking next to his mom. Corrina hadn't noticed him.

"Mom, we can't let our fear hinder what the Lord wants us to do," Eutychus said so quietly that just Corrina could hear him. Corrina didn't respond right away. She struggled with saying it wasn't her fear, when she knew it really was fear that held her back.

Chapter 23
On the Ship

The storm.

The days leading up to the departure to Philippi went by quickly. It was now known by several people in The Way about the trip and several people had come to Corrina and told her that they were praying for her journey. Corrina felt cornered. Yet she also realized that she couldn't deny what was in front of her and that she had to face her own fears. She finally relented and told Eutychus that she would accompany the group going to Philippi. The group had attended another meeting of The Way, and Eirene actually came along with the group. She had attended several meetings before but had always told her mom that those kinds of meetings didn't do anything for her. Corrina didn't push her daughter to go but continued to pray for her. Corrina was surprised when Eirene said she was going to attend the latest meeting. Eirene listened as Nephi and Ruth gave their own personal stories of understanding who Jesus is, and their baptisms, one of water, and one of the Spirit, and as they shared how they now were being taught and guided by the Holy Spirit in their lives.

Eutychus and Milos had been watching the weather. The winds and storms in the fall season could easily become too strong for sailing and the passage could become dangerous. The strong winds on the return trip to Troas made for a quick trip and Milos and the crew had to be very alert and manage the rigging constantly. Eutychus continued to pray and seek the instructions from the Holy

Spirit as to what to bring, and when they needed to depart, and how to pray for the individuals going.

The day came when the group packed up because the ship had arrived at the dock. They awakened before the sunrise to load up and be ready to depart. Milos had advised the group to pack warm clothes and to be ready for possible wet weather on the trip. He felt there was an opening to go, but the possibility of a storm was growing, so the group needed to depart immediately. The boat was loaded and more crowded than normal with six extra bodies on board.

The beginning of the trip was exhilarating for most of them. The strong winds had provided really fast speed. Eirene was beaming and leaning against the rail of the ship enjoying the salt sea spray. Corrina however was sitting down with her head in her hands. Ruth couldn't help thinking about the dream she had had. Her face looked like she was going into battle. Ermias and Eutychus didn't seemed fazed and continued as normal. Nephi was more serious than normal and sat next to Corrina to keep her company.

Later in the morning the winds had grown even stronger, and Milos was beginning to be concerned. He motioned for Eutychus to come. The winds were so strong that he had to talk a little loud to be heard.

"I'm going to head for Imbros, there is a small protected bay on the western side of the island. I've used it before when I had to find shelter from a storm." Milos then pointed east and Eutychus could see the clouds of a storm approaching. "We'll spend as much time on the island as needed until the weather calms down," Milos told Eutychus who just nodded.

In a short while the clouds were overhead and the rain had begun. With the wind the rain was stinging to the skin. Everyone had bundled up and covered as much of their faces as they could. The waves were getting larger and harder to navigate. Milos didn't look concerned, although everyone was looking at him more and more as the conditions worsened.

Ruth kept reminding herself of what the words Jesus had put into her heart after the dream. *Jesus is her Captain, He would never leave her nor forsake her.* The conditions continued to worsen, and Milos was now pushing the crew as adjustments had to be constantly made as the wind and the waves were now really dangerous. Then the hail began. Everyone now wondered if they were going to make it.

Milos was pointing and commanding forcefully to his crew. They had made it to the island dropped sails and rowed into the spit of the bay. They dropped anchors, and the group made several trips in the small rowboat to get everyone off the ship. Corrina slipped on the rope ladder and had fallen into the sea, and Ermias and Eutychus immediately dove in after her. They swam her to the rowboat and helped her in. Nephi had already begun to gather as much firewood as he could find. Once on shore the crew and group worked hard to get the tarps set up and tied down for shelter next to the stone bluff. Under the tarps there was relief from the winds and the rain. Nephi had actually been able to get a fire going with his special fire starter that he had made and brought, that would help start a fire even in the worst of conditions. The crew worked to line the fire with stones and the fire was set just in front of the shelter. Ruth and Eirene had helped Corrina find some privacy in the shelter by putting up some blankets and helped her out of her wet clothing. Ermias and Eutychus had also changed out of their wet clothes. They all dried off and quickly put on another set of clothing.

Corrina was silent and didn't talk much. Eutychus knew his mom was not happy but he was glad for Eirene and Ruth who kept taking care of her and making sure she was okay. The night was hard for the group to sleep, but the crew slept soundly, as most of the men could be heard snoring loudly. Wind, rain, wet clothing, snoring, and strange uncomfortable surroundings made Corrina angry with God.

Why did You send me on this trip?! Why are You doing this to me?! Corrina began blaming God for her misery and uncomfortable conditions.

In the morning Ruth was silently thanking God for saving everyone on the ship as she sat under the tarp looking out into the bay. Nephi was tending the fire and making sure it was being constantly fed. He had moved some coals for a cooking area. Soon breakfast was being made. Much of the crew expressed their thanks for such wonderful food as Ruth and Nephi worked on cooking.

"Do you think we'll be able to leave today?" Eutychus asked Milos when he saw him returning from his hike.

Milos had hiked up the surrounding ridge line in the morning and had been observing the eastern horizon. "Probably not today. I'm hoping maybe tomorrow," Milos said.

"Aren't we going to leave today?" Corrina asked Eutychus as she saw him return from talking to Milos.

Eutychus just shook his head.

Great. Another day, Corrina thought, as her attitude worsened even more. She felt like she just couldn't get warm after her accidental swim in the sea. Ruth and Eirene did their best to take care of Corrina.

Ermias, Eutychus, and Milos met to the assess the situation and weren't concerned as they knew they had plenty of provisions to make it several days more. They all knew that they would have to assess the situation daily.

In the evening the winds had died down some. Milos told Eutychus that they would load up at dawn and head for Neapolis if the storm had completely passed.

Dawn broke with sunlight streaming over the ridge. The group of six were awakened by the crew who had begun to load the ship and take down the tarps. Soon everyone was busy quickly packing up. Corrina was especially careful climbing up the rope ladder to the ship from the rowboat. Soon everyone was on board and the crew rowed the ship out of the bay, sails were unfurled and quickly they were on their way.

Everyone was happy to see the sun and were glad to be headed to their destination, except Corrina. She was now sneezing and shivering.

With the steady winds they arrived at Neapolis towards the evening. Just after docking Eutychus sent Ermias to find Aabbas. They would need his transportation services in the morning for the group.

Aabbas arrived at the dock walking quickly in front of Ermias and Dawit. "Your group will stay with us tonight. Andia and Andalee are already preparing for everyone," Aabbas said to Eutychus.

"We are in your debt again, Aabbas. You are so gracious to me. My mother does not feel well, if Andia might have some broth that would help, I'd appreciate it," Eutychus said quietly to Aabbas after he pulled him aside.

"Don't worry my friend, Andia will help her," Aabbas replied and nodded to Eutychus.

Dawit found Eutychus and grabbed him in a bear hug. "My brother says you are doing well. It is good to see you."

"It is so good to see you too. What are you doing here?" Eutychus asked Dawit.

"I'm here for my weekly meeting with Aabbas and family," Dawit replied and smiled.

"Weekly?" Eutychus cocked his head.

"Every week I travel to teach them the scriptures," Dawit said quietly smiling. "They are now part of The Way."

"That's .... wonderful ...Dawit. Wow!" Eutychus was overwhelmed with emotions.

Thank you, Lord Jesus! Thank You, Holy Spirit! Thank You, Father for your grace and mercy to us! Eutychus was shaking his head in amazement as He worshipped God in his heart.

Aabbas was now leading Eirene, Ruth, and Corrina to his tents. Ermias and Dawit followed behind and were walking, talking, and laughing with their arms around each other's shoulders.

"The crew and I will wait here in Neapolis till you give us further instructions," Milos said to Eutychus.

"The moment I have a possible schedule, I will send word through Aabbas to let you know." Eutychus said to Milos and bowed. "Thank you for your skills in saving all of us."

Milos bowed back and said, "I've actually had worse trips. My crew are good men. We can handle the sea and the ship. I'll be waiting for your word."

Eutychus ran to catch up with the group.

Aabbas was encouraging everyone to eat more. He was making sure everyone had plenty of water and wine. Andia had ushered Corrina into a quiet room and had her lay down and put warm fur blankets over her. She then prepared a warm broth for her to drink. Soon Corrina was asleep. Eirene had decided to remain near her mom in case she might need something. Aabbas had quietly slipped in and delivered a large bowl of food for Eirene.

In the main room Andalee was telling Nephi and Ruth her story of how God had healed her when Eutychus first visited them as they all were eating. Nephi and Ruth told Aabbas, Andia, and Andalee about their adventure on the trip to Troas. The feeling of family was so evident, Eutychus pondered as he watched all of his friends enjoying the evening.

In the morning Corrina was feeling somewhat better. Her fever had broken but she still had a runny nose and cough. With some food she was able to say she would be able to make the trip to Philippi. Aabbas had provided his biggest and most luxurious two coaches for the group to use on their trip to Philippi. Aabbas drove one coach and Dawit the other. The women with Andalee went in the newest coach which offered special cushions with Aabbas driving the team of horses. Dawit and Ermias sat together driving the other coach with Nephi and Eutcyhus in the back who were enjoying the countryside views. Andalee played tour guide and was giving the women stories and history of the sites as they traveled the road.

To Nephi, the trip was very enjoyable, seeing the countryside. Both Nephi and Eutychus didn't talk much but just enjoyed the passing scenery. The other coach was a constant state of conversation and questions. Eirene was always asking Andalee questions with Ruth sometimes just trying to get her own questions answered. Everyone was talking except for Corrina who just stared out of the coach. Ruth asked her if she was warm enough. Corrina just responded with a polite half-smile and a nod.

When they finally pulled through the gates and into the courtyard at Lydia's large home, they were greeted by a large gathering of people to welcome them.

"Eutychus, so good to see you!" Euodia said running up to him and gave him a hug. Lydia was greeting Corrina and then led her quickly into the house.

"I've got a room ready for you, we'll get a fire started immediately in the hearth." Lydia motioned to Phoebe who immediately left to prepare the room. "I'll have my cook to make you a warm broth for you to drink."

Lydia then led Corrina down the hall to a large guest room with beautiful furniture and chairs. The room had large windows with very expensive curtains. Corrina was surprised how beautiful and spacious the room was. The fire had just been started and several lamps had been lit.

"This room is so beautiful, Lydia, thank you so much for your hospitality," Corrina said. "I'm sure I'll feel better after getting a good night sleep."

"If you need anything or have any questions, just ring this bell," Lydia said. "Phoebe here will come immediately and see to any of your needs. Her room is right next door." Phoebe just bowed to Corrina and smiled.

The members of the household were unloading the coaches and helping everyone to their rooms. Eutychus and Nephi were shown to the room at the top of the stairs where Eutychus had previously stayed. They then had brought in another single bed. Ruth and Eirene were shown to a larger room on the second floor. Eirene was quite impressed by the furnishings. Ruth just stared at the big beds and expensive beautiful furnishings and wooden cabinets.

"I've never seen ...such a place." Ruth was still just looking around.

"Obviously Lydia has a prosperous business," Eirene responded.

Then a young woman came in and started a fire in the hearth of their room.

"Welcome to our home. My name is Junia. If you need anything during the night, I'm just in the next room. I know that Lydia is having the cook prepare some food and hot tea, so if you're hungry you are very welcome to join us downstairs." Junia smiled and bowed to Ruth and Eirene.

"Thank you, Junia!" Eirene called out to her as Junia left the room.

"Wow. This place is huge and amazing. Do you want to go downstairs?" Ruth asked Eirene.

"Absolutely. I want to check on mom and make sure she is settled in, and then I'll join you. I'm really excited to be here." Eirene had a bounce in her step.

Chapter 24
Back in Philippi
Inspiration.

Ruth awakened in the morning to light streaming through the window. The sun was just rising. She glanced over to Eirene's bed and saw she wasn't there. Ruth got up and went to the balcony and found Eirene sketching the city on papyrus with a piece of charcoal.

"Wow! That's good," Ruth said after looking over the shoulder of Eirene.

"Thanks," Eirene replied. "I couldn't sleep anymore. Something about this place inspires me."

"You're really talented. Do you sell your art?" Ruth asked.

"No!" Eirene laughed shaking her head. "No one knows I do this. I've never shown anyone."

"Seriously Eirene, you have a gift. I think you should use this talent," Ruth said, then added more quietly, "I wish I had such an obvious talent like that."

"You're extremely talented, Ruth! I see so much in you," Eirene responded.

Ruth was surprised and really didn't know how to respond to the compliment from Eirene. "Hey, do you want to see if there is anyone down in the kitchen and making breakfast?" Ruth asked Eirene as she got dressed. "We could help get it going."

"Sure, I'll go with you," Eirene said as she put away the drawing and put on a long-dyed Chiton. "I'll just check on my mom first."

Ruth and Eirene went down the stairs. Eirene headed to her mom's room. Ruth headed to the kitchen but found herself exploring the bottom floor of the large expansive home. Several cooks were already in the kitchen preparing food. Beyond the kitchen there was a large room with couches and large cushions and a long table. The room also had a huge fireplace. People were already gathered in groups in the room and chatting. A roaring fire was already going. The room had tall, broad windows that looked out onto the large patio and to the back of the property which had a large grass area, large trees, and lots of foliage. On the grass just beyond the patio Ruth could see Ermias and Dawit with Eutychus in a furious long staff training exercise. They were spinning and parrying at a very fast pace. She saw Nephi sitting on a bench bundled up and cradling a mug that had steam coming out of it, watching the three going at each other furiously. Ruth went out to the patio and sat on the bench next to Nephi.

"Do they always train?" Ruth asked Nephi.

"I haven't known them much longer than you. You've seen Ermias and Eutychus. You know what they do. Now there's another one just like them." Nephi marveled, shaking his head.

"I'm going to go find Eirene." Ruth got up and went back into the home.

Ruth was surprised by some of the people in the large gathering room who had just begun to sing and play instruments. One had a lyre, another a type of flute, and another had a drum. Ruth found the music and singing very moving. The people were praising Jesus in song. As she stood there staring and listening, she saw Eirene and Corrina enter the room.

"How are you this morning Corrina?" Ruth asked as she walked over to the two.

"Feeling a little better" Corrina replied.

"We heard the music and singing," Eirene said as she stood watching and listening. "We both wanted to come and listen."

Lydia came up behind the three and just stood silently listening to the music. "They're good aren't they?" Lydia said.

The three turned around to see who had said that.

"Very good," Eirene replied. Corrina nodded.

"They usually practice in the morning for the night's worship time," Lydia explained.

"Worship time?" Ruth asked.

"Yes. We have a worship time for anyone who wants to join us in worshipping God," Lydia said. "This room and the entire patio are usually filled with people. We do it twice a week after dinner. In the evening on Lord's day and once at mid-week." Lydia motioned the group to the kitchen. "Let's have breakfast. There's no formal eating time together for breakfast, everyone has their own schedule, so people just eat as they need and go."

Lydia walked with Corrina to check on how she was feeling. The four picked up plates of food that were spread out on the kitchen table. After making their selections, they walked back into the large gathering room and sat on cushions along the large table together facing the room.

"Lydia, your home and hospitality is overwhelming. It's so beautiful here." Corrina told Lydia.

"I hope you will feel welcome here," Lydia told Corrina. "Your son is quite the man. I really haven't met anyone like him. He seems to be an 'old soul' and wise beyond his years."

"This last year I've prayed for him a lot. My mother's heart was greatly concerned for him." Corrina had tears beginning to form in her eyes. "I guess I have to confess it was worry much of the time. Since he's been back I've seen so many changes in him. He's still my Eutychus, but he's got so much more confidence in areas he didn't have before. Like in the spiritual area. He has changed…"

"You are happy for him, but still feel like you are losing him," Lydia said quietly.

"Yes," Corrina said with a catch in her voice.

"I have watched several of my friends go through the same transition with their adult children. It isn't easy." Lydia put her hand on Corrina's arm. "He's safe here, Corrina, many here love him. And Ermias and Dawit are very protective of him, more than I've ever seen them with anyone else. And that's really saying something because those two give of their lives to everyone so much around here," Lydia said, quietly patting Corrina's arm.

"I'm so grateful to you and your influence in his life," Corrina said. "And I'm so grateful that you have welcomed my daughter and I so richly without any notice."

"Your entire household is welcome here at any time." Lydia smiled at Corrina, and she paused and looked directly into Corrina's eyes. "Eutychus and your family's business has expanded our operation to levels that are amazing. With the leading of the Holy Spirit, our operation has more than doubled in the last year. I have doubled the number of people I employ now. I wish I could meet your husband. Is it true he is not part of The Way yet?"

"Neither Nikias nor my older son Nicolaos are. I pray for them daily," Corrina said and then motioned towards Eirene who was deep in conversation with Ruth who were both watching the worship team practice. "Neither is she," Corrina whispered to Lydia.

"Well, then I definitely know how to pray then!" Lydia's eyes seemed to sparkle with determination.

Eutcychus abruptly came into the room from the patio followed by Ermias and Dawit. They strolled through on their way to the kitchen. Ermias and Dawit were laughing and talking loudly but quickly quieted down when they heard the music. They made obvious comic-like movements to tiptoe through the room.

"I've never seen Ermias this happy," Ruth said to Eirene.

Eutychus and the brothers brought plates piled high with food and sat down on cushions across the table from Ruth and Eirene.

"What's the plan today?" Ermias asked, smiling to the two young women.

"I've never seen you this happy, Ermias," Ruth said.

"I love being home with my brother, and there is no danger here that I have to be wary of, and I can relax and enjoy everyone here. Plus, the food!" Ermias said and Dawit laughed.

Eutychus was too busy stuffing his face and he just nodded with a full mouth.

"Eutychus, did you know your sister is an artist?" Ruth asked. Eirene tried to shush her. Ruth just ignored her. "She's got a great eye, and her sketches are amazing. You should see them."

Eirene shook her head "no" to Ruth's observations.

"My sister is very talented and creative," Eutychus said in between bites of food. "I do know that."

"Is my brother a good student?" Eirene quickly asked the brothers trying to change the subject.

"Eutychus still has much to learn," Dawit said. "But he's learning."

Ermias nodded. "He needs to keep eating, he's got to put on some more muscle," Ermias said punching Eutychus in the shoulder.

"I'm trying," Eutychus said with a mouthful of food.

"Could you two please accompany us to the warehouse this morning?" Lydia was looking at Ermias and Dawit. "I'd like to give our guests a tour of our operation here, for anyone who wants to see it."

"Absolutely. Just let us know when you want to go," Dawit responded to Lydia.

"I was hoping to get to see it. Thank you, Lydia," Eirene said immediately.

Lydia turned and looked at Corrina, smiled and raised her eyebrows. "Let's plan to leave in just a bit. After everyone has finished eating and had chance to get fully ready," Lydia said.

Ermias and Dawit nodded.

"I'm going to come too. I want to see how you've expanded things," Eutychus said.

Later that morning Dawit had gotten a wagon ready to go, and now it was full of people headed to the warehouse. Eirene was looking at all the homes and buildings as they traveled through the streets and just trying to put all of it into her memory. Ruth also was marveling at how rich the city and citizens looked. It wasn't like Smyrna at all, as everyone here seemed to be so happy and smiling. She was surprised at how many people happily waved to them. *How my life has changed. Thank you, Jesus.* Ruth found herself thanking Jesus and praying so much more here in Philippi.

Dawit stopped at a long large warehouse just inside the city wall. People got out of the wagon.

"Is this a different warehouse?" Eutychus asked Lydia.

"This is another warehouse. The old warehouse is in use too. We've more than doubled our space," Lydia explained.

Lydia led the group through the entire operation. They toured both warehouses and their river operation. Nephi was continually impressed. He marveled how well the all the employees were working hard yet seemed to be enjoying their jobs. When he got to the final room storing the finished product, he was in awe. All the different hues of purple and textures of cloth was overwhelming to Nephi.

"I wish I could show my father what you are doing here. This is the biggest and finest operation of this type that I have ever seen. It would be my honor to represent this cloth to all of Africa and beyond." Nephi bowed low to Lydia.

"Nephi, my brother, the Lord obviously had plans for both of us. Let's see where He leads us.," Lydia said, returning the bow. Then Lydia came close and whispered just to Nephi, "I have plans to expand into new colors as well, I've been experimenting." Lydia winked at Nephi.

Nephi's eyes got really big at hearing this. He put his hand over his mouth as his jaw had dropped.

"This is amazing," Eirene leaned into and quietly said to Ruth.

"This is truly inspiring. I never thought a woman could run such a huge organization," Ruth said with her mouth open in awe.

"I want to ask Lydia so many questions," Ruth said to Eirene.

"Then ask her. Don't waste this opportunity. Be bold and just ask her," Eirene told Ruth.

"Excuse me, Lydia?" Ruth had actually spoken up.

Lydia turned and walked to Ruth and Eirene. "Yes? What can I do for you two?" Lydia was smiling at them.

"Have you tried your dyes on leather?" Ruth asked.

Lydia was surprised at the question. Her eyebrows went up and she cocked her head to one side. "That, my dear ...is an excellent question. I have not tried that ... yet. But because you asked... I will now!" Lydia was obviously pleased with Ruth's question.

Ruth got a little bolder. "I was thinking about sandal straps and small coin purses, made of colored leather, and maybe even larger leather bags." Ruth was slow in her talking while she was thinking at the same time.

"Maybe even some thick canvas bags, too," Eirene said.

"Oh my! The possibilities!" Lydia looked really intrigued.

"Okay, when we get back home I want to take you two to my very secret experimenting room where I try different things and methods. I usually don't take anyone there, but you two... are definitely stirring my creative side," Lydia said this very quietly to Ruth and Eirene.

Eirene just looked at Ruth excitedly and rubbed her hands together. Ruth decided to be even more bold.

"Lydia, Eirene here has a real gift. Her drawings are excellent. Maybe you have some paints she could try?" Ruth asked.

Lydia looked at Eirene and smiled. "A budding artist. Excellent. I now know definitely we're going to spend some time together." Lydia looked directly at Eirene and nodded.

Corrina noticed on the ride back to Lydia's home Ruth and Eirene were huddled together in the back of the wagon and were talking fast and excited. *Oh Lord, please reach out to my daughter.* Corrina was surprised how clear an answer came back to her mind.

I have plans for her.

"Looks like your daughter and Ruth are becoming quite close," Nephi said to Corrina.

"Please pray, Nephi, that she would come to know Jesus as we do," Corrina pleaded with her eyes at Nephi.

"I already have been." Nephi smiled and nodded. Corrina just smiled back at him. Nephi saw her eyes begin to fill up with tears as she turned her head away.

When the group arrived back at Lydia's large home, everyone went their separate ways. Ruth and Eirene hung back. Lydia motioned for them to follow her. They followed Lydia around the side of the house to the back and they continued through the patio area and into the grass towards the trees. As they got closer, they saw a small path that led through the foliage and bushes. Through the bushes the came to a small building with a couple of small windows at the very back of the property that was set next to the wall that surrounded the entire property. It couldn't be seen by any place on the property, it was completely hidden. Lydia opened the skinny door and motioned them inside.

In the building they saw shelves and tables and pots and lots of different containers of all sizes. There was a small fireplace on one end that was used for heating pots and containers. There were strips of all sorts of cloth hanging from the rafters.

Eirene just looked and looked. Obviously this was a place of great experimenting.

Ruth was in awe of the space. She looked in containers and saw minerals, and dried plants, and what looked like shells, and different things from the sea. It seemed every container had a different interesting item inside.

Lydia just watched them and prayed. *Lord, I know You have plans for both of these young women. Help me to know what to say to them. Help me to know what to do with them. Help me to know what to show them. Guide me, Lord.*

Lydia went to the wall and took down some longer thick canvas sheets with a hole in them. She put one on like an apron over her head and handed two more to Ruth and Eirene. They watched her put it on and they did the same.

"Are you ready to go to work, girls?" Lydia asked the two.

Ruth and Eirene looked at each other. Each were beaming from ear to ear. Eirene rubbed her hands together.

Chapter 25
The Way Meetings
Testimonies.

The afternoon flew by as the three worked together in Lydia's little building. They experimented with coloring leather along with other textiles and items to see what worked well and what didn't.

"Hey, is there anyone in there that wants to eat?" came the shouting voice from outside of the little shop building.

"Oh my, this always happens to me. I get busy in here and time just flies by. Let's go get some dinner." Lydia motioned to Ruth and Eirene as she hung up her apron.

"That was fun!" Eirene said to Ruth as they walked together behind Lydia back to the house.

"It was fun for me," too," Ruth replied. "I want to try all sorts of other things as well. I wonder if Lydia will allow us more time to experiment?"

"I sure would hope both of you will join me quite often in my shop as the Lord allows us time to do so," Lydia said without turning around. Ruth and Eirene just looked at one another and smiled.

Dinner at the house amazed Eirene and Ruth. So many people showed up. So many workers and friends. So much food. There were people sitting everywhere, inside and out on the patio. Outside on the patio the fire pit had been lit as well as inside the fireplace. People were coming up and constantly introducing themselves to the Troas group.

"On worship night my entire crew is invited to dinner and to stay for worship if they want," Lydia was explaining to Corrina.

"Are they all part of The Way?" Corrina asked Lydia with an increasingly surprised look on her face as the number of people showing up.

"Oh, no. I'd say maybe two thirds of my employees now are part of The Way. This last year I've had to hire more workers," Lydia explained to Corrina, "and the number of people who wanted to be part of our company was almost triple of the positions I was opening. But with each mid-week dinner and worship service more employees accept Jesus as Lord of their lives. We've seen a few encounters during worship times that many say are miracles." Lydia added with a serious look on her face, "We've also had several infiltrators try to enter our group. But the Holy Spirit always points them out. They don't last long. We've learned to listen to Him about people and who to trust."

Dinner was winding down and others were still showing up for the worship night. Then Eutychus spotted Aabbas, Andia, and Andalee walk onto the patio, and he immediately got up to greet them.

"It so good to see you three!" And everyone was hugging.

"We now come every mid-week," Aabbas was telling Eutychus. "Dawit invited us after we made Jesus our Master. I also rent an apartment here in Philippi for all of us as it just made sense with our expanding business. Lydia has given us much more business. And some of my employees have also become part of The Way."

"That's great, Aabbas, and amazing, it's wonderful to see you here." Eutychus couldn't stop smiling.

"Okay, brothers and sisters, let's come together for worship." Lydia stood on a chair and was almost shouting to everyone.

People on the patio came inside and those in the main room where moving furniture into the hallway to make room for more people. Soon the entire room was packed with people with everyone sitting on the floor. Some were handed cushions. Eventually everyone eyes turned towards Lydia.

"When praying and asking the Holy Spirit as to what I was to speak to you all about tonight, the second letter from Paul to the Thessalonians kept coming to my mind. So, I will read a page or two to you now." Lydia began to read. After she finished reading she began to speak. "Simply I want to say to you and encourage you with... is this... Stand fast in faith to the Lord Jesus and don't be idle. But be listening to the Holy Spirit for the instructions He is giving you personally daily, and then be bold and step out in faith and obedience to those instructions. With everything you do – do it as to our Master Jesus. With excellence, effort, and with everything you have."

There were lots of people nodding in agreement.

"I think now would be a good time to hear from our own Ermias and his companion Eutychus." Lydia then winked at Eutychus. "...on the adventures the Holy Spirit they sent them on."

Ermias looked at Eutychus. Eutychus looked at Ermias with a look of 'go ahead'.

"Whatever you do, do it as to our Lord Jesus under the guidance of His Holy Spirit. This was our lesson each day. Some days we did better than others," Ermias began. He then gave a short account of the churches in Corinth and Ephesus the work the Holy Spirit had them do there. Then he told a little of the trip from Ephesus to Troas mentioning the two new companions they met on the way, Nephi and Ruth.

"I think that Nephi and Ruth should also tell some of how they got here tonight." Ermias motioned at Nephi and Ruth.

Ruth gave a look to Nephi like he was to go first.

Nephi began to speak but his voice sounded nervous and shaky.

"It's okay, Nephi, you've got our support. Take your time," Lydia said.

Nephi went on to tell of meeting Eutychus in Ephesus and how he misjudged him in the beginning. He talked about the conversations they all had in the wagon during the day. And the day he made them stop so that he could make Jesus his Lord. And he talked about the determination to be baptized in a freezing sea. Nephi then just abruptly stopped and everyone could tell he was becoming very emotional. Several put their hands upon Nephi in support.

Ruth then felt like she was to speak. She began with being pretty vague about her past, but just said she was in a dire situation like many of the women

Ermias had said about the women in Corinth and Ephesus, and that Ermias and Eutychus had risked much to rescue her. She then said much of the story was the same that Nephi had told. But she added the beach story of Ermias and Eutychus fighting off bandits. Everyone listened with bigger eyes and ears at Ruth's depiction of the danger she was under and how fast Ermias and Eutychus had knocked out all the men.

"I'm overwhelmed by all the love I've been shown over the past few weeks. First Ermias and Eutychus. Then my new brother in-the-Lord Nephi, and then Corrina and Eirene, and now all of you here... I'm just so speechless." Ruth then too became too emotional to continue.

"I think we now need to worship our God, and our Lord Jesus, and allow the Holy Spirit to flow through us here and now! We have so much to give Him thanks for," Lydia said motioning for the worship team to begin.

The worship team with the instruments began to play. Soon the singers joined the music. Many knew the songs, but those that didn't still listened with joy and many hummed along. People could sense a change in the room. A warm wind and rush of love began swirling in the air above them and through them. Many began to raise their arms and hands into the air in worship. The Presence of the Holy Spirit could now be felt by everyone.

Eirene sat and marveled at what she was experiencing, it was something she had never felt before. She looked over at her mom. Corrina had her arms and hands in the air and was swaying with her eyes closed. She looked at Eutychus. He was now standing in the back of the room with his arms over his head and it looked like he was saying things as he looked out over the crowd, but the sound of the wind, music, and people were too loud to hear what Eutychus was saying. Then the worship team began to sing in a different language almost spontaneously. Eirene looked at Ruth, and she was singing along in a different language too. The love in the room was almost too hard to handle, many were weeping and worshipping at the same time.

This Presence lasted for quite a while and slowly rested in intensity, but the feeling of love remained. A quiet came over everyone in the room. No one moved. The silence was thick with anticipation. Even Eirene could feel Holiness of the Presence in the room. It only lasted a moment, and then lessoned. People could sense the difference and began to relax.

"Obviously He is here tonight," Lydia was saying this very quietly but everyone could still hear her. "Lord, we give You Your place here and in us. We worship the great I AM. Our Father, His son Jesus, and the Holy Spirit." Lydia added quietly, "We need to pray."

Murmurs of agreement were said in response. A small chorus of "Amen" rose up throughout the room.

"I encourage everyone to seek Him now in prayer." Lydia was speaking a little louder now as many had already begun to quietly pray aloud. "If you have something for someone, bring them to the front and pray over them. If anyone wants to join in that effort in praying for that individual you come as well. Everyone else, keep seeking Him in prayer. Let's keep His Kingdom here and going."

Eirene was actually situated where she could hear those who were bringing people to the front to be prayed for. She saw Junia go and get Ruth and bring her to the front. Then she saw Phoebe also join the group to pray for Ruth. Lydia and her mom also came to pray for Ruth. The women gathered around Ruth and Ruth bowed her head.

"I keep getting a name when the Lord was showing me your face in prayer Ruth. Does the name Zosime mean anything to you?" Junia asked Ruth.

Ruth just nodded her head. Ruth was really surprised that her prior name was used.

"He wants you to know that He is very pleased with you and loves you, and that He has plans for you." Junia paused and tilted her head. "I think someone else has more," Junia said.

"He wants you to help others that come from the same type of life you were freed from. No longer a slave to any other earthly master. But free to serve Him in the Kingdom. Their past will be gone as your former name is now gone. You are to help them find purpose and a hope in Jesus," Phoebe said quietly.

"I agree with Junia and Phoebe, He has you here tonight for a reason, He has big plans for you, Ruth," Lydia said as she side-hugged Ruth. By now Ruth was leaking tears and could only respond with a quiet "Thank you."

Aabbas had gotten up and walked over to Nephi and tapped him on the shoulder and nodded towards the front. Nephi got up to walk towards the front. Ermias, Eutychus, and Lydia all joined Aabbas. Eutychus was very surprised when Aabbas had gotten up to pray for Nephi, and immediately wanted to be a part of the prayer.

Everyone remained quiet to allow Aabbas as much time as he needed as they all began to pray and ask the Holy Spirit how to pray for Nephi.

"Brother, I thank God for you. Your courage to step out in bold faith for God. This is the first time I've ever done anything like this. But His hand on me tonight was stronger than I've ever encountered before, and He began to talk about you. So, if I get it wrong please forgive me – because I'm new at this kind of thing. I think He wants you to be a messenger of His to your family and people. I saw you on a ship headed to Alexandria. He wants you to tell your story to many others." Aabbas paused and then said, "There's just one more thing. When I saw you on the ship I think Ermias was next to you. That's all I have I hope this helps you." Aabbas stepped back to allow others to come in closer. Lydia nodded and smiled at Aabbas in approval.

Ermias had now come closer to Nephi.

"Nephi, my brother. I will go with you if you feel it is what the Lord wants for you. I can't get the story out of my heart and head that you told of Matthew. I'm feeling drawn to go back to Ethiopia and to help Matthew there. . . yet my new family is here. But the calling of the Lord cannot be swayed in me. I know I must go ... home." Ermias now was too emotional to continue.

Eutychus had never seen such emotion before in Ermias. Eutychus reactively put his arms around Ermias. Ermias grabbed Eutychus fiercely in a hug. Then Dawit joined the hug.

Lydia then tapped Eutychus on the shoulder. Eutychus was let go by the brothers and kneeled down and bowed his head.

"I see Roma. Your time to go is soon. Your mission will be completed there. Jesus is waiting for your reunion with Him. This will be the longest and most difficult mission of your life." Lydia began praying and prophesying over Eutychus. Corrina had been listening and wondering what it all meant. Eutychus had a strong emotional response of relief, surprise, wonder, warmth, determination, and trepidation all at the same time.

"Holy Spirit help me," was all Eutychus could say in response.

Eirene listened in awe to all that was going on around her. She too wondered about what Lydia had said to Eutychus and what it all meant. So many things she had experienced this evening was tugging on her soul.

Eirene tugged on Ruth's garment. Ruth turned to Eirene with a questioning look.

"How do I make Jesus my Lord?" Eirene asked Ruth quietly. Ruth gathered the others around Eirene.

Chapter 26

Decisions and New Ventures

Growth.

A parchment arrived late morning to the household of Lydia from one of Aabbas' employees addressed to Corrina. It read: "Members and Family of The Shield of Iraklidis from Milos: I see an opportunity to return to Troas. Weather seems favorable. We will be leaving Neapolis port tomorrow midday. Please send correspondence."

Corrina read the parchment and quickly went to find Eutychus.

"I'm not sure what to do. I don't want to have the kind of experience I had on the way here, and I'm not sure about Eirene, I'm pretty sure she'd want to stay with all that just happened to her. But I don't want your father to worry about us." Corrina was talking fast and not giving Eutychus any chance to respond, so he just waited.

"Mother..." Eutychus slowly and gently began to speak after Corrina had finally stopped. "Father will be fine. Eirene will be fine. I am fine. As a family we are incredibly blessed. I agree that Eirene will want to stay and I think she should stay at least till spring when it will be safer to travel on the sea with better weather. If you could stand it, I think you should stay as well, I know I want you to." Eutychus was speaking as calmly as he could to his mother. "I'm sure Lydia won't mind us staying until spring, in fact I've got some proposals and ideas for both of you that I'd like to address to both of you. I've been praying about them for the past few days. If it makes you feel any better we can ask Lydia and Aabbas about renting an apartment till spring here in Philippi. Let's go find Lydia and tell her of your correspondence from Milos." Eutychus smiled at his mom and motioned for her to follow him.

"Rent an apartment? No. You will stay here." Lydia was firm in her voice and her eyes sparkled with joy and determination. "I actually need Eirene and Ruth in some of my new creative endeavors. Having someone to always go find her when I finally have the time will be too inconvenient for me. Eirene needs to stay here. Corrina, I also really am enjoying having another woman of 'our generation' and wisdom to share with, please stay. Send a letter to your husband that you will be staying 'til spring when it will be safer for you to return." Lydia looked directly at Corrina. Corrina paused and stood still and silent as she thought and internally prayed for guidance. She then nodded.

"Thank you, Lydia, for your invitation and warm hospitality to all of us. I want to go and tell Eirene about our plans and have Eutychus write a letter to Nikias to be sent back with our ship captain." Corrina hugged Lydia and then went to find Eirene.

When Corrina told Eirene the plans that they were staying 'til spring, Eirene actually jumped for joy. Eirene then ran to find Ruth and tell her the news.

Eutychus had went to Nephi and Ermias and told them of captain Milo's plans to depart the next day.

"I need to leave with him," Nephi said firmly.

"I'm with you, brother," Ermias nodded at Nephi.

"I'll go find Aabbas and tell him you will need transport to the port before midday tomorrow," Eutychus said.

Nephi and Ermias went to pack for tomorrow's departure. Eutychus went to find Aabbas in the city.

When Eutychus arrived back at the house, Corrina pulled him aside.

"I need you to write a letter for me to your father to send with Milos."

"Let's go to my room, I've got parchment there." Eutychus then led his mother up the stairs.

Corrina dictated the letter to Eutychus.

"Dear Nikias, everyone here is healthy and well. For safety reasons we will be staying until spring when travel is much safer. We love you and miss you. Corrina."

"I will send this with Ermias and Nephi," Eutychus said to his mom.

"They are returning with Milos?" Corrina asked with a shocked voice.

"Yes," Eutychus said with a nod. "Nephi feels he needs to leave as soon as possible, with great urgency he felt God's call on his life last night as we prayed for him. Ermias feels the need to go with Nephi and then on to Ethiopia, his home, to help Matthew."

"Wow. It's amazing how fast things move here," Corrina remarked as she got up to go downstairs.

Eutychus then wrote another letter to Steven asking for him to send the tent from Aquila and the leather goods they had brought from Ephesus on the next available ship to Philippi, as well as an order to Aquila for another two tents and the twice amount of leather goods to be sent from Ephesus to Troas. Funds for the order were to be drawn from his personal account. Eutychus rolled up the letter to Steven and put in the same roll with the letter to his father.

Eutychus then found Ermias in his room and handed him the letters. "I'm going to miss you, Master Ermias. You've taught me so much." Eutychus then grabbed Ermias and hugged him tight.

Ermias tightly held Eutychus for a moment. When he let Eutychus go, he stepped back with his hands remaining on the shoulders of Eutychus. "You will always be my ... brother." Eutychus could barely see the water forming in Ermias' eyes because his own eyes were now filled with tears.

"It has been my honor ... to be your student. I will see you in the Kingdom," Eutychus said as his voice broke.

"I think it's better we do this now before tomorrow morning." Ermias laughed.

"When I was with Him, Jesus said it would just be a ... few minutes till I'm with Him again," Eutychus said with emotion. "I think about that more and more, as I am here in this place. My hope swells in my heart to know I will be with you again … brother."

"The great reunion when we will all be changed," Ermias said while pondering.

"But for now… faithfulness and obedience to His instructions to us, to the end of each of our races," Ermias said with forcefulness.

Eutychus grabbed Ermias in a quick hug and turned and left the room.

I'm going to miss that guy. Help me, Lord, to help Nephi and be with Eutychus. Ermias then turned and continued his packing.

Early the next morning, the entire household stood in the courtyard saying their goodbyes to Ermias and Nephi. There were lots of hugs and tears. Dawit had decided to go with them to the port to see his brother off. Aabbas drove the carriage himself.

As the carriage rolled away, Lydia called everyone to breakfast. Everyone was sitting at the table when Eutychus said he'd like to have a meeting this morning with Lydia, his mom, his sister, and Ruth.

"Let's do it now. Let's go sit by the fire." Lydia motioned the group to the couches near the fireplace. "Okay, Eutychus, what's this about?" Lydia asked.

"First, I've sent to letter to Steven asking him to send me all of Aquila's leather goods on the next ship to Neapolis. Plus, I've given Steven an order to be sent to Aquila for two more tents plus twice the leather goods when it can be sent to our warehouse in Troas." Everyone was now interested and listening carefully. "This is what I see as possibilities, obviously with all of your approval. One. We set up Ruth to start her own business here in Philippi with the help of my sister and her designs selling your new creations, which all of you have been creating out there in your secret building Lydia." Eutychus winked at Lydia.

"Second. We expand into other cities with the help of Priscilla, and my mom here with Ruth managing the growth of inventory and shipments to other vendors that we set up via our warehouse." Eutychus now had all of them looking at each other and smiling.

"Three. This will mean lessons in reading and writing for all involved. I already know Ruth wants to learn more. Lydia, I hope you will help me with this, as I am willing to commit time every day to this teaching, and I know I can't do it alone. You know that people in business must be able to read and write well." Eutychus finished and looked at Lydia.

"This sounds like the Holy Spirit is again way out in front of us. Eutychus … I had been thinking about some of these very same things. Although I had not considered the writing and it's need, but of course I do now. Yes, of course I will help. I suggest we get started today. What does everyone think?" Lydia looked at the other women.

"I'm not sure how I could help," Corrina said hesitantly.

"Your help will come with correspondence with Priscilla and Lydia as we help women out of slavery by giving them new lives and opportunities. I also would like to see you learn to read and write as well," Eutychus said gently. "I also want to talk to you and Lydia about beginning some orphanages here in Philippi and Troas as part of The Way's ministry to their cities and people," Eutychus said with emotion. "We need to reach out to these children who are just destined to slavery and give them a chance for a better life."

"Ermias and I were involved with Priscilla and The Way in Ephesus in starting one there, and it was highly needed and one of the most meaningful things they were doing. We need to do that in both our cities." Eutychus said.

"That sounds like a big undertaking," Corrina said.

"It is," Eutychus said with a nod, "and a lot of work too. But the rewards are worth it."

"That has more than once crossed my mind, Eutychus, I just didn't know how to begin it with all of the other projects and businesses I had going," Lydia said with enthusiasm. "But with yours and Corrina's help I am very much in support of whatever you need."

"This all sounds so great, except the part where I have to take lessons from my brother," Eirene said. They all laughed.

"I'm not sure what to say, Eutychus, this is beyond my biggest dreams. It sounds almost scary and I don't know if I can do it," Ruth confessed.

"You're not doing it alone, Ruth," Eutychus replied.

"Exactly, your designer will be right beside you." Eirene winked and smiled.

"Everyone here will work to see this is a success, it's not just you." Lydia nodded and smiled.

"I know you'll be great, Ruth. You've got the skills I've seen them already," Eirene said.

Ruth had tears forming and wiped her eyes. "I've never had a family before. Is this what it's like?" Ruth said through her tears. "And Eutychus?" Ruth paused.

Eutychus looked at her and listened patiently.

"Anything, and I mean anything, you think I can help with for those orphanages, I will do. Maybe if one existed when I was a child..." Ruth stopped and wiped her eyes again.

Corrina leaned over and hugged Ruth. "Okay I'm in," Corrina said.

"I'm curious, Eutychus, why did you order more from Aquila already?" Lydia asked Eutychus. "I can see we may need them sometime in the future, but I think you might have other reasons as well?"

Everyone then turned and looked at Eutychus.

"I would like to be your first vendor in Roma, Ruth," Eutychus said clearly and firmly. "I'm going to need a business there and income while I serve the Lord's instructions there so I can fund His directions to me. And since Lydia already has a vendor there for her cloth, that opportunity is already taken. This is what sits right in my heart to do. I've ordered those materials from Aquila out of my personal funds. I believe in you, Ruth, and the talent of my little sister." Eutychus looked at the women. "And I'm planning on leaving sometime this summer for Roma. So, we better get started on this now, if everyone agrees."

"Well, I like it," Lydia said. "Let's get going today. Ruth and Eirene, let's meet in the shop today after lunch and we'll decide what's best will fit our immediate needs in the way of products. Then in late afternoon, we'll begin reading and writing lessons."

Lydia, Ruth, and Eirene got up and went to their rooms to collect items they wanted to experiment with while Corrina and Eutychus remained seated by the fire.

"How does all of this sound to you mom?" Eutychus asked quietly.

"I'm amazed at you, Eutychus. I wonder where my little boy went. You've become such a man of God and a businessman. Honestly, I feel a little sad, and at the same time excited to see what the Lord Jesus is doing through you. I don't know how much I can do, but I know I need to try," Corrina confessed.

"Lydia will help you. She really likes you, I can tell," Eutychus replied. "And this time will be good for Eirene to grow in her faith, in a place that isn't her 'home' where she now can see herself growing into a woman of God. At home she would be just the 'little sister' and the youngest child. Here she will be a business partner, using her creative skills, and a friend growing in faith with a group that isn't just her family and friends she grew up with. And she will be learning all sorts of new skills to help her with all of her God given talents." Eutychus was explaining to his mom.

"Yes, this is the right thing to do. But I'm just the mom," Corrina said.

"Yes, you are my mom, but you are so much more," Eutychus looked at his mom.

"Ruth never really had a mom. She needs to know what it's like even at her age. And there are so many others that need a 'mom'. You're an awesome mom. You can be so much to so many people," Eutychus said with encouragement.

"I love you, son."

"I love you too, Mom."

The days flew by. Everyone was busy working, planning, and learning new skills. Even Eutychus had continued his daily self-defense disciplines except now with Dawit as his teacher and master. Dawit was more nuanced in the closeup skills of knife defense. Ermias was the master of the staff. Dawit was the master of the short blade. Eutychus was being stretched to learn new habits and skills.

In the late afternoon there was a class on reading and writing, and more women in Lydia's household had joined to learn literacy skills. Corrina had also joined the class. The participants all worked on copying the letter to the Romans by Paul. Working on copying the letters helped them understand at a quicker pace. Soon they were copying the other letters of Paul and James as well.

Eutychus also had begun a small group teaching about the very nature of the Holy Spirit by having the group go through the nine fruit of the Spirit found in Paul's letter to the Galatians. The participants then would ask the Holy Spirit each day how He wanted to work on that particular fruit in their lives. Soon there were other groups formed from the graduates of the first group. Eirene had joined in the second wave of groups. Eirene still had issues seeing her brother as many others saw him.

Corrina and Eutychus along with Andia had actually begun to search the city for a good spot for the orphanage project. Andia had already appealed to Aabbas as she had already taken in two orphan children from Neapolis. When she heard of the plans for an orphanage in Philippi, she wanted immediately to be a part of the work. Andia and Andalee as well had also secretly joined the reading and writing class.

The design group of Lydia, Ruth, and Eirene had produced some remarkable products. Sandal designs especially for women. Smaller ornate leather bags, with intricate designs on the leather, as well as bags and sandals with bead work. Some sandal designs had colored leather straps. Some sandals were a whole new style that didn't require the person to tie the straps, one could just slip into the sandal. The main strap had a different color with small seashells woven to the top. When the products were presented to the women of Philippi, they sold out immediately. Eirene and Ruth could be seen dancing and hugging behind the vendor stall as they were so excited to see their work be so accepted and desired. When the shipment from Aquila came, then vendor stall had the professional look they all wanted. Plus, there was a lot more leather products that could be changed into their own specific designs. Ruth would only sell their products one day a week out of the tent. When they arrived at the tent in the morning on sale day, there was always a line of women waiting. Ruth and Eirene were working hard to produce enough products so that they could possibly open for two days a week. Lydia had told them they might need to find a space to begin making the products with the help of workers. There were so many learning lessons for Ruth and Eirene in those first few weeks and months. Lessons of reading and writing. Creating, designing, and selling. Pricing, and inventory. Supply and demand.

Life in Philippi was extremely busy for the household of Lydia that winter.

Chapter 27
On the Ship to Roma
Nikolaos.

Eutychus was leaning over the side of the ship enjoying the speed and salty sea spray. It was now midsummer and the weather was good and the trip to Roma had been secured with Nicolaos as captain of the largest ship in the Shield of Iraklidis fleet. Eutychus and Dawit had secured the shipment from Ephesus from Aquila and loaded all the latest products that Lydia, Ruth, and Eirene had newly designed and manufactured for sale. They had been on the sea now for four days, and just settling into the three-week journey to Roma. Eutychus had continued his regular daily discipline of exercise with his new training master Dawit, and they went through the different forms and combat exercises each morning. Dawit was pushing Eutychus to learn new techniques and Eutychus was having to unlearn some habits that were hindering his progress.

"This is like life, Eutychus. We are always learning new things from the Holy Spirit, which requires us to change our ways and old habits. He never wants us to stop growing and listening to Him." Dawit talked as he spun wielding the wooden short practice knife as he circled Eutychus.

Eutychus was having to focus all the more as Dawit seemed to be moving faster and faster. It was taking all of his concentration on defensive moves and he couldn't respond to what Dawit had just said.

"Always having to learn new things keeps us humble which is what He wants ... Eutychus." Dawit had spun quick and had swept the leg of Eutychus who was now on his back and found the wooden knife to his throat.

Dawit helped Eutychus to sit up.

"What was that distraction move you just did? Can you show me that again?" Eutychus asked Dawit.

Nicolaos enjoyed watching the two go through the exercises.

"Enough for today. Go over our last exercise in your mind. Ask the Holy Spirit about it. See what He says to you." Dawit began gathering up the practice weapons.

Eutychus sat on the deck of the ship thinking about all that had just happened. He began to ask the Holy Spirit in his mind what He wanted to say to him, when the whole conversation he had had with Nicolaos just before landing in Corinth over a year ago came rushing back to his mind.

Ooof. You want me to confess to Nicolaos that he was right, and that my pride got the better of me?

Yes, humble yourself before him, came the immediate response in his mind.

Eutychus stood up and walked over to Nicolaos.

"Can we talk?" Eutychus asked.

"What can I help you with?" Nicolaos said with his usual straight face.

"I need to tell you... you were right. Your advice to me over a year ago about Corinth was correct. My pride became my downfall that same day we left the dock. God had to show me where my pride made me mess up. I repented before Him and he restored me. But it wasn't an easy or quick process for me because I thought more of myself than I should. I just want to thank you for that advice, I should have listened to you better." Eutychus was being as humble as he could be.

"Well, you should listen to me, I've got a lot more experience than you with these cities," Nicolaos said with somewhat of an air of superiority.

"I also want to tell you that I've been praying for you," Eutychus said quietly.

"Keep your prayers. I'm doing fine," Nicolaos said as he began to walk away from the conversation.

"Wait, Nicolaos, there's more I'd like to share with you. It's about our sister."

Nicolaos stopped and turned around. "What about Eirene?" Nicolaos said with almost an irritation in his voice.

"Our little sister is becoming quite the designer and businessperson," Eutychus said with a smile. "Here, come with me." Eutychus motioned for Nicolaos to follow him. Eutychus led him to the supplies that they had brought with them. Eutychus opened a box and showed him a leather bag that was very ornate and colored designed. It had extensive bead work on it. It looked very expensive.

"Eirene designed this." Eutychus handed the bag to Nicolaos.

Nicolaos turned the bag over and over in his hands. He noticed the fine scrolling and bead work on the leather. He also noticed the color was actually a purple hue and not the natural leather tan color.

"Eirene made this?" Nicolaos looked at Eutychus with his eyebrows furrowed.

"Obviously she had help. Lydia, Ruth, and Eirene are all working together to produce these items. But the design is Eirene's. There's a lot of different items here. I'm going to begin to sell them in Roma. They already are the must-have items in all of Philippi with all the wealthier women. But they also have designed some for the common woman as well. I will price those accordingly," Eutychus said.

"She definitely has talent, that's obvious," Nicolaos said.

"I want to tell you just one more thing..." Eutychus was praying to the Holy Spirit in his mind at the same time ... *Give me the right words to say here.* "Eirene has become part of The Way now too. She has joined Mom and I with her faith in Jesus," Eutychus said directly.

Nicolaos frowned.

"This isn't about religion, Nicolaos, but an actual relationship with God through the indwelling Presence of the Holy Spirit," Eutychus explained. "It isn't about visiting a building, temple, or even a meeting, but it's about a personal intimate daily connection with God though the Holy Spirit."

Nicolaos just turned and walked away.

The days continued as usual with the regular daily maneuverings and chores of a larger sailing ship. Eutychus and Dawit had their regular exercise time. The only difference was Eutychus was finding Nicolaos becoming more and more short with him. Nicolaos seemed very irritated and gruff all the time.

Finally, Eutychus asked Nicolaos, "Are you okay?"

Nicolaos replied with anger. "I'm fine. Leave me alone."

He's not sleeping well. The words you spoke to him, I am reminding him of them every night. I'm working on his soul. The Holy Spirit was telling Eutychus what was actually going on.

What exactly do you want me to do? Eutychus asked the Holy Spirit.

Just keep praying for him as I lead you, came the immediate response to his mind.

It was around day eighteen when Nicolaos caught Eutychus alone and stopped him. He began to speak very quietly.

"How does a person exactly encounter this .... Holy Spirit.. you keep talking about?" Nicolaos said with a frown on his face.

Eutychus almost jumped physically, but remained exactly the same standing very still, hoping his face didn't give away his joy.

"The answer is quite simple," Eutychus began slowly.

"First you believe in your heart that Jesus is who He said He is. You believe His message. Then you repent of your ways you know have displeased Him. Then you ask Him simply to baptize you with the Holy Spirit," Eutychus said plainly.

Nicolaos just listened and didn't say anything in response. So Eutychus continued.

"Once you asked Jesus to baptize you with the Holy Spirit. You ask Him to help you hear His Voice with clarity in your mind. This can sometimes take some time. I know I didn't understand this right away. But you keep pursuing Him every morning asking every morning for His guidance and instructions." Eutychus paused, thinking maybe Nicolaos might have more questions, but he just stood there not saying anything.

"After you've established that relationship and communication with Him you listen for his instructions for that day. Remember that day I confessed to you about how I messed up and you were right? That was the Holy Spirit directing me to do that. To humble myself before you." Eutychus looked at Nicolaos in the eyes. "What's normal for me are daily lessons in humility, and gratefulness. And repenting for the things I got wrong. The Holy Spirit has no problem pointing those things out to anyone who asks with a pure heart. And we know He loves us, so we listen. He convicts me all the time of the things I need to correct in my life," Eutychus confessed. "I search the scriptures for the ways God wants us to live. The Holy Spirit guides me with understanding with what I'm reading. He teaches us all individually ... inwardly. I search the scriptures almost daily learning from Him."

"So I have to sit under another man's teachings? Become a crazy person? Where I have to wear a weird gown or be a part of a weird cult?" Nicolaos finally asked with a cutting edge in his voice.

"No." Eutychus was calm and speaking slow and gently.

"Have you seen Dawit and I dressing differently? Don't you know Dawit is also part of The Way? It's the Holy Spirit that guides you in ultimately understanding the scriptures, ... not men. It's His direct Voice to your heart in which your faith's foundation is set and grown." Eutychus was attempting to be as gentle and humble as possible in his tone. "Here's the thing with me, Nicolaos, that I can't deny. Heaven is real. Jesus is alive. And I've personally met Him there. I'm now terminally committed to Christ Jesus for whatever duration of days He has for me here. I willingly chose to be His messenger and servant to be sent back here to serve Him. And I will gladly go home to be with Him when He says my time here is done. This isn't about religion, Nicolaos, it's about reality and our soul's eternal existence and where it will reside, either with Him ... or not." Eutychus was trying to speak from his heart and plainly.

"So once a person becomes ... one of you ... part of The Way... as you called it, then they all get along great and are like blind sheep following along whatever way the leader tells them to go?" Nicolaos still had that cutting edge to his voice.

Eutychus couldn't keep the laugh from escaping his body. "All get along? Follow blindly, not exactly. We're still human, with very different personalities, and thoughts, and abilities. Actually, in Philippi there are these two women in The Way that are almost always debating one another. Euodia and Syntyche are always coming from two different perspectives. Sometimes the conversations get quite heated. But I love both of them. Their personal perspectives almost always drive me to the Holy Spirit with more questions," Eutychus replied. "And Eirene doesn't exactly follow me around now either or seek me out for … teaching or advice. I'm still her …sibling. Just as I'm sure you still see me as the 'little brother' who doesn't know much." Eutychus was being straightforward in his words.

"I try not to deceive myself and believe things that aren't so. The indwelling Presence of the Holy Spirit helps me with that. He shows me the way and points out the truth of things. He tries to keep me humble. If I'm brave enough I ask Him to tell me where I'm missing it with Him. Because if I ask – then He is real with me and tells me where I've fallen short of His desire for me. That isn't always easy to be shown your faults and weaknesses," Eutychus said quietly and honestly.

"We as followers of Jesus in The Way have to learn to ask for forgiveness and admit our faults to one another. That's not easy because of our natural pride, and we have to admit that to God and ask Him to work on His fruit in our lives. That's why I confessed to you at the beginning of this trip, as I said the Holy Spirit was pushing me to tell you," Eutychus confessed quietly.

"Yeah, I got that. You repeated yourself with that incident," Nicolaos said as he walked away.

Please, Holy Spirit, speak to him! Eutychus genuinely prayed for his brother.

"What was that all about?" Dawit asked as he walked up to Eutychus.

"He asked about how one gets to know the Holy Spirit."

"Oh boy. The Holy Spirit has been giving him a hard time." Dawit shook his head. "That's a rough time having to deal with one's … prideful ways," Dawit said under his breath.

"I certainly know that by painful experience," Eutychus agreed.

"I will definitely seek the Holy Spirit on how to pray for our beloved Captain."

"Thank you, brother." Eutychus then hugged Dawit. "Why are family often so hard to deal with?" Eutychus asked Dawit.

"Familiarity. We knew them before. We know them better than others do. We know the real changes in them when we see it. Believe me, Eutychus, your brother sees the changes in you. But we also see the same traits we've always seen in them, which sometimes clouds our opinions of them. We know before anyone else when they are just being themselves instead of being led by the Spirit of God. We have to remember that the Lord loves them just as much as He loves us. And we are to love them with His love not just our own." Dawit had his hand on Eutychus' shoulder.

"And that's why you are my trainer. The wisdom of the Holy Spirit is so evident in you, Dawit... and your brother Ermias," Eutychus said thankfully.

"Now let's see if you'll still like me after today's training." Dawit chuckled as he walked away smiling.

Oh boy, I think I'm in for another difficult lesson, Eutychus thought to himself.

"Hey, I may love you but that certainly doesn't mean I always ... like you," Eutychus called out loudly to Dawit while laughing.

Chapter 28
The Harbors
Passage to Roma.

"**O**stia harbor is in view," Nicolaos called out to his crew. "Make ready the ship."

It was about midday. The crew went quickly to bring down the sails and stow them and get in place to row into the harbor. Eutychus had never seen so many ships outside of a harbor. It was going to be tricky getting into the port as the shipping traffic was so heavy. Dawit had joined the crew at the oars.

Eutychus stood beside his brother looking at the harbor in wonder. *And I thought Troas was busy.* "What advice do you have for me, brother?"

"Oh, you are far from being done with me today," Nicolaos said. "We will unload this ship and load the ferry for the trip up the Tiber to the city. We won't be getting into the city until after dark. Which will be right, as no carriages or wagons are allowed on the streets during daylight. You'll obviously need a porter with a wagon for all the supplies and goods you've brought."

"Why no wagons during the day?" Eutychus asked.

"Too many people in the streets, makes it too dangerous, and now it's against the law," Nicolaos replied. "If you have the means, you are carried in a litter by your slaves, from place to place. Over half of the people you see are slaves, and that's a conservative estimate," Nicolaos said plainly.

Whoa. This is going to be different. Father, guide our steps. Show us the way. Eutychus began to pray in his mind.

Eutychus was surprised how skillful the crew was in navigating around all the other ships. And then to dock with such skill in such a tight place. Nicolaos was greeted by a man on the dock calling out to him.

"The honorable Shield of Iraklidis arriving again! Welcome, Captain Nicolaos."

"We'll need the skills of Abd al-Karim for the trip into the city. Is he still available?" Nicolaos called back.

"Yes, he is still here, I will call for him," the man called back. He then motioned to a young man who ran off.

As the crew were completing the tying down of the ship, a dark complected finely dressed looking man came walking down the dock.

"Captain Nicolaos, how may I serve you?" The man bowed low.

"We've got a big shipment into the city this trip. We'll need two stops this trip," Nicolaos replied.

The man then turned and signaled and several men came running.

Soon two crews were unloading the ship and loading the ferry boat. Nicolaos' crew would be staying in the port while Nicolaos, Eutychus, and Dawit went with the ferry upriver. Soon the crew of the ferry were using their long poles and rowers to move up the river.

Eutychus stared and looked at both sides of the banks of the river. He had never seen a place or a river so filled with docks, and people.

"Not exactly Troas, is it?" Nicolaos said to Eutychus with a smirk on his face.

Eutychus didn't respond right away. Hours later, he asked, "How was this ferry still available?"

"This ferry is one of the largest and most expensive in the harbor. Granted they are the best, so they charge accordingly." Nicolaos replied. "Not everyone can afford the services of Abd al-Karim," Nicolaos said plainly before continuing. "We will stop at the central dock for the Aventinus quarter where you will unload. I then will continue upriver to the northern dock for the Campus Martius quarter. Hopefully my regular porter for central dock will still be available for you. You of all people should know I've been bringing in regular loads of purple cloth to Roma."

"Thank you, brother, for all your help," Eutychus said genuinely.

Nicolaos just nodded.

"Obviously we will be shipping a lot more supplies in the near future," Eutychus said, "so an updated shipping schedule will be appreciated."

"Obviously," Nicolaos said and pulled out a clay tablet from his bag. "This is the proposed schedule for this summer for Roma." Nicolaos handed it to Eutychus who took it and put it into his own bag. "Just contact Abd al-Harim's man at central dock for any outgoing messages you will want to send to me. They will be held by the dock master in Ostia till my next arrival if I am not there."

The crew was now headed to the dock on the east side of the river as the sun had already gone down. As they were tying the ferry to the dock, Nicolaos waved to one of the porters. The dock was lighted by oil lamps. The man came running.

"Captain Nicolaos, an honor, how may I serve you this fine evening?" The man bowed low. He looked fair skinned, stocky, with a full beard.

"We need your wagon tonight, Odo. A large shipment again to the Aventinus quarter, two passengers. This is my younger brother Eutychus and his man Dawit. Treat him well. Help them and all their goods get safely to their destination," Nicolaos said with an authority.

The man then bowed, and then turned and waved his hand and several other men who ran up to help unload the ferry shipment into a large wagon.

Nicolaos then gave Odo a bag of coins, climbed back onto the ferry. He waved at Eutychus and said, "See you later, little brother, don't get into any trouble, I won't be here to save you."

Eutychus just waved back. He then turned to the porter and gave him the address of where he wanted to go.

Odo raised his eyebrows then quickly said, "A very fine home, not far from here. I've been there many times. Please climb aboard the wagon, we're ready to go."

Eutychus and Dawit climbed into the wagon and sat down. The streets were lit up with oil lamps. Both Eutychus and Dawit were surprised by all of the light.

Even the wagon had a lamp. In just a short while they were in front of a home on a street of fairly large homes. But unlike other cites these homes didn't have any front courtyards, but a large set of doors and windows that were closed for the night with wooden shutters with iron over them.

"This is your destination." Odo pointed to the home.

Eutychus jumped down and went to the front door and knocked. A boy soon came to the door and opened it and was surprised at the wagon and men standing at the door.

"We are from Philippi, and we are looking for Epaphroditus. My name is Eutychus and this is Dawit."

"I will go get Epaphroditus," the boy said and closed the door.

The door opened again and an older muscular man with short gray hair asked, "Eutychus are you my replacement? Has Lydia sent me a replacement ...finally?" The man was smiling and walked towards Eutychus.

"Epaphroditus?" Eutychus asked.

"Yes, welcome to the home of Priscilla," Epaphroditus said warmly. "Let's get your goods inside and get you settled." Epaphroditus went to help unload the wagon at the surprise of Odo.

"Master, I've got the shipment, no need to strain yourself," Odo said quickly. "I almost always unload your shipment myself."

"It will go faster with my help ...my friend," Epaphroditus said as he easily lifted one the boxes onto his shoulder. Eutychus and then Dawit also began to help unload the wagon.

"Masters, this is highly unusual, I can get this load very easily by myself," Odo said.

"Don't worry, friend, we don't mind helping this time." Epaphroditus then whispered to Odo, "It won't affect your gratuity." Epaphroditus then winked at Odo. Soon the shipment was in the home's Atrium stacked in a pile.

Epaphroditus and Eutychus both handed Odo a coin and Odo's eyes were big and he replied, "May the gods favor you. If you ever need my services at any time just send for me at the dock." Odo bowed low and Epaphroditus followed him out and locked the front door.

Eutychus and Dawit were admiring the size and spaciousness of the home when Epaphroditus came back and said, "I'll show you to your rooms, we've got plenty of space. I'll introduce you to the family in the morning. I'm sure you're ready to just lie down and rest. I'll bring some water, bread, and grapes to your rooms in a bit." Epaphroditus led them through the home up the stairs to the second floor and gave them separate rooms.

Each room had a bed and desk with a chair and also a long couch with cushions. It was bigger than they expected. The bed had lots of pillows and warm blankets. It had windows that looked out towards the inner courtyard and one on the far wall that looked out towards the city. It had both external and internal wooden shutters.

"This is so much more than I expected, thank you Epaphroditus," Eutychus said as he looked around the room.

"We'll get acquainted in the morning and share our stories. Till then rest well. I'll bring you some food in a bit." Epaphroditus turned and left the room.

Eutychus followed him out and went into the room given to Dawit. "What do you think?" Eutychus asked.

"The Lord has blessed us. I am very grateful for His lavishness towards me," Dawit replied. Dawit's room looked about the same as Eutychus' room.

Epaphroditus then walked in and set down a tray of food and a pitcher of water. "Your food and water are in your room." Epaphroditus was looking at Eutychus. "See you brothers in the morning. Rest well." Epaphroditus then walked out.

In the early morning, Eutychus was awakened by Dawit's voice in his room. "Get up. You've got training to do," Dawit said quietly.

Eutychus slowly got up and stumbled out of the door onto the balcony overlooking the inner courtyard. He saw Dawit down in the courtyard doing his warmup and stretching exercises.

"Be down in a bit." Eutychus waved to Dawit.

When Eutychus finally got to the courtyard Dawit told him quietly, "Today's lessons will include the discipline of silence and stealth. You are to make no sound as we go through the exercises. This is so you learn to control your movements and breath. And it will help to not wake up anyone else in the home this morning."

Dawit and Eutychus went through the exercises as quietly as possible. Even as Dawit took Eutychus to the floor, they both tried to do it silently. As Eutychus rolled away from Dawit he spied behind a pillar two small eyes watching him. Eutychus looked at Dawit and cocked his head towards the pillar. Dawit just nodded as he had also seen their small audience.

As Eutychus got up he looked at the pillar and asked very quietly, "And what beauty do I have the honor of addressing? My name is Eutychus."

A little girl boldly stepped around the pillar and said very matter-a-factly, "I'm Chrysiis, why are you here wrestling with that man in our courtyard?

"That man's name is Dawit and he is my friend and trainer. He is teaching me many things. We arrived last night, and we'll be staying here with you in your home for a while, if that's okay with you?" Eutychus replied quietly.

"Oh, you'll have to ask my daddy that question," Chrysiis said and then she ran to a man who was coming to the courtyard and wrapped his legs in a hug.

"Greetings, brothers," the man said. "Epaphroditus told me you arrived last night. Hesiod is my name. I see you've already met my youngest daughter."

Both Eutychus and Dawit got up and walked over to greet Hesiod.

"My wife, Polymnia, is already preparing the morning meal. Come let's break bread together." Hesiod motioned for them to follow him. Chrysiis kept a hand on her father's clothes.

They followed him to a large room just off the courtyard that had a very large table and cushions. A doorway opened to another room which had a kitchen. Just then another little girl a few years older than Chrysiis came into the dining room from the kitchen with a bowl of food and put it on the table.

"This is my daughter, Phaedra," Hesiod said. Just then a boy came into the dining room with a large platter of food and set it on the table. "And this is my son Eliud."

"Yes, we met him last night. He came to the door," Eutychus remarked.

"And this is my wife, Polymnia," Hesiod said as a beautiful woman came into the dining room with several pitchers.

Both Dawit and Eutychus quickly stood up.

"Thank you so much for your hospitality and preparations here for us," Eutychus said politely.

"It is our honor to serve you," Polymnia said quietly and turned to go back into the kitchen.

All three came back into the dining room with more food and then sat down around the table.

"I'm Eutychus and this is Dawit. We just came from Philippi, from Lydia's home. We are so blessed to be here with you," Eutychus said just as Epaphroditus came into the dining room.

"Oh good, now I don't have to make introductions. This looks fantastic Polymnia, thank you." And Epaphroditus sat down at the table.

After breakfast the children and Polymnia cleared the table.

"I guess I'll begin by giving you a little background as I'm not sure what all Lydia has told you about me and this house." Epaphroditus was looking at Dawit and Eutychus. Polymnia then came back and sat down next to Hesiod. The children had gone off somewhere else. "This is the city home of Priscilla. Her family had this home as well as a large villa outside of the city near the coast. She sold the villa but kept this home when Claudius expelled the Jews and that included the followers of Jesus as he saw them as the same group ten years ago. She and Aquila then went to Corinth and then with Paul onto Ephesus."

"Yes, I've met Priscilla in Ephesus in their home with Dawit's brother, Ermias," Eutychus interjected.

"Good. Good. Then you know firsthand what kind of people they are. They allow this home to be used by the followers of Jesus, and the biggest meeting of The Way in Roma happens in this home weekly. Hesiod and Polymnia act as the hosts and elders for that meeting. He's quite the musician as well."

"How did you come to this home, Epaphroditus?" Eutychus asked.

"I was getting to that. I'm a retired Roman Praetorian Tribune who had retired to Philippi to live out the rest of my life in ease. Then along came this woman Lydia." Epaphroditus paused. "Well, one thing led to another. Then this man Paul came to visit Lydia. I was invited to come to Lydia's home to hear this man Paul and his message. Well, seeing Paul and hearing Paul is one thing, but watching the miracles happen was astounding to my nature. I knew I was seeing the power of God. I began to attend the weekly meetings at Lydia's home. The Presence of God was so thick in that place. I knew that Jesus was real and wanted this old man to follow Him. So, I gave my life to Him as my Lord and Master. Paul and I had many long talks. He became a good friend to me."

"That's incredible, Epaphroditus. I'm so glad to be here with all of you," Eutychus said.

"When Lydia asked for someone to be her broker of her cloth in Roma, I knew I was to be the one. I had the contacts and knowledge to really get the business going in the right directions. So, I volunteered, but I told her that once I had the business established, I wanted her to find me a replacement because I wanted to come back to Philippi and my villa there. Before I left for Roma. I helped Lydia set up security measures for her business and meetings. Then when she traveled with me to Roma to get the business going, she had the opportunity to acquire both Dawit and Ermias, which you know. Of course, they were freed immediately and voluntarily joined her purpose in the Lord and went back to Philippi with her. Looks like they both became part of The Way as well." Epaphroditus looked at Dawit.

"We both accepted Jesus as our Master on the trip back to Philippi. Our lives are forever changed because of her sacrifice and the sacrifice Jesus made for us," Dawit said quietly with emotion.

"And now I've have had the honor of training under both of them," Eutychus said.

Epaphroditus' eyes got wider. "I thought in your tradition you don't train others in your fighting ways." Epaphroditus looked at Dawit.

"The Holy Spirit is our Master now and instructs us in what we are to do. His instructions go beyond tradition," Dawit said plainly.

"I agree with that. I also have personal experience in that," Epaphroditus said nodding.

"Well, that's enough of talk for now. It's time we open the shop doors, Hesiod." Epaphroditus got up with Hesiod and the others followed them to the front of the home. Epaphroditus and Hesiod began to open the windows to the street. Two rooms faced the street that acted as a shop where they sold Lydia's purple cloth. One room was used for the merchants and the other was for the public. Epaphroditus looked over the merchant room and Hesiod and Polymnia opened the other room for the public.

"This room stays closed until a merchant comes to pick up their order. I usually sit in the public room most of the day. After Hesiod opens he goes to work. Sometimes Polymnia relieves me if I have an appointment elsewhere, and if not I just close the shop for that time," Epaphroditus said to Eutychus.

"There isn't much here," replied Eutychus as he scanned the public room. "I'll soon take care of that."

Chapter 29
The Way in Roma
New family.

"Dawit, I think we're to change our routine this morning," Eutychus said quietly.

"I agree. The Holy Spirit is filling my mind with instructions," Dawit responded.

Dawit and Eutychus sat facing one another with crossed legs on the floor in the inner courtyard of the home where they usually did their early morning self-defense training.

"Let's spend this time in prayer together and share what we are receiving from Him," Eutychus suggested.

"Father, we seek You above all else. You are our highest goal. To know You. To serve You. Please guide us in the way we should go." Dawit had launched straight into prayer.

"I agree, Father. Come Holy Spirit and give us Your plans for us," Eutychus prayed.

"Here is what my heart is being moved by... to help more people to become like me. Not in the sense of what makes me unique, but in the sense of ... being free and independent to follow Him. Ever since we arrived back in Roma I've had these feelings." Dawit was trying hard to put words to his feelings.

"Oh, Dawit, that is totally in line of what is on my heart too. Except I am getting the sense that half of the proceeds of this new business for now should be to buy the freedom of slaves. And then ask them if they would like to go to Philippi or Troas to begin a new life," Eutychus said.

Thank you, Jesus! Praise You Father! Come Holy Spirit and empower us! Dawit was rejoicing inside.

"We are in agreement with Him! And I keep seeing myself giving self-defense training to groups of people in this place." Dawit pondered the images he was seeing in his mind.

"Yes! That is so needed. Maybe three different groups? Younger children, women, and young men?" Eutychus suggested.

"That makes sense," Dawit agreed.

"And I know I'm to begin reading and writing classes again. Probably the same groups that I mentioned you should train," Eutychus pondered aloud.

"And you are to begin the Holy Spirit training groups with your study of His fruit found in Paul's letter to the Galatians and I'm supposed to help with that," Dawit suggested.

"And I need to begin prison visits. Giving words of encouragement to those who seem to have no hope. Bring the words of Jesus to them," Eutychus said with emotion. "It's my task from Jesus."

"Absolutely. I'm here to help you with that in any way I can," Dawit responded.

"Now I'm seeing two areas where we are to sell the new products. One in the general marketplace of the forum using Aquila's tent and selling to the common people. And the high-end products in the public shop here at the home." Eutychus was trying to describe the pictures in his mind.

"That means we'll need more helpers Eutychus," Dawit said quickly and again went immediately into prayer. "Father, guide us to those who are to work beside us, who You've called and equipped for this work You want us to complete for Your glory and Name."

"I agree, Father – guide us to the people You want in this work and the people You want freed by this work!" Eutychus prayed.

"Yes, yes, yes, thank You Holy Spirit for giving us Your plans! Now empower us to carry them out as You want us to!" Dawit prayed with excitement.

"Wow," Eutychus said. "Do we have our work set out in front of us! I'm excited Dawit, this will be challenging and filled with adventure, but also a lot of work."

"But now we have the plan. Let's share it with Epaphroditus and Hesiod," Dawit suggested. "I'm pretty sure they'll play a big part in all of this."

"Agreed. Let's go find them." Eutychus got up and Dawit followed in search of the other two.

Epaphroditus and Hesiod came walking from the front of the home and met Eutychus and Dawit walking towards them.

"I suggest we get at the huge pile in the atrium you brought with you," Epaphroditus said to Eutychus as they walked up.

"Why don't you three begin on that and I'll go get some food from the kitchen that we can eat while we work," Hesiod suggested.

"Sounds great, brothers," Eutychus said. "Dawit and I have much to share with both of you. We can talk as we open everything and organize the inventory."

Hesiod came back with a tray of food, as the other three were opening all the boxes and bags and were sorting it all out.

"Why don't you begin by telling us how you became part of The Way and your encounters since then while we work," Epaphroditus said to Eutychus.

Eutychus launched into his family history, his family's visit to Ephesus and his mom and his encounter with Paul, and their acceptance of Jesus. He talked about helping his father with the warehouse, and then the night he fell out of the third story window at one of the meetings when Paul was teaching the Troas city group of The Way. At that point of Eutychus' story Epaphroditus interrupted.

"Wait. What? You fell out of a third story window and ..." Epaphroditus was speaking slower. Everyone stopped working and turned towards Eutychus. Dawit was smiling, he always loved this part of Eutychus' story.

"Yes. And I was immediately in another place..." Eutychus continued.

Dawit watched the faces of Epaphroditus and Hesiod as Eutychus talked about his encounter of meeting Jesus. Epaphroditus' face was intense, and totally focused on every word Eutychus was saying. Hesiod was wide eyed and was leaning forward.

"... then when I opened my eyes I was in Paul's arms," Eutychus ended.

"That's a story like I've never heard before," Epaphroditus said. "And I believe you too." Epaphroditus scratched his beard. "All my life I've been trained to know when someone is telling the truth or not. I have not sensed any deception in you."

"The Spirit always confirms this encounter in my heart and spirit when he tells it," Dawit confirmed.

"I don't know how – but I feel the same. There was no deception in him while he told his story," Hesiod agreed.

Dawit and Eutychus went on to tell Epaphroditus and Hesiod about all the plans they had received that morning from the Holy Spirit.

Epaphroditus had stopped working and had sat down.

"Are you okay?" Eutychus had come over to check on Epaphroditus.

When Epaphroditus looked up at Eutychus, Eutychus could see the tears in his eyes. "The Lord is so Present with me right now," said Epaphroditus. "He's moving on my heart. The plans He has given you here ... I want to be a part of and help, but I also sense He has something else for me in the near future as well. So many things are stirring in my heart I can't make sense of it all just now."

Eutychus put his hand on Epaphroditus' shoulder and began to pray out loud. "Father, thank You for this faithful servant who has been such a blessing to us here. Guide him. Speak to him. Show him Your plans for him. Thank You Father for men like Epaphroditus who are like earthly fathers to us in Your Body. We need more like him." Eutychus had actually began to tear up as he prayed, feeling the Holy Spirit's love for Epaphroditus. When Eutychus had finished he opened his eyes to see that Dawit and Hesiod had also come over and had put their hands on Epaphroditus as well.

"I agree, Father, give us more men like Epaphroditus," Dawit prayed.

"I love him, Father, he's been such a blessing and example to me and my family, strengthen him, Father," Hesiod prayed as he also could feel the tears welling up in his eyes.

Epaphroditus stood up and took some deep breaths and let them out slowly. His face showed determination and focus.

"We are in His favor! Let's be about Him today in everything we do!" Epaphroditus said plainly.

"Let's get the shops open Hesiod. Maybe you could pick out some items for the shop today Eutychus from this new stock?" Epaphroditus asked.

Eutychus nodded. The four began moving and working with new energy, determination, and speed.

"Here it is," Eutychus said as he picked up a small package from inside one of the boxes. "This is for you from Lydia." Eutychus held it out to Epaphroditus.

"I'll open it later in my room at the end of the day. Thank you, Eutychus, for bringing it." Epaphroditus nodded at Eutychus.

As Hesiod and Eutychus worked on a display of new products in the shop for the public at the front of the house, Eutychus asked him for help.

"Hesiod, do you think you could introduce me to some of the other groups of The Way here in Roma and on the outskirts of the city, so that if any of their number end up in prison that they would notify us so I could go visit them?" Eutychus asked. "Also pray about who in your group here might be the Lord's choice to help us in the sale of these new products and possibly help with their sale in the main marketplace utilizing the tent we brought with us as a booth for the sales. We'll need both men and women. I think the Lord is about to expand our business here in Roma."

"Ever since you mentioned your plans this morning my mind has been running and thinking of possible helpers from within our group. I'm going to pray and ask the Lord about it," Hesiod said.

"That's the Holy Spirit again. Coordinating us in His work. He still surprises me ... every day." Eutychus was shaking his head.

"I feel His energy today, it's different than I'm use to. It's like there's a power vibrating in my bones. It's hard to describe." Hesiod was talking in spurts.

"He works in us in ways that are still a mystery to me. But I know it's Him when I feel my love for Jesus deepening. At least that's the way I can kind of explain it," Eutychus confirmed.

"Yes," Hesiod said. "Ever since I heard about your encounter with Him, my heart yearns to meet Him too. I so want to be with Him."

"But for now, we have our assignments to do here. Let's be faithful giving our all in these things He has set before us to do." Eutychus nodded.

Eutychus walked over to the other shop for the merchants to talk to Epaphroditus. Dawit was there helping stack and hang large sections of cloth in the shop. They had brought with them new hues of purple cloth that had yet to be introduced to the public.

"Epaphroditus, do you think you could help me with getting into the prison to talk to people for the assignment Jesus has given me?" Eutychus asked. "I'll need the favor from the Roman officer in charge of the prison if I'm to be making regular visits."

"I'm not sure who is assigned there now, but we could take a walk this afternoon and find out. If Dawit will watch the shop while we're gone," Epaphroditus suggested.

"I'm here to help, Epaphroditus, whatever you need," Dawit said, nodding.

"That would be great! I'll be ready to go whenever you are," Eutychus replied.

"I don't know what the Lord has in store for me ... but I think I'm supposed to sit down with you Eutychus and go over the entire business with you here in Roma. The complete merchant list, and my evaluation of each merchant, and the level of trust I have or don't have with each person. I'm thinking you are my replacement. And maybe I should make plans to return to Philippi?" Epaphroditus was pondering all sorts of things.

"I certainly would love to have you stick around longer. There is so much I could learn from you. Lots more about life than just the business end of things. I see His wisdom in you Epaphroditus, but I also don't want to be selfish and get in the way of His path or plans for you." Eutychus was being honest.

"Maybe until next spring, when the weather will be better for a sea voyage? That would give me some time to plan." Epaphroditus was pondering out loud.

"I know all of us would love that, Epaphroditus," Eutychus almost said pleadingly. "There is so much you can help us here with. Especially now with all of these new projects and assignments He has given us here in Roma."

"What's gotten into you today?" Polymnia asked Hesiod after he came into the kitchen humming and being very affectionate towards her.

"I love you," Hesiod said to her, as he grabbed her and kissed her.

"Okay. What's up?" Polymnia asked after the passionate kiss.

"I haven't felt the Lord's Presence like this ever before in my life! It's so exhilarating and exciting!" Hesiod explained.

"And....?" Polymnia waited for more.

"There are lots and lots of good things coming, my dearest Polymnia." Hesiod was smiling.

"You're still not making any sense. But I like that you're feeling good." Polymnia was still somewhat skeptical and smiling.

Just then Chrysiis walked into the kitchen. Hesiod picked her up and stepped out of the kitchen into the courtyard and began to swing her around. Chrysiis began to laugh uncontrollably. Phaedra walked up to the spinning duo and said, "Me next, Daddy, me next!"

Late in the afternoon Epaphroditus and Eutychus walked to the bottom of Capitoline Hill where the Carcer was located just above the forum. The prison building was not for the faint of heart. Epaphroditus inquired of the guard at the entrance. The guard took one look at the ring Epaphroditus wore on his hand and quickly escorted him inside. Eutychus sat down and waited outside for Epaphroditus.

Finally, Epaphroditus emerged from the building. Eutychus got up and followed him as he began to walk back home.

"So...?" Eutychus asked quietly.

Epaphroditus stopped and pulled Eutychus to where they couldn't be seen by anyone. Epaphroditus then put something into Eutychus' hand. "This coin will get you in any time you visit. Just show the guards the coin and they'll let you in and give you access to the two holding rooms, the one above and the one beneath. Do not let this coin out of your hand. Show it only to the Roman guards but don't let any one of them take it from you," Epaphroditus said quietly.

"Is this a secret? Is it dangerous?" Eutychus was sensing that this was not a normal situation.

"The officer in charge owes me his life. This should never be allowed, but I made him give me this favor. He reluctantly agreed. He could lose his post if any one higher up ever found out. So, show it sparingly to the guards and no one else. I'm hoping once they get use to you, you won't have to show it at all." Epaphroditus was being very serious in his tone. "I'm no fan of the current 'boy' who is currently in power of this nation. Many in the Praetorian Guard also have my same sentiments. But saying so out loud would mean death." Epaphroditus was speaking at a whisper level.

"Let's get home, Epaphroditus, and not talk any more of this here." Eutychus then turned and followed Epaphroditus feeling the coin in his hand wondering what the Lord had in store for the future and the prison.

Chapter 30

The Warning Dream

Fire.

Eutychus was awakened to the sound of screams. He got up and looked out the window. It was still night, but the entire horizon was glowing orange. Then he heard people yelling, "Fire!" Eutychus ran out of his room and began to wake up the others in the home. "We've got to get out of here... NOW!" Soon they were rushing out of the home in the direction of the river. The streets were filled with running people full of panic and fear.

Eutychus found himself thrashing about in bed. He awoke with a start and found himself sweating. That was a dream. *Lord, what was that all about?* Eutychus was still breathing heavy and trying to calm down.

Dawit stood in his doorway. "What was that all about Eutychus? I heard you yelling."

"It was a dream," Eutychus replied. "A very vivid dream. I'm still trying to process it."

"Do you want to talk about it?" Dawit inquired.

"In my dream, I awakened to screams. I went to the window and could see the city on fire. I went to everyone in the home and got them up and out of the home, and then we were all running towards the river. The street was filled with lots of panic and fearful people. I need to have the Lord give me the reason I had this dream," Eutychus explained.

"Yes, the Lord will need to tell you why you had this dream. Do you have a sense of when or if it will happen?" Dawit asked.

"Not exactly. I'm still trying to remember and concentrate on what I saw, it was all so fast." Eutychus was finally calming down.

"Holy Spirit, speak to my brother, Eutychus, and give him the answers and instructions he needs from this dream. Let me know if I can do anything to help."

"You're already doing it. Thank you, brother," Eutychus responded.

"This morning will be our first meeting here in the home with The Way. It should be interesting to learn what He has for us here. Obviously you'll be in prayer now and I think I now need to go spend some time alone with Him in prayer. See you at breakfast." Dawit then turned and left.

Everyone was at the table and enjoying the morning food Polymnia had prepared except for Eutychus who had not yet joined them.

"Where's Eutychus?" Epaphroditus asked.

"He had a pretty disturbing dream early this morning," Dawit explained, "and I'm pretty sure he's spending time in prayer inquiring of the Lord about its meaning. I think we need to give him some time."

"There is a lot to do this morning. Will you help us get ready for the meeting today?" Hesiod asked Dawit.

"Absolutely. It would be my honor," Dawit replied. "Just tell me what you need."

It was the biggest gathering of people of The Way that Dawit and Eutychus had ever experienced. Eutychus still was somewhat subdued throughout the meeting, as he was still pondering the dream. He was jolted back to the present when he noticed Dawit getting up and was motioning for him to stand up as well. Dawit then began walking to the front and Eutychus followed him. Epaphroditus introduced them as members of The Way from Philippi and Troas.

"Greetings in the Name of Jesus Christ," Dawit began. "We are honored and blessed to be among you this morning. The Holy Spirit has given us instructions on serving here. I would like to offer my skills and knowledge by beginning self-defense training classes here. Eutychus will also be starting classes on reading and writing. Together we will also begin small group trainings on the Fruit of the Holy Spirit and being able to hear His Voice with greater clarity in your life. So, if any of you feel the Lord's prompting on any of those things, please come greet us afterwards. Thank you." Dawit and Eutychus then went back to where they were sitting and sat down.

"I'm sorry I didn't help you," Eutychus whispered to Dawit.

"I'm fine. What needed to be said was said," Dawit whispered in reply and smiled.

After the meeting there was a large crowd gathered around Dawit and Eutychus wanting and waiting to talk to them. Eutychus was writing down names of people for the different classes and groups people wanted to be a part of. They told everyone to come tomorrow late afternoon for general instructions and find out when all the classes would begin and what days and evenings.

"Well, it looks like classes will start tomorrow," Dawit said. "I'm going to meet with everyone who wants self-defense training tomorrow and then set up the different groups and times. I think we need to do the same with the other classes as well. Looks like all the classes will be full."

"A very big response," Eutychus responded. "Obviously the Lord is moving on people's hearts. We will definitely need His help."

After the formal meeting of the gathering in the morning, people stayed though midday and into the early afternoon, with fellowship, food, and conversation, people were leaving when they needed to but there was no rush or requirement to leave. Many were continuing to stay and come up to Eutychus and Dawit to greet them and welcome them to their group.

A grey-haired, older, short, plump woman came up to Eutychus and asked if she could speak to him somewhat privately. Eutychus was intrigued and felt no check from the Holy Spirit, so he walked with her to a less crowded area.

"How can I help you?" Eutychus asked the older woman.

"My name is Devorah and I'm a widow. While I was in prayer yesterday the Holy Spirit told me to come this morning to meet someone new. He then pointed you out to me. This might sound strange but He was telling me I'm to help you in your business. I'm not a businessperson, so I don't have any idea exactly what He is meaning. Does this mean anything to you? When your friend mentioned your classes, I thought 'oh the Lord wants me to help you with your classes', and He immediately responded to me, 'No! I want you to help him with his business.' I hope you understand I'm just being obedient here to what the Lord is instructing me with." Devorah half smiled.

Eutychus smiled back at Devorah. He paused and looked down and then up and into Devorah's eyes. "The Lord continues to surprise me. He moves in ways that still are a mystery to me. Yes, I need to find people to help in this business He has had us begin here. If you're willing and available, could you come in the morning tomorrow and we'll pray together and see what His plans are for us together?" Eutychus quietly and calmly said.

"Yes, I can come tomorrow morning. You never said what kind of business. Can you share with me a little what the business is?" Devorah asked.

"I'm sorry, yes. We are bringing new leather products that come from Ephesus which are then shipped to Philippi and redesigned and remade specifically for women," Eutychus explained. "Sandals, bags, belts, and different purple cloth items. Lydia, my friend Ruth, and my sister are doing the redesigning. They are working to build a manufacturing facility in Philippi if the products are what the women like. So far we've gotten great demand and sales in Philippi. I think they'll be very popular here as well."

"Well, this should be interesting," Devorah said. "I don't have any experience in sales, the Lord mainly uses me these days to pray for people. To pray His heart and will over them while I'm alone with Him. As a widow, I live a very simple life."

Eutychus could feel the Holy Spirit rising within him and flooding him with His love for Devorah. *She is one of my special prayer warriors. You will need her skills and gifts. She is who I want you to support. Pay her as I instruct you.*

"Oh, how the Lord loves you, Devorah. Come tomorrow and you'll begin working in our shop. With that position will come a good salary. I've already been instructed to take care of you." Eutychus had tears forming in his eyes as he spoke these words.

Devorah then gently put her hand on Eutychus' head and began to pray, "Father, bless this young man with your power and anointing. Guide our steps together."

"Why am I seeing you in jail? You're going to be visiting people in jail?" Devorah asked Eutychus with a surprised look on her face.

"There is much we will talk about tomorrow. You're not wrong," Eutychus replied and the gave Devorah a hug. *Thank you, Lord Jesus, for bringing her to me.*

Devorah and Eutychus rejoined the crowd talking in the courtyard. Eutychus was then approached by Eliud.

"Am I too young to help with your business? Could you use my help?" Eliud asked.

"You are not too young. I started helping my father in our family business when I was younger than you are now. I can use you, but you'll need to get your parents approval first. And a requirement will be that you enroll in the first round of reading and writing classes as well. Do you agree to those terms?" Eutychus was speaking to Eliud like a peer and an adult.

"Yes, I agree!" Eliud said, smiled big and then quickly ran off to find his dad.

By late afternoon the people had gone and the family was cleaning and straightening up after the meeting.

While they were working and cleaning, Eutychus asked Epaphroditus, "What did Lydia send to you? If it's not private."

"She sent me my favorite concentrated oil," Epaphroditus replied. "Its fragrance helps to clear my mind and calms me. She also sent me a note about you." Epaphroditus smiled. "You've made quite an impression on her. It's clear to me now that you are to be my replacement. She didn't say that exactly, she just told me that I am to help you."

"The Lord seems to be sending elders to help me. Since I never knew any of my grandparents, it seems he is providing some now," Eutychus said under his breath.

"I may be old but my hearing is still good," Epaphroditus said. "Life experience is more valuable in my mind now than ever before. I often scoffed at the older generation. Now I somewhat understand the value age and experience and scars bring."

"While Dawit and I were in prayer together the other morning. we got the instructions we were to use some of the proceeds from the sales to buy certain individual's freedom from slavery. And then asking them if they would like to relocate to Philippi and Troas. I'm sure the Lord will confirm who it is we are to approach. What do you think about that?" Eutychus asked.

"I already have a person in my mind. I've been waiting on specific instructions from the Lord on how I should approach the situation," Epaphroditus said with caution. "Actually, I'm sure it is from the Lord, but we will need to be very patient and get very detailed instructions from Him on each person and His timing. These are delicate matters and could stir lots of unwanted attention from the authorities. The slave trade is by far the biggest money enterprise in Roma."

"Then we need to pray together and find out how we are to begin with the person He has already pointed out to you," Eutychus responded. "I'm willing to proceed with using any funds needed as we get the go ahead from the Lord."

"I will look into it as much as I can with this certain individual, and then I will report back and we can pray for further instructions," Epaphroditus agreed.

"My son tells me he is going to work for you." Hesiod came walking up to Eutychus.

"Only with your approval and if he joins the first round of reading and writing classes," Eutychus responded.

"He didn't say any of those requirements." Hesiod laughed.

"Actually, I didn't want to overstep my bounds here in this home, but I was wondering if you yourself would like to be involved. I'm not sure what kind of work you are currently in, but it has crossed my thoughts that you would be good at the business." Eutychus looked at Hesiod.

"I'm not sure I'd be good at selling items to women," Hesiod confessed.

"My thoughts have always been on the merchant side of the business for you. You know Epaphroditus has been looking to return to Philippi and now he's thinking I'm his replacement, and I'm thinking I'll need a lot of help as the Lord is continuing to load my day's plate with more than one person can do. Would you be willing to sit down with Epaphroditus and myself and go over all of the merchant's side of the business?" Eutychus asked.

"Well, I would need to talk to my current employer and give him some notice that I'll be leaving his business," Hesiod replied. "I definitely will ask the Lord and Polymnia as to what I should be doing."

"Actually... I also thought of Polymnia helping as well," Eutychus said half smiling.

"We will need someone to be in the forum marketplace to sell items to the regular common crowd. We've got designs for the common person and priced low enough for almost everyone," Eutychus explained.

"Wow. Well... then I really do need to have a conversation with her. Those are some big changes in our lives. Then we'll have to figure out what to do with our girls during the day," Hesiod said scratching his head. "I would want some kind of protection for Polymnia," Hesiod said thinking about it.

"I was thinking of Dawit at least at the beginning, until the Lord provides a replacement for him. I totally agree Polymnia should not be alone in the marketplace," Eutychus quickly responded. "As to your girls, I'm sure that can be arranged as well. You should know what the Lord thinks of children. He'll provide for their needs and send us just the right people to help. Phaedra actually is getting to that age to be a help to her mother. I suggest she begins reading and writing classes as well."

"That young?" Hesiod asked with surprise on his face.

"Yes. You'd be surprised how quick she will pick it up," Eutychus nodded.

"Sounds like our group here in the home is going to expand soon," Hesiod remarked.

"In the Lord's timing. But I do think it will be very soon," Eutychus responded.

That night around the dinner table Eutychus mentioned his dream to the family there. After telling portions of the dream so as the children wouldn't be too frightened, he made some suggestions to the group.

"I think all of us should take this dream to the Lord in prayer. And ask Him what we should have if at any moment He called us to leave and go. I will provide bags than you can use to have to be ready to be packed or already packed if the Lord calls us to leave in a moment's notice," Eutychus explained.

"Do you think that the fire will be soon?" Polymnia asked.

"Honestly, I don't know. First I get the dream, and then I have all these instructions about the expanding business and classes, which also will take some time. But I think He wants us prepared more than we are now. At least to begin to consider our days with Him. And be ready at a moment's notice to move if He says to go," Eutychus said while shrugging his shoulders.

"I guess it wouldn't hurt to prepare some bags that each of us will carry and be ready to go," Hesiod said with others nodding in agreement.

"It could be farther in the future that some of us will already be called to someplace else by Him, even before the fire. But I think there is a lesson in this about staying very close to the Lord daily and asking for His instructions," Eutychus said.

After the dinner and all the dishes had been cleaned and put away, Epaphroditus called Eutychus over to his room.

"I asked you here to talk about the... small groups you do on hearing the Lord's Voice with greater clarity," Epaphroditus said slowly.

Eutychus waited to reply, not knowing what Epaphroditus wanted to say or know.

"Would you be willing to have an older man join your first group?" Epaphroditus asked.

Eutychus was kind of surprised but also honored. "Anyone. And I mean anyone... is invited. To be very clear and open with you, I myself learn from the Holy Spirit and everyone involved every time I coach a group and go through this study and exercise," Eutychus said. "I say coach because the Holy Spirit really is the Teacher. I just guide the group to seek Him. I am always learning there are deeper levels of intimacy with Him. I would be honored to have you in the first group. I think you will have a lot of wisdom to share with the group. I'm excited to learn from you."

Chapter 31
The Coin
Tribune authority.

"This column is the cost of goods. This column is the cost of transport. This column is the cost of employee wages. This column is Roman taxes. And finally, this column is profit." Eutychus was going over the books with Eliud who had shown an amazing ability with numbers while working with Devorah in the shop. Devorah mentioned Eliud's ability to Eutychus who was now showing him how the financial and inventory tracking of the businesses worked. Eliud caught on very quickly and already had suggestions on how to improve the tracking of costs and inventory.

"I may not be the best at languages but numbers make sense to me," Eliud said.

"That has become very clear to everyone around you," Eutychus replied.

"Do you think you would like to be our account bookkeeper?" Eutychus asked Eliud. "That will mean working after everyone is done for the day and collecting monies and inventory numbers every evening and then recording it all."

"That sounds fun!" Eliud said quickly.

"Okay. You will be with me for the first week watching everything I do at the end of the day with these three accounts: the marketplace account, the Merchant wholesale account, and the shop account. Then next week I will shadow you as you do all of the work. Then finally on week three you will do it yourself without my help and I will check your work at the end of the week. Do you understand?" Eutychus asked Eliud.

"That sounds like a long time," Eliud responded with a disappointed look.

"Believe me, you will encounter things where you won't know how to process them. It always happens, and you just have to figure it out," Eutychus explained. "And it helps to have someone with more experience to ask questions concerning about the situation you are in."

"Okay fine," Eliud responded with a sigh.

Devorah had shown an amazing ability in the shop in making the women feel at home. She confessed to Eutychus that she was praying for every woman that came into the shop and asking the Holy Spirit what He loved about them. Then she asked the Holy Spirit what to say and what to show the woman. Only a couple of women were almost explosive in attitude as they walked into the shop, as everything irritated them. Devorah was very aware of the presence that they were carrying with them. Devorah had remarked how much joy she was having in the shop as God was so present throughout the entire day with her. And the sales showed it. The leather products were a hit with the women of Roma. And Devorah actually had asked for Chrysiis to join her in the shop in the mornings and was teaching her about display and talked to her about the Lord.

A young teenage girl from another family in The Way had offered to watch Chrysiis and Phaedra during the day, as Polymnia had accepted Eutychus' business proposal and began working the marketplace tent selling the leather items designed for the everyday woman in Roma. Dawit and Polymnia had been quick to learn how to transport the items and quickly set up the stall. The sales of items had been very popular and sold quickly and easily.

Hesiod was working beside Epaphroditus with the merchant cloth accounts. They had shown several of the merchants the new colors of cloth and they had sold out quickly. Hesiod then continued to work on the purple cloth accounts. Sales had actually risen with the 'word' getting out of new cloth availability. And merchants had been placing orders for future shipments. Hesoid and Epaphroditus began requiring a deposit on future orders as the demand had risen dramatically.

Eutychus had sent a quick message to go to Nicolaos and back to Philippi and Lydia and company.

"Huge success. Send all you can as soon as you can. Expand! Expand! Expand! On your approval, monies will be set aside for buying more slaves like Dawit and Ermias." Eutychus knew Lydia would understand the inference of buying slaves for the purpose of freeing them.

Dawit's classes of self-defense had begun. But because of his duties with Polymnia, the classes were either before daybreak or after sunset. That had reduced the number of people who wanted to attend. So, they were all praying for the person who was to help Polymnia at the marketplace. The solution was solved in just two months as they had sold out of items for the marketplace, as the next shipment had not yet arrived. Both Polymnia and Dawit then focused on the classes that were going to go on during the day now in the home. Polymnia and Phaedra had actually been attending the reading and writing classes Eutychus had been giving in the evenings.

After the reading and writing classes in the evening, the class on hearing with better clarity the Voice of the Holy Spirit began. Eutychus had been given instructions from the Holy Spirit as to whom should be a part of the first group. It was only a group of ten people. Everyone else had been told that they would be a part of the second round of classes. Eutychus could tell the first members each had a specific role in being part of the group. He marveled at how the Holy Spirit arranged the group and their talents and giftings. He knew almost all of the first group would become coaches for the next groups. Epaphroditus had shown an amazing insight to the things the Holy Spirit was bringing up with him. The entire group always wanted to hear what the Holy Spirit was teaching Epaphroditus.

Eutychus' days had become very long and busy. He was continually asking the Lord as to whom was to replace him in the many duties he was trying to accomplish every day. The group that lived in the home began having weekly meetings to discuss the various financial and other activities that were currently happening within the group. With the sales being so successful, the financial accounts were well supplied, but everyone agreed to live on a modest means until the shipments could be well established and regular. Hesiod and Polymnia were very happy to be part of the business. And everyone was astounded at Eliud and his ability with numbers.

Priscilla's home in Roma had become very busy with activities.

"Eutychus, I need to talk to you." Hesiod had walked up to Eutychus' room late one evening.

"What can I help you with Hesiod?" Eutychus asked.

"Remember when you asked me to share with you about possible people that might have relatives currently in jail?"

"Yes."

"I was approached at our last Way meeting by a woman who mentioned she had an older brother who did not know the Lord Jesus. He was convicted as a thief and is now sitting in jail this week. His sentence is supposed to be carried out in two days from today. She mentioned it to me so that I could ask people to pray for him. She didn't know about your request," Hesiod explained.

"Did she give you his name?"

"Demetrios."

"Thank you. I will ask the Lord about him," Eutychus replied.

Eutychus knew immediately that he was supposed to visit Demetrios the next day. *Lord, guide my steps. Give me the words to say to Demetrios.*

The next day after getting through all the questions and needs that were presented to him, Eutychus finally had a break and knew the Holy Spirit was pushing him out the door to get to the jail. Eutychus left the home and began the short walk to the Carcer. The entire way, Eutychus was in prayer asking the Holy Spirit for His help and wisdom. As he began to approach the prison, he got the coin out of his bag and clutched it tightly in his fist. "Lord, guide my steps. Be with me. Cover me. Open the way before." Eutychus was praying quietly under his breath.

He held the coin between his thumb and fore finger showing both sides to the guard standing outside at the prison. The guard's reaction was one of complete surprise. The guard then reached out to take the coin but Eutychus quickly stepped back. "I was told by the tribune to never let this coin leave my person," Eutychus said with authority.

The guard then turned with a frown and motioned for Eutychus to follow him. The guard whispered something to the guard at the gate and it was then unlocked and opened. Eutychus then followed the inner guard to another iron gate. It opened to a semi large room with prisoners who were all shackled by their hands and ankles together about a man's total arm span from each other. The chains ran from prisoner to prisoner through iron loops that were in the stone walls. The guard then followed Eutychus into the room and stood at the doorway. The prisoners lined the complete room's wall. The only open space was the doorway and in the very middle of the room. There definitely was never going to be any private conversation with anyone. There was one very small window high up on the wall near the doorway that let in the only light. Certainly no one could see in or out of that window as to its placement and height.

"Who is Demetrios?" Eutychus said while he stood in the room. All eyes were focused on him ever since he stepped foot into the room.

"What do you want?" came a reply with anger and scorn.

"You're just a boy," came another reply. Soon the insults and yelling began.

The guard in the room slammed the door shut. Everyone got quiet.

"Is there a Demetrios here?" Eutychus asked again quietly.

"Over here," came a response.

Eutychus walked over to the man just out of arms reach and looked down at him. "I'm here to deliver a message to you."

"What message will do me any good now?" Demetrios said with his head down quietly.

"You need to know that your sister still cares for you and is praying for you. It's because of her care for you and another person that I've come to deliver this message to you," Eutychus said quietly. He could tell everyone was listening.

"What other person?" Demetrios said dejectedly.

"Have you heard of Jesus?" Eutychus asked.

"That Jew who the Romans crucified thirty some years ago? Yeah, I kind of heard that story," Demetrios said dismissively. "My sister wouldn't shut up about him."

"Well, I have met Him, and He gave me a task, and one of those tasks was to visit people like you," Eutychus explained.

Laughter around the room immediately broke out in the room.

"That man deserved to die. He wasn't anyone," came a voice shouting over the laughter from the other side of the room.

Right then the Holy Spirit told Eutychus in his mind very clearly and loudly, *Tell the spirits to be quiet in the Name of Jesus.*

Eutychus immediately said loudly, "In the Name of Jesus, spirits be quiet!"

The laughter slowly subsided.

"Demetrios, you do know that one of the men crucified next to Jesus was a thief? And that he even recognized who Jesus was and acknowledged who He was and asked Jesus to remember him when He came into His kingdom?" Eutychus paused and there was complete silence in the room. "And Jesus told him that he would be with Jesus that day in paradise. When I fell out of the third story window a few years ago and hit the stones... I died. An instant later, I met Jesus in His kingdom. He sent me back to this world to bring words of comfort to people just like you who are in the position you are currently in, facing death in a short time. You, too, Demetrios can be with Jesus in His kingdom very shortly."

"He wouldn't want me," Demetrios said quietly.

"He is always willing to forgive anyone who has a repentant heart and asks Him," Eutychus said quietly.

"I've done awful things."

"We've all done awful things, Demetrios. Everyone in this room, including myself. The law of God is not Man's law. Sin is sin. He is willing to forgive us even of those awful things if we ask Him to," Eutychus said quietly. "That's why He died. To pay our eternal debts for each of us before God. He offers eternal life to those who will accept His price He paid for each of us."

Demetrios was now looking at Eutychus with a look of surprise on his face. Demetrios felt a warmth in his chest that he had never experienced before.

"Jesus loves you, Demetrios. He sent me to you. To give you this message."

"What does He want from me?" Demetrios said this with a break in his voice.

"Will you ask for His forgiveness?" Eutychus said very quietly.

"Yes. I need His forgiveness," Demetrios whispered before crying out in a loud voice, "Jesus, please forgive me!" His voice echoed in the room.

The room was completely silent. No one moved.

"I know you feel Him right now," Eutychus said at the lowest level of voice he could.

Demetrios just began to weep. Huge spasms of shaking were coursing through Demetrios as he wept loudly. No one said anything. Eutychus kept his eyes on Demetrios. When Demetrios finally stopped he looked up at Eutychus. "I know He has forgiven me. How ...I can't explain to you, but I just know he has forgiven me."

"And tomorrow you will be with Him in His kingdom," Eutychus said.

"I can feel Him! I can feel Him! Such peace!" Demetrios was now saying this very loudly. Everyone in the room heard him. Demetrios had a smile on his face. "Thank you for bringing me this message. What is your name?" Demetrios asked.

"You'll find that out tomorrow. My name isn't that important." Eutychus smiled large at Demetrios and then turned and walked out of the prisoner filled cell.

The guard slammed the cell door behind them and followed Eutychus to the front of the prison. The front gate was unlocked and Eutychus exited the Carcer.

Thank you, Jesus, for this privilege! This was incredible. Thank you, Holy Spirit, for giving the words and instructions! Eutychus was almost bouncing in his step. Then the Holy Spirit began to respond to Eutychus.

It won't always be this easy. Some will reject My Words. But I still want to offer it to them. Just be obedient and go as I lead you.

Eutychus began to realize and feel the weight of the choices everyone had been given in even a greater depth that he had before. God had given free will to all of mankind. A choice.

Eutychus was lost in thought while he walked, pondering all of the things that had just happened. All the lessons of situational awareness that were taught to him by Ermias and Dawit were far from his mind. He then looked up and saw three men walking straight towards him as he had turned down a narrow street. He quickly looked behind him as saw three other men coming up behind him.

Oh boy. Help me, Holy Spirit!

Eutychus began to run forward. Then one of the three in front of him tackled him to the ground. Eutychus went straight into ground moves and quickly twisted out of the man's hold, getting in a few well-placed elbow shots. The other two had begun to kick him while he was down. Eutychus moved quick and got to his feet and somehow had gotten around the three and began to run down the street as fast as he could. Soon there were six men chasing him. Eutychus turned into the bigger street and found a Roman soldier standing by a door and stood next to him. The six men slowed their run to a walk and then stopped and were watching Eutychus from a distance.

The Roman guard asked Eutychus, "Are you a thief?"

"No. I was being mugged by those men. I guess they thought I'd be easy prey," Eutychus replied through his heavy breathing.

The Roman soldier looked in the direction Eutychus had pointed, then he tapped on the door he stood in front of with the butt of his sword. The door opened and another Roman solider came out. "Supposedly this young man was almost mugged by those men." The soldier pointed at the six men who quickly turned and left the street.

"What's your business here today?" the second soldier asked Eutychus.

"I was on an errand of mercy for a friend."

"What friend?" The first soldier asked.

"I was delivering a message to a brother from his sister."

"Family matters. Figures." The soldier rolled his eyes. The other soldier just laughed.

Eutychus then just turned and walked away being hyper aware of his surroundings. When he got home in the early afternoon he was unconsciously limping.

"What happened to you?" Dawit asked when he saw Eutychus limping.

"Got jumped on the way home from the prison," Eutychus said. "I was so overwhelmed at what had just happened in the jail that my mind forgot where I was and my situational awareness was very bad. All these lessons you and Ermias have given me, and I'm still messing it up." Eutychus sat down dejectedly.

"Well, let me take a look at you and see if I can help your wounds. Can you make it to your room?" Dawit asked.

"I think my wounds are more mental than physical. You're training actually saved me, Dawit," Eutychus said as he groaned when he stood up and slowly walked to the stairway.

"I'm going to take a look anyway." Dawit was right behind Eutychus on the stairs.

"How can I get it so right one moment and so wrong the very next moment?" Eutychus asked Dawit as they entered his room.

"That my friend is ... life." Dawit responded. "Life ... sure keeps me humble. Especially when the Holy Spirit is present. I can think I've got it all going right and in the next moment mess it all up," Dawit confessed. "And I think we have to remember that there are many forces that want us not to succeed, that are waiting to find a weakness in us and then punish us for that weakness. And attack us especially when we've just had a victory. I've come to realize the spiritual warfare is real," Dawit said as he helped Eutychus out of his clothing and was inspecting the bruises. "It was a victory …wasn't it? At the prison?" Dawit asked.

"Oh, Dawit. It was amazing what the Lord Jesus did," Eutychus said with a huge smile.

Just then Hesiod came into Eutychus' room.

"Are you alright? I saw you limping." Hesiod asked.

"He'll live. His pride has mainly been injured," Dawit replied.

"Tell the woman that her brother will greet her in Heaven," Eutychus told Hesiod.

"What?! What? That's… that's … wonderful. Thank you, Lord!" Hesiod then clapped his hands together in joy. "I'm going to get you lunch!" Hesoid shouted as he bounded down the stairs.

Eutychus smirked after Hesiod's exit. "People say the weirdest things when they're happy. Have you noticed that, Dawit?"

Chapter 32
Paul and Luke
Old friends.

It was springtime and the blossoms had burst onto on trees and surrounding foliage. Priscilla's home in Roma was extremely busy. People were coming and going for classes. The shops were extremely busy because the biggest shipment from Philippi had just arrived a month prior. It required two ships specifically designated for that cargo. Everyone in the home was excited to see familiar products as well as the new designs. Devorah had become the overseer of the public shop in the home and now had two assistants helping her as well. Polymnia as well had two more helpers and a new protector for the marketplace tent. Dawit had been very impressed by with his abilities and his great situational awareness. Eutychus had been able to step back from most of the direct teaching of the classes as many graduates from the previous rounds had stepped into teaching and coaching roles. Hesiod and Epaphroditus still worked together, but more and more, Hesiod was doing most of the work. Eliud had become the bookkeeper for the entire operation and Eutychus marveled how Eliud had improved the record keeping and analysis way beyond what he was doing previously. Eliud provided weekly and monthly reports to all involved in the home's businesses. Eliud had organized the inventory room into an extremely efficient manner.

"Devorah, a man just walked into the shop asking for Epaphroditus. Should I go get him?" The young woman shop assistant had somewhat of a concerned look.

"I'll go get him. Just go back into the shop." Devorah smiled as she patted her arm.

Soon Devorah and Epaphroditus walked together into the public shop. Epaphroditus was immediately excited and had a huge smile on his face when he saw the man.

"Luke! It's so good to see you. What are you doing here?" Epaphroditus then led Luke into the home and to the courtyard where they sat down.

"This is the situation, Epaphroditus. Paul is under house arrest," Luke began to explain. "He appealed to Caesar. So, he was brought here to Roma. We were shipwrecked and had to stay in Melita for the winter, but that's another story. God is definitely guiding our steps and watching over us. Paul is being kept in a lower room in a large apartment right next to the Praetorian fortress."

"I know that building very well. That building just outside of the military fortress is specifically used for Praetorian related purposes. He is there now?" Epaphroditus asked.

"Yes, and Aristarchus is with him now and will stay with him for the duration of whatever God deems the time will be for Paul to be here. I will also try to procure an apartment in the building to be close to Paul for any needs he might want from me. I am close to finishing the book God has given me the assignment to write. The Holy Spirit is so on me to finish it. And I know Paul has been given an assignment from the Holy Spirit to write while he is bound within this situation. I'd expect to see Paul begin writing letters to the churches and encouraging them in the Lord and Holy Spirit. I come with requests. Can you supply writing materials to both of us? And I will probably have other requests as they come up." Luke finally sat back leaning on a cushion.

"Absolutely. I'll get you those supplies before you leave today. We will help in any way that we can. Can I walk back with you for a visit?" Epaphroditus asked. "I'd love to greet my brother Paul."

"I'd love your company. Thank you for all your support." Luke smiled in return.

"I'll send word to Lydia immediately about your company's arrival and Paul's situation. Our home and group here will be at your complete disposal. Whatever you need. Don't leave just yet, allow me to get you some refreshment and let me get you those supplies and get some correspondence ready," Epaphroditus said and immediately got up to get things going.

"Eliud, here is a letter for Lydia that needs to go out as soon as possible." Epaphroditus had come into the office room where Eliud was working.

"It will go out today with our latest order," Eliud responded. "Eutychus is sending the same order as last time. We should see another massive shipment again in a month and a half."

"Can I please have these supplies?" Epaphroditus was gathering up quills, ink, and parchment paper by the stacks.

Eliud's eyes were getting big as he watched Epaphroditus gathering such a large amount. "I guess? For what purpose? So, I can at least put it into my records?"

"Put it under missionary support for Paul and Luke," Epaphroditus replied.

"Paul and Luke? They're here... now?" Eliud said with a surprised look on his face. Eliud had heard many stories about them and had studied all the letters they had from Paul.

"Luke is in the courtyard now, and Paul is in house arrest next to the Praetorian fortress," Epaphroditus said quickly on his way out the door.

Eliud then went and stood in the doorway looking at the man sitting in the courtyard. *So ...that is Luke. Wow.*

Phaedra had brought Luke some food while he waited and fresh fruit juice on Epaphroditus' request. Soon Epaphroditus was walking into the courtyard with a large leather bag filled with supplies.

"You ready to go?" Epaphroditus asked Luke.

"This home exudes the peace of God. It is amazing here. And yes, just let me finish this juice." Luke took a long drink from the clay mug.

"Okay, let's go." Luke rose from his chair and walked with Epaphroditus out of the home. They were laughing together as they walked out of the home.

"Hesiod, was that Luke I just saw?" Eutychus asked as he walked into the merchant's shop. He had just come from visiting the Carcer.

"I don't know, I was busy going over all the latest orders," Hesiod replied. "My head was in these receipts. Sorry."

"So, how's it going?" Eutychus asked Hesiod.

"Really busy," Hesiod responded. "Epaphroditus says he's never seen it this busy. I've got at least ten more new merchants wanting cloth."

"Good. I've sent another order for the same amount from Philippi. We should see it in about forty-five days, weather permitting," Eutychus said to Hesiod.

"So how was your visit at the jail today? Fruitful?" Hesiod asked Eutychus.

"I'm just His messenger, He is the Gardener, and the One that determines the harvest. But it was encouraging as many listened ...so much seed was scattered and hopefully some will find good ground. And every time I go there I'm dealing with spiritual entities wanting to keep the individuals from hearing me. It is a spiritual battle every time I step into that building. At least now all of the guards know me, I never have to show Epaphroditus' coin anymore," Eutychus replied.

Eutychus came closer to Hesiod and began to talk quieter.

"I had the fire dream again last night," Eutychus said.

"That's about every week now ... right?" Hesiod asked.

"Yes. I'm really waiting for the Lord to give me further details and instructions on the dream," Eutychus said. "But all I get ... is a sense to hold things lightly and be prepared for whatever He has for me. Which I guess it is a good thing as everything right now seems to be going so well. It would be really easy to get complacent and comfortable as everything and everyone is doing so well."

Days and weeks followed and showed great expansion in people learning in the classes and the businesses all seemed to be extremely successful. Sure, there were the minor arguments over trivial matters as always seem to happen when there is so such growth and new employees.

Epaphroditus had been daily walking to and from Paul's incarceration apartment and visiting with him. Eutychus had begun to notice that Epaphroditus was getting thinner and walking slower than usual in the past weeks. He just figured it was just the amount of walking Epaphroditus was doing every day.

Each return trip to Philippi on the ships from the Shield of Iraklidis now included one or two new passengers from the home of Priscilla who had been procured by the proceeds of the sales. There were quite a few procured individuals living with them in the home and who were now helping out with the increasing needs of running the home and businesses. These individuals were given their documented freedom immediately and offered places in any of the classes they wanted to attend. The selection process of these individuals had been through much prayer and interviews as well as research. But ultimately it came down to what the Holy Spirit was telling the group. Many were already followers of Jesus and wanted to leave Roma and begin a new life. The waiting list to leave had been growing. But the some of the ones with families in the area hesitated to leave immediately. They were one's most okay with being further down the list to leave and often gave up their spot to someone who wanted to leave earlier.

Philippi had also sent a care package for Paul to be delivered by Epaphroditus that came along with the latest shipment. Lydia had included many very personal favorite items that Paul liked and enjoyed. The Church in Philippi had also sent a monetary gift for the support of Paul as everyone there wanted to contribute to the gift Lydia was sending.

The fall weather had begun but still Epaphroditus walked almost every day to see Paul. And his health had continued to deteriorate. He often just waved anyone off who mentioned it. And everyone figured it was just Epaphroditus' military training and lifestyle that kept him going and shrugging off the growing discomfort he was having. But privately, several in the home were becoming concerned and had begun to pray and inquire of the Lord concerning Epaphroditus' health.

Devorah had come to Eutychus and wanted to sit down to discuss a matter that had been increasingly becoming heavier on her heart. Eutychus asked Devorah to follow him and they sat down together in the dining room.

"Son, my heart is growing weary," Devorah said quietly.

"What is it, Devorah?" Eutychus looked concerned, as he knew of Devorah's gifts and intimacy with the Lord in prayer.

"You need prayer cover every time you go to visit the Carcer. I've listened to your reports. And it definitely sounds like the spiritual battle has increased with your work there. We need specific individuals to be in prayer for you the entire time you leave this house until you step back into it. You need prayer cover. Obviously our enemy knows of your efforts there and here. And I shouldn't have to remind you of your encounter after your very first visit."

"But I'm obviously much more careful and am aware now as I travel the streets," Eutychus said.

"Of course, that is necessary," Devorah replied, "but that doesn't mean that our enemy has stopped planning to attack you in regard to your efforts."

"Please allow me to gather some others together for the plan of covering you with prayer every time you visit that place. I know this means you'll have to notify us before you go, and it might make your trips take a little more planning, but I think the results will be worth the inconvenience for you. Your safety and efforts are a big part of my life now. I want to help and see you successful in everything you do." Devorah had placed her hand on Eutychus' arm.

"I love you like a son, Eutychus. Or maybe because of my age ...my grandson." Devorah smiled and chuckled.

"You are right, Devorah. Go ahead and gather your prayer team. I'll try to give you as much advanced notice as possible before I visit the Carcer." Eutychus put his hand on top of Devorah's.

"Now let me ask you a question. What do you think is going on with Epaphroditus' health situation?" Eutychus asked as he looked at Devorah with concern. "Has the Lord Jesus or the Holy Spirit told you anything about it?"

"I have noticed that Epaphroditus hasn't been looking that well," Devorah answered, "and I have sensed there has been an evil plot against him, but I haven't been given any of the details about it. I think you might need to shadow him on one of his trips to visit Paul. You probably need to pray about the timing of it. He probably wouldn't like it if he felt like you thought he needed help. You know Epaphroditus. That Roman military attitude is still there, we all catch glimpses of it. I love him dearly. And he's going to become a target of my new intercessor group to pray for his safety and health, whether he likes that idea or not."

"Good." Eutychus nodded. "And let me know if the Lord says anything about that situation. I need your wisdom, gifts, and life experience. I think your plan to start a ... what did you call it?"

"An intercessory prayer group," Devorah said.

"Yeah... that is what is needed more and more around here. I need to tell you that my recurring dream is still very much with me. The Lord has not given me any further details about it, but it sits on my mind and heart every day," Eutychus agreed.

"Your fire dream?" Devorah asked.

"Yes. Maybe once a week that dream keeps coming in my sleep," Eutychus explained.

"I think the plan to have a gifted focused prayer team in this home is from the Lord, Devorah. Please set it up and gather the individuals the Lord tells you to." Eutychus patted Devorah's hand.

"And I'll let you know if I'll need any further help in the shop. I'm not sure what this new assignment of this prayer group will take," Devorah said.

"Whatever you need ...just let me know," Eutychus said as they rose from the table and Eutychus gave Devorah a hug.

Chapter 33

Epaphroditus' Condition

Sickness.

"Life in the Spirit is like eating an orange. Once you've eaten it, you know exactly what's it's like. But when others who are from the religious side try to convince you what is right and spiritual, yet have never even tasted the Spirit like that orange, it's blaringly obvious ... isn't it?" Epaphroditus was sitting and talking with Paul in Paul's apartment home.

"To be carnally and fleshly minded is death; but to be spiritually minded is life and peace," Paul responded to Epaphroditus with a slow voice and thought. "So, then they that are in the flesh cannot please God. But you are not in the flesh, but in the Spirit, because the Spirit of God dwells in you. Now if any man has not the Spirit of Christ, he is none of His."

The two sat talking for a time each day usually after Paul had finished his writing for the day. Aristarchus had gathered up all the writing materials and prepared food for Paul when Epaphroditus finally came to visit. Epaphroditus was showing up a little later each day, and Paul was beginning to notice Epaphroditus wasn't looking as well as he was when he first began visiting him.

Paul always left Epaphroditus in a contemplative mood. He often walked home going over the conversations in his mind. But the change in Epaphroditus wasn't the biggest change happening in the room. The Roman Praetorian guards sitting in that room with them heard every word. The talk back in the fortress was quite filled with discussions. As they learned of fellow hard cases, who were of the filthiest mouth, and crudest lifestyles, and were the most cutthroat among them had become disciples and followers of this Jesus. Epaphroditus told Paul story after story of Roman Praetorian soldiers coming to believe in Jesus. The impact of the discussions between Epaphroditus and Paul were causing quite the controversial dissension within the ranks of the Praetorian guard.

Finally the day came during the first of the year when the Holy Spirit gave Eutychus the instructions to join Epaphroditus on his walk to visit Paul. The intercessor group had been praying for Epaphroditus. They sensed a working of an evil that had been burrowing on the inside of Epaphroditus that was causing his illness, without Epaphroditus even knowing it was there. It had concealed itself deep within Epaphroditus. This information was extremely troubling to Eutychus and he didn't know how to reveal it to Epaphroditus, and first he had to learn what that evil actually was. Because if someone has no knowledge of what is happening to them, then how do you help them reveal it or expose it? Eutychus knew it would have to be the Holy Spirit Himself revealing it to Epaphroditus. But there was also the very reality of his physical health being greatly and continually affected.

The walk was very revealing to Eutychus in many ways. Epaphroditus was walking much slower than he expected, and he had to continually take rests and stop along the way. When they finally got to Paul's apartment, Eutychus greeted Paul and Aristarchus briefly. Aristarchus and Eutychus talked a little about their first meeting in Troas at the warehouse years ago. But soon Eutychus excused himself and went outside to pray. His own spirit was wrestling on knowing what really was happening with his friend Epaphroditus.

Just listen to Me. I will reveal it to you today. Be aware and awake. Epaphroditus will see and agree. The Holy Spirit was trying to comfort Eutychus, but also help him to see the importance of listening to Him.

On the walk back home as they got to the center of the city, Epaphroditus went to a food vendor's cart that served a roasted meat on a stick.

"I always have a little snack here for energy before I continue my walk," Epaphroditus said to Eutychus. "It's just the right price and sweet."

Everything inside of Eutychus was going off like alarm bells. *DON'T EAT THAT MEAT!*

"Let's not eat here today, Epaphroditus. Let's go to that fruit vendor over there." Eutychus was trying to distract Epaphroditus while he was trying to understand why he was having such an aversion to that meat vendor and what the Holy Spirit wanted to explain to him.

"But that meat vendor is my friend from my olden days," Epaphroditus said to Eutychus. "He always cuts the price for me. He always gives me the choicest pieces."

"Let's just get you home. I'll have Polymnia cook up some very tender meat when we get back," Eutychus said to Epaphroditus as he gently guided him away.

Eventually the two got back to the house, Hesiod and Polymnia and Devorah took care of Epaphroditus as his stomach hurt him. He was very tired when they led him to his room.

The Holy Spirit was directing Eutychus with urgency. *Run back to the meat vendor... NOW!*

Eutychus left the home in a sprint. When he finally reached the vendor's cart, the Holy Spirit began giving Eutychus questions he needed to ask the vendor.

"Which god has this meat been sacrificed to?" Eutychus was very direct.

"Well... uh...." The vendor was being hesitant.

"It has been sacrificed to the gods. It varies from day to day. It is my honor to serve it to good Roman citizens." The vendor had taken a very prideful tone.

"Does Epaphroditus know? Did you tell him?" Eutychus asked directly.

"Of course not," the vendor said plainly. "But everyone should just know." The vendor bragged, "It's what us Roman's do."

Eutychus then just walked away shaking his head. But the Holy Spirit kept up His urgency with Eutychus. *Go get Luke now. Bring him back to the home. He will need to help Epaphroditus.*

Eutychus turned around and began running towards the building both Paul and Luke were staying in. When he got to Paul's apartment he was greeted at the door by Aristarchus.

"Which apartment is Luke staying in? I need him now to come with me to help Epaphroditus," Eutychus said. "It's urgent."

"He's here now, I'll go get him," Aristarchus said as he turned and went back into the apartment.

"Aristarchus said Epaphroditus urgently needed my help, what's going on?" Luke asked Eutychus as he came out of the door.

"Let's go quickly, I'll explain as we go," Eutychus said as he turned and walked at a very fast pace. Luke and Eutychus even began to jog back to the home. Eutychus told Luke the conversation with the meat vendor.

"There are certain things that are very unhealthy for the body in eating that meat. The toxins in the blood that could be in the animal can still remain within the meat, especially with some of the different ritual sacrifices they do while slaughtering the animal," Luke was explaining to Eutychus. "And that doesn't even cover the spiritual aspects that will affect the person. Paul was just mentioning me today that he sensed there was something wrong with Epaphroditus. That he was looking more and more feeble. It's what we actually talking about when you came to the door."

"We were about to pray about this issue together and ask the Holy Spirit. We all love Epaphroditus. His work and service are so precious to us," Luke said.

"He's like the grandfather I never had. We all love him so dearly. Let's move faster," Eutychus said and began jogging again.

When Luke and Eutychus returned to the home, they found everyone in the room of Epaphroditus standing gathered around his bed.

"How is he?" Eutychus said as they entered the room. Everyone turned and moved so Luke could come directly to the bed.

"He's feverish and incoherent. Polymnia just went to get some cool cloths for his head," Hesiod explained.

"He's in serious condition. Please, everyone, let's give Epaphroditus some space." Luke was being firm. "I suggest you get everyone together and begin to pray. I will ask the Holy Spirit what I need to do for his body."

Luke worked with Polymnia giving her instructions of the different herbs to acquire and the different things he needed to treat Epaphroditus.

Devorah had brought the intercessor group together and they went to battle in prayer for Epaphroditus now that they knew the instrument used against him. Eutychus and several others joined the prayer group in praying for Epaphroditus. In that room where they met, there was always someone praying for Epaphroditus. Prayer warriors eventually took breaks and returned when they could. The prayer continued night and day without stopping for Epaphroditus.

When Devorah and Eutychus had left the room together for a break Eutychus pulled Devorah aside and asked her a question.

"How does one who is filled with the Spirit end up trapped like Epaphroditus? Yes, I know myself all the mistakes I have made and continue to make. But this is Epaphroditus. Older and wiser and so willing to serve and love?" Eutychus was almost pleading with Devorah.

"Son. Age doesn't take away our ability to make mistakes. Age doesn't mean we don't have weaknesses," Devorah said. "Our enemy is a crafty one. He will use any and every weakness in us to bring us down and attack us. We all have blind spots in us that the Holy Spirit needs to reveal to us. But it's His timing."

"So how come someone else can see our blind spots and not us ourselves?" Eutychus asked.

"We are all wonderfully and beautifully made. And each of us are unique. And we all have many life experiences that shape us. Some for the good and some for the bad. The Holy Spirit is loving, and gentle, and good, and kind, and especially patient with us. And often revealing the deep truth about ourselves to us can be too much for us to understand and even accept at the moment we want it. So, the Holy Spirit knows the perfect way to deal with us and He has perfect time, because He knows us better than we even know ourselves. I must confess Eutychus there is still so much that is a mystery about Him with me.

But I know He loves me. So, I trust Him and believe Him." Devorah patted Eutychus on the hand.

"I so don't want to lose Epaphroditus," Eutychus said honestly.

"You of all people should know, our time is not our own. And that if the Lord decides to bring Epaphroditus home to Him – then He knows best. It's our hearts currently that would feel the loss. But as you also know we will see each other again in a ... short time," Devorah said.

"But he could still have so much to do... for Jesus..." Eutychus mused.

"Only He knows when the proper time, and what usefulness we can be for Him. You know this, Eutychus," Devorah said as gently as she could. "But we pray to defeat the enemy's schemes and ways. Especially with those we love. And we all love Epaphroditus," Devorah added quietly.

A month later, Epaphroditus finally emerged from his room to the cheers of everyone. Luke had his volunteers from the home going day and night taking care Epaphroditus. Slowly Luke was able to help Epaphroditus' body clear all of the toxins and help it recover. The prayer group was ecstatic and ... tired.

When Epaphroditus was finally strong enough to visit Paul some six weeks after his previous visit, Paul gently pleaded with Epaphroditus to return to Philippi. Epaphroditus agreed with Paul and said he would go back to his villa in Philippi. But Epaphroditus also had Paul promise him he would visit him if he ever made it back to Philippi.

"I'm so glad the Lord Jesus will use you more here with us," Eutychus said to Epaphroditus.

"Through the summer. In late summer I'll be returning to my villa in Philippi. I've almost finished my work here in Roma," Epaphroditus said to Eutychus.

"The others here have grown so much. I'll be leaving this work in good hands." Epaphroditus smiled and patted Eutychus on the shoulder. There was a greater peace now evident in him. He was okay with moving slower now and sitting and talking with others in the home. Everyone noticed the change in Epaphroditus. He was no longer in a hurry.

"I've learned a lot from you, young man," Epaphroditus said to Eutychus.

"Not as much as I've learned from you," Eutychus said quickly in return.

"I was blind but now I see... kind of..." Epaphroditus laughed.

"You know, Eutychus, after talking with the Holy Spirit about this whole thing, He reminded me that He warned me about that meat on the very first walk home from visiting Paul. But the Spirit's Voice was so gentle and quiet, I dismissed it. I knew better...that vendor was my old friend. I'm glad you listened to the Holy Spirit for me," Epaphroditus said genuinely.

"That's a lesson I too seem to always be learning the hard way. I guess that's why we need each other. One part helping the other ...like in the Body," Eutychus said.

"That still small Voice.... we've got to listen," Epaphroditus said.

The summer days past by quickly and the busyness of the home and businesses continued to keep everyone with lots to do. Eventually the time had come for Epaphroditus to take the trip back to Philippi. Eutychus was surprised to find Dawit had packed up all of his belongings.

"I'm accompanying Epaphroditus back to Philippi," Dawit said as he grabbed Eutychus in a hug. "It's time for me to return as well."

"But..." Eutychus couldn't find the words. But he knew Dawit was right.

There were lots of tears as the residents of Priscilla's home waved goodbye to Epaphroditus and Dawit. Two more from the list were joining them for the trip and already Epaphroditus had his arm around one of their shoulders talking to him on the wagon ride.

"We'll see them again soon," Eutychus said to himself while feeling the hole in his gut.

As they group went back inside, Eutychus pulled Devorah aside. "I think I want to have you to take on the role of prayer coordinator for the home. I can sense we have the need to have that prayer room going all the time now. People need to learn how to pray as well. You can teach them that. It should become part of our class schedule."

"Yes, it is time," Devorah confirmed. "I've been waiting for this time. I've felt like it would be soon."

"Who should be your replacement in the shop?" Eutychus asked.

"I've already trained her. She's been doing all my manger's work for the past six months now anyway." Devorah laughed.

Eutychus just looked at Devorah and raised his eyebrows.

"We need to talk more often. There isn't anything I can tell you that you don't already know."

"What we need to talk about ... is your fire dream," Devorah said. "That time is coming soon. And there is much the Spirit wants to reveal to us to prepare us for what is coming."

"My problem still is as I'm here on this earth is understanding what exactly 'soon' means to Him. Even when I was with Him in His kingdom for the very short time my understanding of His time was far beyond me," Eutychus confessed to Devorah.

Just then a shop assistant came to Devorah and Eutychus. "There are two men in the shop asking for you, Eutychus."

Eutychus and Devorah walked back to the shop.

"Timothy!! Tychicus!!" Eutychus grabbed both of them in a huge hug. "You just missed Epaphroditus and Dawit. They just left for Philippi. Just a bit ago. What are you doing here?"

"We're here visiting Paul, Luke, and Aristarchus," Timothy said. "Luke sent a letter to us saying Paul had some letters he wanted to send to different churches and that he would like to speak to both of us. So, we made the journey. None of us know what will happen with Paul with Nero's current moods. Luke mentioned you were here in Priscilla's home in Roma and we wanted to come and see you. This was the first chance we got."

"Do you have a place to stay?" Eutychus asked. "We've got room if you need it."

"We're with Luke is his place for now," Timothy replied. "But if the Lord allows ... we might stay here with you a few nights while were here in Roma. I just miss you and would love to hear about all what the Lord is doing in your life now."

"Can you stay for dinner?" Eutychus looked back and forth at the both of them.

"Sure. That will give us some time to talk," Tychicus said after watching Timothy nod his head.

Eutychus led his friends into the home.

Chapter 34

Friends and Discipleship

The Word distributed.

As the weeks and months flew by, Eutychus was visiting Timothy and Tychicus at least once a week. And they too had shown up at Priscilla's house on occasion to visit him. Eutychus was excited for the work Timothy and Tychicus were doing. Along with Aristarchus, the two were copying the letters Paul had written and the long book Luke had just finished. They were all making as many copies as time would allow. They each checked the other's work to make sure any mistakes were caught in the process. Eutychus was so excited to finally get a copy of each of Paul's letters and Luke's book. He dove into them every morning, relishing the stories and wisdom found in the words. The Holy Spirit was guiding and teaching him right alongside him as he read and pondered the words. And then it hit him hard: *I've got to make many more copies, everyone who has been through the classes here need to be invited to come back and help in making copies of these letters and book.*

The call went out to all students from the home to come back for this current assignment. Many arrived and were excited to participate in the work. Soon there was an entire production of copies being made. Eutychus and Devorah and Eliud became the mistake catchers. Each copy was closely scrutinized three times before it was allowed to be put on the finished pile. Each person working on the project was promised a personal copy for themselves. Each day and long into the night people worked on copies. Everyone was so excited when reading and copying. In fact, the gifts of the Holy Spirit seemed to be breaking out in all directions.

After reading the letter to the Ephesians, Devorah immediately set up a class on spiritual warfare, that went alongside her class on prayer. The prayer room was now a day and all-night running operation that never stopped. Intercessors were there constantly praying. Many could feel the difference in the home. There was a special holiness and calm that made one very aware of God's Presence in the home. Soon many were asking for groups to discuss and talk about the letters Paul and book Luke wrote. It seemed the home was busier than ever.

Paul had finally asked for an audience with Nero. And suddenly the order came down for Paul's release. Everyone was shocked. Paul didn't get his audience with Nero face to face. But the small company didn't waste any time. Paul, Luke, and Aristarchus got on a ship with passage to Spain. Timothy, and Tychicus went to visit Eutychus to stay a few days in Priscilla's home.

"Wow! Your group has made so many copies so fast," Timothy said wide eyed looking at the stack of finished copies.

"It helps to have many students who are so diligent and dedicated. I promised a personal copy to everyone who volunteered for this project. Each copy is checked three times. And as you can see we're still at it," Eutychus replied.

"Paul's given me the task of delivering them to the different churches," Tychicus said.

"Do you need help finding passage? I know my brother could help you with a shipping schedule of our ships and their various ports and expected times and routes," Eutychus offered to Tychicus.

"That would be extremely helpful," Tychicus said with a huge smile.

"I'm headed back to Ephesus," Timothy said. "I'll be sure to give a full report to Aquila and Priscilla about all of your work here. They're going to be amazed."

Eutychus laughed.

"Why the laugh?" Timothy asked.

"I'm sure Aquila will mention how busy we've kept him. His products sent to Lydia's operation, who in turn redesign and add to the products. This home has sold so much of their work and talents. Be sure to thank them for me. They've played a big part of our success and ability to touch so many lives. I'm also sure some have arrived there from here to begin their new lives," Eutychus replied and pondered over the past few years in Roma.

"So how are your prison efforts going?" Timothy asked.

"I'm still going," Eutychus replied. "There have been quite a few who have been sent to meet with Jesus in His Kingdom. But the spiritual warfare has been intense. That's one of the reasons we have a prayer room going all the time now."

"That's so good to hear," Timothy said. "I'm always amazed at what the Lord Jesus has given you to do. I'm inspired and blessed every time I get to talk to you. You are amazing, Eutychus."

"I can't agree more. Your work all along has been incredible. Thank you for all of your help to me personally," Tychicus said. "Eutychus I have a question," Tychicus said, looking focused.

"Yes?" Eutychus waited.

"What's the Lord's plan for all of these copies your group is producing?" Tychicus asked.

"Beyond our own personal use within our group and home, that is the question. It is something we're praying about," Eutychus answered.

"I'm thinking that there are many other groups of The Way here around Roma proper that would love to have a copy. Do you think the Lord is calling you to deliver them personally?" Tychicus asked.

"Well now I do," Eutychus said, laughing. Timothy and Tychicus laughed too.

That began the work of finding all the groups of The Way that were meeting in the vicinity of the city of Roma. Hesiod worked with Eutychus in compiling the list. Eliud and Hesiod worked on confirming the meeting places. Everyday Eutychus attempted to find a member of one of those groups. It meant a lot of walking for Eutychus. He came home most everyday really tired. The distances each day were requiring greater and greater efforts. Polymnia had begun putting together a bag of food every morning for Eutychus for him to take. Some nights he arrived home very late.

But the copies were being distributed, and they were all welcomed with such enthusiasm and thankfulness. But Eutychus began to see so many groups who were really struggling just to have enough food to meet the needs of families. He had begun to bring extra money with him along with the copies to give to the different groups as the Holy Spirit instructed him. Eliud one night then told Eutychus his personal monies were getting low, that Eutychus' personal account was almost empty.

"But there are so many needs. I look into those children's eyes and I know I have to help in any way I can. The Holy Spirit continues to remind me to keep trusting Him for the supply, Eliud," Eutychus said late one evening after Eliud brought his report.

"Maybe we need to let the group here know of the needs. I'm sure there are many here who would join your efforts. Either by walking with you, or providing funds, or even praying for those families," Eliud offered.

"Yes, you are right... again. I've been so busy just working at it each day. I need to update the group here of what I've been experiencing and seeing every day," Eutychus said with a tired sigh.

That Sunday Eutychus made sure to be at the meeting of The Way in the home. He gave his report to the entire group. After the meeting, many people came to sign up to see how they could help. Three lists were provided. A prayer list, a financial donation list, and "willing to go with Eutychus" list. Then Devorah added a fourth list. A clothing donation list. The next time Eutychus left the home to find a new group of The Way, he had three in company with him. And they carried supplies of food and clothing, as well as money that had been hidden on each member. It seemed everyday as he left there were different members going with him as well as one or two constant regulars. The other groups were greatly encouraged and blessed by the group in Priscilla's home. Some of those who had joined Eutychus promised to return to those groups to help in starting various classes and teaching. Soon there was more than one group leaving the home every morning for many different purposes in equipping and supplying the various groups of The Way around Roma. The discipleship was growing fast in Roma.

One very late evening, Devorah knocked on Eutychus' bedroom door in the home.

"Are you awake?"

"Yes. Come on in," came the reply.

Devorah found Eutychus half laying on some cushions reading one of the letters. Eutychus sat up.

"The Lord is impressing on me the urgency of the dream you've had ...the fire dream. It is almost time. It seems very close," Devorah said quietly.

"I can see His hand in all of this. What He's been doing these last few months and past year. The distribution of His Word. The connection of all of the Body. The real and vital help being brought to the least of the families. It's like He's getting us ready to be spread abroad in a big way," Devorah pondered aloud.

"That's very ... insightful. That makes perfect sense." Eutychus really pondered Devorah's words. "So what else do you think we should be doing?"

"That's where I'm not sure," Devorah said. "I don't have any real tangible directions as of yet from the Holy Spirit. That's why I wanted to talk to you.

To see if you're sensing or hearing about anything like this. We can't be the only ones sensing this."

"I'm thinking now that there have been many who have been with you and seen the work firsthand, that you might need to pull back and hand off these latest duties as well and go back to your original calling. The prison ministry," Devorah suggested.

"Hmmm... again you're making perfect sense." Eutychus rubbed his head.

"Well, let's pray right now and ask Him," Eutychus said. Devorah suggested that Eutychus and her should go to the prayer room and ask those praying currently in the room to join with them in seeking the Lord for the future of the work here. Both Eutychus and Devorah headed to the prayer room.

It surprised Eutychus as they prayed that one of the members said they were seeing a big fire in their mind rushing through the city, that it was almost here and they needed to prepare and be very attentive to the Voice of the Holy Spirit to be ready at a moment's notice. Several others confirmed that there was an increasing need to prepare for the time that was very near ahead.

Devorah nodded at Eutychus. Eutychus nodded back. Things were going to heat up—literally.

Eutychus quietly slipped out of the prayer room and Devorah followed him.

"I'm just so tired," Eutychus said to Devorah. "I've got to get some sleep."

"You go sleep," Devorah said. "Let's talk to the elders and leadership here in the morning about what's next. And put everyone on an increased alertness to the Holy Spirit about being prepared if a fire was to come any day."

Eutychus nodded and headed back up to his room.

The next morning a leadership meeting had been called and those that could make it came. Polymnia had passed off the duties of the marketplace just in the last few months and now stayed in the home teaching the growing group of children in the home the basics of reading and writing and math. She had Eliud try to help with the math teaching, be he often got too frustrated with the children's questions.

There were at least twelve people sitting around the dining table in the morning. Eutychus and Devorah brought their report and the visions and prayers the prayer room intercessors had been seeing and hearing from the Lord. Everyone was in a very serious mood. Some of them had heard types of reports like this but didn't realize the imminent possibility.

"I think we need to begin to ask the Lord if we are to spread our valuables and supplies in various locations outside of this home," Eliud suggested.

Several nodded at that suggestion.

"What about thinking about other possible locations to meet at ... if and when the fire comes?" Another asked.

"Maybe multiple locations?" Another said.

"These are all good suggestions. Now we need His direction. As I think everyone is feeling the urgency now, and we all need to be bringing these things before Him in our prayers," Eutychus suggested. "Let's meet every day now in the morning for a short meeting here in this room and bring anything that seems important enough that all of us would need to know."

"Can I bring my wife to these meetings?" one elder asked.

Eutychus knew them well. "Absolutely," he replied. "I think having several locations to go to if we have to go at any moment is really a high priority for us to begin to explore."

Everyone nodded in agreement.

"Okay, see everyone tomorrow," Eutychus said and dismissed everyone.

"Wait. Wait," Devorah said.

Everyone stopped moving.

"Lord, we ask you be with each and every one of us here and now," Devorah prayed. "Speak to each one of us today. In Jesus precious Name."

Amens were heard from everyone and then they all left the room.

"Thank you, Devorah. I sure appreciate you," Eutychus said as he gave her a hug.

Chapter 35

The Fire

The test.

The group in Priscilla's home were very busy reaching out to all the groups of The Way surrounding the city of Roma. Copies of Paul's letters and a copy of the book that Luke wrote were distributed to every group that could be found. This meant the production of the copies continued. They were providing the groups help in any way that they could. The elders continued to meet every morning for prayer and gave any updates that needed to be shared. It had been decided that the people in the home would travel southwest when the time came to leave the residence due to any disaster or danger that called for it. They had established a very good connection with groups in Ostia and in between the two cities. They thought that having access to the port if and when needed to possibly escape was also was a good strategy. Eutychus kept a close contact with Nicolaos on the updated shipping schedules. Both Timothy and Tychicus had already left the home in early spring on their assignments from Paul.

The fire came in the night in mid-July. When Eutychus was awakened, he thought he was still dreaming, as the actual event and sounds were so close to the re-occurring dream he had so often. Eutychus had run out of his room to awaken the household but found many were already up and getting ready to leave. So, he went back into his room to gather up what he had already prepared to take with him.

When Eutychus went downstairs he found Hesiod and family already waiting in the Atrium for the rest of the residents in the home. Soon everyone was accounted for and they left the home watching the flames coming towards them. Every adult had multiple leather bags around their bodies. Children also if they were old enough also had a bag on their back. They kept together as they headed south on the road out of the city. All around them there were panicked people, running and screaming. They also saw groups of men that were obviously taking advantage of the chaos and were looting homes. Eutychus and Hesiod took opposite ends of the group. Hesiod led the way with Eutychus bringing up the very rear. They were encouraging everyone to keep up the fast-walking pace, but several of the older members like Devorah could only go so fast. Hesiod kept checking to make sure the group didn't get to strung out but remained as a tighter group. Certainly, they were very aware that they could be targets for attack. Eutychus walked with a staff just in case. But with all of the panic they were left alone, and once they got out of the city Hesiod slowed down the pace. The sun had come up while they were walking and they could see the smoke from the city. They finally had reached a farm just outside of Ostia that belonged to one of the members of the group of The Way where they had already stored several of Aquila's tents. They were greeted by the family with open arms and together they all watched the smoke and prayed together. They then began the task of setting up the tents and making a place to stay. The farmer named Rusticus showed them the best places to set up.

"Tomorrow we'll go find our elders and let them know that you are here and how we can help any refuges from The Way," Rusticus told Hesiod and Eutychus. Both Hesiod and Eutychus thanked Rusticus and his wife so much for their help. Polymnia and their daughters talked about how they would feed the group. Soon a campfire area was built and cooking began. The well on the farm was very close by and the water was plentiful. It didn't take long to get everything set up, as the group had been preparing for this event for so long. That first day once the tents were set up, most of the children went inside to sleep. For them it had been a very long after an exhausting night.

The topic began to turn to the aftermath and what the Lord wanted them to do in the immediate future. They watched the smoke for six days until it seemed to be dying out. And then it seemed to begin again farther west in the city for another three days. All the time the group was asking the Lord what He wanted for them and how they needed to prepare for the future. Several families had come to bring food and other items from the groups of The Way in Ostia, as the group from Roma had touched many of their lives with help and now they could give back to the group now as they needed it. There were several other families who were a part of the group in Roma of The Way but lived outside of the home that had eventually joined Eutychus' small group. Other members had arrived in the city of Ostia where they had already made friends and preparations. Some members remained in the city since their apartment buildings had not been as close to the fire and not affected. The group of The Way in Roma proper that met in Priscilla's home for worship and weekly classes and meetings were now spread in many directions and places.

One of the members of The Way in Ostia had a close contact within the Roman military and was gathering information from him to learn of the news from Roma. The current news was that fire was supposedly started in the Circus Maximus stables. This was just a couple of blocks away from Priscilla's home. Much of the richer areas of Roma had been burned. Later that week the gossip had been that Nero himself had started the fire because of his constant hatred of so many of the senators and wanting their property for himself, and thus the burning down their districts. Then there were rumors that groups of men were seen carrying torches and lighting fires on certain homes. The gossip was flying through the people and so many were very angry. And much of that anger was pointed at Nero, which made the rumors about him spread all the faster. At the end of the fire at least two thirds of the city of Roma had been burned.

In reality, Nero wasn't even in the city at the time, but that didn't stop the rumors as people said he paid people to start the fires. There were so many displaced people now living just outside of the city in temporary camps. Eutychus' group had traveled farther away from Roma than most of the displaced people. The Roman military were called out to maintain order on all the roads surrounding the city. Checkpoints were established and security became tight entering the city. Many people were not allowed back in the city once they had left. At least during the first few weeks in the aftermath of the fire. Looting and stealing in the city was the main reason for a high military presence.

In the first part of August, it had been decided that Eutychus, Hesiod, and Eliud would attempt to go back to Priscilla's home, at least what was left of it, and secure certain hidden heavier items that they were unable to carry on the first night. They had borrowed Rusticus' farm wagon and mule and were headed back into the city. When they came to the military checkpoint, Eutychus showed the coin Epaphroditus had given him to the soldier and they were waved through. They were looking at so much devastation. The roads were mainly filled with Roman wagons carrying off debris from the burnt homes. The huge amount of the debris was hauled to the marshes just outside of the city. Their small farm wagon wasn't given any attention as the three headed to where Pricilla's home once stood. The stopped in front the fallen rubble that was once their home, and then they went to work. They carefully stepped through the burnt debris moving stones and tiles till they got to the front office and they cleared away the floor the best they could. Eliud then got out two thin metal hooks and pushed them into slots on the sides of one tile in the floor and he lifted the tile up. Under the tile was a stone area which held the home's money. The pulled out the bags of coins and talked about how to conceal them for the ride back to the farm. This money would support the immediate group and pay the passage for any who needed to leave the country on ships. The ride out of the city was hard for the three – for the realization was now directly in front of them and all around them that their lives in Roma were most likely over in the way that they were used to. The checkpoint at the edge of the city just waved them through as their wagon looked basically empty except for a few clay pots. They told the soldiers there was very little left of the home. The soldiers looked in the pots which were empty. The bags of coins had been hidden under the wagon in between the wooden beams wrapped in cloth and tied so they wouldn't make any sound.

The group was relieved to see the three returning that evening. At the evening meal they were told the latest news. Nero had now claimed that "Christians," followers of Jesus, who were part of the cult called The Way, were responsible for the fire. And that they were now deemed 'enemies of Roma'. Everyone now wondered what their next moves should be.

"Obviously, everyone needs to find out what the Lord Jesus and the Holy Spirit is telling them individually and what He wants them to do, and how He wants them to serve Him," Eutychus said.

"This is very serious, as all of us now have been placed under a death sentence, by Nero. But we don't serve Nero, we serve the Lord Jesus and we will be faithful to Him no matter what He calls us to do and wherever He has us to our very end here," Devorah said with conviction.

"We need to pray. All of us. And seek Him with all our hearts and be listening to Him for what He wants to tell each one of us. We should not be fearful but obedient to His words to us. How many times have we heard these things from our brother Eutychus?" Hesiod said to the group.

That night it was very hard for many to sleep, and most were gathered together in small groups of two or three in prayer.

In the morning the group began to see more and more people they recognized walking by the farm on their way to Ostia. They could see that there were more and more people were beginning to leave Roma. Then began the raids on known homes of Jesus followers in the city of Ostia by squads of Roman soldiers. Long lines of prisoners tied with ropes were seen being led into the city of Roma. The military effort to find the people of The Way had become their main objective and orders from Nero. Now instead of strong security restricting entrance into the city, the security became very hard for anyone attempting to leave the city. The Praetorian Guard had been seen with large squads of soldiers going house to house. Neighbors and others began to turn in those who had been suspected of being part of The Way. Inside the city of Roma, the military swept through the homes like the fire did just a month earlier. And a huge temporary prison camp was built right next to the Carcer to hold the growing number of prisoners condemned to death.

Eutychus and group had become a part of the work in getting believers out of the country on ships from Eutychus' family company. They couldn't use the port so small fishing boats launched off the coast about an hour's walk south in a small cove loaded with several people met up with the ships at night after the main ship had left the port. The group became a smuggling ring for believers to get people out of the country. Many of Eutychus' main group including Devorah had finally left on one of Nicolaos' ships. Hesiod and family after praying felt they needed to help people leave until the Holy Spirit would direct them differently. They had abandoned the farm tents and now were hiding in a cave on the bluffs hidden by trees and bushes close to the cove to still help others get out on the ships. The area around Roma had become extremely dangerous for believers of Jesus. They had also learned that Nero had decreed that the Apostles Paul and Peter were to be apprehended at all costs. They were to be found and brought to Roma for execution.

Eutychus and the Hesiod family were talking quietly in the evening trying to figure out the next steps they needed to take.

"Has anyone gotten instructions that they are to leave this country yet?" Eutychus asked the family.

"I think the Lord will have me leave, I just don't know when, He has told me that my work isn't over," Eliud said.

Hesiod, Polymnia, Phaedra, and Chrysiis all replied that they hadn't gotten any further instructions yet. Phaedra and Chrysiis were now young women and Eliud had become a full-grown man and now actually was a year older than Eutychus when he had met Jesus in heaven. It was only the five of them left now that had stayed together.

"One of us will need to see if there are any others that have arrived at the farm looking for help," Eutychus said to the family. "Of course, I will go at the third watch of the night."

"I'll go with you and see if there is any food I can bring back," Eliud nodded at Eutychus.

Chapter 36

Ostracized and On the Run

Brutality unchecked.

"**I**'m tired of this. That 'boy' has gone off the deep end," the officer said in a low voice to another officer. They were washing off the day's blood from their bodies. The bath area in the Praetorian fortress was having to be drained every few hours and refilled as the water was now too contaminated with blood. Most officers preferred to be washed by water being poured over them while they stood than be submersed in any standing water.

"I've actually got blisters from the hammer usage," the other officer said in response. "I don't know if my hands will take much more. Now I'm just going to order someone else to hammer the spikes."

"That's if you can get someone assigned to help you," the first officer said. "We've had no luck trying to get any of the condemned to help us in anyway, they'd rather just die right there by any other method. We're all so short staffed now. That 'boy' has spread us so thin with all his orders. And the burn piles smell so bad. We've had to learn by experience what is too big of a pile of bodies."

"You think that smell is bad?" the second officer said. "Well, at least you haven't been put on torch duty." Torch duty was being assigned to the squad that had the duty of taking people and tying them to a pole, raising the pole up, dousing them with oil, and then lighting them on fire. At first Nero did this just in his garden area for his evening festivities. Then he liked the idea so much he began to line certain city streets with human torches every night.

Everyday there were believers of Jesus being captured and put into the prisoner camp and everyday there were those being taken out and executed. The Roman execution squads could barely keep up with the methods required for execution. The had gone to extra measures with crucifixion, and not allowing the person to die on their own time, because there wasn't enough space or materials. They needed the crosses and spikes for the next person. They were usually piercing the lungs of the newly crucified individual with a spear or breaking their legs so that they would die much faster. Of course, Nero was loving his new hobby and had become more and more devious in his methods. He loved his new role of executioner and he began to wear the armor of a charioteer. At one point he began to have the Roman soldiers sew pig skins onto men and then release dogs to chase them, catch them, and devour them for his guests who were invited to his garden 'parties'. The sheer brutal and cruel methods of torture and death being devised by Nero and ordered to be carried out by the Roman military was beginning to have an effect on them and the public who were witnessing such evil and cruelty. Nero's reputation was again losing ground, but the executions and the rounding up of those he wanted to blame for the fire continued at an alarming pace.

Eliud and Eutychus had carefully made their way back to the farm and scanned it from a distance. But in the dark it was hard to see if there were any new people there. They decided to move closer and walk through the farm area as quietly as they could. They found two children hiding under a tree.

"Where are your parents?" Eutychus asked quietly.

"Taken," the older child answered barely with a whisper.

"Okay, follow us. We must get you to safety," Eutychus said as he and Eliud held out their hands.

"Let's get them to the cave. Hopefully they can go out on the next ship," Eutychus whispered to Eliud.

The two eventually ended up carrying the children for over half the distance, because the children complained too much and were making too much noise.

When they got back to the cave, Eliud's sisters wanted to know if Eliud had found any food. Eliud just shook his head.

"We'll get them out tomorrow night on the next ship, hopefully," Hesiod said.

Nicolaos had begun to change the shipping schedule to accommodate the need of having a ship leave almost every evening to help his brother's plans. He was having his ships take shorter and smaller loads, which put them back into the port at Ostia more often. Eutychus promised him that it wouldn't be much longer, as most had been captured or already fled the area.

"Let's go and see if we can find some food," Eutychus said to Eliud. Eutychus went to the final money bag and took out a few coins. "Just in case we can find someone to sell us some," Eutychus said to Phaedra.

Eutychus and Eliud again left the cave and went in search of food. As the sun rose, Eutychus and Eliud pulled their cloaks over their heads and headed into the outer rim of the city of Ostia. They headed to the poorer side of the city. They found a vendor with bread and paid him more than they ever would have before for two loaves which they quickly put into their clothes.

"Hey you! What's your business here!" A Roman soldier called out to the two of them. They stopped and turned around to see two soldiers of regular rank walking towards them.

"What can I do for you?" Eutychus asked the soldier.

"What's your business here in Ostia?" the soldier said, frowning at Eutychus.

"I was going to the port to see if my brother was there," Eutychus replied. "He is a captain of a ship."

"And...?"

"I'm on official business for a Roman officer," Eutychus offered.

"Really, now..." the soldier said in a mocking tone. At that point Eutychus went into his small leather bag inside his waist and pulled out Epaphroditus' coin. He held it up in his fingers and turned it so the soldier could see both sides.

The soldier took one look at the coin and immediately reached out to take it. Eutychus stepped back quick.

"I was told to never allow this coin to leave my person," Eutychus said with authority. He was glaring at the soldier. "What's your name ...soldier? Do you want me to report back to my benefactor that you were holding up his official business?" Eutychus said with even more of an authoritative voice.

"Fine. Move along. NOW!" The soldier then turned and quickly walked away.

"I don't think he wanted to give you his name," Eliud said to Eutychus very quietly and barely smiling.

"Using this coin is dangerous now. I'm going to have to be really careful. But your sisters and mom and dad need this bread. We've got two coins left, let's see if we can't get some fruit with them," Eutychus said quietly.

They had found a vendor with potatoes and bought a larger bag of them with the two coins. Eliud threw the bag over his shoulder and they began the long walk back to the cave. They constantly were alert to see if they were ever being followed or seen. The meandered on the route and made sure to only turn in another direction when no one could see them.

When they arrived back at the cave in the late afternoon, the young women were so glad to see the bread. Eliud put down the sack of potatoes and Polymnia smiled.

"That will last us a while," she said with a nod at Eliud. Polymnia then went to get a pot to begin to boil them.

"I'll wait till this evening before I start a fire. I just want to be ready," Polymnia said to Hesiod.

The small group spent the afternoon in prayer together. They encouraged the children to join in, and eventually the children began to pray with them. After praying for a while, the children began to ask them questions.

"What do you think is happening to my mom and dad?" asked the older child.

Everyone immediately began to pray and ask the Holy Spirit for help in knowing how to answer this precious child's question. The pause was longer than the child wanted and looked back and forth between the six.

"Your parents will be meeting Jesus," Eutychus finally replied.

Everyone else let out a quiet sigh knowing they wouldn't have to answer.

"Is Jesus in the camp too?" the younger child asked.

This question led Eutychus to share a shortened version of his meeting with Jesus that he had with the children.

"We don't need to fear death when we know Jesus," Eutychus explained.

The group then went on to tell their stories of Jesus. They had so many more now that they all had read Luke's book. The children were wide eyed as story after story was told. Soon the sun had set and Polymnia worked on boiling some potatoes. They all gathered around and Hesiod prayed, blessing the food and thanking Jesus for supplying their every need. Hesiod broke the bread and passed small portions to each member and child.

"Let's see how long we can make this last." Hesiod smiled. They all smiled back knowing how precious it was.

"And after dinner children we need to get you ready to travel," Hesiod told them.

"Where are we going?" the older child asked.

"You two will be going on a large ship and sailing to another city away from the danger here," Hesiod explained.

"How are we going to get on the ship?" asked the older child. "There's no dock around here."

"We'll take you by our small fishing boat and we're going to meet the ship on the water," Eutychus answered. "You'll need to be very quiet as we go in our boat. You'll be hiding under a fishing net until we get to the ship, and then they bring you onto their ship."

About an hour later Hesiod, got up with Eutychus and Eliud to have the children go with them down to the cove. They put the fishing net over the children and began to row out into the sea. This part of the plan was always difficult. It was hard to see small craft at night. But the captains had learned to stop at a fairly precise place using shore bluff outlines and distances. They had developed a code with phrases that allowed each party to verify each other. And another coded sentence to allow the other party to know that they currently were under compromise.

Eutychus and Eliud began to row out into the sea. The ship hadn't arrived yet, and they really didn't know if one would arrive or not, so they just prayed while they waited once they got out far enough from the shore. After a while Eliud saw a ship being rowed towards them. As the ship stopped rowing, they heard the coded sentence. They replied with the proper response. Soon a rope was being lowered and the first child was being hauled onto the ship. The younger child had to be reminded to stay quiet. Soon the children were on board and the ship was raising its sails and rowing away.

The Roman soldier was talking to other soldiers in their squad at the end of the day. "Have any of you guys ever seen a tribune coin?"

"Nope. Nor do I think I want to. You don't mess with that rank," another soldier replied.

"I saw one today. The man looked young and wouldn't let me take it. And he knew what he had. He didn't come by it by accident. Obviously he wasn't a tribune," the first soldier said.

"How would someone else have a tribune coin?" the second soldier said without thinking.

"How should I know?" the first soldier said angrily.

A Centurion had been listening to the conversation when his ears heard "tribune". He was remembering a story from another Centurion who was in charge of the Carcer about a young man who had used a tribune coin for getting access to the prisoners, and he was definitely a Jesus follower.

The Centurion called the first soldier over to him. The soldier jumped up and walked over.

"Sir." The soldier saluted.

"The next time you see that young man that had that tribune coin, arrest him," the Centurion ordered.

The soldier remained silent and didn't move. But the Centurion could tell the soldier was really uneasy with his order.

"Just bring him directly to me. I'll deal with him... and his coin," the Centurion said. The soldier just saluted and turned and left.

When Eutychus and Eliud got back to the cave after beaching and hiding the fishing boat, they fell right to sleep. Neither of them hadn't been getting much sleep as so much had to be done at night so as not to be seen.

"Finally they're asleep. They sure need it. Do any of you have any further instructions from the Lord? Have any of you heard if we are to leave soon?" Hesiod was asking Polymnia and his daughters.

"I thought by now we'd have already been told to leave. But another two children were just saved. I pretty sure the Holy Spirit will direct us when our assignment here is done," Phaedra said.

Chyrsiis just nodded in agreement.

"I'm so proud of both of you. I love you so much. Your bravery and courage inspire me every day," Hesiod said looking at his daughters.

"I often think about Eutychus' heaven story and his meeting of Jesus. I don't think I'd mind meeting Jesus soon, if that's what He wanted from me. I'm less scared each day. The Holy Spirit has been giving a kind of peace that I've not experienced before. I know He is with us," Chrysiis said quietly.

"You amaze me," Polymnia said to Chrysiis, smiling and reached over to give her a hug.

Chapter 37
Caught
Prisoners.

Eutychus and Eliud were laying on the ground and watching from a distance, totally hidden by the bushes. The Roman soldiers were going into the cave where Hesiod and family were hiding. Eutychus wanted to run and somehow rescue them, and he was praying furiously trying to hear instructions of what to do.

Calm. They are in My hands. I have plans for Eliud, now is the time to give him your letters, and the coin. You know the calling I gave you. You are now to go with the family. In the camp there will be the final people I've called you to speak to and encourage. You already have been seeing the things I showed you when you were with Me in my Kingdom. Now it's almost time to come home. Just a few more days and you'll be with Me. Help others to rejoice in Me. I AM the Resurrection and the Life.

The Voice of Jesus was calm and gentle but firm in the mind of Eutychus. He breathed some deep breaths and exhaled slowly, then slowly moved back from the spot where they were watching. He motioned for Eliud to follow him. They went behind a large rock where no one could see them. Eutychus took off his day bag and pulled out a small bundle of letters. He then reached into his waist band and pulled out the small leather purse which held Epaphroditus' coin and a few other gold coins. Eliud watched Eutychus carefully. Eutychus handed these things to him.

"What are you doing?" Eliud asked in a whisper.

"I need you to take these letters to Philippi and my family. And this is Epaphroditus' coin. Don't use it without the Holy Spirit's approval and instructions. It's too dangerous to use now without the help from the Holy Spirit. I suggest you get to Tarracina, it's at least four days' walk. And stay hidden. Then find one of our ships eventually headed back to Troas. From there you'll be able to get to Philippi. Ask for Steven at our warehouse, he'll help you." Eutychus handed the clay piece that had the family's shipping schedule, it was old but he figured it might help. Eliud knew what Eutychus was telling him was correct but the feeling of wanting to go and fight for his family was so strong as well.

I will be with them as I will be with you. Now go south. The Holy Spirit was loud and firm in the mind of Eliud.

Eliud took the bag and began to put all the items into it. When he looked up at Eutychus, he had tears filling his eyes. Eutychus' eyes were also filling with tears.

"It will only be a short while and we'll all be back together again." Eutychus tried to smile, and Eliud tried to smile back.

Eliud grabbed Eutychus in a fierce hug. "Tell my family I love them," he said through a broken voice.

"I will," Eutychus said in a whisper.

"Now go, and don't look back. Your assignment for the Lord Jesus is ahead. Listen carefully to the Holy Spirit. He'll guide you," Eutychus said quietly.

Eutychus watched as Eliud crouched and began to walk east to the southern road to Tarracina.

Watch over him, Lord. Help him, Eutychus prayed for Eliud. *Lord, now give me Your strength and words.* Eutychus was praying in his mind. He got up and walked around the rock and waited by the path. Eventually he saw the group emerge from the cave and he watched as the four were being marched down the path all tied in a line by rope. Hesiod was in back, and Chrysiis was in front. Two soldiers were in front and one was behind.

"You there, state your business," a soldier shouted at Eutychus.

"I'm with the family you have wrongly arrested," Eutychus said plainly.

"These are Jesus followers and have been helping others escape. If you're one of them, then you too are under arrest by the order of Caesar." The soldier came up to Eutychus who stood there with his wrists already held together out in front of him.

Hesiod was crying, "No!" as the soldiers tied Eutychus' hands and wrists and attached him by rope behind him in the line. Chrysiis and Phaedra looked at Eutychus with tears in their eyes and smiled slightly as he passed them. No one wanted to mention anything about Eliud for fear of exposing him.

"These followers of Jesus are such a weird bunch," one soldier said to the other. "You never know what they're going to do. They are the most unpredictable people I've ever encountered."

"Did this guy have anything on him?" the other soldier asked, hoping that they might actually garner a few more coins.

"Nothing. Again, it's weird, it's like he wanted to be arrested," the soldier replied.

"Why would anyone want to be arrested knowing that they would die?" the soldier asked.

"Like I said, these are a weird bunch of people," the soldier replied. "So obviously I don't have a clue why they do what they do."

The march to the city was a hard one. But the group was joined to another line of prisoners being marched into the city. And on the second day, they were thrown into the prison camp. Immediately they were met by other prisoners who gave them a drink of the water they had somehow saved. The guard's practice had been to throw several water bags into the camp over the fence once a day. They figured to allow the prisoners to sort out the pecking line of who would get to drink first and how much. When they had begun to first do that in the previous weeks, there had been some real fights, but now it seemed like the remaining prisoners had a much different demeanor and set of rules among them.

Eutychus and the family found a spot near the back by the fence and sat down and rubbed their wrists. They were sore and hungry from the long walk. But at least they had had some water.

"What's going to happen now?" Chrysiis asked looking at her family.

"We're going to meet Jesus," Eutychus said quietly. "But until that hour comes, I suggest we all ask Him for His strength and words that He wants us to speak to others here as an encouragement to them."

Many of the other families in the camp were also huddled together. There were a few who had no one by them. Some of the single persons were slowly pacing. It was almost evening when the gate swung open and four soldiers came into the camp. They began grabbing certain men and women, about twenty, and dragged them out. The family watched and prayed for the ones taken.

It was now dark but no one slept in the camp. Sobs could be heard in the distance. Hesiod and group were sitting in a circle and praying quietly.

"I've got a weird thought and it won't go away," Chrysiis whispered to her family.

Hesiod asked quietly, "What is it?"

"I think He wants me to sing," Chrysiis said. "I keep remembering the story of Paul and Silas in prison and how they sang hymns to the Lord in Luke's book. And a song from our fellowship keeps ringing in my heart."

"This one?" Phaedra asked and then began to sing a hymn quietly.

Chrysiis nodded and began to sing with her. Then the rest of the family joined in but with louder voices. Soon there were many other prisoners joining with them in the song. The guards were stunned.

"They're singing?!" a soldier said to another soldier.

The song ended and Phaedra began another one. And again, the prisoners joined in in praising Jesus in song. The entire night continued with singing. In the night, the other prisoners had come closer to the little group and joined their circle.

In the morning Eutychus, began to share with the prisoners his encounter with Jesus in heaven and encouraged them that they too would see Him very shortly, and to ask Him for His strength to make it through the next few hours. Many were asking Eutychus about what heaven looked like and what Jesus was like. Eutychus felt no check from the Holy Spirit in sharing any of his experience with Jesus in heaven and answered all their questions the best he could.

And again, the gate was opened and soldiers came in and began to grab people and drag them away. This was the regular event that everyone was dealing with throughout each day.

"Can you believe these people?" a soldier said to the soldier next to him as he was helping raise another cross into the vertical position with the person spiked to it. There were three lines of twenty crosses in the forum all with people dying on them. The soldiers weren't as fast in exchanging the people on the crosses in the dark of the early morning. But at daybreak when the new squad came to relieve them the process started all over.

"This bunch is kind of different than the first ones," the other replied.

"Yeah, most of them are not as scared as the first ones. Some even praise their god at the strangest times," a soldier said.

"I'm really beginning to hate this duty," another soldier said.

"Why do we have to go through all this trouble and then speed it up by breaking their legs? It doesn't make any sense," another soldier replied.

"Nero wants his daily quota." Another soldier spat on the ground.

"It would be so much easier by the sword to the throat, then all of this never ending ... work," another soldier said.

The sound of the hammering of spikes seemed to never stop. People had stopped even walking by the Forum because they were tired of seeing the spectacle. People now went out of their way to walk further around so as not to have to see the orders of Nero still being carried out with such brutality. People were tired of smelling the smoke from the fires of bodies being burned when the wind turned and blew it in the direction of the city.

Incoming prisoners were becoming less and less, as the crowd inside the fence was no longer growing as more people were being taken away than coming in. Everyone knew they would be chosen soon.

"Thank You, Father, for spreading Your Word to the farthest reaches of our world. Thank You for Your faithful Body here and their witness to the world. May our stories be known as being faithful to You to the very end." Eutychus was standing and praying in a loud voice so that others could actually hear him.

Phaedra and Chysiis were quietly praying in their prayer language as Eutychus prayed aloud. Other prisoners had joined them on their knees in prayer.

"You hear that one praying?" A soldier said to his fellow soldier.

"Yeah, definitely not the kind of people were usually ... spiking ... from the other campaigns I've been on," The other soldier replied.

"I have to give it to this bunch though, most, of them never break. It's really quite remarkable. I've never seen such women so committed to a ... religion and so strong. And I've known quite a few women from the temples who were committed to their religion, but certainly not like these," the soldier was saying to the other soldier as they raised another cross.

Eutychus and Hesiod were now bringing the water bags that had just been thrown over the fence to each of the families not part of the larger group and encouraging them to come and pray with the group at the back of the camp. Chrysiis, Phaedra, and Polymnia were praying for other women and laying their hands on them.

Eutychus could be heard breaking out in loud prayers for everyone in the camp. He was praying for strength and faithfulness to Jesus. He was heard praising Jesus loudly. Then Eutychus began to loudly pray for the soldiers who were executing them. Several people jerked their head around when they heard Eutychus praying for the soldiers.

"Lord Jesus, touch the hearts of these men. We forgive them, Father, as You have forgiven us."

"You hear what that guy is praying now?" Oone soldier remarked to the other guard.

"Never heard anything like that. Not in all of my days in service," the guard said.

"Now he's praying that a 'spirit' come and reach us?" the first soldier said.

"It doesn't sound like a curse that I've ever heard before," the guard said.

"I don't think he's cursing us ... he's asking his god to forgive us. This is definitely some weird stuff," the first soldier said.

Then the gate was opened again and the soldiers came to Hesiod's family and Eutychus and grabbed them along with some others. Several of the other prisoners tried to hold onto them but were roughly thrown aside by the soldiers.

The five just looked at one another the best they could. Their eyes showed their love and encouragement to each other.

Chapter 38
A Cloud of Witnesses
Heaven's gaze.

There was a great crowd of witnesses that day. Not on earth but from above. They were gathered to marvel at the courage and faith of those whose whole hearts were fully given to the King of Kings. Heaven paused to witness and mark it.

Hesiod and Polymnia were taken with Eutychus by one soldier and Phaedra and Chrysiis by another. They were pulled away from one another in different directions. The soldier that was taking the sisters pushed them forward in front of him and was grumbling under his breath. He was so tired of swinging the hammer. He told the sisters to stop. He took out his sword. At that moment the other soldier who had the other three shouted at him to stop, which made the three also turn to look at Phaedra and Chrysiis. The soldier with very fast two expert moves sliced the throat of each sister. They never even saw the blade, and they fell immediately to the ground, never making a sound.

"Why did you defy the Emperor?" the other solder asked.

"I'm tired of being brutal. They deserved a quick and virtually painless death. What good would it be for anyone to witness their agony? No one sees this anymore but us. Everyone in the city avoids this place now. The 'boy' certainly won't see it. I'm done," the soldier said in a tired voice.

"Go back to the camp and get two more," the other soldier said.

"Why? The next two would have to wait anyway, there's no space open for them yet," the tired soldier replied.

The other soldier just turned back to Hesiod, Polymnia, and Eutychus and pushed them towards the three crosses lying on the ground. He understood the other soldier's weariness and agreed with him, even though he hadn't gotten to that level of conviction yet.

"Strip," the soldier said. They took off their clothes and stood shivering.

"One, two, three. Lie down." The soldier pointed to each cross.

Crucifixion is a brutal death. It is one of asphyxiation. Eventually the individual is unable to lift themselves anymore to allow themselves to take a breath. The pain is far too great in the feet and hands to pull and push anymore. But this can take days, depending on the strength of the individual and much too long for the Emperor's daily quotas he was demanding of his execution squads. Just enduring the spiking process will usually cause blackouts due to the excruciating pain, to eventually awaken in the vertical torture of trying to breathe. So, to speed up the process a spear to the torso into the lung area or the breaking of the legs making it impossible to push themselves up will make the process a few minutes of torture rather than many hours of torturous, excruciating breaths.

When the three regained consciousness, Eutychus struggled to speak. His voice was hoarse from no water, but he was still able to get the words out.

"Thank You, Jesus, for Your mercy to Phaedra and Chrysiis. Help us now, Lord. To You ... we ... commit ... our ... lives."

"Yes.... Lord ...Jesus," Hesiod said with his all his strength.

"Lord Jesus ... we love You!" Polymnia said.

The soldier sighed. These three will be another long process. They were showing too much strength of will. He thought of getting the club for their legs but got the spear instead. The spear had less of a chance of making a mistake and usually the process went even quicker.

There was a sharp instant of pain in his side and Eutychus' eyes were almost blinded by the intensity of the light. He immediately and instinctively looked down. He saw his feet standing on green grass.

Wait ... I know this place! The air was alive. Everywhere there was life. Everything was filled with life. Eutychus looked up and ... saw Him. He was standing just twenty steps from him. The moment Eutychus saw Him, Jesus ran to Eutychus and hugged him hard, lifting Eutychus off the ground. He set Eutychus down stepped back, keeping His Hands on Eutychus' shoulders and said, "Well done, Eutychus! Well DONE! You know you wouldn't have needed to look down, but I understand you're just not use to this place yet or your new abilities." Jesus had the biggest smile on His face.

"Are the others here too?" Eutychus asked.

"What did I tell you when you were here last time just a few minutes ago? There's no need to rush here. And there's no need for concern. Just relax and breathe!" And Jesus laughed.

"I'll try." And Eutychus took a huge breath in and slowly let it out. He could feel the life in the air that went inside him. It was a strange but wonderful feeling.

"Now that I've got you alone all to Myself ... do you have any questions?" Jesus asked playfully. Jesus actually spun around as He said this.

"Um.. uh... not really?" Eutychus was just in ... awe ... of ... everything. Of course, Jesus laughed again.

"Okay, let's go. There are a lot of people waiting to greet you and talk to you, and I'm sure you're going to be surrounded by so many familiar faces." Jesus began to walk towards the hill and crowd of people. Eutychus noticed the magnificent buildings nestled in the hills and a massive shining city in the distance. Everywhere there were trees larger than he had ever seen. Flowers and bushes with flowers that were so vibrant. And they sang, well, he thought it sounded like singing kind of ... because they made their own individual music ... somehow. And again, there were those children running and rolling down the grassy hills, laughing and playing.

They walked up the hill with Jesus' arm over Eutychus' shoulder.

"There he is!" Two young women ran up to Eutychus and threw their arms around him in a huge hug. Phaedra and Chrysiis were laughing and jumping up and down all the while hugging Eutychus. It looked pretty funny. It made Jesus laugh. Eutychus caught sight of Hesiod with the biggest grin on his face.

"Your stories were good, but not THIS good!" Hesiod motioned with arms moving them in all directions while laughing.

"This place is kind of hard to explain ... down there," Eutychus said while still being hugged by the sisters.

"Okay, girls, give this woman a chance," Polymnia said and they let go and allowed their mom to smother Eutychus in a hug. "Thank you for showing us ... the way." Polymnia said with the full warmth of joy and love in her voice.

"I'm so glad to be here with you too," Eutychus answered.

"You've got quite a line." Polymnia nodded her head to the crowd behind her.

Another young woman came and hugged Eutychus, but gently. "Thank you for bringing Jesus to me in that cell."

"Chloe??!!!" Eutychus shouted and grabbed her in a fierce hug.

"It looks like I wasn't the only one." Chloe laughed.

"Well, here he is and just minutes after me. Thank you for your persistence with me, buddy. Obviously it paid off for my benefit."

"Yes, Demetrios, and for MY benefit!" Jesus said loudly.

"Demetrios?!" Eutychus didn't recognize him for he looked so different now.

And that's the way it went for what seemed a long time, but one can never quite understand time in the first moments in that place. So many from jail after jail. So many conversations that led them to make Jesus their Lord and Savior. Eutychus was so surprised at the number.

Eutychus then felt a tap on his shoulder. He turned around and Nicolaos grabbed him in a huge hug.

"Wait... what... YOU'RE HERE!!!" Eutychus shouted.

"How? What? But I just got here myself?" Eutychus said in total surprise.

"I just spent quite a while talking with Jesus, and He filled me in with a few missing details I didn't know," Nicolaos said. Jesus nodded His head and smiled at Eutychus while standing behind Nicolaos. Eutychus looked at Nicolaos and then at Jesus and back and forth. Jesus just winked at Eutychus with a half grin on His face.

"I did get your letter, Eutychus. And I read it. And then I had all these men somehow find me and talk to me. Epaphroditus, Aabbas, Dawit, and then the kid Eliud who gave me your letter. Their words kept ringing in my ears. I realize now that the Holy Spirit kept repeating them in my brain. And the night of the storm, I gave my life to Jesus. And then I was here. And ... you say you just got here? But you died about four years ago .... down ...there." Nicolaos had a look on his face Eutychus had really never seen. Nicolaos was truly his brother now. Nicolaos and Eutychus turned and looked at Jesus.

"You're now on My time, guys," And Jesus just smiled at them.

Then the crowd just started clapping and surrounded Hesiod, Polymnia, Phaedra, Chrysiis, Eutychus, and Nicolaos.

"Okay, I prepared a treat for all of you. Chloe, will you show them the way please?" Jesus said to the entire group.

Chloe then had the entire crowd follow her. Distance somehow became something Eutychus didn't quite understand because they were all of sudden walking on streets of pure gold in that huge city. How they got there so fast he didn't quite know. He looked down at the street. The street was translucent. Eutychus could see through the gold which was layer upon layer. Then they came upon a huge, magnificent round building. There were gaps in the walls which allowed a large crowd to enter. That led right and left to another gap in the inner wall which opened to a large, round auditorium which sloped down to a cylindrical stage in the center. Aisles led to seats. The building was huge. Chrysiis and Phaedra sat on either side of Eutychus. Hesiod and Polymnia were just in the seats next to their daughters. Nicolaos was next to Hesiod. The complete auditorium was filled without one seat empty. On the stage were musical instruments that Eutychus had never seen and the players were also quite the surprise. About half of the players were human and the other half were...

"Angels. They look so shiny," Chrysiis said with a giggle.

As the musicians began to play, everyone stood up.

"Hey, I recognize this ..." Chrysiis said.

The musicians began to play the hymn Phaedra and Chrysiis began to first sing in the camp that night. Soon the entire crowd was singing along. The music moved through them like they had never experienced before. They could feel the music literally going into them as they listened and they sang. But it took them a few brief moments to realize that the music that was now coming out of their mouths had an actual substance like almost a liquid, translucent blue mist with gold shining flakes in it. The music was so full and rich and beautiful. The worship was pure and full of such love and joy. And the auditorium began to fill up with the praise and worship which literally could be seen and felt until the entire huge building was saturated completely. Then all of a sudden an opening in the top of the building opened up and the worship flowed up and out at a tremendous speed. Everyone was now shouting and cheering and laughing and hugging and turning absolutely joyous, jumping up and down. After quite a time they settled down and someone yelled, "Another one!!!" Soon everyone was asking for the same thing.

And the musicians began playing the next song Phaedra and Chrysiis sang that night. And the whole experience was repeated again. This was repeated until the entire list of songs they had sang that night in the prison camp had been sung again in Heaven.

"Wow ...that was .. incredible," Eutychus said to Chloe as they all slowly walked out of the building.

"That was amazing! That worship stream flying up to the Father's Throne. All of you were just awesome!" Jesus was saying this as He came up to the crowd.

"Enjoy yourselves!! I'm off to meet new arrivals," And with that Jesus was just ... gone.

"You'll get use to it." Chloe said. "If you need Him, He's right there. And then in the next moment when you're just thinking about what He was just saying ... He's off greeting more arrivals. We've just begun to understand ... He moves beyond us."

"You want to see something you've never seen before?" Chloe asked Eutychus.

"Follow me." Chloe motioned and Eutychus followed. As they walked Chloe tried to explain some things. "As you've already noticed, time isn't the same here. Same with traveling distances. As to the principles behind it ... I'm still learning. But it is amazing isn't it?"

"Definitely." Eutychus' head was like it was on a swivel. Everywhere he looked there seemed to be things he could look at for hours. Such beauty, such creativity, such ... life.

"You'll get to meet all sorts of interesting people. Like Steven. He's amazing," Chloe said while they walked.

"You mean Steven ... the one where Paul held his coat and Jesus stood?" Eutychus asked.

"The very one," Chloe said. "But the one that really gets me is Adam. He wasn't like I expected."

"How?" Eutychus asked.

"You'll get to talk to him, then you'll see." Chloe grinned.

"Hey, mind if a tag along?" Chrysiis came running up.

"Everyone is welcome. That's the way it is here." Chloe smiled.

"You have to try running, Eutychus ...it's so different than what we're all use to," Chrysiis said.

"Isn't it?! Yeah the first time I ran here ... I was like ...woah," Chloe was saying excitedly.

"So much to learn. So much to explore. This is so ... fun!" Eutychus said with a big smile.

"Yeah, and the great thing is ... you've got all the time you need," Chloe said with a grin.

Chapter 39
Letters
From the heart of Eutychus.

The following are the letters of Eutychus sent with Eliud.

Eutychus' letter to Nikias his father.

Dad, I love you. You've been a great father to me. I've tried to listen to your advice and instructions, but obviously I've missed it more than once. I've disregarded your advice and wisdom more than I should have. For that, please forgive me.

You've shown me what it means to be a good man and businessman. Honor and respect were clearly taught by you. Thank you for not giving up on me. I was proud to say I was your son. And I was proud to call you my father.

The night I died when I fell out of the window changed me again in ways it's hard to describe. My faith in Christ was an intellectual one until that night. I firmly believed Jesus is who He says He is, but that night I met Him in person in His kingdom. He then gave me a choice: to remain with Him or be sent back to earth on assignment for Him. I actually asked Him when I was there about you. I love you and want you too to be in heaven with us. Jesus said that my further service to Him on earth would allow me greater opportunities to be an example to my family of what it meant to live for Him.

Dad, I hope you saw some of those examples in me. I hope you were able to see what the Holy Spirit was doing in me and changing me to the man He created me to be. You had a hand in some of that, whether you knew it or not.

Dad, will you please go speak with Epaphroditus and Dawit in Philippi, and Aabbas in Neapolis, and ask what Jesus means to them? Nephi was also greatly changed by Jesus, and if you ever see him again, ask him as well. Mom and I have been praying for you for a long time. Why? Because we love you and care for you, and want you to know the joy that we know.

Dad, if you're reading this, I'm now in heaven with Jesus. I've finished my race and assignment for Him. And I know I'm loving being there with Him, as I've been there before and know somewhat what that place is like. But I know on earth the feeling of loss is real, and grief is hard to deal with. But knowing that we can be together again for eternity is the hope that sustains our further work for Him as we remain in His service there.

Ask Mom to tell you about her time in Philippi. Ask her to share what really happened to Eirene. Those experiences are significant and worth knowing about. Ask Steven and Ruth about their lives in Jesus.

You may not know it, but there are many people praying for you because we love you.

Love your son, Eutychus.

Eutychus' letter to his mother.

Mom.

Oh, how I love you! I think you are awesome! I know getting this letter is hard. But you know how much my "window" event changed my life and that Jesus was my sole focus from that moment on. His assignment was my passion and goal. Life in the Holy Spirit is always an adventure! I think your adventure with Him is still growing and has many more fruitful years.

I think you need to establish regular communication with Lydia and Priscilla. You three women are powerful tools in the hands of Jesus. Plus, you three can encourage one another in those assignments the Holy Spirit is giving all of you. And I know that they can be scary and look really huge, because they are. But with Him ALL things are possible. You know this. It's His strength and abilities not ours. We just join Him for the ride.

So keep being a mom. The world needs moms who are filled with His love, His Spirit, and wisdom. I know that knowing you were there praying and loving me was a HUGE foundation for the assignments He was giving me. You are valuable beyond what you understand, especially now for Nicolaos and Eirene. I'm sure I don't have to remind you to continue to pray for Nicolaos, as I also pray every day for him to come to know Jesus Christ. Obviously we've both been praying for Dad in the same way.

Just know I am happy. Beyond happy that I have finished my race for Him. And there when we meet again – and we will never again have to be apart. And I know by heaven's time that will be soon.

I love you so much mom.

Eutychus

Eutychus' letter to his older brother Nicolaos.

Nicolaos.

If you're reading this, I am now dead in earthy terms. But know I am still alive! I am in heaven with Jesus currently. You should know that when I fell out of that window, I died and met Jesus in His kingdom. That event totally changed my life's trajectory. Jesus IS who He says He is. And there is no other way to His Kingdom but THROUGH Him. Accepting Him into your heart, asking for forgiveness for the things you've done against Him, and, yes, you'll know what those are. Don't deny it. Be honest with yourself and Him.

I know the Holy Spirit is bringing many words to your mind as a reminder, along with all of the conversations we've had in the past in these last few years.

You need to know I've been praying for you every day. I want you to know the joy in Christ as I and Mom and Eirene know it.

You've been a faithful big brother. Thank you for all the help you've given me, but more so thank you for giving so much help to my friends and fellow believers in Jesus. I know it was a big risk for you.

If any of my friends come to talk to you, please give them time and your ear and truly listen to them. They are incredible people and I value them so much. So as my older brother do this for me: listen to them and don't dismiss what they have to say. For I know Jesus will be sending people to talk to you.

I hope to see you soon.

Eutychus

Eutychus' letter to his younger sister Eirene.

To my wonderful, creative, and talented sister Eirene.

I am so happy to know you are now pushing into Jesus and being led by the Holy Spirit and becoming who the Father created you to be. I'm so thankful to you the way you have shown love to Ruth and accepting her like a sister. And as you now know she really is your sister in the Lord!

Keep going! Keep pushing into the creative and be like your Heavenly Father, the ultimate Creator. Keep going in the adventure in the pursuit of His love and its unfathomable depths.

Know this, sister, I am so happy to be with Jesus now. I've finished my race and am waiting with great joy till you join me here. I know that time can be somewhat difficult to deal with there. Just know that all of time is in His hands, and we'll see each other soon.

You are so beautiful and talented and awesome in my eyes, and I'm proud to be called your brother.

Your fan and brother who loves you!

Eutychus

Eutychus' letter to the believer's and Church in Philippi.

Greetings to my wonderful family in Philippi!

I've made it! I've finished my race for Him! Rejoice in the Lord with me!

I've sent Eliud with this letter. Please accept him into the family there. He is an incredible brother of mine. He has awesome skills and talents and gifts that would be an asset to any organization or group. Hopefully others from our group here in Roma might have made it to your fellowship as well.

So many of you there mean so much to me, and I won't list the many, many names so as not to make anyone feel slighted as I might do as I would list and list so many of you. This letter would become too long that way and thinking of this is making me laugh. That reminds me of Jesus laughing. He definitely is One who laughs, all the time. He is joy personified.

Keep going, my family! Keep being His light and love to that entire city and the world beyond. I so look forward to seeing all of you again in heaven. I promise I will be there for each of you when you arrive in that place to welcome you after Jesus gets His time with you.

Keep pressing into Him. Keep allowing the Holy Spirit to lead each of your lives every day and every moment. Time is precious, so use what you are given well. Listen to His Voice.

The one thing I ask of all of you is to please pray for my father, Nikias, and my older brother, Nicolaos, to know Jesus Christ. Ask the Holy Spirit for messages that you are to speak to them. Seek them out and be faithful to share what the Holy Spirit is giving you for them. As all of us desire our own families to know the joy we all have and live in Jesus with the indwelling Presence of the Holy Spirit. Keep being the awesome people all of you are. I love you all.

Your friend and brother in Jesus Christ.

Eutychus

Chapter 40

Epilogue
What happened.

7 0 AD. It has been five years since the death of Eutychus.

Both apostles Paul and Peter have been captured and martyred.

Nicolaos was lost at sea a year ago during a large storm with the entire ship and crew. We do know where he ended up. Milos took over Nicolaos' responsibilities of the shipping scheduling and captaincy of the Shield of Iraklidis' largest ship.

Ermias and the apostle Matthew were martyred in Ethiopia for their faith just months after the death of Eutychus.

Nephi continues his work in Alexandria, both in the cloth and leather business and has a large work with discipleship of believers of The Way in the city. He has become a highly successful businessman and usually sends a large jewel to Corrina in Troas by courier once a year to be sold for the funding of the orphanages in Troas and Philippi. He also sends a jewel to Ruth at the same time for the funding of the freeing of women from their former lives, called the Ruth Initiative.

Epaphroditus has settled into his villa in Philippi and has a group of believers almost the size of Lydia's meeting several times a week, as well as many weekly group trainings. Epaphroditus has continued Eutychus' training on the Holy Spirit and now calls the training the Holy Spirit boot camp. It is a three-month intensive of learning how to hear His Voice and begin the individual internal character work by studying the fruit of the Holy Spirit listed in Paul's letter to the Galatians. After reading the letter from Eutychus sent to Philippi, Epaphroditus prayed and received a message to give to Nicolaos and was diligent to meet with Nicolaos every time he docked in Neapolis. Epaphroditus usually called Dawit and Aabbas to join him in meeting with Nicolaos.

Steven, Nikias' main manager and friend to Eutychus, and Ruth were married a just months after the death of Eutychus. They have one child, a boy named Eutychus, and Ruth is currently pregnant with their second. Steven now is half owner with Eirene in the Shield of Iraklidis. Ruth has leather businesses in over six cities in addition to Troas, all run by women as they are all employed through the Ruth Initiative, which exists to help women become free of slavery and find a new life in Jesus Christ. Steven promoted Carpus to become the main manager of the daily warehouse business after he and Ruth were given half ownership of the company. Steven now spends his efforts expanding the entire business and is being mentored by Nikias. Carpus was able to meet Paul, as he still maintained a box in the warehouse before a Roman squad was able to arrest Paul and deliver him back to Roma.

Eirene lives in a large home in Philippi and is married and has three children and is currently pregnant with number four. She is the main designer for all of Lydia's company's products. Her husband runs the complete daily operations of Lydia's companies.

Aabbas, Andia, and Andalee who is now married and pregnant with her first child, live near Philippi now, and the transport business has grown three times as large between Philippi and Neapolis. They live just outside of the city proper on a large estate of acreage where Aabbas is raising horses and has enough space for all of the transport vehicles for the business.

Devorah lives in the villa of Epaphroditus and has a large group of intercessors which now pray daily for the entire world and the work of the Body of Christ.

Eliud now lives in Lydia's home in the room where Paul and Eutychus stayed. He is in charge of the complete finances of all of Lydia's companies. He is not married and is continually a source of entertainment for Lydia as so many single women are trying to get his attention. And he still carries Epaphroditus' tribune coin that Eutychus gave him as a reminder to follow the Holy Spirit's leading every day and hour.

Timothy, Tychicus, and Luke are all based out of Ephesus and continuing the work the Holy Spirit gives them.

Corrina is very busy running the orphanage in Troas and works closely with the Ruth Initiative. Corrina, Priscilla, and Lydia have an annual gathering to talk and pray about what the Holy Spirit would have them do. They have a monthly correspondence with each other utilizing the ships of the Shield of Iraklidis.

Nikias, after reading the letter from Eutychus, met regularly with Epaphroditus, Dawit, and Aabbas in Philippi. He spent time with Eirene and Lydia with Corrina. While attending one of the large meetings at Lydia's home, he gave his heart to Jesus and asked Him to baptize him with the Holy Spirit. One of the very first things the Holy Spirit asked Nikias to do was to give up ownership of the Shield of Iraklidis and to pass it to the next generation and become a mentor pouring out his life for Christ and the generations below him. Corrina had already officially adopted Ruth legally as her daughter in the previous year, so the ownership was split between the two families. Steven and Ruth run all of the business in Troas because Eirene and her husband are busy running Lydia's operation in Philippi. Nikias and Epaphroditus have become very good friends, and Nikias was one of the first participants in Epaphroditus' Holy Spirit boot camps. Nikias has also become very good friends with Aquila while the three women meet for the annual get togethers.

... and Eutychus? Well, with Ermias and Nicolaos, they all are wildly exploring heaven and helping Jesus make ready for their family's very soon arrival... because, as you know, it's a time thing.

*C*haracter bios (R=Real historical person / F=Fictional character)

As many actual facts or traditional information about the real characters were used, but still many facts are fictional (which could be their age) about them. Character ages are at the time they join the story. The story has a seven-year span from 58AD – 65AD. Epilogue is set at 70AD.

In order of appearance:

R – Eutychus / Greek man / 17 years old at the beginning of the story

F – Nikias / Greek Father to Eutychus / 42 years old

F – Gaius / Roman soldier / 28 years old

F – Nicolaos / Greek Older brother to Eutychus / 20 years old

F – Corrina / Greek Mother to Eutychus / 38 years old

F – Xenia / Greek woman 45 years old / part of The Way

R – Timothy / ½ Greek ½ Hebrew man / part of Paul's group / 41 years old

R – Tychicus / Greek man / part of Paul's group / 36 years old

R – Aristarchus / Greek man / part of Paul's group / 48 years old

F – Crispus / Roman Soldier 25 years old

F – Eirene / Greek / younger sister to Eutychus 15 years old

F – Steven / Hebrew man / warehouse worker 20 years old / Part of The Way

R – Paul / Jewish Pharisee man / converted to Christ / 54 years old

R – Jesus / 1/3rd of the Divine Trinity / Godhead / fully human / fully God / in Heaven

R – Holy Spirit / 1/3rd of the Divine Trinity / Godhead

R – Lydia / Greek woman / Purple cloth Entrepreneur businesswoman / 50 years old

R – Luke / Greek Physician man / Writer of the Gospel of Luke and Acts / 58 years old

F – Martha / Hebrew woman servant / cook for Corrina and Nikias' household / 44 years old

F – Atticus / Greek man / worker in warehouse / 21 years old

F – Aabbas / Arab man / owner of a Transportation business / 31 years old

F – Andia / Arab Wife to Aabbas / 29 years old

F – Andalee / Arab Daughter of Aabbas and Andia / 12 years old

R – Euodia / Greek woman in Lydia's household / 21 years old

F – Ermias / Ethiopian man / Warrior / 28 years old / brother to Dawit

F – Dawit / Ethiopian man / Warrior / 30 years old / brother to Ermias

F – Phaedra / Greek woman in Lydia's household / 20 years old

F – Nikita / Greek woman in Lydia's household / 22 years old

F – Lia / Greek woman who works in the kitchen in Lydia's household / 25 years old

R – Syntyche / Greek woman in Lydia's household / 22 years old

F – Junia / Greek woman in Lydia's household / 27 years old

R – Father / 1/3rd of the Divine Trinity / Godhead

F – Regulus / Roman man / Lydia's contact in Corinth / 45 years old

F – Chloe / Greek woman condemned to death in prison / 17 years old

F – Dimitra / Greek woman intercessor in Corinth / 31 years old

F – Prophyrius / Greek man / Elder in Corinth / 35 years old

F – Flavius Aeneas

R – Priscilla / Roman woman married to Aquila / 43 years old

R – Aquila / Hebrew man married to Priscilla / tent maker / 45 years old

F – James / Hebrew man / helper in Aquila's business / 17 years old

R – James / Hebrew man / Half-brother of Jesus / 53 years old

? – Theophilus / Unknown origin / The person Luke to whom he wrote his book

F – Nephi / Egyptian / 25 years old

F – Sheikh Masud / Father to Nephi / Sheikh of great wealth and status / 50 years old

R – Adam / as mentioned in the Bible

R – Noah / as mentioned in the Bible

R – Abraham / Abram / as mentioned in the Bible

R – Matthew / Hebrew disciple / apostle of Jesus / 49 years old

R – Solomon / As mentioned in the Bible

F – Dashan / Hebrew man / Aquila's contact in Smyrna / 32 years old

F – Joseph / Hebrew man / Worker in warehouse in Smyrna / elder in The Way / 33 years old

F – Alexius / Greek man / Worker in the warehouse in Symrna / 22 years old

F – Zosime / Ruth / Greek / Runaway slave in Smyrna / 15 years old

F – Heron / Greek man / Elder in The Way in Pergamum

F – Gaius / Roman man / Elder in The Way in Pergamum

R – Antipas / Greek man / Elder in The Way in Pergamum / 54 years old

F – Miriam / Hebrew woman / Wife to Anitpas / 50 years old

F – Alrazi / ½ Greek ½ Persian man / Roman citizen / wealthy jewel dealer

F – Milos / Greek man / Captain in the fleet of ships for Nikias' business / 23 years old

F – Annella / Greek woman / Part of The Way in Troas / 32 years old

F – Anat / Greek woman / Part of The Way in Troas / 42 years old

F – Abd al-Karim / Arab man / Ferry owner on the Tiber river / 42 years old

F – Odo / German man / Transporter in Roma / 41 years old

R – Epaphroditus / Roman retired Praetorian Tribune / 57 years old

F – Chrysiis / Roman girl / Daughter of Hesiod and Polymnia / 7 years old

F – Hesiod / Roman man / elder in The Way in Roma / 38 years old

F – Polymnia / Roman woman / Wife to Hesiod / 37 years old

F – Phaedra / Roman girl / Daughter to Hesiod and Polymnia / 10 years old

F – Eliud / Roman boy / Son to Hesiod and Polymnia / 13 years old

F – Devorah / Hebrew woman / widow / Intercessor in The Way in Roma / 60 years old

F – Demetrios / Greek man / prisoner / thief / condemned to die / 32 years old

F – Rusticus / Roman man / farmer near Ostia / 40 years old

R – Nero / Roman Emperor / 26 years old at the time of the fire in Roma

R- Carpus / Greek man / Worker in the warehouse in Troas / Promoted to manager after Steven becomes owner

About The Author

J. Pauls

Joseph was given a terminal diagnosis early in life with only six months to live. After opting out of all therapies, Joseph was healed by Jesus in a single day. The term "Terminally Committed to Christ" began with that experience. TC^2 is a response to the call of Jesus to take up one's cross and follow Him with the promise that those who lose their lives for His sake shall find new life in Him–"for it is no longer I who live, but Christ who lives in me."

Connect with J. Pauls online **(feel free to send him your questions or comments):**

Website & Blog: www.terminallycommitted.com

Instagram: @terminallycommitted